PRAISE FOR AMANDA BRITTANY

'**An exciting new voice** – Brittany reels readers in with this twisty, clever thriller that will have you second-guessing everything …'

Phoebe Morgan, author of *The Doll House*

'**Brilliant, pacey,** and will leave you suspecting everyone is involved!'

Darren O'Sullivan, author of *Our Little Secret*

'I was drawn in right from the rather original prologue and **did not see that twist coming!**'

Diane Jeffrey, author of *Those Who Lie*'

AMANDA BRITTANY lives in Hertfordshire with her husband and two dogs. When she's not writing, she loves spending time with family, travelling, walking, reading & sunny days. Her debut novel *Her Last Lie* reached the Kindle top 100 in the US and Australia and was a #1 Bestseller in the UK. All her eBook royalties for *Her Last Lie* are being donated to Cancer Research UK, in memory of her sister who lost her battle with cancer in July 2017. It has so far raised almost £7,000.

Visit amandabrittany.co.uk to find out more.

Also by Amanda Brittany

Her Last Lie

Tell The Truth

AMANDA BRITTANY

ONE PLACE. MANY STORIES

HQ
An imprint of HarperCollins*Publishers* Ltd
1 London Bridge Street
London SE1 9GF

This paperback edition 2019

1
First published in Great Britain by
HQ, an imprint of HarperCollins*Publishers* Ltd 2019

ISBN: 9780008323042

MIX
Paper from
responsible sources
FSC
www.fsc.org   FSC® C007454

This book is produced from independently certified FSC™ paper
to ensure responsible forest management.

For more information visit: www.harpercollins.co.uk/green

Typeset by Palimpsest Book Production Ltd, Falkirk, Stirlingshire
Printed and bound in Great Britain by
CPI Group (UK) Ltd, Melksham, SN12 6TR

With loving thanks to my mum, for always
believing in me.
And to my dad for proudly reading
everything I wrote –
I wish you were here to read *Tell the Truth*.

Prologue

Born or made? In my genes, or was it what happened to me as a child? Maybe I was dropped on my head at birth.

I laugh inside. They tried to find out once: the shrinks. They talked to me for hours, those who thought they knew. They couldn't see I would kill again.

I never meant to kill the first time – extinguish a life. Yes, the anger bubbled even then, but it wasn't meant to end in death.

The second kill was different. I sent David and Janet Green up in smoke like a Guy Fawkes effigy. They deserved to die. To scream as flames licked their bodies, and thick, black smoke invaded their lungs.

It was the same with Ronan, and again with Flora.

They all deserved to die.

Now there are more lives to take. But this time I'm going to make a game of it – have some fun. And when the game is over, I will drop off the edge of the world, into oblivion, my job here done.

Chapter 1

December 2017

The soft sofa felt as though it might swallow me. Suffocate me in its bright yellow fabric. I wasn't keen on yellow, unless worn by a daffodil or buttercup. It tended to reflect off my normally healthy-looking skin, giving me an unflattering jaundiced complexion that clashed with my blood-red hair.

It was hot in the TV studio, but it was too late to remove my hoodie. The clock said almost eleven, and Emmy – the nation's favourite morning presenter – had flicked me the nod. She was about to introduce me.

But I was crumbling, anxiety flooding through my veins. I had an excuse. Lawrence had left me.

A cameraman slid his heavy camera across the studio floor towards me. It seemed threatening somehow – a metal monster. I rolled my tongue over my dry lips, my throat closing up. Was I going to cope? I reached for the glass of sparkling water beside me, and gulped it back. I was about to talk about childhood memories to millions of people sitting in front of their TV sets at home. How was I going to do that, when I couldn't shake Lawrence's departure last night from my head?

Emmy finished telling the viewers about Stephen King's latest novel – another nod in my direction. She had a pile of hardbacks on the table in front of her: Stephen King, Paula Hawkins, and Felix T Clarke. If she'd asked for my opinion I would have told her I love them all. That I adored Inspector Bronte, Felix T Clarke's character who had come to life in over ten novels.

I scanned the studio, trying to stop my knee from jumping, still amazed Emmy had swung it for me to be here.

'You're perfect, Rachel,' the producer had said when I met her. 'The public will love your casual style, and your pixie cut is appealing – you've got a bit of a post-Hermione Emma Watson thing going on.'

I wish.

Five years ago, Lawrence loved my look, which, come to think of it, hadn't changed since then. Perhaps that's why he left. But then he'd once loved that I was a casual kind of gal, who lived in jeans, T-shirts, and hoodies. They say opposites attract, so when did I start to repel him? When did I pass my sell-by date in Lawrence's eyes? When was the first time he suggested I wore heels, or that I might look good in a figure-hugging dress?

'I want Grace in my life, Rach,' he'd said last night about our four-year-old daughter, folding his arms across his toned chest. He didn't have to say *but not you* – the words were in his eyes.

I admit I over-reacted, fired abuse at him, hoping to inflict pain. 'I'll move away. You won't see Grace, if I have anything to do with it.'

He said I was over-reacting – that I should calm down. 'I'll get my solicitor onto it right away,' he'd gone on, far too calm. 'We'll sort something out to suit us both. This can work. We can stay friends.' And then he'd disappeared through the front door without a backward glance.

I confess to getting pretty angry with some inanimate objects after a couple – five – glasses of wine. But the truth was I'd been thinking for a while that our relationship wasn't right. He worked

4

long hours. I barely saw him. I'd wondered more than once if we were only together for Grace's sake. But it still hurt. The memories of when things seemed perfect kept prodding my mind. And his timing was awful. How could he leave when he knew what I was going through with Mum? Or was that partly why he left?

'We are lucky to have brilliant psychotherapist Rachel Hogan, who once worked for the prestigious Bell and Brooks Clinic in Kensington, in the studio with us today,' Emmy was saying, bringing me out of my reverie. She didn't mention that I now ran a private practice in a summerhouse at the foot of the long, narrow garden of my rented end-terrace in Finsbury Park.

The camera was on me, and my heart hammered in my chest. *You can do this, Rachel. You can do this.* The point was, if I did this right, they might ask me back for a regular slot – that's what Emmy had said – so I needed to throw a metaphoric bucket of cold water over my feelings, and get on with it.

Emmy had been one of my clients for about a year. Looking at her now – her pale ginger hair spiralling over her shoulders, her sparkly green eyes, the sprinkle of freckles on her nose, her beaming smile – you would never have guessed the torment she'd been through. The persona she'd created for TV never gave that away. Although for a time, the medication had helped pull it off.

'Hi, guys,' I said, waving at the camera, trying not to imagine the number of people watching. 'I'm here to talk about childhood memories. We've all got them, but how real are they? And what about those we've repressed, ones that lurk in the dark corners of our minds? In our subconscious.'

My confidence grew as I spoke – it was a subject I knew well.

Emmy chipped in. 'I remember my second birthday party. My parents bought me a toy monkey with a huge red bow. And when I was three I had a little pushchair for my dolls, and I would take them for walks round the garden.'

5

I was wrong-footed. She'd lost her mum when she was a child, and now, in front of millions, I was about to extinguish her recollections.

'Sadly, it's unlikely they are real memories,' I said, running my finger over my dry lips, as I looked her way.

'Oh,' she said, raising a brow, and giving a strange little laugh. 'So, you're saying I don't remember my second birthday party?' She'd lost her smile.

'Well, it is possible, but rare to recall things from before the age of three or four. In fact, few memories are stored before the age of six. You may have kept the monkey and pushchair for years.'

'I did, yes, Vanessa the monkey was my favourite toy until I was about twelve.' Her smile was back – always so professional. 'And before you ask, I've no idea why I chose that name.'

'Maybe you've seen photographs of you pushing the push-chair?'

'Oh yes, tons. My mum took mountains of pictures of me when I was little.'

There was a slight dip in her voice that only I would pick up on. I felt awful. I knew I'd hurt her, and wanted her to look my way so I could mouth that I was sorry, but she didn't catch my eye.

Once the camera was back on me, I said, 'I had a toy rabbit called Mr Snookum as a child.' I smiled. 'I still have him stashed away in my loft. My mother told me she gave him to me on my fifth birthday, and I'm sure I remember her handing him over and telling me to always take care of him.' My voice quavered, and a lump rose in my throat. *My poor mum. My poor, poor mum.* I swallowed, and took a breath. 'But I can't be sure the memory is real. Vivid recollections of my childhood start much later, particularly her painting on the beach at Southwold.' I gave a little cough to ward off my stupid emotions. 'She's an artist.' *Why am I sharing this with the nation?*

My slot seemed to go on for ages, as I continued to discuss childhood amnesia, and the different methods of retrieving infant memories. I did my best to put on a front, hoping I was making a good impression.

Then it was the phone-in. The bit I'd dreaded most.

A woman suffering from post-traumatic stress disorder came on the line, and I went through breathing and muscle relaxing exercises with her, and suggested meditation and yoga. 'Spending time with nature can be beneficial too,' I concluded.

Next, a man suffering with agoraphobia called in.

'Do you think it's something in my childhood that I can't recall, causing me to stay in my apartment day in, day out?' He sounded defeated, on the verge of tears.

What a ridiculous position I was in. How was I meant to answer someone I knew nothing about?

'Could be,' I said. 'Call your doctor as soon as possible. They can advise you.' *Pathetic!*

'We have John Burton on the line, Rachel,' Emmy said, once the agoraphobic man had hung up. She pressed her finger to her ear, as though listening through her earpiece.

'Hello, John,' I said. 'How can I help?'

'Polly put the kettle on,' he sang. 'Polly put the kettle on, Polly put the kettle on, we'll all have tea.'

'Do you remember that nursery rhyme from your childhood, John?' I said, feeling uneasy, and glancing over at Emmy.

There was a pause, before he said, 'Yes.'

Emmy furrowed her brow, and shrugged. Surely they would cut him off. Blame a poor connection.

'What age do you think you were when you heard it?' I asked, trying to sound professional.

'Suki take it off again, Suki take it off again, Suki take it off again, they've all gone away.'

The hairs on my arms rose, despite the heat of the studio.

'I'm crying out,' he said. 'But they won't listen. And now you

7

must pay, Rachel.' The line went dead, and within moments we went to a commercial break.

'Oh my God,' Emmy said as soon as we were off the air, jumping up and dashing over. She plonked down next to me, and put her arm around my shoulder. 'Why the hell did they keep him on the line so long?'

I didn't reply; instead, I dashed off set, barely looking at the concerned faces following me through the door. I rushed through the labyrinth of corridors, desperately seeking an exit, my heart thumping. Eventually I spotted the automatic doors that led to the car park, and raced through them, freezing air hitting me like a smack. I stood for some moments, my eyes darting around the area, trying to catch my breath.

I drove home, relieved Emmy was still on the air and couldn't call me. I needed time to process what had happened, before discussing it. I collected Grace from Angela, keeping the conversation with my next-door neighbour brief so she didn't see how anxious I was. 'You knocked them dead, sweetie,' she said in her throaty middle-class way, as I dashed down her path, holding Grace's hand.

'Thanks,' I called back, certain she couldn't have seen the live show.

Inside my house, with the bolts pulled across the door and the deadlock on, my heartbeat slowed to a normal rate. Grace settled herself in the lounge, building with Lego, and I padded into the kitchen to make tea, the song 'Polly put the Kettle on' worming its way into my head on repeat, driving up my anxiety.

I rummaged in the freezer for fish fingers for Grace's lunch. As I closed the freezer door, I noticed a photo of Lawrence and me on holiday a couple of years ago, pinned amongst the magnetic letters. I couldn't tear my eyes away, and touched Lawrence's face with my outstretched fingertip. We were happy once. Weren't we?

'Mummy!'

I jumped at the sound of my daughter's voice, dropping the

box of fish fingers to the floor with a thud. I fell to my knees.

'Are you OK, Mummy?' Grace said, running over and crouching beside me, as I shoved broken fish fingers back into the box with shaking hands. She craned her neck to see my face, touching my cheek softly, and I realised tears were filling my eyes.

'Don't cry,' she said.

'I'm not crying, lovely. I've got something in my eye.'

What the hell was the matter with me? Was it Lawrence taking off, or the stupid call? I took a deep breath, trying to escape the silly nursery rhyme in my head. *It's just some weirdo. A troll. Nothing personal.*

I rose and slipped the battered box onto the worktop, and lifted Grace up into my arms, burying my nose into her dark curls. She smelt of strawberry shampoo. 'So did you have a lovely time with Angela?' I said, as the kettle boiled.

***

The phone blasted on my bedside table. It was 7 a.m. Only one person would ring so early – someone who got up at five.

'Emmy,' I said as I answered the call, my voice croaky.

'I'm so sorry about the odd phone call yesterday, Rachel,' she said. If she'd been angry about my comments on air about her childhood, she'd let it go.

'It wasn't your fault. And I'm sorry too … for rushing off like that.'

'No worries. You dealt with it all amazingly while you were on air. After the break we had that cute contestant from *The Bake Off* on, and carried on as though nothing had happened. There's been a few tweets about it, but nothing major.'

'Thank God.'

'Live TV, especially phone-ins, can be a nightmare.' She paused for a moment. 'Are you sure you're OK?'

'I'm fine, honestly,' I said, pulling myself up to a sitting position, and propping myself against the headboard.

'I still can't believe they let him stay on the line for so long.' Her TV persona was confident, loud and bubbly, yet the real Emmy – the one on the other end of the line, was softly spoken. 'The guys handling the phone lines said he sounded upbeat and friendly when he called in. Had a great question to ask you.'

'It doesn't matter,' I said, raking my fingers through my hair. Despite 'Polly put the Kettle on' playing in my head during the night, I felt sure I was over the call. Lawrence had left. My mum was ill. I wasn't about to let some creepy caller add another layer of worry to my life. 'It was just some fool with nothing better to do,' I said, sounding strong. 'I'm sure the call wasn't aimed at me personally.'

'I'm not so sure, Rach,' she said. Words I didn't want to hear. The phone line went quiet for a few moments, and I imagined her twirling a curl of her hair around her finger, forming the words she sometimes struggled to get out. A trauma twelve months ago had triggered a childhood stammer, although she could mainly control it now and rarely stuttered on air. 'The thing is …'

'What is it, Emmy?' I leaned forward on the bed, and threw back my quilt, suddenly hot. 'What's happened?'

'Nothing's happened exactly,' she went on. 'And to be honest, I've been deliberating over whether to tell you – but then I feel you should know. Just in case.'

'Just in case what?' The hairs on my arms rose.

'The thing is, a man came to the studio looking for you earlier this morning.'

'Was it the man who called in?' *Is that fear in my voice?*

'No. Well, I don't think so. I don't know who he was, but he was quite normal, nothing like the bloke on the phone. He was waiting outside when I arrived. He'd been there a while, as he was soaked through.'

'It's raining?' I glanced at the window. Part of me didn't want to hear what she had to say. *Let's talk about the weather instead.*

'It's dried up now. Rach, are you taking this in? Did you hear what I said?'

I nodded, as though she could see me, before rising and pacing the room. 'Of course. Yes.'

'He didn't tell me his name, despite me asking several times.' Another pause. 'Just that he was desperate to talk to you. I hope I've done the right thing in telling you. I thought you should know.'

Just in case.

'Yes, yes thanks, Emmy. You did the right thing.'

'He looked nice. Normal,' she said. 'I'm sure it's nothing to worry about, Rachel. Listen, I must go, I'm back on the air in five. Talk soon. And please don't worry.' She ended the call before I could answer.

It's nothing, I told myself, continuing to pace the bedroom. *I'd been on TV. Things like this happen all the time.* But my neck tingled, and a chill ran through my body. Had it been the same man who called in to the studio?

And if it was, why was he looking for me?

Chapter 2

February 2018

We were on our way. Zoe driving, me holding on to the overhead handle, knuckles turning white.

She always drove too fast, and was taking the car to seventy mph along dark, narrow roads. Twigs, like bony fingers, scraped the window as she raced past the hedgerow, barely missing oncoming traffic. Despite the harrowing journey, I was looking forward to the evening ahead with my friend. It would be good to unwind, and I loved being with Zoe. She was the tonic to my gin.

It had been a long two months since Lawrence left. At first I was grieving, I supposed – well, I'd certainly wanted him dead. But after an initial love affair with gin and chocolate – a useless attempt to shave off the sharp edges of my crap life – I'd *almost* accepted we were over, and my sadness was now fully focused on my mum.

I still hadn't come to terms with her early onset dementia, and wasn't sure I ever would. In fact, sometimes, on bad days, it was as though I'd already lost her, and yet she was still here, reminding me of the life we'd once had together.

I'd first noticed the signs a year ago, just before her fiftieth birthday. The confusion and forgetfulness I'd witnessed back then would later be attributed to Alzheimer's. It hadn't seemed possible, and her rapid decline had made it even crueller.

Zoe reached over and turned up the radio, as she sang along to 'Bohemian Rhapsody'. It was as though she'd forgotten I was there. Zoned in to her singing, she continued to swing her red Clio along the spiralling country roads towards the spa, seeming oblivious to the frosty February evening – the chance of ice on the road. A sprinkling of snow had coated the pavement earlier, and the forecast promised snowstorms heading from Siberia. *Slow down! Please.*

I stared her way, and as though sensing my eyes on her, she turned, and stopped mid-Galileo.

'You OK, Rachel?' she said, tucking her chestnut-brown hair behind her ears with both hands.

'Hands on the wheel, Zoe, for Christ's sake,' I yelled.

'Jeez, you don't have to shout,' she said, doing as I asked. 'Are you OK?' she repeated.

'Of course.' I smiled. Tonight I was determined to purge thoughts of Mum's illness from my head and de-stress. Enjoy myself. Lawrence had Grace for the weekend, and the care home had my mobile number. I could relax. It was Friday night. Surely I was allowed to chill every so often, uncoil my tension.

'Almost there,' Zoe said, slowing down. 'I've booked us both in for a facial and a head massage, and maybe we could swim too.' She didn't wait for a response. She knew what she'd said. 'Oh God.' She covered her mouth. 'I'm such an idiot.'

'It's OK. It's no big deal.' I smiled, and patted her arm, wishing I hadn't told her about my fear of water – I didn't like to make a fuss about it. 'Actually, I fancy a long read on a hotbed. I've brought my Kindle.'

Her eyes were glued on me as I spoke, and her car veered to the right. 'Keep your eyes on the road or you'll kill something,' I cried, although I felt sure it would be us if we didn't reach our destination soon.

I was relieved when she indicated and pulled onto a sweeping drive, lit by white lights. She manoeuvred into a space in front of Mulberry Hall. I hadn't been here since it became a spa.

As she pulled on the handbrake, I picked up my bag from the car well, unzipped it, and rummaged for my phone. I found myself constantly checking for missed calls from the care home. My mum had nobody but me. She'd never been one for making friends – a bit of a recluse in many ways – and my grandparents had died before I was born in a car accident. She'd never been close with them anyway, she told me once.

There were no missed calls, only a notification on Facebook. I clicked on the app. 'Ooh, I've got a friend request.'

Zoe glanced over. 'Well it can wait, can't it?' she said, getting out. 'We totally need pampering.'

I slipped my phone back in my bag, and jumped from the car, eyes scanning the prestigious Victorian building. Both the spa and the luxury apartments had once been an insane asylum, and later a psychiatric hospital.

'I fancied buying one of those apartments when I moved this way,' Zoe said, nodding towards Mulberry Hall. 'But allegedly it's haunted by old patients.' She wiggled her fingers and made a howling, ghost-like sound.

'Oh for God's sake, Zoe.' She looked amazing in a red three-quarter-length coat with a fur trim, over tight-fitting leggings and expensive trainers. She was tall, slim, elegant; whereas I was small, and a whisker away from chubby when I'd been on a chocolate binge. A flash of memory came and went – Lawrence telling me that 'with a bit of effort' I could look as good as Zoe.

I zipped up my hoodie and hunched my shoulders against the cold, my teeth chattering.

'They used to do awful things here in the late 1800s,' she said, her eyes skittering over the building. 'What a terrible time to have lived if you showed any signs of not fitting the mould.'

'Mmm.' I glanced at the towering building. 'Put in asylums for no good reason half the time.'

'I know. You could have been admitted for anything from novel-reading to nymphomania – so that's me admitted.'

'I didn't know you read novels.'

'I don't.' She burst out laughing, and I laughed too. 'Seriously though,' she said, sighing. 'They would even admit poor souls for grieving.'

'It's hard to believe now how terrible the mental health system was back then.'

'The treatments were awful. They would immerse patients in ponds until they were unconscious, or tie them naked to a chair and pour cold water over them.' She looked about her and shivered. 'I wouldn't want to be out here alone,' she said. 'There's something spooky about this place, don't you think?'

I shrugged. It was quiet, yes – but it seemed peaceful, and the apartments were stunning. Anyway, I didn't believe in ghosts. Truth was, I was more scared of the living.

'I saw a ghost once,' she said. 'When I was a child, I slept with my arm dangling out of the bed. I woke one night feeling certain something cold had touched my hand.' She shuddered. 'A girl in blue stood by my bed.'

'A dream?' Tingles crawled up my neck, despite my determination not to believe in the paranormal.

'It must have been. Although I never slept with my arm out of the bed after that.' She laughed. 'Let's go inside before we freeze to death.'

I looked over my shoulder, trying to imagine lost souls looking down from the many apartment windows. And despite only seeing the stunning apartments, lit by what I imagined were happy dwellers, I couldn't help wondering what secrets the walls held.

As we walked, Zoe nodded towards the lower building we were

15

heading for, built from the same mustard-coloured brick as the apartments. 'Apparently the swimming pool is where the morgue used to be,' she said, reaching the door.

'Good God,' I said with a laugh. 'I'm actually glad I don't swim.'

'Hello, ladies,' said the man behind the counter as we approached, his Irish accent charming. He was in his early forties, with a sprinkling of grey in his dark hair.

'I'm the manager, Connor Mahoney.' His eyes drifted to Zoe, a look of appreciation on his face. Men seemed to like her.

'Zoe Marsh,' she said.

While he glanced at his computer screen and tapped on his keyboard, I studied Zoe's perfectly made-up face, her blemish-free skin, her full lips, and her perfect eyebrows. I tended to hide my brows under my fringe. I'd never got the hang of plucking, and now power-brows were the in thing, and I hadn't got the first clue how to shape and fill them. I'd been a bit of a tomboy when I was a kid, so never acquired the skills to be feminine – but it had never bothered me.

Zoe owned a salon in Islington, so knew ways to highlight her beauty, and make men notice. 'Come along to my salon sometime,' she'd often said. 'I could do your colours.' I never had. I suppose I was happy as I was, with my boxed hair dye, and my cheap-as-chips make-up.

We'd met at a yoga group about six months ago and hit it off. I'd seen her a few times before we finally got chatting, and admired how she'd managed to make all the moves look so graceful. Whereas I'd made the mountain pose look more like a molehill. I was quite sporty – fastest in my class at the hundred-metre sprint when I was twelve – but elegant yoga poses, I struggled with.

'So you're both booked in for a facial in an hour,' Connor said, looking up from the screen.

'I don't suppose you could book me in for a full-body massage,' Zoe said. Her words were tangibly flirtatious.

'Sorry, we're fully booked,' he said, his eyes locking with hers.

There was an instant chemistry, and I suddenly felt like a ham sandwich at a vegan wedding.

He handed us robes and towels, and gestured for us to go through the frosted-glass doors. 'We'll just take some details and then you can enjoy your evening.'

As we headed towards the hotbeds, Zoe smiled. 'He's rather nice, don't you think?'

'I guess so,' I said, and then whispered, 'But what about Hank?'

She stopped suddenly and covered her mouth with her hand, her chin crinkling.

'What is it? What's wrong?' I said, stopping, and two women walked into us. 'Sorry,' I said, as they skirted round us, rolling their eyes and muttering. 'We should have brake lights,' I called after them, but they didn't look back. 'What's wrong?' I repeated, my attention back on Zoe, whose eyes had filled with tears.

'We broke up.' She removed her hand from her mouth, and slapped the tears from her cheeks. Straightening her back, she carried on walking.

'I'm so sorry.'

'I was going to tell you earlier, but didn't want to ruin the evening. I still love him, Rach. Always will. But I can't handle it any more.'

'The drugs?'

She nodded. 'I've tried so hard. You know that, right?'

'I know you have, lovely,' I said, linking arms with her and pulling her close, so we walked as one.

'He's never going to listen. The other day I found him so out of it, I thought he was dead.'

'Oh God, Zoe. You can't live like that.'

'I know.' She sniffed, her eyes still watery. 'It was the final straw. I can't bear to think that one day I *will* find him dead.' She dashed another tear from her cheek with the back of her hand.

'Of course you can't.'

I'd only seen Hank a few times. He would pace the pavement

17

some distance away, while waiting for Zoe to finish yoga. And even from across a busy road, I noticed his skin was far too pale, his clothes dishevelled, and his whole demeanour agitated.

'He still refuses to get help, so for my own sanity I walked out on Tuesday.'

'You've done the right thing, lovely,' I said, fishing a tissue from my bag and handing it to her. 'You've done everything you can.'

'Thanks. You've no idea how much I appreciate your support,' she said, dabbing her cheeks. 'And I know I sound a bit cold flirting with Connor – but I need the distraction, and I suppose the comfort. It's been hell with Hank for a long time.'

'You have to do what's right for you,' was all I could muster.

'Life's short and all that,' she said.

It wasn't until later, as I relaxed on a lounger, that I looked at the friend request I'd received earlier. My heart sank as I opened it. I was expecting a long-lost friend, or even a boyfriend wanting to meet up because he'd heard about my breakup with Lawrence – but it wasn't a name I recognised.

David Green: CONFIRM/DELETE REQUEST

It was no big deal, I told myself. Lots of people got requests from strangers. But then I'd never had anything like it before. My anxiety rose, though I couldn't put my finger on why.

The temptation was too much. I clicked on his profile. David Green's profile picture was an image of a lake. His cover photo was of a row of grey houses with red front doors, the words 'Mandan Road, County Sligo' at the foot of the picture. He had no friends that I could see, and his timeline only revealed one status update:

Here comes a candle to light you to bed
Here comes a chopper to chop off your head

Below the words was a cartoon gif of a blazing fire.

I shuddered, trying to convince myself it must be a mistake, or some kind of joke. But my heart hammered in my chest. I was born in County Sligo. My mother grew up there. Was it a coincidence? And if so, why did I suddenly feel so vulnerable?

Chapter 3

July 1995

The flames dance like magical beings – telling me I'm right – telling me they deserve to die.

They'd left the back door open, so it was all so easy.

And now I can see David from my window. He can't get out of the bedroom. I wedged a chair under the door handle.

'Help!' he cries as he presses on the glass; well, I think that's what he's yelling. I can't be sure. I'm too far away to hear.

'Nobody will help you,' I whisper.

He looks down and I wonder if he's going to leap from the bedroom window, but the fire grips his pyjamas, and his face changes shape as he cries out in agony. He slips out of sight.

I draw the curtains, rest my head on the pillow, and close my eyes.

Chapter 4

February 1987

Laura let herself into the house she grew up in. It was hers now. The house her father built, with its oversized windows and oddly angled sloping roof, far too modern for the stunning surroundings. The towering trees and wildlife looked on and laughed at it – that's what she'd thought as a child.

A flick of the light switch illuminated the lounge, the paintings on the walls, the vases cradling dead flowers. The wealth was tangible. Her parents had had far too much: spoilt children wanting more, more, more. Except they'd never wanted her, had they?

Laura flung her denim jacket onto the sprawling leather sofa, and attempted to push the creases of the journey from her orange kaftan. She'd been staying at a hotel in Sligo Town for two weeks. Now she was here, and the shock of her parents' death was slowly wearing off, bubbles of anger rose in her chest.

She dived towards the drinks cabinet, poured vodka into a cut-glass tumbler, and placed it to her lips. With a jolt, she remembered.

You're pregnant. You fool.

She abandoned the drink and padded towards the window, barely able to see into the darkness – just a reflection of the room and her still-willowy shape. She would be isolated here, in this ridiculous house she'd inherited, along with far too much money. She would sell soon – once she felt she could move on with her life.

Thoughts of Jude swam into her head. 'There's been an accident,' she'd told him three weeks ago. And when he took her into his arms, she'd buried her head in his shoulder, breathing in the smell of his Brut aftershave, and Consulate cigarettes. She'd hoped at that moment he'd changed his mind. That he would put her and their unborn child before his law degree, before his monstrous parents. That he would care enough to stay.

'They're in intensive care,' she'd gone on. 'Will you come to Sligo with me? I need you, Jude.'

He'd pulled away, his grey eyes cold – the shock of finding out a few days before that he would be a father still reflecting on his handsome face. He looked too young to be a parent, but then she was young too.

'You know I can't, Laura. I'm sorry. Please think about a termination.' He'd said it so softly, that the word termination didn't sound so bad. But the truth was, she was already attached to the baby growing inside her – even if it was only the size of a peanut. This would be her and Jude's child.

She'd cried as he pulled on his jacket, and dragged his woollen hat over his dark curls. And with a final, 'I'm so sorry,' he opened the door, and disappeared into the night.

Controlling her desire to race after him, she'd dashed up the stairs to her rented room, flopped onto her bed, and cried into the early hours.

The following morning, her holdall slung over her shoulder, she headed for Connolly Station, and boarded a train for the three-hour journey to Sligo.

She'd told no one she was pregnant. Not that there was anyone to tell. The people she'd rented with had never been close, and although she had friends at university in her first year, falling for Jude meant she'd let them slip away. Even before uni, growing up in her parents' isolated house meant she'd had few friends – and part of her liked it that way.

As the train rattled along the tracks, she placed her hands on her stomach, imagining her child with Jude's curls and cute nose, rather than her straw-like hair and sharp features. But it would have her blue eyes – an amazing child that Jude wouldn't be able to resist, once he'd had time to reflect. He would love their baby. They would be happy. The three of them.

'Your mother's gone,' the nurse had told her when she reached the hospital. 'I'm so sorry for your loss.'

A crushing numbness took over. *She'll never love me now.* Her eyes ached, but no tears came. She'd dreamt that one day she would be close to her mother – that they might even become friends. It had been a ludicrous dream.

The nurse touched her arm gently. 'Would you like to see your father?' she said, after a few moments. 'Although I must warn you, he's in a poor way.'

The week that followed had been long and painful. Her father was attached to drips, and the beeps of the monitor penetrated Laura's head, making it ache. He had been an arrogant man – so vain. Yet now he was swollen and bruised, and she cursed the wicked thought that invaded her head, as she sat by his side. *You deserve this.*

But still she visited each day, waiting for it all to be over.

'Why?' she asked him on day five, a question that spanned so much. But he never woke.

Why did you always drive so fast? Had it been for Mum? Her mother had loved the wind in her hair, as he treated back roads like racetracks.

23

Laura had been told the woman coming the other way had died instantly. That the child strapped in the back had survived. *A child lost her mother because of you.*

It was on the seventh day she asked, 'Why didn't you want me?' A tear finally rolled down her cheek, and she imagined for a moment that he squeezed her hand – that he was saying he was sorry. But there was no way he could have. He'd died ten minutes earlier.

And now, Laura stood in her parents' house, her hair damp from a shower and loose about her shoulders, her feet bare on the cold wooden floor. She knew she wouldn't go back to university – to the room her parents had paid for. It was time for her to get off the merry-go-round of life, pause time until she had the strength to climb back on – and what better place to come to terms with her parents' death, her pregnancy, and Jude letting her down, than here in this isolated house in the middle of nowhere?

The phone blasted, bringing her out of her reverie, and she raced to pick it up.

'Jude,' she said, twirling the phone cord around her fingers. He was the only one she'd given her parents' number to.

'It's Abi.'

Laura froze. She'd been friendly with Abi in her first year, but she didn't need her right now.

'I just wondered if you're OK,' Abi went on. 'Jude told me about your parents. He gave me this number – I hope you don't mind me calling.'

'I'm fine, Abi. Honestly. I just need some time out, that's all.'

'Well, give me a call, won't you, if you need anything. I can come up and see you at the weekend, if you'd like me to.'

'No.' It came out too sharp. Abi was a good person. 'Sorry. It's just I'm fine. I don't need anyone right now.'

'Well, OK then. But you know where I am …'

'I do. Thanks.'

Laura ended the call. The only person she needed right now was Jude.

She cupped her hand over her eyes, and peered through the window, and into the woods, her nose touching the glass. The lake where she'd swum as a child was visible through the glade. There had been some happy moments, hadn't there?

She narrowed her eyes. Someone was out there, by a distant tree. She blinked. She was tired, imagining things. The area had been deserted when she first arrived, and the nearest life a farm half a mile away. It was the shadows – the shapes of the hedgerow playing tricks.

She lowered the blind and spun round, her eyes skittering around the room. An oil painting of her parents filled the wall above the fireplace. That would have to go. In fact she would bag up most of their stuff and give it to charity. Her father would die again if he knew.

She grabbed her holdall and climbed the twisting staircase, and then stood in the doorway of her old room for the first time in two years. When she'd gone off to the University of Dublin to study art, she'd never looked back, never called – not once. Deep sadness consumed her.

She padded into the room, lifting books from the shelves. They were all educational – no *Noddy* or *Famous Five*. Her parents had expected so much of her. It was probably for the best they'd never known about the baby – that she'd made the decision to drop out of university.

Laura had begged her parents for a toy rabbit when she was a child, like Jenny's at school. 'Babyish,' her father had said. She'd been seven at the time.

My child will have toys – all the toys they desire.

She flopped onto the bed, eyes wide and looking at the ceiling, imagining her parents' awful accident on Devil's Corner – and how the poor woman had died. Had it been instant? Had the little girl in the back seat witnessed it, or had she been sleeping? How would such a young child cope without her mother?

She felt suddenly cold, and pulled the duvet over her. She curled into a tight ball, cradling her knees.

'We'll be OK, little one,' she told her unborn child, her eyes growing heavy. 'When Daddy comes, everything will be all right.'

Chapter 5

February 2018

'It's a bit weird, that's all.' I stared at the kettle, urging it to boil, feeling cross with myself for making too much of the friend request, and for showing it to Angela. 'I'm sure it's nothing to worry about. Just someone having a joke.'

'Jokes are meant to be funny, Rachel. Aren't they?' Angela heaved herself onto the kitchen stool, and rested her elbows on the breakfast bar, gazing my way.

She'd moved in next door about a year ago, and we'd hit it off immediately. I liked to think it was because we both liked Imagine Dragons and drinking rhubarb gin, but sometimes wondered if it was more than that. She was around my mum's age. Was I looking for a replacement mother figure, or perhaps a gran for Grace? I certainly couldn't rely on Lawrence's parents to fill that role; they'd started a new life in Australia before I met him, and he rarely spoke to them.

I swallowed a lump in my throat, guilt rising that I would ever consider replacing my mother, and I attempted to bat down memories of the last time I'd visited her. 'What a delightful little girl,' Mum had said, as Grace sat in the communal lounge with her colouring book and crayons, pausing every now and then to suck orange juice through a straw. 'Is she yours?'

It was those kinds of moments that held the most regret. Regret that I hadn't made more of the second chance I'd been given when Mum had a heart attack ten years ago. I'd promised myself at the time that I would make the most of every moment – and I did, for a while, visiting her often. But then I met Lawrence, and worked long hours in Kensington, and later we had Grace. Weeks sometimes turned into months. I should have called her more, visited more, especially as she would never have travelled to London.

'Well, I still think you should take the request seriously, Rachel,' Angela continued, cutting into my thoughts.

I bit back tears. 'I'm sure it's nothing.'

'It's pretty odd, if you ask me. Do you think it's connected to the call-in at the TV studio?'

Well, I do now. 'Why the hell would it be?'

She shrugged. 'Hey, keep your hair on, I just wondered, that's all. Have you tried searching for this David Green on the Internet?'

'Yes.' I spooned coffee into mugs, refusing to catch her eye. 'Last night, but the name is far too common. There are millions of results on Google.' I'd even searched random LinkedIn profiles, Twitter, and Instagram to see if I could find him, with no luck.

'Did you add Mandan Road and Sligo to your search?'

I nodded. 'Still nothing.' I felt a wave of anxiety wash over me. Sometimes, like now, Angela drove me crazy with her worrying. 'Anyway, lots of people get requests from strangers,' I went on, needing her to back up that theory, not raise more concerns.

'None for me!' She held up her hand as I rammed a teaspoon into the sugar bowl. 'I need to lose a couple of stone.'

I splashed scalding water into the mugs, and handed her a steaming sugar-free coffee. 'But you look great,' I said, controlling my desire to ask her to leave.

She tweaked my cheek. 'You're such a sweetie.'

'I mean it.' I did. Her weight had yo-yoed since I'd known her. Sometimes, like now, she was curvy, and looked great in jeans and a flowing, funky top – the kind my mum loved. Other times, she looked too thin. Today, her highlighted hair fell in layers to her shoulders, and her pleasant round face carried a smile. 'Are you going anywhere nice?' I asked, realising she was more made-up than usual.

'Another attempt at meeting Mr Right, this time for lunch – hopefully in liquid form.' She rolled her eyes. She'd signed up to a dating agency she'd seen advertised on TV, but so far it had been a disaster. 'It's costing a fortune to meet idiots and bores, quite frankly. Let me tell you, Rachel, chivalry is dead. I've paid my own way every single time.'

'That's the way it's done these days,' I said, with a smile.

She blew on her coffee, and took a delicate sip. She'd told me before how she'd taken early retirement, and recently she'd felt a bit lost. 'I just want someone to share my evenings with, Rachel. Is that too much to ask?' she'd said. 'It's lonely spending twenty-four hours a day in your own company.'

Now she glanced over her shoulder, and into my lounge: a square room with an original fireplace I adored. Toys were put away in the wicker chest, and I'd straightened the cushions and throws, put the books on the crammed shelf in height order, and dashed the hoover over the grey carpet. I was grateful the room looked tidy. Angela's house was always spotless. Not that she judged me.

'I'm guessing Lawrence has Grace?' she said.

'Mmm. They won't be back until Sunday evening, so I'm hoping to drive down to see my mum shortly. I prefer not to take Grace any more.' Another stab of guilt – what about the times Mum recognised her? 'It hurts … you know,' I went on. 'When Mum doesn't know us.' Sharp tears prodded my eyes, and I took a deep breath. I'd done far too much crying.

29

Angela reached over and patted my arm. 'I know, sweetie,' she said, her voice soft and warm. 'I know.'

***

Dream Meadows Residential Care Home was deep in the Suffolk countryside, and my mother seemed happy there, as far as I could tell.

I parked and headed into the front entrance, spotting Margo, a care assistant with a permanent smile and short silver-grey hair. 'Are you looking for your mum, dear?' she asked breezily, hurrying across the reception area. She'd taken a shine to my mother, and Mum liked her too. 'She was sleeping when I last put my head round her door. Go up. She's had a busy day today, but she'll be delighted to see you.' She went on her way, straightening her navy tunic over her midriff, as I climbed the stairs.

Mum's was a cosy room: a single bed, and a wardrobe and chest of drawers in antique pine. The surfaces were filled with framed photos jostling for space with trinkets Mum had asked me to bring from her house.

She was asleep on the bed, a duvet with lilac butterflies pulled over her, her breathing shallow. I stepped towards the window, and dragged back the thin curtains that matched the quilt cover.

Fields extended for miles – sheep and cows no bigger than ants dotted in the distance, and I imagined Mum painting the scene.

She stirred behind me, and I went over and perched on the edge of the bed near her head, watching her sleep, my body tensing as I pretended she was fine. Her quiet breaths were rapid, her eyes moving under closed lids. *What are you dreaming about, Mum? Is it the times we spent together when I was young? Trips to Southwold – eating chips – flying kites – walking along the beach? Should I wake her?*

As though sensing me, her eyes flickered and opened. 'Rachel,' she said, and my heart sang. It was a good day. *Thank God it's a good day.*

She pulled herself to a sitting position and leaned her head against the wall behind her. She was wearing a faded orange kaftan dress that was creased from sleep. I remembered her wearing it when I was young, yet it still fitted perfectly; she'd never gained weight over the years. I remembered visiting her house a few years ago, and trying to get her to throw a few things out. She'd been horrified when I suggested the dress should go, clutching it to her like a security blanket.

Now she pulled her plait over her shoulder, reminding me of a character from a Brontë novel.

'It's so lovely to see you, darling,' she said, burying her fists into her eyes and rubbing them, childlike. She leaned forward, and I took her into my arms and hugged her close, breathing her in.

'Where's Grace?' she said, when I released her.

'She's with Lawrence.' I hadn't told her we'd broken up. Not yet. I wanted to save her from that. 'Are you getting up? We could go for a walk in the grounds. It's cold but bright.'

'Yes. Yes, let's do that.' She swung her legs round, and a furry toy rabbit in a waistcoat fell to the floor.

I picked it up. 'Mr Snookum,' I said, placing a kiss on his head. 'I haven't seen you for years.' I thought he was in my attic.

She took him from me, and began fiddling with his ears. 'I gave him to you when you were little, remember?'

'Yes,' I said, raising a brow. 'I didn't realise you had him.'

She placed the love-worn rabbit on her pillow, and covered his small body with the duvet, so just his head poked out. Then she slipped her bare feet into canvas shoes.

'Will you be warm enough? It's been snowing.'

'In summer?'

'It's winter, Mum. You'll be cold.'

'Of course I won't,' she said, standing and pulling on a long, thick cardigan that brushed against her ankles. 'Let's go,' she said, and I followed her from the room, closing the door behind me.

We strolled around the grounds for about half an hour, our arms linked as we pointed out crocuses and snowdrops pushing their way through the cold earth. We talked about art – her favourite subject, and how different areas in the grounds would make beautiful paintings. Bare trees lined up against a pale sky in the distance with a hint of sunlight glowing around the branches, caught her attention. 'I'll paint those,' she said.

'I love you, Mum,' I said, resting my head on her shoulder, wanting to capture the lucid moment – a second of clarity amongst her sea of confusion. I wanted to bottle it so I could drink it in whenever I felt down. I couldn't bear that I was losing her, and battled down tears.

'Love you more, Rachel,' she said, as I brushed my cheek with the back of my hand. 'You're not crying, are you?'

'No, no, of course not,' I said, breathing deeply.

'Is this because Lawrence left you?'

I shook my head. *How did she know?* We stopped and stared at each other for several moments, her blue eyes shimmering. She took hold of my wrist, her hand freezing. And there it was, that look. I was losing her again. 'There are things you should know about the past, Rachel,' she said. 'Before I go.'

'Where are you going, Mum?'

'Laura.' Margo was dashing across the grass towards us, a little breathless. 'It's time for your heart tablets, love.'

To my frustration, Mum released her grip on my arm. 'I don't want to take them. They're poison,' she said, as Margo took her arm and led her away.

Our conversation was over for the day.

Chapter 6

February 2018

'She said there are things I should know about my past,' I said, as Angela and I sat next to each other on my sofa. I admit, I'd have preferred to be with Zoe, who I could rely on to pull me round and tell me I was daft to worry, but she was always so busy with work and her new romance with Connor – who was so cute she could eat him, apparently.

Angela's eyes were fixed on mine. Her curiosity, or maybe the wine, made them sparkle. 'What do you think she meant?'

I shrugged. 'She gets confused,' I said, stating the obvious.

'I know, sweetie. It must be dreadful for you both.' Angela leaned forward and filled our wine glasses for the third time, before handing me my glass. I wasn't sure I wanted another. I certainly didn't need a hangover tomorrow. But I took it anyway.

'She isn't herself at all,' I said. Another obvious.

'How much do you know about your past?' she asked.

I shrugged again. 'I was born in Ireland, County Sligo, but I can't remember that far back. We moved to Suffolk when I was about four, I think.'

33

'So, you're Irish?' she said, leaning forward, elbows on knees, as though the topic fascinated her.

'Half Irish – although my father could have been Irish, I guess.'

'You don't know who he is?'

Angela had asked about my dad before, but I'd changed the subject. I hadn't known her well enough at the time to discuss my personal life. She often pried into areas I wasn't ready to share with her. In fact, she'd only lived next door a week when she brought round moussaka that I could *pop into the oven, gas mark 5*, and a bottle of wine. She'd seen Lawrence go out for the third time that week, and thought I'd be glad of the company. I'd invited her in, not wanting to hurt her feelings.

But despite her flaws, she'd become a good friend. A friend I relied on to look after Grace.

I shook my head. 'I've asked my mother lots of times over the years who my father was, tried prodding her memory – but she's always insisted he was a one-night stand, and she'd been too drunk to even remember his name.'

'Do you know where in Sligo you lived as a child?'

I shook my head again.

'Could you ask your grandparents?'

'They died in a car accident before I was born. My mum was never close with them. And I have no other family.'

I tried to shake my mum's comment from my head. I liked that my memories started in Suffolk, that they were such happy times spent with my mum. But now I felt my curiosity rise, drawn to Ireland – to Sligo.

'You should find out more about your grandparents, at least. I've done a family tree, and it's been fascinating discovering things I never knew.'

'But they may not be relevant to what Mum said. I think I just need to talk to her next time I visit, wait for one of her more lucid moments, and ask her what she meant – before it's too late.'

My mood was spiralling downwards, like a child on a helter-skelter. I needed to change the subject, and managed to pluck a smile from somewhere. 'Anyway. Enough about me. How's the dating going?'

'Awful,' she said, leaning back, and peering over her almost empty glass. She was drinking too fast – and I wasn't far behind her. 'I feel like a fool selling myself to strangers. And the bra and knickers stage scares me half to death.'

I laughed. 'It's not easy,' I agreed. 'Have you met anyone you like?'

She shrugged. 'There was one bloke. But after a couple of dates he told me he was married. Separated, he insisted, but I couldn't face being part of a love triangle. I've been there before.'

'You have?'

'Mmm.' She nodded. 'A long time ago.'

'Was it serious?' I said, clutching at the opportunity to find out more about her. For a person who was so inquisitive about my life, she'd given little away about her own.

She closed her eyes and sighed. 'Anyway.' Her eyes sprung open, and I knew the little insight into her past had ended. 'There was another bloke I quite liked. He was a bit young though.'

I raised a brow. 'How young exactly?'

'Thirty – give or take a few years.'

'Oh my God, Angela, you devil.'

'I felt like his sugar mummy.'

I smiled. 'Is there such a thing?'

She shook her head. 'A panther then …'

'Cougar.'

We burst into laughter, my mood lifting.

'I think I'll be alone forever,' she said, fiddling with her earring as she drained her glass.

'You and me both.'

'But you will always have Grace.' She unscrewed the lid of the third bottle, and filled our glasses.

'Yes, Grace keeps me going,' I said, rubbing my forehead with the tips of my fingers. 'Although I worry about her, you know, how my breakup with Lawrence is affecting her. Nursery said she's been a bit quiet lately, but they have no concerns.'

'She loves you both very much, and you love her. She'll be just fine.'

'I hope so,' I said, my mind drifting.

And as though sensing she was losing me, Angela put down the bottle, looped her arm around me, and pulled my head in to her shoulder. She smelt of Chanel No.5 – Mum's favourite. 'Is there anything else bothering you, Rachel?' she said.

'Just Mum.' But in truth it was more than that. It was Lawrence. It was the fact I was letting the friend request from David Green blow out of proportion. And I'd definitely had far too much wine.

'I'll deactivate my Facebook account,' I said. 'Then the friend request can't bother me any more. And the truth is I look at Lawrence's timeline far too often. That can't be healthy, especially as he seems to be having more fun than me – which isn't that difficult.'

'Do you miss him?'

I shrugged. *Do I miss him?* 'I miss bits of him,' I said. 'The good bits.' And there had been good bits. We had a beautiful daughter together. He would surprise me with flowers and a bottle of Prosecco, and lead me upstairs where we'd stay for hours. Yes, there'd been good times. Lots of them.

But there had been bad times too, and his voice suddenly hammered in my head: *'You always over-react, Rachel.' 'The place is a pigsty.' 'You're a mess.' 'Aren't you getting a bit old for bright red hair?' 'Your mum isn't going to improve, and you have to accept it, and just get on with it.' 'I'll be late tonight.' 'I'll be late tonight.' 'I'll be late tonight.'*

I grabbed my open laptop, thumped it down on my knees, and clicked into Facebook, determined to close my account. 'Oh God, I've got another friend request,' I cried, peering at the little symbol at the top of the screen.

'Don't look at it,' Angela insisted, trying to pull the laptop from me.

I tugged it back. 'No, no, I'm not going to.' But I was already clicking on the symbol with shaking fingers.

Relief surged through my body, and I let out a small laugh.

'Who's it from?' she said, looking over my shoulder at the screen.

'You, you doughnut.'

She'd said a few weeks back that she was going to sign up, *to stalk the men on the dating site*, she'd joked. I gave another laugh as my heart, which I hadn't realised was racing, slowed to an even beat.

'Oh, yes, I forgot about that.' She laughed too. 'I don't suppose I'll use it that much. It took me all afternoon to work out how to set up a bloody profile.'

I accepted her friend request.

'But I thought you were going to deactivate.' Her forehead furrowed.

I shrugged, confused. 'To be honest I feel a teeny bit pissed – not the best time to make such a life-changing decision.' I giggled, picked up my glass, and drained it in two gulps, even though a nagging voice in my head was telling me not to.

Angela yawned and, stretching her arms above her head, glanced at the time on her phone.

'Oh my God,' I said, looking at the clock on the wall. 'It's gone midnight. I've kept you up.'

'No problem,' she said, rising. 'It's been fun. Better than a blind date any day.'

Five minutes later we hugged goodbye and, from my front door, I watched her stagger towards her house. Once she was safely inside, I closed and bolted my door, hating that I was alone – and hating even more that I hated being alone. I flumped down on the sofa, and picked up my phone, moving my index finger over the screen. Would Lawrence be up? Would he mind if I called? He'd said we could be friends.

I squeezed my hand into a fist. It was a ridiculous idea. If I called him after midnight he would be put out. He'd always told me he needed his beauty sleep if I ever woke him in the night desperate to talk about Mum.

I reached for the half-drunk bottle of red, unscrewed the lid, and refilled my glass. As I drank, I couldn't expel Lawrence from my head. How happy we'd been in the early days. We'd met at an art exhibition I'd put on for Mum, in a small gallery in London. He'd bought a study of Lough Gill in Ireland.

'It's the lake mentioned by Yeats in his poetry,' he'd said, locking me in with his grey gaze.

'You like Yeats?' I'd asked.

He'd nodded, and there was something about him that had captured my interest. Maybe it was simply because my mother had read Yeats and other romantic poetry to me when I was young.

I finished the wine and, my good sense heading out the door, brought up his number on my phone. I pressed call. It rang and rang, and I was expecting it go to voicemail when it was picked up. 'Lawrence Templeman's phone.'

It was a woman. American. *Why has a woman picked up his phone after midnight?*

'Hello,' she continued when I remained silent. 'Is that you, Rachel?'

Damn you, caller-ID. 'Sorry, yes, who is this?'

'It's Farrah.' It was as though I should know exactly who she was. 'Lawrence is asleep, I'm afraid. I heard his phone and, well …' She paused. 'Is everything OK? Is your mother OK?'

I bristled. Why had Lawrence told this woman, whoever she was, about my mum?

'Is Grace OK?' The sudden thought of a strange woman in the same house as my daughter angered me.

'Yes, she's been asleep since seven, bless her heart. She's an absolute delight. You must be so proud.'

I wanted to yell that I was coming to get my daughter, and how dare Lawrence let her into Grace's life without my permission? But I said nothing.

Farrah clearly picked up on my silence. 'Are you OK?'

'Yes, yes, I'm fine. Listen, I shouldn't have called.' My voice trembled, and I knew it carried a slur. 'I'll ring back in the morning.' And before she could respond, I ended the call.

A surge of tears hit my eyes as my thumbs thumped the screen and I sent a text to Lawrence:

How dare you let someone new into Grace's life without telling me!

Oh God, would Farrah read the text? I let out an exasperated wail, raced upstairs, chucked my phone onto the bedside unit, and threw myself onto the bed like a lovelorn teenager. The room spun.

Eventually sleep saved me from my chaotic emotions.

Later, I woke from a vivid nightmare, certain something had stirred me. I was thirsty, my head throbbed, and the quilt was tangled around me like a cocoon. I normally planted a glass of water on my bedside table if I'd been drinking, but in my silly stupor a few hours earlier, I'd forgotten. I was still in my clothes.

I lay for a few moments listening, but the only sounds were familiar creaks of the old building, and the distant rumble of a train. It was odd how when Grace wasn't with me, I felt more insecure.

I untangled the quilt, sat up, and swung my legs round, stuffing my feet into my slippers. I needed water before my tongue stuck to the roof of my mouth.

Flicking on the bedside light, I picked up my phone: 3 a.m.

I thought again about Lawrence. Were there photos of Farrah on his Facebook timeline that I'd missed? I dragged my fingers through my hair, still feeling pretty pissed. Water could wait. I clicked into Facebook on my mobile.

It was then that I saw it – another friend request. My heart bounced around my chest.

Ronan Murphy: CONFIRM/DELETE REQUEST

I clicked on his profile. As before, he didn't appear to have any friends. His profile picture was another view, a mountain this time – and I knew it was Benbulbin in Sligo. The cover picture was of a building that reminded me of a workhouse, and it had a sign outside that read 'Glastons Insurance. Dublin'.

I scrolled down his timeline. Just one status update:

Ronan, Ronan is no good
Chop him up for firewood

But this time I noticed he'd sent me a message.

Chapter 7

Incessant rain hammers against the window – a clap of thunder rings out. It doesn't wake him.

One strike to his head, so he doesn't fight back – but now he wakes, dazed – tries to speak – no words come out.

I plunge the knife deep into his flesh – once, twice, three times. The blood sprays and spurts like a bright red fountain, covering me – metallic on my lips.

He's holding on to life – too young to die – refusing to let go, reaching up to me, eyes pleading. He thinks I'll stop. Poor Ronan.

I lurch forward. The knife goes in one final time – deeper, and I twist, hearing his ribs crack.

They'll know it's me this time, but I don't care.

Ronan Murphy deserves to die.

Chapter 8

March 1987

Kneeling in front of the loo, Laura buried her head in her hands, waiting for another wave of nausea to hit. It would soon pass, once the digestive biscuit she'd eaten on waking took effect.

She rose, padded to the sink, and splashed her face with cold water. This would be so much easier if Jude was with her – but he hadn't replied to her calls. And she'd already stayed at her parents' house longer than she'd envisaged, unable to find the strength to put it on the market and move on. For now the woods and lake felt different to when she was a lonely child. She liked the solitude. The isolation.

She'd received a couple of letters from acquaintances at university, asking if she was OK, was there anything they could do, but she hadn't replied. Paralysed by the twin poles of grief – the loss of the parents who never loved her, and Jude not changing his mind – she found she couldn't reach out them.

She headed down the stairs, tightening her robe, knowing her face was the colour of dough. She needed to shower, to clean her teeth, but first, some coffee.

Despite liking the quiet of the area, the house still felt far too big. Sometimes it was as though she was on display – an exhibit in a glass case. Why had her parents loved this house so much? Her father had said the window gave them a splendid view of the lake, and she supposed it did, but what about feeling vulnerable on the other side of the glass?

She drifted into the kitchen and put the kettle on. Should she try to get hold of Jude again? Was she beginning to act like a stalker? Never giving up when she knew, deep down, it was over.

She'd tried the number of his digs so many times, but either it went to answer machine, or his roommate answered and promised to pass on a message. But Jude had never got back to her. She'd even tried his parents' house, but his father had picked up and told her with a bark to stop calling.

She made herself a mug of coffee – she'd gone off tea – and stood at the kitchen window sipping it. The kitchen looked out onto a lonely country road. It was a rarity to see a car pass by – it was too quiet at times, just as it had been when she was a child. She'd had no friends nearby back then, and travelled a fair distance to school by bus.

A postman appeared, cycling round the bend, and her heart almost lit up at the sight of another human being.

Maybe she should get herself a cat. At least she could speak to it, even if it didn't answer – it was better than talking to herself, which seemed to be happening more and more.

'It's Postman Pat,' she said, rubbing a hand over her stomach, which barely showed a baby was growing inside her. 'He's coming to see us, peanut,' she added, as he propped his bike against the wall.

There was a clatter, as three letters dropped through the letterbox and onto the mat. She headed over and picked them up. There was a letter from her solicitor sorting out the ownership of the house and the money her parents had left her, a phone bill, and a handwritten expensive-looking envelope. She ripped open the final letter, her eyes filling with tears as she read the words:

Dear Miss Hogan,

It's come to our attention that you are carrying our son's baby. We realise you are probably concerned and distressed too and so we would like to offer you the money to have a termination in a private clinic and a lump sum for you to make a fresh start; on the condition you no longer contact Jude. He has a bright future ahead of him, which I'm sure you already know, and I'm also sure you want a similarly bright future for yourself, without trying to raise a baby on your own. We all agree it's for the best if you and he have no more to do with each other. It was foolish of you to get into this predicament. But it's easily rectified. Please contact us at your earliest convenience, so we can arrange an appointment.

Sincerely,
Bruce Henshaw

She ripped the letter into shreds, dropping to her knees as she sobbed. How could they?

The tears stopped eventually, and she laid her head down on the floor and closed her eyes, small sobs escaping as she drifted off to sleep.

It was dark when she woke. Realising she'd slept all day, she blinked to clear the sleep from her eyes and stretched her aching limbs. The pain from reading the letter had subsided, replaced with anger.

She walked through the house, moonlight touching the dark lounge as she made her way through the shadows and the pockets of pure black. She moved closer to the window and looked out at the lake. Someone was out there – just as they had been on the first night. She'd dismissed it then as a trick of the light, but tonight, there was no doubting the silhouette she'd seen.

The solitary figure would have unnerved her once, but she

didn't care any more. *Come and get me if you dare. You can't hurt me. I'm already destroyed.*

The figure darted behind a tree, as though he'd heard her thoughts.

'Who are you?' she called, her words trapped behind the triple-glazed glass. Without a second thought, she raced to the kitchen and picked up a carving knife. 'Right, you bastard,' she whispered, heading for the patio door, and throwing it open. 'It's time someone paid.'

She stood for some moments, her robe dancing about her ankles in the wind, her eyes skittering around the area, knife clenched in her hand. 'What the hell do you want?'

A silent figure peered from behind the tree. It was too dark to make out his features.

'I've got a knife,' she yelled, raising it like a warrior. 'And I'm not afraid to use it.'

'I just want to talk,' a voice called back. He sounded young, a teenager perhaps. 'Wanted to find out who'd moved in.'

'Come here then.' She clenched the knife tighter, but as he approached and stepped into the light, she knew she wouldn't use it. He was just a child, no more than twelve – scruffy and unkempt, his dark hair tangled, his face grey with grime.

'Dillon O'Brian,' he said, hands deep in the pockets of grubby jeans. 'That's me name, case you was wondering.'

She looked into the woods. 'Where do you live?'

He took his hands from his pockets and pointed eastwards. 'Lough End Farm, with me ma and da, and Bridie and Caitlin.' He was Irish, his accent thicker than her own, and his green eyes looked dull and vacant.

Laura remembered the farm from her childhood. It had stood empty for years – was empty when she set off for university. 'When did you move in?' she asked.

'Almost two years now.' He sniffed, and wiped his cuff across his nose. 'Bridie's a year old, Caitlin's two months. They cry a lot.'

She placed the knife on the patio table, keeping her eyes on the lad, who nibbled at his thumbnail and scraped his heavy boots through the leaves and twigs.

'So you want to talk,' she said.

'I do. Yeah.'

'About?'

He shrugged. 'I just …' He stopped, screwing up his nose, and nodding towards the house. 'Did you know the couple who lived here?'

She nodded.

'They would tell me to piss off if I came up this end of the woods. They thought they owned it, but I told 'em they can't own a fecking wood.' He kicked a stone, and it flew up and hit the patio table, the clatter echoing into the darkness.

'You're right,' she said. 'But they thought they could do what they liked.'

'How did you know them?'

'They were my parents.'

'Christ! I thought I had it bad.' His face broke into a smile as he glanced towards an owl on a branch of a high tree, its eyes wide and haunting, and then he looked back at Laura.

'I'm Laura,' she said. 'Do you want a glass of lemonade or something?' And deciding the boy could do with a treat she added, 'I've got chocolate biscuits.'

He shook his head. 'I should get back before Da notices I'm gone. Ma always says he'll beat the shite out of me if I'm too long.'

'Surely not.'

He shrugged. 'He hasn't yet, but I ain't risking it. Listen, can I come by again some time? Would you mind?'

She smiled. It would be good to have the company. She was already feeling the isolation of the place. 'I'd like that,' she said.

'Grand,' he said, and took off, small and wiry, zigzagging through the trees.

46

Chapter 9

February 2018

I hated Sundays as a child. The thought of school the following day meant my hours at home were ruined, whatever we did. If I'd had my way, I would have stayed with my mother every day, watching her paint.

Sometimes, although never in depth, she would talk about her parents. 'We were never close,' she told me once, touching my cheek. 'Not like us, Rachel – we're different. It's you and me against the world.'

'I love you, Mum,' I would say.

'Love you more,' she would reply, as I leant my head on her knee.

If I was honest, I wasn't a fan of Sundays even now, especially today. Grace would be with Lawrence until six o'clock, and I had nothing planned. Plus I was woozy and fatigued from drinking too much. And with the weird things that had been happening, it really did have all the hallmarks of being a pretty rotten Sunday.

Needing someone to talk to, I'd messaged Zoe and Angela at four in the morning. Why I thought they'd be awake, I had no idea. But now the sun was up, its rays streaming through the kitchen window, and they still hadn't replied – I thought maybe they were miffed I'd disturbed their sleep.

Lawrence hadn't replied to my stroppy text either. Had Farrah deleted it, or perhaps suggested he shouldn't respond to his crazy ex?

Nibbling on a piece of dry toast, swallowing it down with sweet tea and painkillers, promising myself I would never drink again, I stared, trancelike, out of the kitchen window. My eyes fell on the summerhouse where I worked most weekday mornings, and I wondered what right I had to offer psychological help to others when I couldn't seem to manage my own life at the moment. Tomorrow, Emmy would arrive on her morning off from the TV studio, and I wasn't even sure I could face her.

Perhaps I should move out of Finsbury Park – start again somewhere new.

We'd moved nearer to central London when I worked in Kensington, and Lawrence worked in the finance district as a Software Development Engineer. Later, when he suggested we didn't need my salary, and I could be a stay-at-home mum, I'd had no objections. I adored spending time with Grace – being a mum. But after a while I missed working. So, over-riding Lawrence's objections at the time, I set up a business from home to fit around Grace.

I stared down at my phone. I hadn't opened the message from Ronan Murphy, convinced that if I did, whoever had sent me the request would know I'd looked at it. But now I needed to know.

I grabbed my phone, and opened the message, my hand trembling. Just two lonely words:

Hi, Rachel.

I tapped the screen:

Who is this?

Seconds later an attachment flew into my inbox. I opened it, heart thumping, oblivious to any thought it might hold a virus. It was a photograph of a pretty, pale pink cottage, with roses around the door. At the foot of the photograph were the words: **Evermore Farmhouse**, followed by an address in County Sligo.

'For God's sake,' I whispered. *What the hell's going on?*

Within moments I was Googling Ronan Murphy, adding the name of the insurance company, followed by the name of the farmhouse. Then I tried keying his name into LinkedIn, Instagram, and Twitter. But as with David Green, it was impossible to find him.

By nine o'clock, I felt calmer, and the painkillers had kicked in. I'd showered, pulled on leggings and a long, baggy jumper that touched my knees, and attempted to do something with my hair, which needed cutting badly.

My phone pinged. It was Angela.

Oh, sweetie. Do you want me to come round? X

I didn't. The desperate need for a friend in the small hours had vanished.

Maybe later. Thank you X

A red heart appeared on the screen, along with a row of kisses. At least I had friends I could rely on.

Phone in my hand, I brought up Lawrence's number. Should I call him? Ask to speak to Grace? I stopped myself. I was still fuming about Farrah, and the last thing I wanted to do was upset my daughter. Instead I rose and took the stairs two at a time, deciding to distract myself by clearing out my wardrobe. De-cluttering and filling a bag for charity would make me feel better, I felt sure of it.

I'd been working for about an hour when the doorbell rang. I raced downstairs to see a large envelope on the doormat. I reached to pick it up.

It was addressed to me.

Inside was a canvas, folded twice. The painting was in my mother's unique style, although unsigned. But it was ruined. Flakes of dried paint lay in its creases, and splodges of black filled the pale blue sky – a childlike attempt at clouds, perhaps. I tipped the envelope upside down, but there was no letter – no clue who sent it.

But I recognised the farmhouse immediately. It was same as the one in the photograph from Ronan Murphy earlier, although the building in the painting looked run-down. Had Ronan Murphy posted it through my door? Was it by my mother?

I flung open the front door, and looked up and down the road. Two cars – a red and a black – were indicating to turn left at the end of the road, and a white van was travelling in the other direction. A young couple stood at the bus stop, and a man with a briefcase hurried along the pavement. I had no way of telling who had delivered the letter.

I slammed the door and leaned my back against it. When had my mother painted this strange painting?

I hadn't seen all of my mum's work – many of her paintings were sold when I was young – but as I looked at the picture of the farmhouse, something stirred inside me. I'd seen a similar painting before in a pile I'd brought from Mum's house in Suffolk, when I'd collected things she'd needed in the care home. I'd intended to hang some – but they'd ended up propped up in the corner of the lounge for ages, and later been transferred to the loft.

I dashed upstairs, pulled down the loft ladder, and looked up, my stomach tipping. There were so many memories up there. Would it be upsetting to start wading through my childhood memorabilia, or souvenirs of happier times with Lawrence? I took a deep breath and climbed the metal steps. I would look at the paintings and come straight back down.

It smelt musty, and always felt odd in the attic, as I shared the space with Angela. No divide had been put up when the house was built, and although Lawrence had said he would sort it out, he never had.

The light illuminated twenty or so boxes crammed in our section, whereas Angela's side was almost empty. Just a pile of books – mainly medical – a holdall, and somehow Mum's pictures were leaning against her back wall. I hadn't been up there for so long, I could only think Lawrence must have moved them when he was trying to sort things out, and forgot to put them back.

I clambered over the boxes, and knelt down in front of the paintings. There was a stunning painting of Southwold's brightly coloured beach huts; one of the remains of Greyfriars Priory in Dunwich, the sky intense grey, as though it might start to rain; another depicting a fish and chip shop in Aldeburgh, a queue of people waiting – and I could almost taste the chips with lashings of salt and vinegar. They were all studies of where we'd visited when I was a child. Despite never travelling far from home – I never went abroad as a child – my mother loved Suffolk.

And then I saw it: a painting of the same farmhouse – but this time four children stood outside, three girls and an older boy. A memory fluttered. I knew this house. I'd been inside it, could smell the damp, the cigarette smoke, and what was that? Bleach? I dropped the painting, a surge of fear filling my senses.

Something terrible had happened there.

I rose, suddenly breathless, and clambered my way across the loft, knocking my knee against one of the boxes and letting out a cry, almost falling.

By the hatch I saw a box marked 'Rachel's Childhood'. Mum had given it to me many years ago, and despite knowing I needed to get out of the loft, the temptation was too much. I lifted the lid, and began rummaging.

I picked up a naked, tangle-haired Barbie. I'd had all her accessories too – although I hadn't wanted them that much. I'd been happiest with a football or a cricket bat, but a friend had a Barbie so I'd asked for one too. I continued to rummage through the fluffy toys that had once lined my bed, and found a game of Monopoly. I smiled at a memory of Mum and I playing. She'd joked that she'd wanted to buy Whitechapel and Old Kent Road to do them up, but I'd bought Mayfair and Park Lane, putting paid to her renovating ideas.

'Mr Snookum?' I whispered, nearing the bottom, and spotting his soft body. I lifted the toy rabbit out, and adjusted his waistcoat, before placing him against my nose, and breathing deeply.

And then it hit me.

Mum had him when I last visited. She'd tucked him under her duvet. How the hell had he got back into my loft?

I put him back in the box and snapped the lid shut, before climbing down the metal steps, my heart thudding.

Once downstairs, I put on my thick socks and boots and grabbed my parka, shoving the painting that had arrived earlier into my pocket.

I scooped up my car keys from the plate near the door. I knew I had to visit Mum.

Chapter 10

July 1987

Laura dangled her feet in the lake, the hot sun stroking her neck. The house her father built stood behind her as though determined to cast its shadow over her.

But it was a beautiful day, and the sun's rays danced on the water like shimmering diamonds. Anglers on the banks in the far distance looked like tiny dolls set up by a child. A sailboat glided across the lake, carried by the breeze.

Laura nibbled on a blade of grass, as she gazed through her sunglasses, her corduroy maternity dungarees tight across her stomach.

The jerking movements of her unborn child brought her out of her trance. She touched her stomach, but instead of how she'd hoped she might feel by now – amazed and bewildered by the miracle growing inside her – it was as though she was carrying an alien. An alien that reminded her daily that Jude let her down.

Seven months she'd carried the little stranger, and now she'd stopped hoping Jude would call. She'd accepted he never would, and any love she'd first felt for their unborn child had been replaced with fear. Thoughts of moving away, starting a new life, were a distant memory. She hadn't got the strength to move on – not right now. Perhaps she should have told her GP she dreaded the birth of her child. But how do you explain something so awful? How do you say those words?

She clung to the rapidly fading glimmer of hope that maybe, when she held her child in her arms, her motherly instincts would kick in. Burst through and outweigh anything she'd ever felt for Jude. Maybe their baby would become the love of her life, and together they would start a new life somewhere else.

Twigs snapped behind her. She turned, but there was nothing to see. She knew it was Dillon. She'd seen him several times over the past few months, when they would drink lemonade and talk. She had learnt not to ask too many questions about his home life because each time she had, he'd clouded over and clammed up.

He was an imaginative, animated boy, lighting up as he described the monster in the lake, and the werewolves in the woods – giving Laura's life a much-needed magical boost. He'd been flattering too – telling her he could talk to her more easily than he could to anyone else. And he'd loved her paintings.

Laura had enjoyed painting since childhood, and despite dropping out of university, she'd loved studying art. And now painting had become her go-to – her escapism from her grief and isolation.

'They're fecking brilliant,' he'd said, scanning her walls. (They'd taken ages to put up – a rebellious act against her parents.) 'Maybe you could paint one of me and me sisters?'

'One day,' she'd said.

'Dillon,' she called now, her gaze skimming over the cluster of trees, blinking as a beam of sunlight hurt her eyes. 'Is that you?'

The sun drifted behind a fluffy white cloud, and Laura pulled on her cardigan and shivered. 'Dillon, don't be silly,' she called over her shoulder. 'Come and talk to me.'

He appeared on the bank behind her, and she patted the ground moaning as she twisted her baby bump, a twinge crossing her stomach. 'Sit with me,' she said, and he ran and dropped down beside her, stretching out as the sun crept out once more – his hands behind his head like a pillow, and eyes closed.

'Did you know the mayfly only lives twenty-four hours?' he said.

'I did not know that,' she said with a smile.

'And did you know the dragonfly doesn't bite or sting? Although it looks pretty scary.' He pulled himself to a sitting position, and she noticed his eyes were bloodshot and red.

'Are you OK, Dillon?'

'Yep, course. Why?' He avoided her gaze.

She placed her hand on his arm. 'You know you can tell me anything, don't you?'

'I said, I'm fine.' He pushed her hand away. 'Don't go all soft on me, Laura.'

'OK, sorry. I didn't mean to be nosy. So tell me more about the dragonfly.'

He rubbed his face hard, and his eyes shimmered. She wanted to ask again if he was OK, but felt it might scare him away.

'Did you know fox pups stay with their parents until they're seven months old? They make great parents. I like foxes. I often see one out here.'

'You're so clever. How do you know all this stuff?'

He shrugged, and turned to look at her, eyes serious.

'What is it, Dillon? Please tell me.'

'I can't. If he knew …'

'Who knew?'

He dropped his head, fiddling with his fingers. 'You have to promise on your baby's life you won't say anything.'

'OK.'

'It's just … sometimes I find my sister Bridie in the cupboard. I hear her sobbing sometimes because it's dark in there, and she can't get out. Ma has the key.'

'Oh my God, Dillon,' she said, her heartbeat speeding up.

'Ma says me da puts her in there before he heads off to work, as a punishment. And ma says she daren't get her out because he'd go mad, and hit her.' He paused, now picking at a scab on his knee. 'But Bridie's only little, Laura.' The scab came away in his fingers, and blood trickled. 'I don't know what's wrong with me da. He's always been a bit of a shouter, but now it's as if the divil's gotten into him.'

Laura studied the boy, shocked something so awful could be happening – was he telling the truth? He'd never mentioned anything like it before.

'I swear on my sisters' lives it's true,' he said, as though he knew what she was thinking.

Laura's mind spun. 'Shall I come over?'

'Jaysus and all his angels, no.' Dillon narrowed his eyes, and wiped away the blood on his knee with his sleeve. 'You can't come to the farmhouse, Laura.' He shot to his feet. 'If Da or Ma find out I've been talking …' He looked towards her, fear in his eyes. 'There's nothing you can do, anyway. I once called the Guards on Da, because Ma said he hit her. But Ma wouldn't let them in. Denied it, and they just believed her. Never came back. I just needed to tell someone, Laura, but there's nothing you can do. Promise you won't do anything.'

'OK, I won't. I promise. Sit, please, Dillon,' she said. 'Tell me more about the wildlife.'

A sudden stir in the trees seemed to unsettle him. 'I'd best get going,' he said, and before she could say another word, he made a bolt for it, and it wasn't long before he was out of sight.

Laura edged forward on her bottom, and dangled her bare feet in the clear, cold water, as a swan drifted by. Ten minutes passed in a daze, as she thought about Dillon, Caitlin, and Bridie.

Were the children OK? Did Dillon even go to school? He'd told her he did, but she couldn't be sure – he was often about during the day. Should she try to find out more about the children's life at home? Introduce herself as their neighbour, perhaps?

It was almost seven, and she knew she would need to move fast if she wanted to get to the farm and back before dark. She dried her feet on the grass, slipped them into flip-flops, and grabbed her hessian bag.

It was dusk by the time she found the farm, a dilapidated two-storey farmhouse. A couple of run-down sheds stood nearby, and a small apple tree grew near the lake, near a moored rowing boat. She remained a good distance away, obscured by trees, watching as a small, dark-haired woman of around her own age gathered towelling diapers from a makeshift washing line. Hens darted around her feet, almost toppling her over, as she folded the diapers into a wicker basket.

Laura wanted to go over, introduce herself, but her legs refused to move; the woman looked stern, unapproachable, and anyway, she'd promised Dillon. As she watched on, the last of the sun went down, coating distant trees like liquid gold. The woman wedged the basket onto her hip, just as the front door was flung open, and a little girl toddled out, her head full of dark curls – one of the braces of her red dungarees was undone, flapping about as she moved.

'Bridie!' It was Dillon, following her out. He lifted her up and swung her round and round, and the little girl giggled.

From what Laura could see, they seemed happy enough – a normal family. A little rough around the edges, but she knew that much.

The woman looked about her, and ushered Dillon, with the girl tucked under his arm, inside, as though she sensed a storm coming. Moments later the door slammed behind them. If it hadn't been for the hens scurrying about, pecking the ground, it would have felt as though nobody lived there at all.

The sun had dipped behind the horizon, and Laura hitched her bag further onto her shoulder, and turned for home. But as she stepped forward a searing pain made her tense. She grabbed her stomach, and bent over.

'You spying?' It was a male voice some distance away.

Laura stood upright, and looked about her, the pain easing.

'I asked you a question,' came the voice.

'I was just out walking. I live about half a mile away,' she called, trying to pick out the man in the darkness.

'Lough End Farm is private property,' he called. 'You're trespassing.'

'Yes, sorry. I'll be on my way.'

'What's your name?'

'Laura. Laura Hogan.'

'The daughter of that couple who died at Devil's Corner? I heard you'd moved in.'

She shuffled. 'I should get back.'

'I'm Tierney O'Brian.' He was still out of view, although his shape was moving towards her through the darkness, tall and broad – still too far away to make out his features. 'Just keep away from here in future.'

'Yes, yes, of course.' She dashed into the woods, another pain gripping her, as though someone had grabbed her around the middle and squeezed. She stopped, crying out, and grabbed a tree branch.

'You OK?' she heard Tierney call out, his footfalls approaching.

'Fine,' she called. *Surely it isn't a contraction, not this early.*

She sucked in a breath, and hurried through the darkness, nerves jangling, Dillon's words about Bridie being locked in a cupboard still in her head.

She picked up speed, weaving in and out of the trees, a sudden movement of a low-flying bat causing her to cry out. What the hell was wrong with her?

Relieved to see the welcoming porch light of her house, she

fumbled with her key. Once inside, she pulled the bolt across and leaned against the door. The family at the farm looked perfectly happy, didn't they? She could stop worrying about the children, couldn't she?

Another painful contraction ripped across her stomach.

'Oh God, no,' she cried, as she slid to the floor in agony, her waters breaking.

Chapter 11

February 2018

I arrived at Dream Meadows Care Home at two o'clock. Mum was in the communal lounge, a peaceful place looking out over the grounds.

I made my way through the people dotted about on chairs and sofas, reading, sleeping, or doing crossword puzzles, and sat down beside her.

Her blonde hair, not a trace of grey, hung loose and damp, from a recent shower I suspected. She looked younger than her years. Pretty in a flowing purple top with a ruffled hem, that I'd bought her for Christmas, over navy leggings, and a pair of fluffy slippers.

'Mum,' I said, taking hold of her hand, and she looked up, her eyes wide and vacant. I knew before she said a word that she didn't know who I was.

'Hello,' she said, locking her eyes on mine. 'I'm Laura Hogan. Do I know you?' The question always stung. But before I could answer, my mother continued, 'My daughter's at school at the moment – she's very clever. She came to see me this morning.'

I sighed inside. 'Can I get you a drink?' I said, trying to control the usual surge of tears burning behind my eyes. 'Coffee?'

'Are you my carer?' She looked about her. 'Where's Margo today? I like Margo.'

'I'm not your carer, Mum. It's me. Rachel.' I swallowed a lump rising in my throat. I had to keep from crying, for her sake.

'I don't want any …' She stopped, and tapped her knee with her free hand, as though she was sending Morse code to her brain. 'I don't want any brown hot water … thank you. I've had several cups already. It keeps me awake at night.'

I squeezed her hand, wanting to ask her what she'd wanted to say the last time I was here, ask her about Mr Snookum, show her the painting, but what good would it do?

'I love you,' I whispered.

'Love you more,' she said, eyes still closed.

'It's still you and me against the world, Mum. It always will be.'

Her eyes flickered and opened, and she broke into a smile. 'Would you get me a coffee, please? My daughter might come later, and I want to be awake when she does.'

For an hour I sat by her side, reading aloud *Alice's Adventures in Wonderland*, one of her favourite books. It was far easier to read than attempt to talk, and the words of Lewis Carroll seemed fitting somehow. My mother had disappeared down a rabbit hole and into another world, just like Alice.

Finally, I got up to leave, and kissed her cheek. I pulled on my coat, and as I tucked my hand in my pocket, I felt the picture, and questions darted around my head. Should I show it to her? Would she recognise the farmhouse? Would her older memories be easier to reach? I didn't want to upset her, but desperately needed to know. I pulled it out, unfolded it, and placed it on her knees. 'I wondered if you remember this place, Mum?'

She looked down, and her eyes filled with tears, as she ran shaking fingers over the black clouds and down the creases. 'Rachel added the clouds.'

'Did I?' I couldn't remember.

She stared at the picture for some time before a sudden desperate sob came from deep inside her. 'The cuts,' she cried. 'They were the same size. They should have been different, you see. I should have said something.'

I reached over, folded the picture, and stuffed it back in my pocket, as Margo rushed over to comfort her, pulling her into a hug.

'Mum,' I said. 'Mum, tell me what's wrong. What is it you wanted to tell me last time I was here?'

But as quickly as her tears came, they stopped. She pulled away from Margo, and her eyes, vacant once more, focused on the window.

It was time for me to leave.

***

Snow fell thick and fast on the journey home, settling on the grass verges, and I began to panic that I wouldn't get back in time for Lawrence bringing Grace home, but thankfully I skidded to a stop outside my house the same time as he did.

'Mummy,' Grace called once he'd unstrapped her from the car seat, and plonked her down on the snow-covered pavement.

'Hello, my lovely girl,' I said, crouching and holding out my arms. She padded across the snow towards me, wrapped in her winter coat, a wool hat with a fur pom-pom covering dark curls. She'd inherited her hair from Lawrence, although he kept his short these days.

I took her into my arms and squeezed, breathing her in. 'I've missed you so much.'

'I've missed you more,' she said, as I released her. She looked up at the dark sky, and a snowflake landed on her nose. 'Can we build a snowman?' she said, eyes back on me.

'Maybe later,' I said.

She crouched down, and began scooping snow into her gloved hands, singing 'Do you want to build a snowman?' from *Frozen* at the top of her voice.

Lawrence approached, tall, slim, and handsome, in a smart jacket with jeans and a green woollen hat with an oversized pom-pom. I glanced at the car. Someone was sitting in the passenger seat. *Farrah?*

'I got your text,' he said, folding his arms.

'Yes, well, I was angry.' I looked up at him and stuffed my hands in my pockets, conscious I looked a mess. 'You should have talked to me before introducing fucking Farrah to our daughter.' I never swore much, and it always sounded a bit lame – silly – like I was a child trying out the word for the first time.

'Don't be pathetic, Rachel.' He'd said that to me a lot in the weeks leading up to our breakup. 'Her name's Farrah Bright.'

'Of course it is.'

He glanced over his shoulder at Grace. 'Listen, I think it's only fair you should know.' He paused for a moment. 'The thing is …' He scratched his eyebrow. 'The truth is, I've been seeing Farrah for over a year now, and we're pretty serious. I'm sorry, Rach …'

'A year?' I cut in. 'Jeez, Lawrence, how could you?' I felt my chin wobble. 'You were seeing her when we were together?' My stomach heaved. I'd had no idea.

'Not seriously.'

'Well, that's OK then,' I spat.

'I'm sorry.' He tried to take hold of my hand, but I dodged his, my arms flapping like helicopter propellers as I smacked the cold air, and skidded around on the ice like Bambi.

'I didn't want to hurt you,' he said, catching my elbow.

'Well, that didn't work out for you. Just leave me alone,' I cried, snatching my elbow away, and storming past him, almost slipping again as I fumbled for my keys – desperate to get inside before tears came. 'Grace, come on, lovely girl.'

'Farrah adores Grace,' he called after me. 'She can't have kids, so …'

I turned, glaring at the car. The woman faced forward, a fur-lined hood obscuring my view of her. I wanted to rush over, bang on the glass, scream that she could have Lawrence with knobs on, but Grace belonged to me. 'Keep her away from Grace,' I said calmly.

I opened the front door, and Grace ran to my side. 'Wave to Daddy,' I said, trying hard not to show her how angry I was.

'Bye, Daddy,' she called, waving.

'Bye, chipmunk,' he called back, and it took all of my willpower not to pick up a clump of snow and chuck it at his stupid shiny black car.

Chapter 12

Laura stood in the dense darkness at the water's edge rocking Rachel, hoping the night air would send her daughter to sleep.

'Shh, please,' she whispered, but Rachel continued to yell – a piercing sound, like an incessant dentist drill inside Laura's head, screwing with her mind, twisting her thoughts so they were no longer recognisable as her own.

She couldn't see her baby's face, but knew it would be red and blotchy, coated with tears and snot, because it always was. *It always is.*

The birth had been problematic – a bad start. Laura's hopes that the anger she felt towards Jude would dissipate once she held her child in her arms hadn't happened. Rachel had been premature, with respiratory distress syndrome and severe jaundice. She'd been kept in intensive care for almost a month, and Laura had struggled to bond with her. In fact, she felt nothing. Was she no better than her own parents?

Now Rachel was three months old. The midwife and health visitor were long gone, leaving her to it, believing she was OK. She'd somehow convinced them of that.

She had nobody to turn to. If she'd only kept in contact with the other students at university – accepted Abi's offer of help when she'd called. But it was too late now they'd gone their own ways. In fact, the only people she saw were those behind shop counters, or old ladies who cooed at the child, telling Laura how beautiful her daughter was. She wished she could see what they saw. The consuming guilt was unimaginable.

But she still saw Dillon sometimes – Dillon who'd put up with her tears, and her weirdness. How had it happened that her only friend was a teenage boy?

He hadn't mentioned his family since July, and Laura sometimes felt she should ask, but she was struggling so much with her daughter, she wasn't sure she could take on his problems too.

Laura squeezed the child to her. 'Shh! Shh! Please stop crying,' she said, moving towards the lake. Once there she looked down, her eyes adjusting to the shimmering water, like tar beneath her. 'I'm so tired,' she said, stepping closer still, so close that her toes curled over the edge, and the earth crumbled. If she jumped it would put them both out of their misery.

As though sensing her mother's thoughts, Rachel stopped crying, and drifted off to sleep. Laura looked down at her daughter. This little thing with soft, downy hair, and blue eyes, was an innocent victim of a heartless man and a desperate woman. She hadn't asked to be born.

Laura laid the child, wrapped in a thick blanket, on the ground, and fell down next to her. They would sleep outside tonight.

***

The sun was rising in a cloudless sky when Dillon woke Laura.

'What the feck are you doing out here?' he said, nudging her with his foot as though she was a corpse. He knelt down and picked up the baby. 'What you up to, mischief?' he said to Rachel, touching the child's bare feet that poked from under the blanket. 'Jaysus, your tootsies are freezing.'

He stared at Laura, who was clambering to her feet with the aid of a tree. She ran her fingers through her greasy hair, catching them in tangles, blinking to adjust her eyes to the daylight. 'God, what's the time?' she said.

'About eight – you been out here all night?' He jiggled Rachel up and down, humming 'Hush a bye baby' as the baby attempted to consume her fist.

'Not all night,' she said, avoiding meeting his eye. 'Let's go in – Rachel will be hungry.'

Inside, Dillon gave Rachel her bottle, the baby's hand gripping his little finger as she gulped down the milk, making contented noises. 'You need to see someone, Laura,' he said, sounding far too grown-up for his years. 'You're always crying, and so is this little one. It's not right. Do you even wash?'

'You're a fine one to talk,' Laura said, pushing a pile of newspapers and some dirty mugs across the table, and plonking down a coffee and a can of cola. She sat down beside him.

'I don't know who to turn to, Dillon.' Her eyes filled with tears. She couldn't keep burdening a thirteen-year-old kid – it wasn't fair. 'I can't manage; I know that, but the thought of busybodies interfering – maybe even taking Rachel away – doesn't bear thinking about.'

'I could ask me ma to help?'

Laura stiffened. The woman who allowed a child to be put in a cupboard? 'No, I'll be OK,' she said. 'I'll make an appointment at the doctor's. Honestly.'

'But Ma would be company for you.'

Laura didn't want anyone in her home, finding fault, judging her. And to get involved with Dillon's family worried her. Tierney O'Brian had left her with a cold feeling in the pit of her stomach.

'She could come here when Da's working,' Dillon continued, looking about him at the half-drunk bottles with milk curdling at the bottom, the used diapers that smelt awful, mugs, glasses …

the hellhole she lived in. 'Ma could help tidy up a bit. She's good at keeping things clean.'

Laura looked at Dillon, scruffy and grimy, as ever. She snatched up her mug of coffee and took a gulp. It burned her tongue. 'I'm fine, Dillon,' she said, her eyes on Rachel now sleeping in his arms.

'But she's used to three kids, Laura. She took me on, and that couldn't have been easy.'

'Took you on?'

He rubbed his hand across his mouth, as though he was unsure of the words he wanted to say. 'Imogen ain't me real ma,' he said eventually. 'She just likes me to call her that. I don't mind so much now, but at first it felt wrong.' He placed a tender kiss on Rachel's head.

'Why didn't you tell me?'

'Never came up.' He rose, and placed Rachel into her Moses basket, covering her with a lemon-coloured blanket. 'Me real ma walked out just after we moved to the farm.'

'Oh, Dillon, I'm so sorry.'

'Me real ma invited Imogen to live with us when she was preggers with Bridie. Her parents had kicked her out.' He paused, rubbing his hand across his mouth. 'Can we talk about something else? It's just I don't like talking about it – me real ma never said goodbye.'

'I'm so sorry.'

'It's fine, Laura,' he said, but it clearly wasn't. 'So, should I ask Imogen?'

Laura knew she couldn't carry on as she was. It wasn't fair on the baby. She would either have to accept his offer, or see the GP, who would probably fill her with tablets, or even take Rachel away – she didn't want either. She would bond with the child eventually. She had to. They couldn't go through life like this. Maybe Dillon's stepmother would understand, help her. But the fear of getting involved with the family was too strong.

'I don't need anyone, honestly,' she said. 'Rachel and I will be just fine.'

***

Two days later, Laura sat outside in the rain, soaked and sobbing, while Rachel screamed inside the house as though her tiny heart would break.

Dillon approached through the trees, and stood in front of Laura, his hands deep in his pockets.

She looked up. 'I'm so sorry,' she said, and covered her face with her hands.

He didn't reply, just took off into the woods, reappearing some time later with his stepmother, and his sisters.

'I'm Imogen,' the woman said. She was tiny, her dark hair scraped back in a high ponytail, her fringe uneven. Caitlin, a smiling, pretty baby of eight months, with the same dark hair, was balanced on her hip, and Bridie, more solemn, in grubby dungarees, clung to her mother's blue and white checked dress.

The rain had stopped for now.

Laura brushed away her tears with the back of her hand and got up.

'You poor thing,' Imogen said, stepping closer. 'Dillon said you were in a bit of a pickle. Bad case of the baby blues, I shouldn't wonder. I had it dreadful with Bridie. Couldn't touch the child for months.'

She handed Caitlin to Dillon, and bustled Laura inside. She instantly made the red-faced, screaming Rachel a bottle, and changed her diaper.

'Me ma's pretty good, ain't she?' Dillon's eyes followed Imogen, as she went to work, clearing up, and stuffing washing into the washing machine.

'She is, yes,' Laura agreed. There was no doubting his words, but watching the woman busying herself made her feel more useless than ever.

'Cleanliness is next to godliness, that's what my mother taught me,' Imogen said, as she filled the bottle steriliser with water, and dropped in tablets. 'Not that I believe in God. Well, if there is one, he's let me down.' She headed up the stairs, and Laura followed.

'Help me,' said Imogen, as she changed Laura's bed, and Laura grabbed the pillows and changed the covers. 'That's the idea,' Imogen went on with a smile, as though she was praising a child.

Next, Imogen grabbed a duster and wiped it over the chest of drawers. 'Chanel,' she said, picking up the bottle and spraying her neck. 'Nice for some.'

'Shall we go back downstairs?' Laura said, kicking her dirty underwear under the bed in the hope Imogen wouldn't notice. It all felt far too intrusive.

'In a moment,' Imogen said, leaning down and scooping up the underwear. 'Where's your linen bin?'

'In the bathroom,' Laura said, snatching the knickers from her and leaving the bedroom. 'I can do that.'

Later, when the house was spotless, and Rachel was gurgling happily in her Moses basket – tugging and stretching the foot of her Babygro – Imogen finally collected up her daughters.

'I'd better get home to put Tierney's dinner on,' she said, her eyes skittering over Laura's paintings on the wall. 'These are stunning,' she said. 'Especially this one.' She pointed at one of the lake. 'You're very talented.'

'Thank you,' Laura said, a sudden lift inside her. Perhaps she wasn't as useless as she thought.

'I'll be back soon, I promise,' Imogen said, touching Laura's cheek.

From the window, Laura watched them go, Dillon trotting behind with a stick the size of him, as though he was their protector.

Laura wished she had someone to protect her.

70

Chapter 13

February 2018

By morning, deep snow covered the roads and paths, and a message on my phone at eight-thirty told me Grace's nursery school was closed.

I'd always arranged my appointments to coincide with Grace's nursery sessions. Two clients a day in term time only. At times like these I was grateful to Angela who'd offered as soon as we became friendly to look after Grace if ever I needed her to. Lawrence hadn't been keen on the arrangement. He had a tendency to be suspicious of 'Good Samaritan' strangers. But Grace seemed to like her, and that was good enough for me.

Grace tucked into her cereal, and I approached and sat down beside her. 'What's Farrah like?' I asked, pushing a tendril of her hair behind her ear, wanting her to say she didn't like her. It was selfish of me. If Farrah was going be in her life, it was better that Grace liked her. And she liked Grace. For my daughter's sake, I needed to act like a grown-up about Farrah. Grace seemed to be coping OK with her parents living in different houses; I didn't want to make things harder for her.

71

'She's nice,' Grace said, nodding. 'She smells of flowers, and has hair like a princess.'

It wasn't what I wanted to hear, but I tried not to show it.

'Does she kiss Daddy?' I asked. *Stop asking!* It wasn't fair. I didn't care about Lawrence any more – did I?

She shook her head, so her curls bounced. 'Finished!' Grace dropped her spoon into the empty bowl, and swiped her mouth with the back of her hand.

'You're not going to nursery today, darling,' I said. 'You're going to see Angela.'

She turned up her nose.

'You like Angela, don't you?' *Oh God, please like Angela.*

She shrugged, and slid from the stool. 'She's OK, I suppose. But I want to go to nursery. I like nursery.'

'Well, I'm afraid it's closed today, because of the snow.'

'Snow!' She dashed to the French window, tugged back the curtain, and leaving handprints on the glass, squealed with excitement. 'WOW! Can we build a snowman, Mummy?'

'Later,' I said, feeling a pang of guilt that I hadn't built one with her the night before. 'Promise.'

She glanced over her shoulder at me and pulled a grown-up face. 'Proper promise, or pretend promise?'

'Proper,' I said, through another shot of guilt. 'This afternoon.'

I washed Grace's face and hands, before tugging on her coat and fur-lined boots. We headed for the front door, and I went to grab my spare keys from the bowl in the porch. I always gave them to Angela when she had Grace, just in case I'd forgotten something my daughter needed. But they weren't there. Had Angela returned them last time? I couldn't remember.

We walked across the garden towards her front door, and rang the doorbell.

Angela opened up, a wide smile stretching across her face. 'What a lovely surprise this is,' she said, tugging her robe around her. 'We can play Snakes and Ladders, like last time.' She tweaked Grace's nose.

'And you promise you won't fall asleep,' Grace said, sounding a little precocious, and stepping inside. She dropped onto her bottom and tugged off her snowy boots, clearly remembering Angela's rules of no shoes in the house.

'I was resting my eyes that day.' Angela tipped back her head and laughed. 'I'm not as young as your mummy.'

I laughed too. 'Children can be tiring,' I said, making a mental note to ask Grace more about her time with Angela, who I felt was hardly of an age to need a mid-morning nap.

***

Back home, I had to keep my mind on track – concentrate on my clients – even though I felt I was the one in need of the therapy session. I'd had counselling once, as part of my training. It had been good for me at the time – helped me come to terms with the fact I might never know who my father was.

Despite having all my arrangements in place, my first client cancelled because of the weather, so I trudged down the garden and disappeared into the summerhouse to do some paperwork.

A sharp knock on the window an hour later startled me.

'Rachel, are you in there?' I glanced over my shoulder to see a freckled face appear behind the glass, pale green eyes searching.

'Emmy,' I said, looking at my watch and realising it was time for her appointment. I smiled. At least Emmy would lift my mood. I enjoyed her sessions now, proud of how far she'd travelled. Maybe it was unprofessional, but we'd become good friends.

I opened the door and she stepped in, looking as though she was about to ski down a snowy mountain, dressed in an all-in-one ski-suit, and boots.

'How's things?' she said, and what I wouldn't have given at that moment to tell her everything, unburden myself. But I was here to listen to her. Put her back together again – although most of the stitching had been done. 'God it's hot in here,' she went on, shimmying out of her ski-suit.

'Take a seat,' I said, once she was down to jeans and a cream cashmere jumper. 'Would you like a drink?'

She shook her head, and we slipped effortlessly into therapy. I felt sure this would be her last session.

When she first came, her severe panic attacks, stammering, depression and recurring nightmares were being controlled by medication that helped her cope with her job on morning TV. Her mother had died when she was young, and the tragic stillbirth of Emmy's baby two years ago had triggered memories of her childhood trauma. The desperate need for a mother figure in her life, at a time when she'd come so close to being a mother herself, had seen her fall apart.

Her goal when we first met was to attempt to manage without medication, so she could try for another baby. We were both delighted that she'd now been medication-free for over three months.

'I think we could end our sessions for now, Emmy,' I said at the end of our hour together. 'You're doing so well.'

'I agree.' Her voice was calm and soft. 'And there's something else.' Her eyes shone, as she patted her stomach. 'I'm going to be a m – mu – mum.' I picked up on her slight stammer that was mainly under control, only occurring at times of extreme stress or excitement.

'Oh my God, really?' I squealed.

'Really!' she yelled, cheeks pink.

'Oh, Emmy, that's wonderful news.' I moved in for a hug. This was just the kind of news I needed to lift me. 'I'm totally made up for you.'

'I'm not quite three months, so I shouldn't be telling anyone, especially after … well, you know. But then you're not just anyone, Rachel. You've helped me through the worst time in my life.' Her

74

eyes filled up, and she snatched a couple of tissues from the box and dabbed her eyes. 'I'm not sure where I would be right now if I hadn't booked that first appointment a year ago.'

'I'm just glad I could help,' I said, through a lump in my throat. It was one of those moments when I was proud to be a psychotherapist. 'And if you ever need me, you know where I am.'

'So what about you?' she said, patting my knee. 'Something isn't right. I can tell.'

Was it that obvious? 'We're not here to discuss me, Emmy,' I said, closing her file.

'But our sessions are over. Talk to me.' She leaned forward and stared into my face. 'This isn't to do with that stupid call to the studio, is it?'

'God no, I put that out of my head a long time ago,' I lied.

'If you don't want to tell me, you don't have to.' She leaned back in the chair, and gave a hurt shrug.

'It's just I've had a couple of odd friend requests from strangers on Facebook, and they've unnerved me a bit, that's all.'

She leaned forward once more. 'I used to get them all the time – loads of people do, it's nothing to worry about. In fact, I once got a message from someone saying he was in the forces, and wanted to marry me.' She smiled. 'I've now tweaked my settings to only allow friends of friends to add me. It's easy to do, Rachel. You should get on to that.'

'Yes, yes I will.'

'That's not all, is it?' She furrowed her forehead. 'What's wrong, Rach?'

'It's my mum.' I'd never mentioned her before, keeping my private life private when talking to clients. 'She's in a care home. Has dementia.' I shook my head, wishing the words hadn't tumbled out. It was unprofessional, but then the boundaries between us were already frayed. 'The thing is …' I began, about to tell her about the pictures of the farmhouse, that I thought there were secrets in my mother's past.

'Well, at least she's still alive, Rachel,' she said, cutting me off. 'Make the most of any good times you have left.'

'Yes,' I said, feeling guilty for complaining, when Emmy would have given anything to still have her mother, even if her lucidity was infrequent. 'Yes, you're absolutely right.'

She laid her hand on mine. 'Listen, just call me any time, if you need me.'

'Thank you,' I said, feeling unsettled by the sudden role reversal.

When she'd gone, I sat down at my desk, not sure if I wanted to cry or laugh hysterically at the mess I called my life. I rammed my head into my hands, wishing I could purge the worries about my mum from my head – if only for a while.

My mobile rang, forcing me out of my thoughts. It was a number I didn't recognise.

'Rachel Hogan?' A man's voice – quiet, low, even.

'Yes.'

'This is Martin Walker from Dream Meadows Care Home.' I'd met him a few times. He managed the home. 'I'm afraid I have some bad news,' he continued.

'Oh, God has my mother wandered off?'

'I'm afraid your mother passed away this morning. I'm so sorry.'

It took me a moment to catch my breath. My mum. Dead? 'I don't understand. She wasn't ill. How did she die?'

'A heart attack.'

'But she was on medication for her heart.'

'Miss Hogan, perhaps you could come here … it would be better if I we could talk in person. Could you come to the care home today, and we'll talk here?' His voice had became more insistent as he added, 'As soon as possible.'

Chapter 14

February 2018

'Are you sure you don't mind keeping Grace this afternoon?' I said, standing on Angela's doorstep, stepping from foot to foot, more to control my shaking limbs than to keep warm.

She leaned forward and touched my face. I knew it must look blotchy and puffy from the tears that had followed Martin Walker's call. 'Of course I don't mind,' she said. 'Grace is an absolute angel. I'm just sorry I can't help you more.' Her voice cracked. 'I'm so sorry about your mum.'

'Thanks.' I tugged my parka round me like a protective layer, and stepped backwards. If she tried to hug me, I knew I would cry again. 'I'm afraid I still can't find my spare key, so I hope everything Grace needs is in her bag.'

'No problem at all.'

I was about to leave when Grace trotted into Angela's hallway. I hadn't wanted her to see me in such a state.

'Mummy?' She looked rosy-cheeked from playing in the snow, and was carrying a mug of hot chocolate with marshmallows floating on the top, like lost boats on dark waters. 'Have you come to get me?'

I knelt down in front of her. 'Not yet, lovely girl,' I said. 'That looks delicious.'

'Want some?' she said, offering up the mug, and smiling a chocolaty smile.

'Ooh, yes please.' I took a small sip, enjoying the smooth liquid on my tongue, as she stared wide-eyed. 'Yummy!'

'I'm watching *Peppa Pig*, actually,' she said, and turned and walked down the hall away from me, calling, 'See you later, Mummy. Love you.'

'Love you more,' I called after her, noticing she was wearing a pair of fluffy slippers in the shape of rabbits that were a bit too big for her.

Spotting where my eyes had landed, Angela threw me an awkward smile. 'My sister leaves them here for when she visits with her granddaughter. I hope you don't mind Grace wearing them.'

'Not at all,' I said, attempting to return the smile. She'd never mentioned a sister, but then I knew so little about her.

'Well, I'd better set off,' I said, thanking Angela again, and trudging towards my car.

Despite being a confident driver, I hated driving in the snow, and knowing what I would find at the other end sent a bolt of anxiety through me. 'I hope to be back by six at the latest,' I called over my shoulder.

'I'm so sorry about your mum,' she repeated, before closing her front door.

***

The side roads were icy, but once I was on the main roads, doing a steady fifty, driving got easier, until I reached Suffolk. There, the countryside was treacherous and it took me ages to reach the care home. My head thumped like a bass drum by the time I pulled up in front of it.

I took a couple of painkillers with bottled water, and sat for some moments, trying to calm myself, beating back tears. The care home looked like something from a Jane Austen novel – stately, with rectangular windows, a double front door, and wisteria weaving its way up the walls. It was still hard to believe my mother had been there because Alzheimer's struck long before her time.

And now she'd passed away. Died. My mother was dead. My amazing mother who I loved so much was gone. Not just into her own world, but forever. Tears surged, and I broke down, sobbing over the steering wheel. Loud, breathless cries I couldn't control. I didn't want to go in. If I did it would make it real. I started the engine, and rammed the car into reverse. I couldn't face it today. I couldn't face it ever.

A knock on my side window, before I could press down on the throttle, startled me. It was Margo, huddled into a tartan coat, a scarf wrapped around her neck and half her face. I lowered the window, and a burst of cold air numbered my face.

'Are you coming in, dear?' she said, her voice muffled through her scarf.

'I'm not sure,' I said, with a sniff. Surely she knew how difficult it was for me.

'I know how hard it is for you, Miss Hogan,' she said as though she'd heard my thoughts, leaning in through the window. 'But your mother so enjoys your visits, even if she doesn't always seem to.'

Didn't she know my mother was dead? She'd just arrived for work. Maybe she hadn't heard.

I got out of the car. If we walked in together, perhaps it would be easier.

'That's the spirit,' she said, as we trudged through the snow towards the building, and she linked her arm through mine to steady herself.

We reached the door, and I stopped and turned to her. She

didn't know. I needed to prepare her. 'I've had a call from Martin Walker,' I said. 'And the thing is … the thing is … my mother died this morning.'

'What? Oh, my dear girl, how awful.' To my surprise, she took me in her arms and hugged me close. I didn't pull away, needing the comfort. 'I'm so sorry. I had no idea,' she went on. 'Your mother was an amazing woman. I got on famously with her.'

Once inside, I stood by reception, waiting. Margo had zipped away to 'find somebody to help' and a chill ran down my spine. It felt as though I wasn't in my own body – that this terrible experience was happening to someone else.

My mind cruelly flicked back to the Christmas before last, when we stayed at Mum's, and she was fit and well and seemed happy. Lawrence had been so affectionate back then; we were in love. Flashes of him helping Grace to open her presents, and Mum demanding to know how I'd made the delicious Christmas pudding we'd brought with us, and Lawrence giving away that it was shop-bought. So much happiness, so much laughter, so much normality. And now it was gone, and everything had plunged into chaos and darkness.

'Miss Hogan?' It was Martin's wife, a skinny woman in a tartan kilt and white blouse. Her two-inch heels clipped the quarry tiles as she raced towards me, Margo trying to keep up in her soft shoes. 'Margo tells me you've had a call from my husband.' There was concern in her voice.

'That's right. About my mother.'

'Well, he's away at the moment, so it couldn't have been him,' she said, and now standing by my side, she placed her hand on my elbow.

'I don't understand.'

'Your mother is perfectly well, Miss Hogan. She's in her room, painting.'

I didn't know if it was the shock or lack of food, but the room spun. I grabbed the reception counter, steadying myself. *My mum's alive?* 'I don't understand,' I repeated. *Why would someone call me? Why would someone be so cruel?* 'I need to see her,' I said desperately.

I took a deep breath, and raced up the stairs, throwing open her door. She was sitting in a wing-backed chair looking out of the window, her easel close by, brush in hand.

My eyes fell on her painting, and I held in a gasp. Clouds like cotton-wool balls dipped in blood dotted a vivid yellow sky. Sharp-edged, misshapen metal buildings grew up from emerald green grass.

She turned and placed the brush on the pallet. 'I thought you might be Jude,' she said.

'Jude?'

She tapped her breastbone. 'It's gone, Rachel,' she said.

I approached, battling back tears. 'What's gone, Mum?'

She screwed up her face, and shook her head, continuing to tap her neck. 'Why can't I remember?' Words often teased her, reaching the tip of her tongue, before darting away. She closed her eyes, and opened them again. 'It's been taken.'

'What has, Mum?'

She tapped her breastbone again, the same puzzled look on her face. 'The hanging thing.'

'Your locket?'

'Yes. With Rachel inside.' She picked up her brush once more.

'Who's taken it, Mum?'

She looked towards the ceiling, and shrugged.

'Was it Margo?' I asked. She was the only person I could think of, who Mum saw other than me.

'I need to get it back.' Her eyes filled with tears. 'It's very special.'

'I know it is, Mum,' I said, putting a comforting arm around her shoulders.

'And it's been stolen.'

'I'm sure nobody would take your things.' I glanced around the room, then bent down to look under the bed, wondering if she'd dropped it. Straightening up again, I swept my eyes over her bedside cabinet where there was a photograph of me and a glass of water.

'Well, it's gone,' she said, dipping her brush into the yellow paint, and turning away from me. 'And so have my black shoes with the big gold buckles.'

I dropped onto the bed, my head in my hands. To my knowledge, Mum had never owned a pair of black shoes with big gold buckles.

Chapter 15

February 2018

'Oh God, Rachel, that's awful.'

Desperate to talk to Zoe, I'd pulled off the slippery Suffolk back roads into a lay-by, and called her. I blurted out what had happened as soon as I heard her voice.

'And you're sure it was a hoax call,' she said now. 'I mean what do you know about this Martin Walker?'

'Well, nothing really – I've never met him. His name and photo are on the website, but it's his wife who deals with everything. But it can't be him, Zoe. Why would he do something like that? And the more I think about it, the more I keep thinking the bloke's voice sounded familiar.'

'You think you know him?'

'Yes … no … oh, I don't know.' I sighed, looking out of the front window at the heavy snowflakes twisting and turning in the headlights. 'And I thank God my mum's still here, but I'm so worried about her. They told me to expect deterioration, but …' My throat tightened.

'She's getting worse?'

'Today, she'd painted a really odd picture – nothing like her usual work. It broke my heart to see it. Margo said it's good for her to keep painting, but it's awful to watch how her mind sees things now.' I gripped the steering wheel, not wanting to cry again. 'I'm sorry to burden you, Zoe. I just needed to talk, you know.'

'Don't be daft, hon. You know I'm here for you. In fact, how do you fancy a Chinese and a catch-up?'

'Yes, yes, I'd like that.' I rummaged in my pocket for a tissue, and sniffed into it.

'How about tomorrow night? We could go to the Red Dragon?'

'That would be great.'

'I'll book a table for seven-thirty, shall I?'

'Yes, yes please. Thanks, Zoe, you know, for being there.' I looked about me. I'd parked in a lonely spot, and my stomach tipped. I wasn't normally bothered, but everything that had happened lately made me feel uneasy. I locked my doors with a clunk. 'Listen, I'd better head for home. I said I'd pick Grace up from Angela's at six, and it's already gone five. I'll see you tomorrow.'

'OK, drive carefully, Rach. The roads are dreadful,' she said, as I ended the call.

Knowing it was unlikely I would get home by seven, let alone six, I texted Lawrence:

I'm in Suffolk. Grace is with Angela. Any chance you could pick her up on your way home? I'll collect her from yours.

Next I texted Angela, keeping it brief. I would explain about my mum another time:

Hey, Angela. Sorry to mess you about, I'm still in Suffolk. But I've asked Lawrence to pick up Grace. X

84

She replied instantly:

Please don't worry. Grace is as good as gold. X

I started my engine and skidded out of the lay-by onto the winding road, my wiper blades doing their best to combat the snow. My nerves were in tatters, as everything bounced around my head, like tennis balls on acid.

A rabbit darted out in front of me, and I let out a gasp and slammed on my brakes. The car skidded, tyres screeching, brakes squealing as I came to a stop inches from a deep ditch. My eyes fell on the bundle of grey fur in my rear-view, bouncing into the hedgerow, not caring a whisker that one of us could have been killed.

I thudded my temples three times with my palms, fighting back tears, aware I was close to screaming, my angst at maximum. Was the Martin Walker hoax call connected to the studio call?

I grabbed the bottle of water from my glove compartment and took a swig, staring for a long moment into the cold, dark night.

I knew I wasn't paranoid.

Everything that had happened was painfully real.

The truth was, I had good reason to worry.

***

Since Lawrence moved out, he'd rented a first-floor one-bed apartment near the railway station – just five minutes' walk from my house. I eventually found a parking space after circling the area for some time, and dragged on the handbrake – it was OK for him, he had secured underground parking.

I hurried along the icy pavement, past the closed-up shops, almost skidding over. It would have been as easy to go home and walk, I realised. But it was almost seven. I was here now.

I'd received his text at six o'clock, when I'd pulled into a service station to use the loo.

Collected Grace. We need to talk.

Reaching the apartment, I felt exhausted and hungry. I hadn't eaten all day, and the last thing I needed was a confrontation with Lawrence, or to witness the happy couple.

Did Farrah live with him?

A train thundered by as I pushed the entrance buzzer. 'It's me,' I said, defeat in my voice, as he answered.

He let me in, and I took the stairs like an old woman burdened down with bags, and rang the doorbell.

'She's asleep,' he said, opening the door, and gesturing for me to enter.

'Jeez, she won't sleep tonight, Lawrence, you know that,' I said, passing him, breathing in his familiar aftershave.

Once in the lounge, I noticed his shirt collar was unbuttoned, and a pistachio-green tie lay across the back of the black sofa, but he still looked as though he belonged in his office, in linen trousers and a fitted shirt.

The room was minimalistic. Only what he needed, and nothing more – a widescreen TV, a laptop, old CDs he'd taken when he left. I hadn't argued. I had never been a fan of rhythm and blues, and I rarely played CDs any more. My eyes fell on a vase of fresh flowers on the glass table. 'Is Farrah here?' I asked, preparing myself for a full-on row.

He shook his head. 'Drink?' he asked, pouring gin over ice, and dropping in a slice of lime.

'I just need to get home. I've had a rotten day,' I said, deciding not to tell him about the call about Mum. 'I've been meaning to ask you. Have you visited my mum in the home?'

He shook his head. 'Not since I went with you before we ... Why?' He narrowed his eyes, the glass halfway to his lips.

'I just wondered if you'd told her we'd broken up, that's all.'

He shook his head. 'Nope.'

'So if you didn't tell her, who did?'

He shrugged. 'I've no idea.' He sounded bored of me.

'So, what do you want to talk about?' I asked, remembering his earlier text.

He threw me a crooked smile, as though he was going to enjoy what he was about to say. 'The thing is, Rachel, I don't want you to leave Grace with Angela any more.'

'What?'

'She stank of booze when I picked up Grace.' He took a gulp of gin.

'But you drink in front of her.'

'That's different,' he said, raising his glass. 'She's my daughter, and I never get pissed. Angela was smashed.'

I couldn't believe Angela would do that. Surely she cared too much about Grace. 'She probably had a glass of wine with her dinner. It's not against the law.'

He raised a brow. 'It was more than that. She slurred her words, and staggered. I don't want Grace anywhere near her.'

'For God's sake, you've never liked Angela.' I'd always blamed it on the fact he'd prefer me not to work.

'True, but that has nothing to do with it.'

'I need her in my life. I haven't got anyone else who will look after Grace at short notice, and I must work, Lawrence. Especially now.'

He narrowed his eyes, and took another swig of his drink. 'So you're prepared to put our daughter at risk.'

'No! No, of course not, but I've never seen Angela drunk. Yes, she likes a drink, but don't we all?'

'Functioning alcoholics rarely give themselves away.'

'Oh, but surprise, surprise, she did to you.' I was raising my voice. 'The one day you see her, she just happens to be drunk.'

'Mummy?' It was Grace, rubbing sleep from her eyes and blinking. 'Can we go home now?'

'Yes, darling,' I said, throwing Lawrence a filthy look, as I grabbed Grace's coat.

'Oh and there's something else.' Lawrence smiled at Grace. 'I'd like to take Grace to Disneyland in Paris at half-term.'

'Next week?' I said, manoeuvring Grace's limp arms into the sleeves of her coat. 'That soon?'

'Can I go, Mummy?' Grace looked up at me, her eyes pleading. 'I'd like to see *Beauty and the Beast*.'

I looked back at Lawrence, who took a cigarette from a half-empty box. 'Just the two of you?' I asked.

'Of course,' he said, lighting it, and blowing out a spiral of smoke in our direction. When we lived together he'd smoked in the garden. But now his face said, *I'll do exactly what I like*.

He dragged on his cigarette, as I fastened the toggles on Grace's coat, and turned and glared at him. To think when we first went out I thought smoking made him look sexy.

'What?' he said, widening his eyes. 'My father smoked around me, didn't do me any harm.'

I wanted to say he was a hypocrite, but knew it wasn't fair to argue in front of Grace – plus I would never win. *I never have*.

'Well, I guess she can go to Disneyland,' I said, unable to think of a reason why not, and Grace wrapped her arms around my neck and kissed my cheek.

'Thank you, Mummy,' she said. 'Love you.'

'Love you more,' I said.

***

Once I'd strapped Grace into her car seat, I sat for some moments. Could Lawrence be right about Angela? Had she been drunk when she'd looked after Grace before? Was that why she fell asleep while she was playing with her?

'Do you like Angela?' I said, turning to look at Grace, but she'd fallen asleep again.

I slid the key in the ignition, switched on the engine, and shifted into first gear, feeling sure I would have noticed if Angela had a serious drink problem.

But how well did I really know her?

Chapter 16

July 1988

'It's mostly when he's been down the local, and comes back plastered.' Imogen tugged her cardigan sleeve up to her elbow, and Laura's eyes widened. The cigarette burns on her thin arms ranged from scars to deep red and pus-filled. Laura had suspected, after Dillon's outpouring a year ago, that things weren't right in the farmhouse, that Tierney was a bully, and this confirmed her worst fears.

'Oh, Imogen.' Laura wanted to pull her into a hug, but she knew they weren't at that place. Despite knowing her for eight months, Imogen hadn't been an easy person to reach.

'He …'

'What is it, Imogen?' Laura placed her hand on her arm, but she felt the woman tense, and removed it.

'The thing is … he says he has rights.'

Laura covered her mouth, to stifle a gasp. 'No, Imogen, that's not the way it works,' she said through her fingers.

A gust of children's laughter swept into the kitchen, and Laura turned from where she was sitting with Imogen to see they were on the floor watching a 'Rainbow' video, Caitlin propped on

Dillon's knee sucking on her dummy, and playing with his hair, and Bridie leaning against him, her thumb pressed into her mouth, her eyes heavy.

Rachel was sleeping upstairs.

'You must leave him,' Laura said, her gaze back on Imogen who was pulling down her sleeve, and gripping her cuff in her fist, as though afraid of the secret she'd shared.

'What, and abandon Dillon?' Her eyes swam with tears, and she looked even smaller than her five-foot frame – far too thin. 'What if he gets custody of Bridie and Caitlin?'

'Please tell the Guards, Imogen. Surely they'll do something,' Laura insisted.

'They won't.' Imogen sounded certain. And shaking her head, she stood up and padded towards the kitchen window. 'It's not that easy,' she continued, her eyes penetrating the glass. 'What if Tierney finds out I've contacted them, and then they do nothing? It's not only me I have to think of.' She looked over her shoulder. 'I wish I'd never met him.'

Laura joined her at the window. 'Where did you meet?'

Imogen picked up a cloth and wiped the sink and taps with furious speed. 'In the local when I'd just turned seventeen. He ran the boozer with his wife. Although I rarely saw her at that time.' She paused for a moment. 'He would let all of us drink underage – my parents would have killed me had they known.' She screwed up the cloth and placed it on the work surface, and stared, once more, through the window. 'Tierney seemed a nice bloke, back then. Good-looking, he was – came from a well-off family. His wife told me his parents had had high hopes for him, but then he started getting in with the wrong kind, got into a bit of trouble with the law. They wiped their hands of him.' Imogen's eyes shimmered. 'I wish I'd never set eyes on him.'

'But you ended up living with him.'

She nodded. 'Tierney was left some money when his grand-father died, so he and his Mrs closed the pub and moved to the farmhouse. When my parents threw me out for getting pregnant – I wasn't in a relationship let alone married – it was Mrs O'Brian who said I could come and live with them until I found my feet. She was a kind woman. Dillon adored her.' Imogen flicked a tear from the corner of her eye. 'I've said too much,' she said. 'I should go.'

She went to head across the kitchen, and Laura grabbed her arm. 'Think of the kids, Imogen. What if something awful happens to them? You would never forgive yourself. I would never forgive myself.'

Imogen snatched her arm back, and the look she gave Laura was long and unsettling. 'I *am* thinking of them,' she snapped. 'Dillon!' she yelled, and he was there within moments, Caitlin in his arms, Bridie by his side. 'We're leaving!'

As they made their way to the door, Caitlin smiled sweetly at Laura, as though she didn't have a care in the world.

Laura's mind twisted and turned as she stood at the window, watching them disappear into the woods. Dillon with his usual stick, twirling it in his hands, hurling it high and catching it like a majorette, Imogen carrying Caitlin, taking brisk, sharp steps, Bridie struggling to keep up on her three-year-old legs.

Why wouldn't Imogen tell the Guards about Tierney? Had he got some sort of hold over her?

Rachel let out a yell from upstairs. Laura turned from the window, and blocking her ears with her hands, fell into the armchair. But the child's cries seeped in, along with a surge of guilt. She rose and headed up the stairs.

She lifted Rachel from her cot. She would never be cruel to the child, but even now, after all these months, holding her in her arms she felt nothing but painful loneliness. Jude would have finished his degree by now, and would be getting on with his life without them. It was so unfair. Rachel was his daughter too.

Downstairs, she turned off children's TV – Rachel wouldn't be interested – and slid her daughter into her highchair. She gave her a mug of juice, which the child gulped down, and bread fingers coated with Marmite.

Rachel rarely smiled, and wasn't walking yet. She made noises, but hadn't said her first word, not even 'mama'. But Imogen had told her not to worry, that babies developed at different rates. She was only a year old, after all.

As Rachel squashed the bread into her mouth with damp chubby fingers, Laura smiled and said, 'Is that nice, darling?' But her daughter's eyes seemed lifeless, somehow. Did she know her mother struggled to love her? That her father had abandoned her when she was the size of a peanut?

A knock at the front door startled Laura. She rarely had visitors, and was tempted to bob out of sight.

But whoever it was knocked again, more urgently.

From the kitchen window she saw a smartly dressed man, in a knee-length turquoise mac, stepping from foot to foot. He turned and smiled at her. She had no choice but to open the door.

Close up he looked to be in his thirties, with a round, pale face, and bloodshot eyes. He smiled once more, and dragged his fingers through his short, light ginger hair. 'Laura Hogan?'

'Yes.' She poked her head outside, and glanced up and down the quiet road. A Ford Cortina was bumped up on the grass verge opposite. 'Can I help you?'

'I'm Marcus McCutcheon.' She knew the name instantly. Why was he here, standing on her doorstep? Her parents' accident was over a year ago. 'I can tell you know who I am.'

'Yes,' she said, 'and I'm so sorry.'

'May I come in?' he asked.

The thought of him stepping inside didn't feel right. Although he seemed pleasant enough, she didn't know this man – this man whose life had been ruined by her parents.

'I'm just on my way out, actually,' she said, which was far from the truth. She rarely went out.

'OK, not to worry,' he said, turning to leave.

'What do you want?' she called after him, before he could cross the road.

He turned back and shrugged. 'I don't know.' Another shrug. 'Closure, I suppose. It would be easier if your parents were alive; there would be something to focus on.'

'Focus on?'

'Yolanda's at school now, and I often imagine my wife looking down from the heavens, wondering how her daughter's life can be moving on without her. They were so close. But they forget at that age, don't they? Forget those early years.'

His eyes were swimming with tears, and he looked so helpless, her heart went out to him. 'Come in for a bit,' she said. 'I'll make some coffee.'

He stood behind her, too close, as she spooned coffee into mugs. 'My daughter doesn't need me quite as much these days,' he said. 'I guess she'll need me less and less, as time goes by. I seem to be flapping aimlessly, looking for something to make everything right again.'

Once they had two steaming mugs in front of them on the kitchen table, Marcus told Laura what she already knew. That the bend locals called Devil's Corner was notorious for accidents. 'My wife hated that bend,' he said, blowing on his coffee. 'But, like a fool, I told her she was silly to worry, that if she drove sensibly, which she always did, she would be fine.'

'I'm so sorry,' Laura repeated, as the stranger continued going into the details of how he found out, how the first months were too painful, and how he kept going for Yolanda's sake. When he was done he breathlessly slammed his head into his hands and wept.

Laura pulled tissues from a box and handed them to him, and eventually he calmed down, his eyes skittering around the kitchen as he dabbed his eyes and cheeks. 'Was this their house?' he asked.

'It was. Yes.'

'They must have had money.' *Was this what he wanted? Money?* She was reluctant to answer.

'It's OK, Laura; I'm not after your money. In fact, I'm not sure what it is I want – need – other than someone to pay for what your parents did.'

'You can't blame me, surely.'

His red eyes and wet cheeks made him look vulnerable. 'No, I don't blame you. You're a victim too, I guess. Were you close?'

She shook her head. 'No, not really.'

'A blessing then?'

'Sorry?'

'Not so much pain when they died?'

She wasn't sure how to answer. It had been the most painful time in her life. Losing parents she had hoped one day would love her – and the realisation that *now* they never would. And she'd lost Jude too – her precious Jude – the same week.

Throughout their talk, Rachel had silently tucked into her bread, studying Marcus McCutcheon, but now she let out a cry. Laura rose and lifted her from her highchair, and propped her on her hip, swaying and humming in an attempt to calm the child. She didn't sit back down, hoping Marcus would take the hint and leave. What could she possibly offer him? She hadn't been driving the car that killed his wife.

'I remember when Yolanda was that small,' he said, draining his mug.

'They're hard work,' Laura said, unable to think of anything else to say.

'Jacqueline never thought so.' He got up, and put on his coat. 'She was a great mother.'

'She sounds pretty much perfect.' *Oh God, do I sound sarcastic?* She hadn't meant to.

But his reaction was soft and thoughtful, as he moved towards the door, and opened it. 'Yes, yes she was,' he said. 'Well, I'll leave you to it.'

The slam of the door behind him jolted Rachel into another fit of tears, and she began hitting Laura's face over and over. If she'd been any bigger it would have hurt.

'Calm down, Rachel,' Laura said, wrestling with the child. 'For God's sake, calm down.'

Chapter 17

February 2018

'Chinese delivery!' Zoe laughed, and lifted two paper carrier bags into the air, before stepping into my house.

'I'm so sorry to mess you about,' I said, following her into the kitchen, where she plonked the food on the breakfast bar. 'I'd have loved to go out but …'

'You're too lazy.'

I laughed. 'I wish that was the reason.' I hadn't explained in my earlier text why I'd cancelled our meal at the Red Dragon. It had been too hard to explain in a short message.

We grabbed plates and cutlery, and served ourselves.

'So why couldn't you meet at the restaurant?' Zoe asked, shoving a prawn cracker into her mouth and crunching down on it. 'Grace isn't ill, is she?'

I shook my head, as I scooped prawn chow mein onto my plate. The food smelt delicious, but, quite unlike me, I wasn't hungry. 'The thing is,' I began, 'Lawrence doesn't want Angela to look after Grace any more.'

'What? Why not?'

'It's not important,' I said. Zoe had never met Angela, but I

97

still didn't want to talk about her behind her back. 'It's made things difficult, that's all. I had to postpone two clients this morning, because Grace's nursery school had another snow day.'

'Jeez, Lawrence can be a right bastard at times.'

We finished filling our plates and moved to the table, and sat down.

'Listen, Rach,' she said, waving a fork in my general direction. 'I don't know Angela, but you rate her, don't you?'

I nodded. 'I think so.' *But what if Lawrence is right?*

'And Grace likes her?'

I moved the food around my plate, not meeting her eye. 'Seems to.'

'So who cares what Lawrence thinks?'

I wondered what she would say if she thought Angela could be an alcoholic. And the trouble was, the niggling doubts were in my head now, and I couldn't shake them free.

'More importantly, are you OK?' Zoe asked, pausing from eating and placing her hand over mine. 'I still can't believe some idiot called and said your mum had died. It's sick, that's what it is.'

'I know. And although I'm relieved my mum's OK, I still feel unnerved, especially after everything else that's happened.'

She removed her hand. 'Anyone would be, Rach.'

'I keep wondering if I should call the police.'

'Good idea, although I don't suppose there's much they can do. I read somewhere you should keep a journal of everything that's happening – that's probably what they'll tell you to do. That way, if it gets any worse …'

'Christ, I hope it doesn't.'

'I'm sure it won't, but perhaps you could change your phone number,' she said, shovelling in a mouthful of rice, and chewing.

I shrugged, and laid my cutlery neatly on my plate.

'Not hungry?' She leaned over, speared one of my chicken

balls. and nibbled on it. I wondered if she could really see how much everything was getting to me.

I pushed my plate away from me. 'I'll have it for breakfast,' I said with a smile.

Once Zoe had eaten and we'd cleared away, we settled in the lounge, our legs curled under us, steaming mugs of coffee on the coffee table in front of us.

'Lawrence is taking Grace to Disneyland next week for half-term,' I said, attempting to sound happy about it.

'Wow! Lucky Grace.'

'I know. I'm pleased for her. I thought I might take the opportunity to go away too. A change of scenery and all that.'

'It might do you good.'

'Mmm.'

'Maybe I could take some time off and come with you,' she said. 'Let me know if you fancy that.'

'OK,' I said. 'But I know how busy you are in the salon. Anyway, how's things with Connor?' I said, in an attempt to change the subject. I'd already made up my mind I would go alone, and where I would be heading.

She'd dropped me home after the spa on Friday, and gone on to a nightclub where she'd planned to meet him.

'Yeah, going well, I guess. I still miss Hank – well, the non-drugged-up Hank.'

'It must be hard for you, but you're doing the right thing.'

'I know, I know.' She lowered her head.

'And Connor's pretty cute. You said so yourself.'

'And keen.' She smiled, but I knew she wasn't fully over Hank and still hoped one day he would tackle his addiction.

'Last night Connor and I went to the spa after hours,' she said, as though she'd popped any thought of Hank like a balloon. 'He's got a set of keys, and we went for a swim. And one thing led to another …' She grinned. It would have been my idea of torture.

'It was exciting,' she went on. 'I tried not to think about the room once being a morgue – the spectres of inmates staring at us.'

'There's no such thing as ghosts,' I said.

She laughed. 'I'm seeing him tomorrow too. What can I say? I'm a sucker for an Irish accent.'

A silence fell, but I didn't want the evening to end – to be alone. 'I was wondering if I could make an appointment at your salon,' I said, grabbing a bunch of my hair, and forcing a smile. 'I need a decent cut and colour.'

'I thought your hairdresser came here,' she said. 'And you use a boxed dye, don't you? Which always looks amazing.'

'Normally, but my hairdresser is having a baby, and …'

'Sadly we're fully booked up for the next month, hon.' She leaned over and raked her fingers through my hair. 'But I could cut it for you now, if you like.' She looked at the time on her phone. 'It will only take twenty minutes. I'll have you looking like a pixie before you know it.'

'OK, great,' I said, energised. 'And I'll pick up my usual dye tomorrow.'

'Ah, small problem.' She pulled a face. 'I haven't got my scissors. Tend not to carry them about with me unless I'm planning to commit murder.'

I laughed and jumped to my feet. 'I've got a pair.' I'd bought them to trim Grace's fringe, but only used them once. I hadn't realised how hard it was to get a child's fringe straight.

'Brilliant,' she said rising too. 'Let's do this.'

***

Zoe snipped away at my hair, as I sat on a stool in the kitchen, a towel around my shoulders. She moved round to the front. 'What happened here?' she said, lifting my fringe.

'Where?'

'The scar on your forehead?'

100

'Oh, my ancient war wound,' I said with a smile. 'I fell as child, although I can't remember the traumatic event.' I laughed. 'That's the second reason I have a fringe.'

'What's the first?'

'Have you seen my eyebrows?'

She laughed. 'Well, you've definitely got a bit of a Harry Potter thing going on.'

'Hardly,' I said. 'It's only tiny.'

'Obliviate,' she said, pointing her scissors at it, before moving round to continue snipping the back of my hair.

'You do know you've just wiped my memory,' I said.

She burst out laughing and I jerked backwards.

'Crap' I cried, as pain seared through me. I slapped my hand on my neck, feeling blood wet on my fingers.

'Oh God, I'm so sorry,' she said, grabbing a tea towel, and pressing it against my flesh. I prayed the cut wasn't as bad as it felt.

'My fault,' I said, tears stinging my eyes, 'I shouldn't have moved.'

Zoe removed the tea towel. 'Thank God,' she said. 'It's only a tiny nick. You won't need stitches. Where do you keep your plasters?'

I hurried into the lounge. I needed to see the cut for myself. But once I'd grabbed a hand mirror, and looked at the reflection of my neck in the mirror on the wall, I knew it wasn't too bad.

Back in the kitchen, I rummaged in the cupboard and found a plaster.

'Thank goodness I didn't cut into a vein,' Zoe said, sounding devastated. 'I can't believe I was so unprofessional. So stupid.'

'Please don't worry,' I said, sticking on the plaster. 'It was honestly my fault. I moved back with a jolt.'

I sat down, and once she'd finished cutting my hair, she trotted round to face me and, moving closer, flicked my hair with her fingers and smiled. 'You look gorgeous,' she said.

'Ooh, I thought you were about to kiss me then,' I said, and burst out laughing.

She laughed too. 'I did kiss a woman once. But you're really not my type.'

'Well, I'm offended now,' I joked, rising and heading into the lounge to look in the mirror once more. 'It's great,' I called through. 'Thanks so much, it's exactly how I like it. I'll dye it tomorrow.'

**

'Thanks again,' I said later, dragging my fingers through my hair, as Zoe pulled on her coat. 'I feel so much better.' It was as though I had my identity back – the first step to sorting my life out.

She opened the front door and headed out into the freezing night. 'We must get together again soon,' she said, kissing my cheek. 'Maybe we could go to the spa again sometime.'

I followed her down the path in my slippers, and stood at the gate until she'd pulled away in her car. Arms wrapped around me to ward off the cold, I turned and scurried back down my path, spotting Angela at her front door with a man. I smiled, hoping she'd finally found the one, but quickly realised his voice was raised.

'Stop sending things,' he was saying. 'This has been going on too long. Just stop. Please. Or God help me, I'll take out a restraining order.' He shoved a carrier bag into her hands, and stormed down the path, and away down the road. She looked over at me briefly, closed her eyes as though sapped of all her strength, and then closed her door.

The street was quiet – curtains drawn at the windows of the terraced houses opposite, a marmalade glow radiating from behind them. It hadn't snowed any more, but the cold tingled my fingers.

'Rachel Hogan?' The voice was male and came from the opposite side of the road. Someone was standing at the entrance of an alleyway that led to the station – towards Lawrence's house.

'Yes,' I said, knowing I should go straight inside. I narrowed my eyes, trying to make out the man, but it was too dark to see his features.

'I need to talk to you,' he called, and I felt sure I knew his voice. A feeling of unease washed over me.

'You're a fool,' he yelled, and raced across the road with long determined strides, his hood up and head down. 'Can't you see what's happening? Why it's happening?'

I dived inside, slammed the door closed, and pulled across the bolts, my whole body shaking. I grabbed my phone and thumped in 999, peering through the gap in the curtains.

'Which service please?' a woman on the other end asked.

The road was silent. He'd gone. Disappeared into the shadows.

'Mummy?' I turned to see Grace, hugging her toy rabbit, her hair tangled from sleep. 'What are you looking at?'

'Nothing, darling,' I said, ending the call. 'Nothing at all.'

Chapter 18

November 1989

At two o'clock the sky was a swirl of blacks and greys. In fact, it had barely got light all day. And, like most days that winter, it hung heavy on Laura's shoulders. Slow and mind-numbing. Even painting failed to lift her.

She stood at the lounge window looking out. The lake rippled and lapped in the near distance, vivid through the glade now most of the trees had lost their leaves.

Her voice, low and rhythmic, quietly chanted the words of Yeats's poem 'The Lake Isle of Innisfree' over and over and over.

Was she going crazy? Did she need help? She certainly didn't feel like herself any more. The young woman who had gone to university and fell in love with Jude had disappeared when he never called.

Lately, she was finding it harder and harder to go out. One day inside the house had joined hands with the next and the next. *This place is my prison.*

It had been far too long since she'd ventured further than the lonely woods, and even longer since he had driven into Sligo Town. She ordered her shopping by phone to be delivered by the grocery shop in the village, and everything else she needed she ordered by post. Had she become a recluse? A hermit, living off her parents' money, in her parents' oddly shaped house. She felt sure if she were a man, she would have a beard by now, possibly down to her belly button, and animals would have set up home there.

A loud shrieking mew echoed throughout the house, breaking the silence, and she spun round to see Rachel dragging the stray cat Laura had adopted a few weeks before, into the room by his tail.

'Rachel!' she yelled, racing over, as the child went to bite his tail. 'No!' she said, pulling back the child's tightly gripped fingers from the poor cat. 'What have I told you about being cruel to Rusty?'

As soon as the cat was free he bolted from the room, and Laura stared at her daughter, her hand gripping her wrist. 'Let's go for a walk,' she said, waltzing her into the hall, the child's feet inches from the floor. Laura snatched Rachel's hat and coat from the rack.

'No!' Rachel squealed, wiggling, her free hand bashing against Laura's hip. 'No!'

It was always an effort trying to get the child to put her arms into the coat sleeves, her feet into boots, and Laura had given up so many times before. But today she was determined. 'We're going out, whether you like it or not,' she said, twisting the child's arm and stuffing it into the pink fabric. Rachel screamed out in pain, and began to cry.

'Sorry, sorry,' Laura said, pulling Rachel to her, tears filling her eyes. 'I didn't mean to hurt you. But if you did as you were told, it wouldn't happen.'

Eventually Rachel stopped crying, and they headed out into the woods, hand in hand. Laura breathed in the fresh, cold air. She should come out more. Fight her fear.

She hadn't seen Imogen and the children for over a year, but it hadn't stopped her worrying about them. She'd thought many times about calling someone to check on them – but doubts always nagged at her. What if they came and couldn't see what was happening, and Tierney took it out on Imogen and the children? In the weeks after Imogen had shown her the burns on her arms, Laura had walked the length of the woods several times to watch Lough End Farm from a distance. She would hear Tierney's booming voice, but never saw him hurt the children.

Today she wouldn't go that way. She would take Rachel to the water's edge and teach her about the wildlife. She'd often seen the child stomp the life out of spiders and ladybirds, and wanted her to understand that everything had a right to live, however small.

Once they were sitting by the lake, Rachel smiled up at her, and a flow of warmth wrapped itself around Laura. Maybe their love for each other would grow in time.

'So,' she began, trying to get Rachel's attention. 'As it's winter, lots of animals are asleep.'

'Are they tired?'

'Yes, and they have to save their energy up for the summer months.'

'Aha.'

'There are foxes about though. If we're quiet we might see one. Someone once told me that foxes make great mummies and daddies.'

'Laura?'

She turned to see Dillon standing nearby, and a surge of happiness filled her senses. She'd missed him.

'Hey,' Laura said, lifting her hand. 'I haven't seen you for so long. How are you?'

He looked over his shoulder, and crouched down. 'I'm not meant to be here, but I often come, just in case I see you.'

'How's Imogen? Is she OK?'

He shook his head. 'Not good.'

Laura levered herself to her feet, and walked towards him, twigs crunching under her feet, breaking into the quiet. 'Is there anything I can do?'

He shrugged. 'Dunno. S'pose I came because I thought you could help. But truth be told, how can you? There's nothing anyone can do.' Another glance over his shoulder.

A loud thud behind Laura startled her, and she twisted round to see a young fox scampering away. Rachel was on her feet, laughing. 'Silly fox,' she said.

'She threw a rock at it,' Dillon said. 'I saw her. Da would say she needs taking in hand. A good beating.' He paused for a moment before adding, 'Stupid bastard.'

Laura raced over to her daughter, and crouched down in front of her, taking hold of the girl's muddy hands. Was this Laura's fault? Was her child born like this, or had she made her this way? 'Rachel, you must be kind to animals.'

'Why?' the little girl said.

'Because they have as much right to be in the woods as we do – if not more.'

Laura looked back to where Dillon had been standing, hoping he might help her convince her two-and-half-year-old she should be kind. But he'd gone.

Chapter 19

February 2018

I hadn't slept well, my mind going over and over what the man had said, but I had to push it to the back of mind, at least until Grace was at nursery school. I couldn't let her see me agitated. She needed a strong mum, one who would show her that everything would be OK now her daddy wasn't living with us.

It had been a milder night, and most of the snow and ice had thawed. I felt sure Grace's nursery school wouldn't close for a third day. It had been great spending time with her, but I couldn't afford to lose money by cancelling more of my therapy sessions.

Once the morning ritual of chasing Grace up the stairs to clean her teeth and get dressed was over, and the breakfast table was afloat with Rice Krispies and a puddle of milk, I knew I wasn't going to get a call from the school.

'Looks as though you've got nursery today,' I said, giving her face a second clean with a wet wipe.

'YAY!' she cried, and ran to get her coat and Peppa Pig rucksack.

We walked down the path towards the car, and I noticed Angela's curtain move. I would talk to her later – ask if she was

OK after the man raised his voice at her, and make sure she hadn't taken offence that I hadn't left Grace with her on her snow days.

I strapped Grace into the back of the car, climbed into the front, and was about to start the engine, when my phone pinged. It was a text from an unfamiliar number, and as I read the message my insides turned liquid:

> **Meet me outside the Emirates Stadium, opposite Costa, at noon today. There are things you should know.**

I threw my phone onto the passenger seat, and locked the doors, scanning the road, before pulling away too fast, and skidding across black ice.

'Weeeeeeee,' Grace said, and giggled. 'Do it again, Mummy.'

I turned into the skid and gained control of the car, and drove at a sensible speed to Grace's nursery. Once I'd dropped her off, I sat in the car park gathering my thoughts.

Was it the same man who'd tried to talk to me the night before? Should I meet him? Would he explain the odd things that had been happening?

It was just after nine. My first appointment was at half past, the second at 10.45. I could just make it to the Emirates Stadium if I wasn't picking up Grace at midday. I knew I couldn't take her with me. But I had to go. Whoever he was, he'd picked a busy location. He would hardly hurt me in full view of hundreds of people, would he?

I fumbled in my bag for my phone and called Zoe, desperately needing to talk things through with her before I did anything rash. As soon as she picked up, I told her about the man who approached me the night before.

'And now I've had a text, and I think it's the same man,' I said. 'He says there are things I should know. And there's something else, I keep thinking he's the same man who called the TV studio

– the same man who told me my mother had died. I'm sure it's the same voice.'

'Oh my God, Rachel,' Zoe said, when I came up for breath, but I could tell she was distracted. 'Hold on a sec, lovely. Sorry.' She disappeared, but I could still hear her distant voice. 'Gina, could you finish Mrs Kirbyshire for me?'

'Sorry, Rach.' She was back. 'Listen, have you contacted the police?'

'No. I don't know what I'd say.' But the truth was, I wanted to see this man myself, without involving the police. 'They wouldn't understand.'

'Do you think you should go alone? He could be anybody.'

'I must go, Zoe,' I said with more confidence than I felt. 'I need to know what's going on, and if he knew I'd involved the police it could frighten him off.'

'Not like that, Gina!' she yelled. 'I'm so sorry, Rach, I'm going to have to love you and leave you – you just can't get the staff.' She laughed. 'But promise you'll call tonight. And if you go, please be careful.' And with that she hung up.

I drove home, and by the time I'd pulled up outside my house, time was ticking away. I looked at Angela's front door – white plastic PVC, that didn't quite suit the Victorian terrace. Lawrence once said it was like Jane Austen wearing trainers. Would it be wrong of me to ask Angela to pick Grace up, and look after her for an hour? After all, I'd never seen her drunk, a bit tipsy on occasions, but never drunk, and never when she was looking after Grace.

I got out of the car, walked up her path, and rang her doorbell.

She took a while to answer, and when she did, she peered round the door. She was still in her silk robe and pyjamas, her hair ruffled. 'Rachel,' she said.

'Hey, how are you?'

'Not too bad.' She opened the door wider, and gestured for me to enter. I stepped onto the doormat.

'I saw what happened last night,' I said. 'The man.'

'It was something and nothing.' She flapped her hand dismissively. 'Coffee?'

I shook my head, and stayed on the doormat, so I didn't have to remove my boots. Her front door opened straight onto her lounge – a sea of cream, with snatches of jade, mainly in flower form. 'Better not, my first appointment is in fifteen minutes.'

'Grace back at nursery, then?' she asked, tightening the belt of her robe.

I nodded, hit by a feeling of guilt that I'd let Lawrence influence me. I'd judged her on what he'd told me. It was wrong of me. 'She had yesterday off …'

'Yes, I saw you in the garden. You looked as though you were having fun.' She smiled.

I was beginning to overheat in my coat. 'I didn't have any patients yesterday, so it was nice to spend some time with her,' I lied. I paused for a moment before adding, 'Listen, could I ask a favour?'

Her eyes brightened, as though I was about to offer her the world. 'Of course, anything – you know that.'

'Would you be able to pick Grace up from nursery, and look after her for an hour?'

'Love to,' she said, with a smile. 'No problem at all.'

I lowered my head, thinking about the man who'd called out to me the night before.

'Are you OK?' Angela placed her hand on my arm.

'Not really,' I said. 'The thing is …' I paused for a moment, and then told her everything I'd told Zoe.

'Oh God, Rachel. That's extremely worrying.'

I looked into her concerned eyes, feeling the comfort of her hand stroking my arm.

'He wants me to meet him.'

'You're not going, surely.' She removed her hand, and covered her mouth. 'He could be a serial killer or something.'

111

I knew I should have felt pleased she cared so much, but instead I felt vaguely irritated.

I pulled my phone from my pocket and looked at the time. 'I'd better go, my client won't be long.' I turned and opened the front door, glad to be hit by a blast of cold air – it was always too hot in Angela's house. 'Thanks so much for picking up Grace,' I said, and headed for my morning appointments.

***

I waited by the Emirates Stadium entrance, stepping from foot to foot to keep warm, watching the minutes tick by on my phone, as I occupied myself liking photos on Instagram.

Whoever he was, he'd picked a busy area where people raced along going about their business, and I felt sure I would be safe here. I just wanted answers.

I scrutinised every bloke who passed by, wondering if it was the man who'd led me to the care home with the fake announcement that my mother was dead – the same man who'd called the studio.

I could suddenly hear his voice in my head; *'I'm crying out. But they won't listen. And now you must pay, Rachel.'*

A woman with a stroller rammed my leg, making me jump. 'Sorry,' she said, as she dashed by.

Panic rose from nowhere. What was I doing? It might be crowded, but it would be so easy for him to attack me – thrust a knife into my heart, and run through the crowds.

But I couldn't move, glued to the spot by the desire to know.

As the seconds became minutes, and the clock turned from twelve-fifteen to twelve-thirty, nobody came. But the words, *'And now you must pay,'* played on repeat in my head.

Chapter 20

February 2018

Needing answers, I collected Grace from Angela, who thankfully seemed sober and looked happier than when I'd seen her earlier. I took off on the open road, heading for Mum's house in Suffolk. The house I grew up in.

I'd loved living on the edge of Dunwich as a child. There was something about the peaceful Suffolk countryside that equated to happiness. And although my mum had been a bit of a recluse much of the time, I felt blessed that I'd had the kind of childhood I could look back on and smile.

It was gone two o'clock when I pulled onto a grass verge outside Mum's four-bed Edwardian detached house. With its sash windows and heavy front door, it looked, as it always had, somehow proud, set back from the winding country road ensconced by hedges and trees.

'Are we there yet?' Grace said, waking from a nap in the back of the car. I glanced in my rear-view mirror to see her pink-cheeked and fluffy-haired from sleep. She leaned forward and grabbed the carton of juice I'd given her earlier (along with her lunchbox) and took a long drink through the straw.

'Yes, we're here, sweetheart,' I said, unclipping my seatbelt, and climbing from the car.

Once we were out, we walked hand in hand towards the tall wrought-iron gate, Grace clearly enjoying the crunch of snow under her boots. I scanned the garden through the high fence, childhood memories reaching out to me, and I was glad I hadn't had to sell the place to pay for Mum's home. The fact she'd spent little money over the years, and made so much from the sales of her paintings, meant we'd been able to keep the house.

I'd had Mum's keys since she was admitted, so unlocked and pushed open the gate. It let out a shriek in protest as it travelled over the snow. There were several sets of footprints leading to the door – the postman, perhaps? But then the post-box was on the gate – the gate always locked.

'Is Gran here?' Grace asked, looking up at me with curious eyes as we walked up the path.

'No, sweetheart, she's still in her special house, remember?'

'What about Muffin?'

Mum had got the cat when I went off to university – said it would help fill the void after I left. I admit I was surprised, as I'd never been allowed pets as a child.

I shook my head, and sighed. I'd suggested taking Mum's cat when she went into the home, despite being a bit wary of them, but Lawrence had insisted he was allergic, something he'd never mentioned before. Truth was he didn't like animals that much. But Muffin had been lucky.

'Gran's friend Jessica is caring for him,' I said to Grace.

Jessica was an almost friend of my mother's – a friendly neighbour – who now had fluffy white hair and walked with a stick. She'd lived in the house opposite Mum's since I was a child, where she would look after me when Mum took off every November for a few days. In the early years I would ask Mum where she was going, only to be met with tears. In the end, I gave up asking for fear of upsetting her. It was yet another question I needed to ask her, before it was too late.

I glanced over my shoulder at Jessica's bungalow at the end of a sloping driveway. 'If your mum comes home, I promise to give Muffin back,' she'd said about the cat, when I'd asked if she would care for him. She'd hurried away with the furry bundle as though she'd been waiting for the opportunity. Perhaps it was Jessica who'd made the footprints. She held a key, and kept an eye on the place.

Inside, the house smelt musty, and I rubbed my hands together to ward off the cold. Once in the kitchen, I turned the dial on the central heating, knowing there was power. I hadn't cancelled the utilities, hopeful for a miracle and that Mum would return home one day.

Grace ran into the lounge and I followed and put the TV on. She sat down in front of a black and white film that looked harmless enough, opened her drawing book, and began colouring in a picture of a house she'd started in the car before nodding off. It never ceased to amaze me how children could multi-task.

A lump rose in my throat, as my eyes skittered around the lounge. So many happy memories of my mother flooded in – of her painting – laughing and talking with me – playing board games – reading me poetry.

'This is stupid,' Grace said, looking up at me. 'Someone's squeezed out all the colours. Can I watch something else?'

I picked up the remote control and flicked through the channels, landing on a cartoon.

'Yay!' she said. 'Thank you.'

I went back into the kitchen, made a black coffee, and stood at the window looking out at the back garden, heavy with snow. I'd played out there as a child, spending so much time in the tree-house, which was still in the old oak at the bottom of the garden. It looked a bit weather-battered and sad. The garden circled the house, like a giant hug, and as a child I would run round and round, delighted to end up where I started.

I sipped my drink, noticing more footprints under the window. Someone had been out there. I put down my mug, hurried back to the lounge, and opened the patio doors, letting the cold air sweep in. There were footprints leading from the garden gate to the kitchen window, and then onwards to the patio doors. Whoever had made them, had been looking in – and it must have been recently.

I stepped out, inspecting the area, taking in the apple tree I'd climbed as a child, stripped of its leaves – in fact, the whole garden felt abandoned. I crouched down near the window, and pulling a clean tissue from my pocket, I picked up a cigarette butt. I would take it inside and put it in a plastic bag, like they do on the best cop shows.

I scanned the garden again. The wind was getting up, howling through the hedgerow, lifting a layer of snow so it spun as though dancing, before settling once more. I shivered, the cold numbing my fingers, and as I rose, I heard something move near the bins.

'Hello,' I called out, a quiver in my voice. I darted a look into the house at Grace still happily colouring then peered back towards the bins. 'Hello.'

Muffin shot out from behind the bins, and dashed towards the gate. 'Jesus!' I cried, grabbing my chest.

I raced inside, slammed the doors shut, and pulled across the curtains. Despite knowing it was just the cat, my mind leaped and bounded through scenarios. What if someone had been stalking the place intending to break in? The house had been uninhabited for so long, and in a lonely location. I raced around checking the doors and windows, but there was no evidence that anyone had been inside.

I shook away thoughts of the footprints, and made my way to the heavy sideboard, thick with dust. I'd taken all the framed photographs to Mum at the home. All that was left were a few abandoned ornaments.

Mum had always kept her private things in the sideboard, and she'd made me promise as a child to never look inside. I'd promised, and never had, having far too much respect for her to go against her wishes. But now things were different. She'd said there were things I should know, but her awful condition was stopping her from telling me. I had every right to discover the truth for myself.

I opened the cupboard door, and knelt down. Whatever it was I thought I was looking for, I would find it here.

The cupboard was rammed with shoeboxes full of paperwork, photo albums, notebooks, and files. I unloaded it, methodically checking through everything as I went, snatching glances at Grace tucking into the remains of her lunchbox, eyes glued to the TV.

I was about halfway through, when she padded over. 'What are you doing?' she said, plonking down next to me.

'I'm looking for something,' I said, scanning another notebook.

'Can I help?' She tilted her head.

'If you like. It's a bit boring though. Not as exciting as *Dennis and Gnasher Unleashed.*'

She pulled a face, and dragged a shoebox from the cupboard.

'Be careful, Grace,' I said, as she tipped it upside down and the contents spilled out over the floor, but my eyes fell on the photos and newspaper cuttings, now spread about her.

Grace picked up a photo. 'Is this Gran?' she said, pouting. 'She looks different. And the picture's all burnt.'

I took the photo from her. It was yellowing, and singed down one side. There had once been two people in the picture – a male probably, as a hand was round my mother's shoulders. She looked pretty – her blonde hair hanging past her shoulders, a ring of flowers around her hair, blue eyes sparkling. She could only have been nineteen or twenty. I turned it over, to see the words: *Laura*

117

and Jude in Mum's handwriting, but whoever Jude was, he'd been torched from the picture.

'Jude?' I whispered, trying out the name on my tongue, remembering how my mum had asked if he was going to visit. *Was he my father?* I pushed down the thought – it couldn't be. That would make my mother a liar.

'Who are these children, Mummy?' Grace had found another photo and was handing it to me.

Four children stood in front of a farmhouse, hens around their feet. It was the same house as the one in the paintings. The one in the photo Ronan Murphy sent me.

I knew immediately that I was one of the children – my mum had a similar picture of me in her locket. Here I was wearing a pretty blue dress and cream shoes. Unease trickled like ice-cold water down my collar. Why hadn't Mum told me about the farmhouse, or these children who I must have once known? Who were they? And why had Mum got so upset about the place?

'What's this, Mummy? It smells funny – like mud.'

Grace was holding a yellowing newspaper cutting to her nose.

'I don't know, darling,' I said, taking it from her and reading the headline.

Death Crash at Devil's Corner

The cutting was dated February 1987. I scanned the article:

Four in deadly crash at Devil's Corner. Mother of one, thirty-year-old Jacqueline McCutcheon, who was driving a Morris Marina, died instantly, but her daughter, five-year-old Yolanda McCutcheon escaped unhurt. As well as her daughter, Jacqueline leaves behind her husband, Marcus.

James and Isabella Hogan, who were driving an MG sports car, died later in hospital.

'Oh my God,' I said. Why had my mother kept this from me? Why hadn't she told me everything about the accident? That a woman died?

'What's up, Mummy?' Grace tilted her head again.

'Nothing, sweetheart – nothing to worry about.' I slipped the photos and the newspaper cutting into my pocket, and packed everything else away at speed, before bringing my numb legs from under me.

'Are we going home now?' Grace asked, shuffling her feet.

'No. We're going to see Gran. I'll pick up some chocolate cakes to take. That will be nice, won't it?'

'Yay,' she said, jumping to her feet. 'Will she know who I am this time?'

'I don't know, my little cuppy cake,' I said, kissing her head and taking hold of her hand, trying to hide the sadness in my voice. 'I hope so.'

Outside, I opened the car, and lifted Grace into her car seat.

'Rachel,' came a voice from behind me. I turned to see Jessica, huddled into a chunky pink cardigan, a purple wool hat pulled over her hair, the rim covering her eyebrows. I hadn't heard her approach.

'Hi, Jess,' I said, moving in for a hug. 'How are you?'

'Never mind that,' she said, flapping her hand, always one to come straight to the point. 'I wanted you to know I saw someone hanging about. They climbed over the gate.'

I snatched a look at the house, recalling the footprints. 'When was this? Did you call the police?'

'I did, yes. But whoever it was had taken off before they arrived. Anyway, I felt you should know. You might want to get in touch with an alarm company.'

'Yes, thank you. Did you see what they looked like?'

She shook her head. 'My eyesight isn't what it was.' A pause. 'How is your mum?'

Tears pricked. *Please don't ask.* 'Not good,' was all I could muster. 'I'm going there now.'

119

'Well, send her my love, won't you?' she said, turning and heading towards her house, pausing briefly to wave at me with her stick.

***

Mum's room smelt of incense, and a Genesis track played on her old portable cassette player. She had her back to us, and was swaying to and fro, singing along to 'Ripples' as she looked out of the window.

She turned, seeming to sense us there, and I prayed she would know us.

'Gran,' cried Grace, racing towards her, and hugging her legs, and Mum stroked her hair.

'Hello, darling,' she said. 'How's my favourite granddaughter?'

I sighed with relief.

'I'm your only granddaughter, silly,' Grace said, and they both laughed, a rejoicing sound, like a peal of church bells saying everything will be just fine – for now.

'I've brought some cakes,' I said, putting the box on her bedside table. 'Your favourite.'

'How lovely. Thank you.'

I moved towards her, and took her in my arms, breathing her in. She was wearing Chanel No.5, but the heavy intoxicating smell of incense almost overpowered it.

We went downstairs to the lounge, where we sat by the window and ate the cakes. 'So much snow,' Mum said, looking out. 'Remember how we used to build a snowman and make snow angels, Rachel?'

I nodded, the memories winding round me like a comfort blanket.

'I like making snow angels,' Grace chipped in with a wide chocolatey smile. 'But there's no snow left in London.'

I was enjoying the chatter. The happiness in Grace's eyes, the glow in Mum's cheeks as Grace showed her drawings she'd done earlier.

'You'll be an artist like me one day,' Mum said, stroking Grace's hair.

'Well, it's in her genes,' I said, taking hold of Mum's hand and squeezing. I didn't want to break the spell, but needed to ask Mum questions, before I lost her again.

'Mum,' I said, and she turned to face me. 'I've been wondering who told you I'd broken up with Lawrence.'

She looked up, furrowing her forehead. 'You told me, didn't you? I forget so much these days. I couldn't even remember Margo's name the other morning, but she said I wasn't to worry.'

'Has Lawrence been here?'

'Yes.'

'Recently?'

She shrugged. 'I don't think so.' She placed her slim finger against her lip. 'No, no not lately, not for a long time.' She laid her hand on mine. 'Are you OK, Rachel?'

'Yes, yes of course.' I fiddled with the photographs in my pocket, knowing the one of the farmhouse would upset her – but I needed to know how the children had featured in our lives.

I fished one out, but it was the one of her, where, I assumed, she'd once stood next to Jude. I showed it to her.

'Who is it?' she said.

'Well, this is you.' I pointed at her younger self. 'And I think you were once standing next to Jude.'

'Jude?'

'Yes. Do you know a man called Jude, Mum?'

She shook her head, and turned away. 'No,' she said. 'Not any more.'

'But you did once?' I persisted, but she didn't reply. 'Mum, what is it you wanted to tell me about the past?' I went on. 'Where did you go in November, when I was a child? Tell me about the farmhouse.'

'I'm tired,' she said, stroking Grace's hair, and closing her eyes. And I wondered, this time, if she was pretending.

***

'I don't want to go in the car again,' Grace said, rolling her eyes as we walked towards it, snow crunching beneath our feet. 'What if Gran wakes up? She'll miss us, and wonder where we've gone.' Sometimes she sounded far too grown-up.

'Well, I'm afraid we've got to head for home,' I said. We'd waited for over an hour for my mum to open her eyes, but she hadn't. 'Just think, soon you'll be in Disneyland. How exciting is that?'

'Yay!' she said, stretching her arms above her head, mittens dangling on strings from her sleeves.

***

Once Grace was bathed, and I'd tucked her into bed and read her *The Very Hungry Caterpillar* six times, I headed downstairs, and fired up my laptop.

Evermore Farmhouse hadn't left my mind since leaving Mum, and I knew it was time to take a deep breath and book a bed and breakfast in County Sligo.

I'd never been before, never drawn to the land of my birth. I guess I thought it had nothing to tell me. My mother didn't know who my father was. My grandparents were dead. And my mother had been an only child. But things were different now. I needed to find out about my past.

Chapter 21

January 1990

Laura drove her mother's yellow Ford Capri along the country roads towards the closest village, Rachel asleep in her car seat. Was a mother and toddler group such a good idea? Rachel was a difficult child.

But Laura had known she had to do something. Living a hermit lifestyle was affecting Rachel, and she knew if she didn't force herself to do something about it now – for Rachel's sake – perhaps she never would.

And it was affecting her too. Sometimes she would pick up the phone, place the receiver to her ear, and listen to the hum of the dialling tone, searching her mind for someone to call. She'd even looked up an old school friend a few weeks back in the hope she might be able to meet up with her – but she'd moved away from Sligo a long time ago.

She still hadn't seen Imogen since the day of the cigarette burns, and Dillon hadn't come near the house since November, despite Laura watching out for him. It was as though they'd closed ranks, and sent her into solitary confinement.

Rachel stirred in her car seat, and gave a little grizzle as she rubbed her eyes with clenched fists. Laura pulled into a space along the road, a two-minute walk from the village hall. Despite the short distance, Laura lifted Rachel into her buggy, and headed along the pavement. She opened the wooden doors of the hall and stood, framed in the doorway, as the blast of children's happy squeals and motherly chatter penetrated her eardrums.

'Are you new?' It was a woman in her forties, her fair hair in a Princess Diana style. Laura took her to be the organiser.

'Yes. I called yesterday. I'm Laura Hogan, and this is Rachel.' She pointed down at Rachel in her buggy.

'Well, do come in. Get yourself a cuppa. We're all very friendly.' Her smile was wide and welcoming.

Laura's stomach tipped as she took in the room full of strangers happily sitting on small chairs with cups of tea or coffee, their well-behaved and well-balanced children playing happily. She lifted Rachel from her buggy and put her down on the floor, where the child looked bewildered.

She took her daughter's hand and, chanting *I must do this for Rachel* in her head, made her way towards a plump woman in glasses, who was dressed in a long black jumper with Liquorice Allsorts on the front, and a pair of Oxford Bags she must have had since the Seventies.

'Hi,' Laura braved, sitting down, and putting Rachel on the floor by her legs.

'Hi, I'm Libby.' The woman was confident – her voice deep and strong.

'I'm Laura, and this is Rachel.'

'Pretty name – reminds me of Daphne Du Maurier's *My Cousin Rachel*.'

'Yes, me too.' The conversation felt stilted, and uncomfortable tingles shuddered through Laura's body. She was so far from her comfort zone she needed a telescope to find it. But Rachel seemed fine. She was happily banging on a drum with drumsticks.

'Mine's the red-headed chap.' Libby pointed at a child pushing a metal truck around the carpet, making brumming noises. 'He's two and a half.'

'The same as Rachel.'

'Super age, isn't it?'

Laura nodded, wishing she felt the same.

'Aaron,' Libby called. 'Come and play with Rachel.'

Rachel stopped drumming, and stared at the boy.

'Brum brum,' he said, rolling the truck across the floor towards Rachel.

Laura could hear Libby chatting to her about how she'd just got a desktop computer with a CD-ROM drive from Comet, and how Aaron's favourite toy was his Glo Worm – *won't sleep without it*. But the words were muffled as Laura stared at her daughter and began to overheat, a sense of foreboding washing over her. Was she afraid of what Rachel was capable of? For goodness' sake, she was only two and a half.

There was a thud as Aaron rammed the truck into the drum, and Rachel stopped drumming, and looked at the child.

'I'm afraid Rachel doesn't like trucks,' Laura said, bending forward to see her daughter's face redden. 'Why not go and play with that little boy over there?' Laura went on, pointing to a boy with spiked gelled hair.

But it was too late. Rachel lifted one of the drumsticks and smacked the boy around the face with it, leaving a red welt. His scream was piercing, but before anyone could react, Rachel picked up his truck and smashed it on his forehead.

'Oh my God,' Libby cried, jumping from her chair and picking him up, cuddling him close. 'Hush, darling,' she said, jiggling him up and down as he continued to scream. She stared at Laura. 'Your child is an absolute monster,' she cried, as the friendly Princess Diana woman from earlier bustled over, and other mothers approached, comforting the crying child and his morti-fied mother.

'Is he going to be OK?' Laura said, as a trickle of blood rolled down the child's forehead. 'Can I do anything? Should we take him to hospital?'

'For God's sake! Just take Rosemary's Baby and leave!' Libby yelled.

Laura looked down at Rachel, who smiled up at her. She whipped her up from the floor and dashed from the hall, tears filling her eyes. Once she'd strapped Rachel into her buggy, she left the village hall and raced down the road, her vision blurred from tears. 'What the hell is wrong with you, Rachel?' she muttered through her teeth. 'Why can't you be like normal children?'

'Laura!'

Laura stopped and dashed her sleeve across her eyes to see Marcus McCutcheon, holding a child's hand, blocking her path.

'I'm so sorry, I'm afraid I'm in a bit of a rush,' she said, embarrassed she was in such a state.

'Is everything OK?'

Does it look as though it is? 'Yes, yes, everything's fine,' she said. 'I just need to …'

'You haven't met my daughter, have you?' he interrupted, gesturing to a child of about seven in a dark green school uniform, with pale blue eyes and a sprinkling of freckles. 'She's just been to the dentist.'

'No fillings, I hope,' Laura said, trying for breezy and not succeeding.

'Laura's parents were driving the car that killed Mummy, Yolanda,' Marcus said to his daughter. *Oh God, can this day get any worse?*

'Really?' The girl stared up at Laura.

'Yes. Yes, that's right.' Laura looked at Marcus, but his stare was more penetrating, and she averted her gaze. He was calmer than he'd been the day he came to her house. She glanced down at the child. 'I'm so sorry about your mum.'

'Thank you, it doesn't get any easier,' she said, sounding too grown-up, and Laura knew she'd been listening to her father. 'I know they say it does. But it doesn't.'

'No, I don't suppose it does.'

'You must know what I mean – you lost your parents, didn't you?' She scrutinised Laura from under a neat, honey-blonde fringe. 'That must have been horrendous. At least I still have Daddy.' She looked up at him, smiled, and gripped his hand.

'It's worse for you.' *I was never close with mine.*

'I disagree. I've been told my pain won't last forever, because I'm just a child; it's harder for Daddy – for you.'

Before Laura could answer, Marcus chipped in, 'Well, it was good to see you again. But we should get on. School beckons and all that.' He nodded to a Victorian school with a wrought-iron fence, fifty yards away.

And as they hurried away, leaving Laura staring after them, Rachel began to cry.

Chapter 22

February 2018

Lawrence knocked on the door at eight on Monday morning, just as I was clearing away the cereal bowls, and I confess I was glad I'd dyed my hair, and splashed on a bit of make-up. I didn't want him to fall into my arms or anything, but I needed him to think I was doing OK, even if I wasn't.

It was the first time he'd been inside the house since he'd collected his stuff in December, despite still having a key. Normally we would do our Grace-handover on the doorstep, to avoid him coming in, but today was different. She was going away for six days, and I needed a long goodbye.

Lawrence looked casual in jeans and a black three-quarter-length jacket I'd bought him a couple of Christmases ago. I'd picked it out with such care, knowing it would suit his tall frame.

I wondered if he noticed the ornament he'd bought me for Valentine's Day a few years back – a man and woman hugging – had gone from the mantelpiece. I'd lost my temper and smashed it against the wall the night he walked out, along with a wine glass, and a silver-framed photo of us *oh so happy* in Majorca. I

128

don't know what else I would have broken if Grace hadn't woken and cried out.

But the truth was, Lawrence barely looked around the room, his eyes fixed on his phone as though whatever he was looking at on the screen was more interesting than me.

'Chipmunk,' he said, looking up as Grace came through from the dining room, dragging her Minions case over the flagstones behind her. He crouched down and hugged her for a few moments, saying, 'Ready for Disneyland?'

'Yep,' she said, nodding three times, before padding towards the door. She tugged at her coat on the rack, and it fell onto her head. We both laughed, for her sake.

'I'll drop her back here about five on Saturday,' he said, as I handed him her passport, his eyes falling on my case in the corner. 'You off somewhere too?'

'I am, yes.'

A heavy pause filled the air, as though he was trying to glean my destination. We were both flying from Heathrow, but thankfully our flights were hours apart. The thought of sitting in departures with him wasn't an option.

'Are you going to tell me where you're going?' His eyes were wide with curiosity.

I held on to my words for a few moments longer before saying, 'Ireland. Sligo. Not that it's any of your business.'

'Alone?'

'Again. None of your business.'

'No. You're right.' Another pause as he locked me in a stare. 'Well, I suppose when you start to look a bit like your passport photo, it's time for a break.'

I glared.

'Joke, Rach – what's happened to your sense of humour?'

'It left with you.'

He rolled his eyes. 'Well, have fun in Ireland.'

'I will. You can bank on it.'

Grace was shuffling into her coat, and he bent to help her with her toggles. 'Bye, Mummy,' she said, once they were done up.

'Bye, sweetheart,' I said, kissing her cheek. 'Love you.'

'Love you more.' She reached up and grabbed Lawrence's hand, and I felt a pang of sadness that we had to share her this way, and I knew she felt it too. He opened the front door, and they hurried down the path, Grace pulling her case over the last of the frozen snow.

'Lawrence,' I called after him, and he glanced back over his shoulder. 'It is just you and Grace going, isn't it?'

'Of course,' he said. 'And we're going to have an amazing time.'

I gave Grace a little wave as she climbed into the back seat. 'FaceTime me on Daddy's phone, won't you?'

'Yes, Mummy,' she said.

Once they'd pulled away, I closed the door, my eyes burning with tears, but I stopped myself from crying. This was my life now. I had to accept it.

***

Five hours later, I was through customs and almost on my way to Ireland. I grabbed a pack of sandwiches and some coffee, and found a seat in departures. I didn't mind flying, and had travelled a lot with Lawrence, but now the thought of my flight to Dublin was making me uneasy, to the point where I half-wished I'd taken up Zoe's offer to come with me.

'You're far too busy at your salon,' I'd said when she'd suggested again we could make a girlie holiday of it, even spend time in Dublin trawling the bars – maybe buy a hat with 'I love Guinness' on it.

'It's not why I'm going,' I'd said. Any thought of a *real* holiday had died with everything that had happened. And, truth was, I didn't like Guinness. 'I need to find out about my past. It would be a complete bore for you.'

She'd finally agreed to give it a miss.

You will be fine, I told myself now as I bit into my cheese and pickle sandwich. I knew exactly where I was heading. Everything would be OK.

The call for my flight broke into my thoughts, and I rose and made my way to my gate. It felt like miles, as I hurried along a travelator, and passed several queues of people waiting to show their boarding passes. And then my tummy tipped as I spotted Lawrence and Grace showing a flight steward their boarding passes at gate twenty-three. Their flight must have been delayed.

I picked up speed, wanting to wave one more time to my precious daughter, wanting her to see me, but they were through the glass doors by the time I got there. I stopped and stared as they walked towards their plane. And that's when I saw Lawrence place an affectionate arm on the back of a woman. I couldn't see her face, but I could see my daughter looking up at her with a wide smile.

As they disappeared from view, I fumbled in my pocket for my phone and typed a text with shaking fingers:

I saw you, Lawrence. I bloody saw you.

Anger bubbled like lather. My head throbbed and I wanted to go home. I needed a drink. *I'll fucking kill him.*

Someone bumped into me. 'Sorry,' she said, steering her carry-on case around me. 'But you have stopped in a stupid place.'

I opened my mouth to call after her. This woman was about to get hit with all my anger, when someone else bumped into me. I glanced over my shoulder to see a swarm of people, some pulling cases, all heading my way. I jolted into action, hurrying towards my gate, deciding going to Ireland – running away – was the best thing I could do.

***

From Dublin, I took a train from Connolly Station, and it was late by the time I picked up a hire car in Sligo Town. I'd booked a bed and breakfast just outside Sligo and was *almost* calm by the time I pulled up outside, too tired to hold on to my anger. Plus, I'd almost convinced myself I must have been mistaken – that the woman was a stranger, and Lawrence hadn't lied to me, that my daughter wasn't in Paris with him and his girlfriend. That it was just a father and daughter sharing precious moments.

After all, he'd replied to my text an hour ago:

> *Calm down, Rachel – you need to control that temper of yours. I have no idea what you're talking about.*

I pulled on the car handbrake, and switched off my headlights. I needed a good night's sleep, and tomorrow I would make for Evermore Farmhouse.

It was in the early hours that I felt sure something had woken me – it was as though someone had been staring at me as I slept. I bolted upright, cold, tingly, and disorientated, but there was nobody in the darkness, just murky shadows of my past.

I switched on the lamp, and pulled myself to a sitting position, grabbing my phone to check the time. There was another notification from Facebook. I checked into my account, and my heart picked up speed. Another friend request:

Flora Phillips: CONFIRM/DELETE REQUEST

The profile picture was a nurse's uniform, hanging on a cupboard door; the cover picture a field of daffodils.

As before, there was one status update:

Goosey Goosey Gander, where shall I wander?
Upstairs, downstairs, and in my lady's chamber.
There I met you, Flora, and you caught me unawares,
So, I took you by the left leg and threw you down the stairs.

Chapter 23

December 2015

They can't change their minds. They must believe all is well inside my head, so I will be more careful this time.

'Are you sure you're OK?' Flora asks me, as I approach. But I know she doesn't care – not really – and I want to scream that I'm not OK, that I'm scared of what I'm capable of. That I'm going to kill again. That I'm going to kill her. 'You know I didn't want this to happen,' she goes on. 'You can't choose who you fall in love with. I hope we can be friends.'

'I'm fine,' I say, as I follow her up the stairs. It's dimly lit, and always smells musty. It's cold too. Nobody comes here – that's why it was our meeting place for so long.

The stairs are steep. 'One, two, three, four …' I count under my breath as I follow her up, up, up. Her perfume's strong – she's meeting him.

She turns, as she reaches the top.

'Wait for me,' I call after her. 'I need to talk to you.'

She balances on the edge of the top step in her heels. She looks nice – her hair curled.

'Thanks for waiting,' I say, now at her side, but I see the appre-

hension in her eyes as I push a tendril of her hair from her face. I so want to kiss her, but I know she doesn't want me to. Not any more.

Before she can open her mouth to speak – to tell me not to touch her – I push.

She tumbles, smacking her head against the wall, her legs bending out of shape, as though made of twigs.

The fall breaks her neck. I know because I see a bone poking through her flesh – and the blood, there's so much blood.

Her eyes, wide open and lifeless, stare up at me, as though asking me why. Surely she knows the answer.

'It's because you deserved to die, Flora,' I say, throwing the key down on top of her, before racing away – I can't let anyone catch me here.

Chapter 24

'Happy birthday, Rachel,' Laura said, heading into the lounge with a pile of presents. She'd ordered most of the gifts from catalogues, and bought a few from the village shop. She knew she was overcompensating.

She put the gifts on the floor beside her daughter. 'Open them, Rachel. Find out what's inside,' she said with a fixed smile. 'They're all for you. And this is for you too.' She handed Rachel a card. *One card. A three-year-old with one solitary card – how had she let that happen?*

Rachel stared at the card for over five minutes. It was clear she wasn't going to open it, or her gifts, so Laura tore away the paper, showing Rachel a doll, a teddy, a book of nursery rhymes, Mr Chimney Pot. But Rachel seemed more interested in rubbing a piece of silk ribbon between her fingers.

'And this is Mr Snookum,' Laura said, ripping the paper from a stuffed rabbit with a waistcoat. Rachel turned, widening her eyes, and reached out. 'Do you like Mr Snookum?'

'Yes,' Rachel said, taking him and cuddling him close.

Once all the gifts were open, and the floor was littered with wrapping paper, Laura brought a cake from the kitchen, and sang happy birthday to her daughter. A flicker of a smile crossed Rachel's lips as she watched the flames dance on the candles. Were they bonding?

'Would you like me to read to you?' Laura said, picking up the nursery rhyme book, and moving closer to her daughter.

And as Laura sang the rhymes, Rachel leaned her head on her mother's lap, and for once there were no tears as she slowly drifted off to sleep.

Eventually Laura edged away, put a cushion under her daughter's head, stroked her hair from her face, and covered her with a throw.

For some time she watched her daughter's chest rise and fall, thinking for the first time in a while about Jude. If he hadn't let her down, Rachel would be different. She would be different. It was his fault.

She stood up and opened the heavy sideboard, and rummaged through her photo box until she found a picture of her and Jude. She went into the kitchen and found a box of matches. With one strike, she watched Jude go up in flames, and with every flicker he was purged from her life. When his face and body had curled and melted away, she turned on the tap and extinguished the flames. Tears filled her eyes, but she didn't sob – she'd done too much of that. She knew now it would always be her and their strange little girl, fighting to survive.

Back in the lounge, she turned on the TV, and flicked through channels mindlessly. BBC News was covering an earthquake in the Philippines where at least four hundred had tragically died. She glanced again at Rachel who was snuffling in her sleep – life could be worse, she tried to tell herself.

***

Mid-afternoon, after wrestling Rachel into her coat, Laura and her daughter set out for a walk through the woods, Laura snapping photographs as they went. She'd taken to doing paintings straight from photographs lately, enjoying putting a brush to canvas, after rarely painting for so long.

She captured a picture of a rabbit, a pied wagtail, a sand martin, and snapped studies of Rachel sitting on a log hugging Mr Snookum. Rachel had even raised another smile, seeming to enjoy the attention.

Laura had walked the woods many times now. She knew every trail, so it wasn't accidental she ended up at Lough End Farm. And it wasn't the first time she'd been there in the last two years, never wanting to quite let go of Dillon – always worrying about the children.

She peered through the trees, to see Dillon playing with the girls – they seemed happy, laughing as he chased them. Imogen stood at the kitchen window, but there was no sign of Tierney.

'Mummy.' It was Rachel.

'Just a minute, darling,' Laura said, flapping her hand behind her back at her daughter, not turning. 'I just want to make sure Bridie and Caitlin are OK.'

'There's a squirrel,' Rachel went on, but Laura didn't reply, her eyes fixed on the children. 'Yucky squirrel,' the child continued.

Laura finally turned. 'Rachel? Rachel, where are you?' she called, looking about her, but Rachel had gone.

'Laura?' It was Dillon, appearing through a gap in the trees. 'Can I talk to you? It's about Imogen.'

'Not right now, Dillon,' she said, taking off into the woods, bashing back the hedgerow.

He raced to her side, taller and thinner than when she last saw him, mild acne covering his cheeks, a woolly hat over his curls. He was leaving the boy he once was behind. Chasing the man he would soon become. 'Imogen's ill, Laura,' he said, his tone deeper now his voice had broken.

'I can't do anything, Dillon. You know that. You've all made it perfectly clear I'm not welcome. Now leave me alone – I need to find my daughter.'

'Rachel's missing?'

'She can't have gone far. She was here a moment ago. Rachel!' she yelled.

'Rachel!' Dillon joined in, his eyes darting the trees as they hurried onwards.

'What if someone's taken her?' Laura cried, tears filling her eyes.

'Why would you think that? Did you see someone?'

She shook her head, wondering why her brain had taken her to such a dreadful thought. Was it the complete isolation? 'No,' she said, 'but anyone could hide in these woods. We should call the Guards.'

'Let's look for a bit first, Laura,' he said, reaching out and touching her arm, as she raced through brambles – cutting her leg. 'She could be hiding. You know she's a bit …'

'Troubled?'

As they reached the back of Laura's house, they saw Rachel sitting on the patio, legs outstretched, singing a nursery rhyme.

'Thank God!' Laura screamed, racing towards her and picking her up. Hugging her close. For once, Rachel didn't protest. 'Thank God, you're OK,' she said, kissing her hair.

'I was hiding,' Rachel said.

'You shouldn't hide. I was worried.' She put her daughter down.

'It's my birthday,' Rachel said, taking hold of Dillon's hand.

'Well, happy birthday,' he said, staring deep into her eyes. He looked at Laura. 'I reckon Rachel has the prettiest eyes I've ever seen,' he said with a smile.

Laura was still in shock, her body trembling. 'Has she?' she said, ashamed she'd never really noticed.

Inside the house, Laura plonked Rachel in the lounge with her new toys, and poured herself a brandy. 'Want one?' she asked Dillon. 'You must be old enough, by now.'

'Not quite,' he said, pulling open the fridge, and grabbing a can of cola.

'I sometimes think I'm losing my mind, Dillon.' She knocked back the brandy in one go, and poured another.

'Have you thought about selling up? Starting again somewhere else?'

It was a question she'd asked herself a thousand times. And there were so many reasons why she never had.

'Often,' she said. 'But I haven't got the strength. What if Rachel doesn't fit in? What if I can't cope with the real world any longer?' A pause as she watched him flick open the can, and take a gulp. 'You were telling me about Imogen,' she said. 'That she's ill?'

He nodded. 'She's throwing up every morning, but she won't go to the doctor's – says she knows what the problem is, but it ain't right.'

Laura suspected another baby was coming into the O'Brian family, and it filled her with dread. 'She could be pregnant,' she said, her glass halfway to her lips.

'Christ. I dunno. Maybe.'

'I can't be sure, but it sounds like she could be. Make sure she eats right, help her the best you can, and try to coax her into going to the doctor's.'

'Yeah, yeah, I'll try, but she seems determined not to,' he said. 'Anyway, I guess I'd better go to her.' He thudded the can onto the table. 'I just hope she listens.'

Chapter 25

I woke to sun's rays streaming through a gap in the curtains, and dust particles raining down like a snow shower. I squeezed my eyes closed, having to think for a moment where I was. The sudden realisation I was in Ireland sent a mixture of relief and apprehension through my body. It felt good to be away from my normal life for a few days, but what would I find out while I was here in County Sligo? What would I discover at Evermore Farmhouse?

Then I remembered the friend request I'd received in the early hours, and shot up in bed, grabbing the top of my head, as though my brains might explode.

After a few moments I grabbed the journal I'd been keeping since Zoe suggested it.

I opened up the page where I'd jotted down the friend requests I'd received:

David Green. Cover photo: Mandan Road, County Sligo.
Ronan Murphy. Cover photo: Glastons Insurance Dublin.

I added the latest one:

Flora Phillips. Cover photo: Daffodils.

As with the other requests, it had been impossible to find anything online about Flora Phillips – there just wasn't enough to go on.

I thought about what the odd variations on nursery rhymes could mean, and shuddered. They'd been so creepy, all suggesting someone getting hurt – the fire, the bump on the head, the fall down the stairs.

Suddenly everything that had happened played through my mind like a film on fast forward: the calls, the man who'd wanted to meet me at the Emirates Stadium, my mum's despair when she'd seen the mysterious painting. The photos I'd found at her house.

I slammed closed my notebook. I needed to find out why my mother had kept secrets from me – what happened in Ireland when I was small. And what, if anything, did Evermore Farmhouse have to do with it?

I rose, stretched, and pulled back the drapes to see a clear, pastel-blue sky. There was no doubting it would be cold out, but for a moment, as I pushed my body against the warm radiator under the window, I kidded myself it was summer. That I could go down to the nearby beach in my shorts and T-shirt, and kick off my Converse and wiggle my toes in the warm sand – *not too close to the water*.

Benbulbin stood proud in the distance. My mum had read Yeats's poem about the mountain to me when I was young. It was fascinating to see it for myself, the unusual shape that gave it its local name 'Table Mountain'. Why had Ronan Murphy used it as his profile picture? Was it to lure me here?

I leaned forward, my nose touching the window, attempting to breathe in the peace and solitude on the other side of the glass

– almost forgetting why I was there. Then the moment popped like a balloon, and I was back, ready to find out everything I could about my mum's time in Ireland – everything I could about my past.

I showered, although it was more of a dribble, barely wetting my hair. The bed and breakfast was cosy, and the couple who ran it, friendly, but the place was dated, with swirling patterned carpets in oranges and browns, and a brown Dralon three-piece suite and a hefty-backed TV in the lounge. But then I wasn't here for luxury.

My hair felt light under my fingers as I dried it, and I was thankful that Zoe had cut the weight from it. The nick she'd made with her scissors was now a scab waiting to fall. I dragged on the pair of jeans I'd discarded on the floor the night before, and a clean sweatshirt, along with thick socks and fur-lined ankle boots. My stomach let out a gurgle. I was starving.

The dining room was small, with an old-fashioned sideboard covered with a lace tablecloth, and laden with cereal, fruit, and juices. I served myself, and once I was back at the table a pleasant young waitress brought over a jug of coffee.

Fed and caffeine-fixed, I thumbed through the things I'd taken from my mother's house: the photograph of me and the three other children at Evermore Farmhouse. The newspaper cutting about the crash that killed Jacqueline McCutcheon at Devil's Corner – why hadn't Mum told me more about my grandparents' accident? Didn't she want me looking into her? I pushed down a sudden anger rising inside me. I hated that she'd kept things from me. I hated that I felt I didn't know her at all.

I left the bed and breakfast and hurried along the road towards my hire car, pulling on my parka. According to the satnav, I would be at Evermore Farmhouse in fifteen minutes.

The car took several attempts to start, and I growled inside, but it eventually spluttered into life, and I was on my way, heading along quiet narrow roads, winding my way into the countryside. The ride was pleasant, no snow to speak of, so I turned up the radio, and tried to enjoy the scenery.

It was gone ten when I pulled up next to a set of security gates, and my satnav announced I'd reached my destination – Evermore Farmhouse.

I got out of the car. There were no other buildings close by. No traffic noise – only the chirping of birds, and the rustle of wildlife in a nearby wood. I wasn't afraid of the silence. In fact, I felt energised, full of determination.

I peered through the wrought-iron gate at a pretty farmhouse at the end of a cobbled drive, and pressed the buzzer. I waited … and waited, stomping from foot to foot. Nobody came, and my eyes fell on the side gate. It was ajar. I zipped up my parka, and, before my confidence evaporated, I opened the gate and walked up the drive.

The farmhouse looked more like the photograph sent by Ronan Murphy, very different from my mother's paintings. The place had been renovated and extended since my mother took a brush to canvas. It was pale pink, and a trellis arch framed the front door where, I knew from the photograph, roses grew in summer. There was no sign of hens, or any animals come to that. It didn't appear to be a functioning farm, and I wondered if it ever was. There were a few outbuildings, a double garage, and a patio in a shaded area near the lake with garden furniture, a tree barren of leaves, and a rowing boat moored nearby.

'Can I help you?'

I stopped halfway up the drive, and turned to see a tall man of about sixty, with a shock of greying hair, heading towards me from the wood, a silky, black Labrador by his side.

'Sorry … do you live here?' I said. I knew I was trespassing.

He came closer. 'Yes,' he said. He was Irish, although his accent was watered down, and he seemed vaguely familiar.

'I'm a bit lost,' I said, not sure why I was lying. Why I didn't come right out and tell him why I was there – proceed with questions I was itching to ask about the place. But something stopped me.

'Where were you heading?'

Then it hit me. 'Oh my God, you're Felix T Clarke!' I'd seen him before when he'd signed his novel in my local bookshop, and he'd written a few kind words too. Plus his photograph was on the back of all his books. He'd even played a cameo in the TV dramas based on his novels – a bit like Stan Lee in the Marvel movies, or Colin Dexter in Morse and Lewis.

He smiled, seeming pleased I recognised him. 'That's right,' he said, glancing at the farmhouse. 'I've been cooped up for the last few months hoping to get my next novel finished. My publishers are biting at my heels.'

I confess, I felt awestruck – much like the time I leapt across the organic veg in Sainsbury's to ask for Robbie Williams' autograph. Zoe had almost wet herself laughing when I'd zipped back to where she was waiting with my trolley, with a complete stranger's signature – Mark Bristow, I think his name was.

But there was no doubting this was one of my favourite authors – here, right in front of me. He'd sold millions of books. The dramas were on prime TV.

'Wow! Fancy seeing you here,' I said, knowing I sounded ridiculous. After all, I was the one who'd arrived uninvited.

He smiled and stuck out his leather-gloved hand for me to shake, as his dog sniffed my crotch, which I tried desperately to ignore.

'I adore *The Inspector Bronte Mysteries*,' I went on, as he released my hand. 'I've got all the novels, and the Blu-ray box set – although the early episodes are on Sky now, aren't they? Probably should have saved my money. But they're nice to have.' I was rambling, but didn't seem to be able to stop. 'Lots of people don't bother with Blu-rays these days do they? What with digital downloads – but I'm a bit old-fashioned. Although I own a Kindle and a

Mac, and I never buy CDs any more, so I guess I'm not a complete technophobe.'

Another smile crossed his lips, as I came up for breath. 'Who are you?' he said, raising a brow.

'Ah … well my name's Rachel …'

'Lovely name,' he cut in. 'There was a character named Rachel in one of my books.'

'Yes, I remember – she disappeared.'

'That's right.' He'd lost his smile, and was studying me with dark eyes. 'So you're lost?'

'Yes … well, no.'

'So, which is it?'

'Well, the thing is … I'm doing a bit of family history research.'

'And it brought you here?' Another raised brow.

'Mmm.'

'Well I guess you'd better come in,' he said, striding towards the farmhouse. 'Duke,' he called, and his dog followed. 'I'll put the kettle on,' he said, disappearing inside.

I moved closer to the farmhouse, and peered through the window to see Felix with his back to me, filling a kettle. I placed my palm on the glass, but snatched it away immediately. It was as though it had burnt my skin. Dizzy, I grabbed the windowsill to steady myself, knocking a plant pot to the ground, where it smashed and soil scattered.

Flashes of distorted memories filled my head – blood pooling on the floor, a child, limp and motionless.

I gasped, tears in my eyes as I turned, stumbling away, my stomach turning and churning. Halfway down the drive, I bent over double, retching and coughing.

Are these real memories? Oh God, they can't be.

I continued to stagger onwards, needing to get away.

'Rachel!' It was Felix.

'I'm not feeling well,' I called, not looking back.

I dived through the gate and into the car, tears rolling down my cheeks.

But even as I pushed my foot down on the throttle, desperate to get away, something told me I must go back.

Chapter 26

September 1990

Laura, from her deckchair, captured on canvas the morph of blues and greens in the distance. The way the sun's rays glinted like diamonds on the water. Rachel snuffled in her sleep in her buggy beside her, dressed in a pink polka-dot dress and sunhat.

'Laura.'

Laura turned to see Dillon. It had been over two months since she'd seen him, and her eyes lit up. She put down her brush and rose, desperate to hug him, but too afraid he'd take off if she did. 'It's good to see you,' she said. 'How are you? How's Imogen?'

'You were right. She is pregnant.'

'And she's seen a doctor?'

He shook his head. 'She won't listen.' His chin crinkled. 'It's a real worry, so it is.'

'I'm sure she'll be OK,' she said, but her heart wasn't in her words. She lowered herself back onto the deckchair, looking at the boy. He looked pale and his eyes were bloodshot.

He sat down on the grass, knees touching his chin, fingers entwined around them, and took a deep breath, eyes focused on the water. 'Me da ...'

Was it what she'd always feared? That Tierney had hurt one of them. That she'd done nothing to prevent it. 'Oh God, what has he done?' she cut in.

He gulped, his Adam's apple bobbing. 'He still locks Bridie in the cupboard before he goes off to work if he reckons she's been bad. She doesn't cry any more. Used to it, poor kid.' He turned to catch her in a stare. 'And sometimes Caitlin ends up there too. It's brutal in there, dark, cold – spiders the size of me hand.' He held up his grubby palm. 'Ma's still too scared to argue.' A pause. 'There are so many burns on her arms now, there's no fecking flesh left.'

'Oh God,' Laura said, picturing it, a chill shuddering through her body – the thought of a new baby going into that awful environment making her toes curl. 'Something has to be done, Dillon.'

'I know, but what? What the fuck can I do? I heard Ma screaming the other day. I tried to barge down their bedroom door. I wanted to put him right. But it was locked. He yelled at me to go away. Said it had nothing to do with me. But he's wrong, Laura. I have to protect them.'

'But you can't,' Laura said, trying to sound calm, but feeling far from it. 'He's twice the size of you.'

'I don't care.' He rose, rammed his hands into the pockets of his crumpled shorts, and kicked the dry earth. 'I'm sixteen. I ain't scared of him any more.'

'You're a brave lad, Dillon, but we need to call the Guards.'

He shook his head. 'You know I've called them before – that Ma tells them everything's OK. Tells them to leave us alone.' His eyes were wide, and Laura, despite her earlier reservations, took him in her arms and hugged him close.

'Your mother's afraid of him. Too afraid to do anything,' she said, a note of defeat in her voice. *And now she's carrying another of his children.*

Dillon pulled away, and nodded. 'Imogen told me yesterday

that she thinks he killed me real ma. That me ma didn't take off at all, that he killed her stone dead.' A tear rolled down his cheek.

'What? Why ever would she think that?'

He shrugged. 'She wouldn't say any more, but I'm wondering now if he did. I've never understood why she took off without saying goodbye. I hated her for it, but now …'

'I'm sure it isn't true, Dillon. Imogen's got it wrong – she must have.'

'Maybe,' he said. 'Laura, can we stay with you? Hide away here?' He glanced back at the house, but it was as though he realised even before he'd finished speaking, that it wouldn't work. 'It would be the first place he'd look,' he said, resigned, rubbing his eyes with the heels of his palms.

'Dillon!' It was Imogen, standing some distance away, Caitlin propped on her hip. Bridie was closer to Laura, leaning against a tree, staring with dark, sad eyes. 'I wondered where you'd got to,' Imogen continued, her voice sharp.

'How are you?' Laura called over – she looked so pale.

'Fine!' Imogen snapped. 'Dillon! Home!'

'I'd better go,' he said, racing away, shooting past Imogen, and disappearing into the woods.

'If you ever want to come over,' Laura called, but the woman turned and walked away, leaving Bridie to continue staring.

'You ought to go too, Bridie,' Laura called, but the child didn't move.

Laura's thoughts skittered. How could she help, if Imogen wouldn't let her? Anyway, Laura was no match for Tierney. Perhaps she could call social services? But it was the same worry she'd always had. What if he took it out on the children?

Once Imogen was out of sight, Laura's angst settled a little. She picked up her paintbrush, and dipped it in the blue, glancing every few moments at Bridie still loitering behind her. She would go over soon, make sure she got home OK, but for now the child was dragging a stick along the bark, humming. She seemed happy enough.

Her cat sprung onto Laura's lap. 'Rusty, you startled me,' she said, holding her chest, before stroking the ginger feline's ears. Purring, the cat curled up, making it difficult for her to paint, and he had just closed his eyes when Rachel woke, and let out a cry. He made a quick exit, as Laura lifted Rachel from the buggy and tried to comfort her, but the child kicked and thrashed, as she often did, so she planted her on the ground.

'Stop crying, darling,' she said, as Rachel continued to bellow. 'Please, Rachel. Stop. I've got a headache.' It was true; the sun and the stress of seeing Dillon had been a fatal combination. 'Would you like a lolly?' She took a lollipop from her bag and held it out towards her daughter, but Rachel smacked her hand and upped her volume, so much so a magpie flapped its wings and flew out of a nearby tree.

Laura turned to Bridie. 'Would you like a lolly, darling?' she said, and the child shook her head, her dark hair falling about her face.

Laura looked again at Rachel, and knowing her daughter would only stop crying when she was ready, she picked up her paintbrush once more and attempted lose herself in the view – to enter the picture, and block out the world around her. Was she being selfish?

Rachel's cries died down and she sat for a while on the ground beside Laura, staring out at the water.

Five minutes later, Laura heard a splash – felt the spray of water on her legs. Her first thought was that her daughter had fallen in. She jumped to her feet, the glare of the sun making it impossible to see, as she raced to the lake edge, where Rachel came into focus, gazing down at the water.

'Oh my God!'

The cat meowed and thrashed in the water, trying to stay afloat, his fur soaked to his body. Laura dropped to her knees and fished him out.

'Dead cat?' Rachel said.

Laura wrapped the bedraggled feline in her cardigan, and held him to her chest, hearing the rapid beat of his heart.

'Rachel, what happened?' she yelled. 'Did you push him in? Did you push him? What the hell is the matter with you?'

'She's a troubled girl. You need to get your life in order, Laura.'

Laura turned to see Imogen standing nearby, Caitlin in her arms, and Bridie by her side. She'd clearly returned for her daughter. Laura felt a thundering anger racing through her blood. She was upset. Scared for the cat's life. 'People in glass houses, and all that,' she yelled, as they walked away.

'And what's that supposed to mean?' Imogen said, spinning round.

'It means sort out your own problems, Imogen O'Brian, before you judge me.'

The cat let out a pathetic mew. It would live, thank God, but Laura knew, as she observed her daughter's blue eyes, that he couldn't live with them any more.

***

In the early hours, Laura woke from a vivid nightmare, beads of sweat on her forehead. Needing air, she grabbed her robe, swung her legs round, and shoved her feet into her slippers.

After checking Rachel was sleeping, she slipped a torch into her pocket, and went outside.

Fog whirled around her body as she walked towards the lake, and once there, she stood in the haze of the moon. An owl hooted somewhere in the distance, and an odd shudder ran through her, the kind she felt when someone scraped their fingernails down a blackboard. She glanced over her shoulder, forming shapes out of shadows that dipped in and out of the trees and hedgerow, but still she stood, cool air fresh on her cheeks, her hair dancing in the breeze.

After a while she sat down, and cradled her knees. She would take Rusty to the cats' home tomorrow. Hope they would find him a good family to live with. Their promise to never put a healthy cat down boded well. Someone somewhere would love him, she felt sure of it. She knew she couldn't keep him, and a flood of tears filled her eyes. She'd thought she was finally reaching the child – but it seemed to be one step forward and two back. Had she made Rachel the way she was? Was the damage she'd done irreversible?

Distant voices on the lake disturbed her thoughts. She narrowed her eyes, wondering if it was anglers. She could just make out, with the help of the moonlight breaking through the fog, a rowing boat with two figures inside. Their voices were raised – a male first, then a female – but it was incoherent, muffled. She fumbled with her torch, and was about to switch it on when she heard a splash. An image erupted in her head. The cat panicking as it flailed around in the water earlier. But she knew, this time, something much heavier had hit the water.

Chapter 27

February 2018

My vision blurred as a rush of tears filled my eyes. I could barely grip the steering wheel for shaking. I was driving too fast, and the blast of a car horn as I veered across the road caused my already jangled nerves to shatter. I braked hard, swerved into a lay-by, and sobbed.

Had the visions at the farmhouse been real? *Are they my memories?*

I fumbled in my bag for tissues, and my hand landed on my phone. I pulled it out, wondering whether to call Zoe, and noticed a text from Emmy:

> **Hi Rachel, I wondered if I could arrange another therapy session with you. I'm OK. Just miss our chats – they tend to keep me sane. Sorry to be a pain. Emmy X**

I couldn't face replying. In fact, was I even equipped to carry on as a psychotherapist? I would text her later, suggest meeting for coffee. I threw my phone back into my bag, deciding not to call Zoe either. I would deal with this alone – for now, at least.

I started the engine. I would return to the bed and breakfast. Hide in the sanctuary of my room. Recharge.

By evening, with the help of two glasses of red wine from a bottle I'd picked up from a nearby off-licence, I'd calmed down. Plus a FaceTime session with Grace had helped lift my mood. I'd been tempted to ask her about Farrah, but stopped myself. I didn't want to put Grace in the middle of her father's conspiracy. That's if there was one, and I wasn't simply his paranoid ex.

I opened up my laptop around eight, and searched news stories for Evermore Farmhouse, but it didn't even bring up that Felix lived there – and I assumed he'd kept his private life, private.

It was around nine when I dozed off with the TV on, catching who had gone through on *MasterChef* before my eyelids grew heavy and I couldn't fight sleep any longer.

***

Hailstones hammering the window like marbles woke me the following morning. I threw back the duvet, rose, and headed for the shower – determined once more to find out about the past.

A cooked breakfast inside me, I headed for the nearest village to Evermore Farmhouse, windscreen wipers thrashing.

Although Devil's Corner was a local name for the hazardous bend that had taken my grandparents' lives, I'd managed to track it down on the Internet before I left for Ireland, and knew it wasn't far from the village I was driving towards. Surely someone would remember my mother, or my grandparents' accident – or, more importantly, what happened at Evermore Farmhouse.

Once I'd reached the village, I parked at the side of the road. I dashed along the pavement, hood up, avoiding puddles, and dived into a convenience store. I could tell the teenager behind the counter was too young to recall things that must have happened almost thirty years ago, but decided to ask all the same.

I plonked a bag of crisps and a chocolate bar on the counter.

'Hi,' I said, as she rung up the items on the till, throwing her my best smile.

She looked up from under a green fringe. 'Three euros. Want a bag? They're five cents.'

I shook my head, and handed her five euros. 'Have you lived around here long?'

'Who wants to know?'

'Well, me. I just …'

'Nope.' She handed me my change, and shoved the items towards me with the length of her arm. 'Came here with my parents a year ago. Sod all to do around here.'

'So you wouldn't know anything about Evermore Farmhouse?'

'Where the kid died?'

'A child died there?' I felt my body tense, and my pulse flutter.

She shrugged. 'Apparently, yeah. Old Bob, who was a bit barking according to the residents around here, used to talk about it. He didn't make a lot of sense though, so don't ask me what he was on about.'

'Where can I find him?'

She pointed through the window. 'You go out of here to the end of the road, and turn right.'

'OK, thanks.' I was finally getting somewhere.

'He's the second grave on the far left of the cemetery. Kicked it last June.' She grinned. 'He was gone ninety.'

'Right,' I said, trying to hide my annoyance. 'Is there anyone else in the village who might have lived here thirty years ago?'

Another shrug. 'Some author bloke lives at the farm now, I think. To be honest, most people are new around here. Although I think Marcus McCutcheon's been here a while.'

McCutcheon. 'Do you know where I might find him?'

'Nope.' A pause. 'Anything else?'

'No. No thank you.' I gathered up my items, and headed back into the rain, spotting a tearoom at the end of the street. Deciding I might find locals there, I slipped my phone back into my pocket, and broke off a piece of chocolate and shoved it into my mouth, chewing as I raced through the rain.

A comforting smell of baking greeted me as I made my way towards a vacant table in the tearoom. A gorgeous original feature fireplace housed a flickering fire, and teapots of all shapes and sizes lined a high shelf, which ran the length of the room. Tables with yellow tablecloths and vases of plastic daffodils in the centre – far too much yellow – jostled for space. Music played in the background, sounding a bit like the theme from *Harry Potter.*

A plump woman in her fifties with rosy cheeks smiled from behind the counter. 'I'll be right with you,' she sang, blowing an escaped tendril of black hair from her forehead, as she poured boiling water into a teapot.

I hung my wet coat over the back of the chair, sat down, and picked up a menu.

'Rachel,' came a confident male voice, carrying across the busy tearoom.

I looked up to see Felix sitting by the bay-fronted window, his laptop open, glasses dangling from his hand. I hadn't spotted him when I came in.

'Hi there,' I said, my cheeks suddenly hot with embarrassment that I'd stormed from his house without saying goodbye.

His smile was wide, and seemed genuine, and I mirrored it, as I fiddled with the menu.

'You disappeared quickly, yesterday. Was it something I said?' He put his glasses on. Eyes back on his laptop screen, as though he didn't care how I responded.

'I felt ill all of a sudden. Sorry I rushed off.'

'No need to apologise. I love it when strange people do odd things. It's good fodder for my novels.' He laughed.

'Well, I'm not normally that strange,' I said, running my fingers through my damp hair.

The woman approached, brandishing a notebook and pen. 'So what can I get you?' she said.

'Just a pot of tea, please.'

'Can't tempt you with a slice of carrot cake?' There was a twinkle in her blue eyes, as she nodded towards the counter where a delicious-looking cake called to me from under a glass cover. 'Made it myself.'

'Oh, go on then,' I said, smiling at Felix as she walked away. 'I really shouldn't,' I called over to him. 'I've got a huge bar of chocolate in my bag with my name on it.'

He lifted his cup, blew on it, and took a slow sip.

'So how's the latest novel coming along?' I continued. 'I love Inspector Bronte.'

He took off his glasses again, and overdid rubbing his eyes. 'And I'm sure that has nothing to do with Bentley Ryan playing him in the TV series?'

I laughed. The actor Bentley Ryan was gorgeous. 'No, I read all your novels long before the TV series. I'm a stalwart fan. In fact, I've got a signed copy of *Where are the children?*' But he'd pushed his glasses back on, and his fingers were tapping the keyboard. Our conversation was over.

My tea and cake arrived and, as the woman emptied the goodies from the tray onto my table, I took a deep breath and asked her how long she'd lived in the village.

'Me, love?' she said, shoving the tray under her arm, and rolling her eyes upwards as though searching for the answer. 'Must be twelve years come May. Messy divorce brought me here, but I've shown *him* I'm not just a pretty face.' She glanced about her, admiring her teashop. 'I opened this place ten years ago, and since then it's gone from strength to strength.' She glanced over her shoulder at Felix. 'We even get famous authors in here.'

I smiled. 'It's lovely,' I said, but before I could ask anything else, she zipped away to another table, and began clearing plates.

I poured tea, and found another surge of confidence from somewhere. 'Excuse me,' I called, trying to get her attention once more, desperately wanting to ask if she knew anything about

Evermore Farmhouse, but while Felix was in the café it was a no-go. Instead I decided to concentrate on my grandparents' accident. 'I don't suppose you know Marcus McCutcheon.'

'Yes, I know Marcus,' she said, flicking me a look as she scrubbed the table. 'Comes in here sometimes. Loves my Victoria sponge.'

'Do you know where I could find him?'

'Hmm, now let me think.' She gave her forehead a rub with her fingertips, as though it would release the information. 'I think he lives in Truman Close – not sure what number. Mind you, he collects gnomes.'

'Gnomes?'

'Mmm, can't see the attraction myself – freaky little things, if you ask me. Anyway, he's bound to have some loitering in his front garden, so you'll recognise his house.'

'Gnomes give me the creeps too.' I smiled. 'Anyway, thanks so much,' I said, as she headed away.

I drank my tea, and ate my cake, scrutinising Felix as he typed. I hoped he would look up, and I could bombard him with questions about the farmhouse, but he was so absorbed in his words I didn't disturb him. There would be another time. I would make sure of it.

'Goodbye, Mr Clarke,' I said, once I'd slipped on my coat and opened the door – glad to see the rain had stopped. He didn't look up.

Chapter 28

February 2018

The sky was granite grey as I pulled into Truman Close, a cul-de-sac on the other side of the village, comprising eight semi-detached houses, probably built in the early Seventies.

It was clear which house belonged to Marcus McCutcheon. The woman at the tearoom had been right about the gnomes – they edged his path as though on guard, and seemed to be watching me as I hurried towards the front door. I was being ridiculous, but there was something about gnomes that made me anxious. I felt sure they all stood statue-still when my eyes were on them, moving when I looked away.

I reached the front door, sucked in a breath, and knocked three times.

A small dog yapped, lunging at the frosted glass panel so hard I thought it might knock itself out. Eventually the door was opened, and through a gap of six inches, a pale, freckled face appeared. 'Hello.' He looked to be in his late fifties, with a receding faded-ginger hairline.

'I'm looking for Marcus McCutcheon,' I said, over the dog's bark.

'Trudy, shh,' the man said, agitated, sharp. 'Yes, that's me. What do you want?'

'Oh … well …' I stuttered. 'Hi.' I lifted my hand in a wave, and swallowed hard before continuing. 'The thing is my name's Rachel Hogan. I'm James and Isabella Hogan's grand-daughter.'

'Ah, I see.' He opened the door wider, and gestured for me to enter. 'I've been expecting you. You'd better come in.'

'You have?' I stepped back.

'Well, not today, obviously,' he went on, straightening his cardigan. He gave a small, strange laugh. 'But I knew you would come one day.' He stared into my eyes. 'People always want to know about their past, don't they? Discover who their family were – what they were like?'

'Do they?' I stepped into the house, and he closed the door behind me. Trudy sniffed my feet and looked up at me with chocolate-brown eyes, before trotting away down the hall.

'Come through,' Marcus said.

I followed him into his lounge, feeling wary. He was a stranger, after all, and more than a tad eccentric. Under his cardigan, he wore a crisp white polo shirt over smart, turquoise trousers. His leather slippers looked expensive.

Patio doors stretched across the far wall, and a well-main-tained garden opened up behind the glass, where yet more gnomes had taken over. *Revenge of the Lawn Gnomes*, a *Goosebumps* novel I'd read as a kid, flashed through my mind, making me shudder.

'Coffee?' Marcus asked, and I jumped.

'Please.'

He headed into the adjoining kitchen, where the dog was now curled up in a tartan basket. I turned back to the window, unable to pull my gaze away from those bloody gnomes. I'd never dreamt there were so many types. Some were fishing by a fishpond, others stood by the gate waving signs giving mixed messages: 'welcome' and 'halt'. Under a tree, seven or eight were meditating, and vampire gnomes were perched on the branches.

'Sugar?'

I jumped again – far too anxious. 'No, thank you.'

Moments later he brought through mugs of coffee, and placed them on coasters on a marble coffee table. 'Sit. Please,' he said, dashing back to the kitchen and returning with a plate of chocolate digestive biscuits.

I removed my damp coat, and sat down on the sofa. He took the chair.

'So you've noticed my gnomes,' he said. 'Bit of an obsession of mine.'

'I can see that.' I glanced again out of the window, promising myself it would be the last time. Why did they freak me out so much? 'If I'm honest, I've always had a bit of a gnome phobia.'

He furrowed his forehead, and I knew he was put out. 'My wife loved them.'

'I'm sure lots of people do. Take no notice of me.' I waved my hand apologetically. 'I'm just being silly.'

'We had half a dozen before the accident, and since then I buy a few each year in her memory. I bring them home and show her.' He nodded to a framed photograph on the wall. His late wife looked about my age in the picture, with short, dark hair. She was wearing a black and white checked dress.

'She had a lovely smile,' I said.

'Yes, yes she did.' He looked at his hands, turning his wedding ring around his finger several times. 'I realise collecting so many gnomes might seem a little strange.'

'No. No, not at all,' I lied. It had been over thirty years since his wife died, and yet, as I watched him sip his coffee, I couldn't help feeling desperately sorry. Sorry that life had never been the same since his loss. Sorry that it seemed he'd never moved on. Sorry that my grandparents had been the reason for that.

'I remember your mother,' he said, putting down his coffee.

'You do?'

'Yes. Laura. Not well, but I liked her. I thought once we might … well, that never happened.'

I felt my neck tingle. The conversation felt awkward. I thought back to the newspaper cutting. 'So you have a daughter who survived the crash,' I said, to change the subject.

'Yes, Yolanda. She wasn't so keen on your mum, I'm afraid. She got it in her head that Laura might replace her mother.' He ran his finger around the neck of his collar, a shaft of red crossing his cheeks, and I imagined for a moment him married to my mother – and me, as a child, trying to explain away my peculiar stepfather to my school friends.

'But I told Yolanda more times than I care to remember,' he went on, 'that no one could ever replace her mum.'

I looked around for a photograph of his daughter, and my eyes fell on a child of about six or seven in a green school uniform, with a heavy honey-blonde fringe. There didn't seem to be any recent photos.

'She moved to London to study media and design, and ended up staying, as so many do. She has her own shop in Islington: "Yolanda's Heaven".'

'I have a friend who owns a salon in Islington.'

'Really?' He raised his brows. 'It's a small world, isn't it?'

'I guess so,' I said.

'Yolanda's doing well, she tells me. Says she loves her work – her life.' He let out a sigh, and I knew he was suddenly somewhere else. 'When she was little she wanted to be a ballerina, or an actress like Julia Roberts. I don't see her much, but that's my fault. I should make more of an effort. Trouble is I hate leaving this place, and Yolanda is always so busy.' He took another swig of coffee, looking at me over the mug. 'How is your mother?'

'Unwell,' I said, through a lump rising in my throat, unsure how much to tell him.

'I'm sorry to hear that.' He shook his head, and a pause

followed, broken only by him lifting the plate. 'Why not have a biscuit?' he said.

I took one and bit into it, a cascade of crumbs sprinkling my top. 'I don't suppose you remember where my mother used to live?' I said, my mouth full.

'You don't know?' He didn't wait for a reply. 'She lived in the big house on the edge of the woods in Laurel Road, near the lake. The building looks so out of place, you can't miss it. I'm not sure who lives there now. Your mother moved away years ago, just after the tragedy.'

'The tragedy?' Was he referring to the car crash?

'Yes. Although I've seen your mum a few times over the years.'

'You have?'

'Mmm …' The doorbell rang, and Trudy skidded across the kitchen floor and hurtled towards the door, yapping. Marcus rose, and smoothed his trousers. 'That will be Sue. We're off to The Jester for lunch,' he said, and scooted off.

No, no, no, stay and tell me what tragedy – was it a child? When did you see my mother?

I stood up, desperate for him to carry on talking. But by the time I'd caught up with him in the hall, he'd opened the door and was deep in conversation with a woman in her fifties with pink-tipped hair.

He paused as I reached his side. 'We'll catch up another time, Rachel,' he said.

'But … the tragedy? I …'

'I'm off out now,' he cut in, assertive. 'We'll talk another time.'

I slipped into my coat. 'OK … well I'll leave you to it,' I said. And knowing it was time to go, I pushed past them.

'I'm sure we'll meet again, Rachel,' he said, raising his hand as I raced past the gnomes.

***

As soon as I saw the house where my mother once lived, I knew I'd seen it before. But however much I searched my head, that was where the memory ended.

I got out of my car and approached to see the blinds at the windows pulled down, and I sensed, even before I rang the doorbell, nobody was home. And even if they had been in, my mother sold the house nearly thirty years ago.

I walked around the back and onto a patio, and peered through the cracks in the vertical Venetians, more to provoke memories than anything else, but it was impossible to see.

I turned to take in my surroundings. The heavy rain clouds and tall trees gave it a sombre feel, and the silence, aside from the wildlife, was tangible. I imagined my mum here when I was a baby, and could almost feel the loneliness suffocating her.

An overgrown path leading to the lake pulled me towards it. I pushed my way through the hedgerow, avoiding puddles, and as I reached the water's edge, something moved behind me. I froze for a few moments before turning to see a deer strolling away from me. I pressed my chest, feeling my heart hammering under my fingers.

The peace, now the deer had gone, was breath-taking. It was a setting I recognised from some of my mother's paintings. In fact, the dense, dark clouds pressing down on the lake could have been brushstrokes on one of her canvases.

A sudden memory of a splash, a cat struggling to breathe, Mum rushing to pull it out of the lake.

Unexplainable tears filled my eyes, and I choked them back.

'Rachel, what happened?' It was my mum's voice, and I could see her wrapping the cat in her cardigan, holding the bedraggled animal to her. 'Did you push him in? Did you push him? What the hell is the matter with you?'

Oh God, what the hell had happened here when I was a child?

Chapter 29

September 1990

The boat glided across the lake, silhouetted by the hazy moon. One of the occupants rowed, the other was still. Laura's heart pounded. What had she heard? Whatever hit the water was heavy – a solid mass. Were there smugglers in the area? Fishermen?

But she was pushing down her real fears. The only rowing boat she'd seen since she arrived was the one that had been moored outside Lough End Farm, and that was where the boat was heading now.

She stole a glance over her shoulder at her house. She'd locked up. Rachel was asleep. Laura wouldn't be gone long. She tightened her robe around her, took her torch from her pocket, and flicked it on. Her slippers were hardly suitable for walking through the wood, but if she returned to change them, Rachel might wake.

The torch made little impression on the impenetrable darkness, and the moon was barely visible through the trees. The ground was dry and hard, twigs breaking under her feet. She knew the way now – the direct route. She'd been there so often, watching the children like their guardian angel – hoping they were OK.

An owl hooted, and an animal the size of a mouse darted

about the undergrowth startling her. As she neared the farmhouse she heard hushed, anxious voices, and saw a flicker of torchlight. She continued until she could see and hear clearly, and crouching behind a tree, she turned off her torch.

'I don't like this.' Dillon jumped from the boat, and tugged it to the edge through the liquid black water. He bent to wrap the rope around the mooring post, and Imogen climbed out and stood watching him, her arms folded.

'It's too late now,' she said.

'But what if someone finds out?' He rose to his full height, now several inches taller than Imogen.

'And who would that someone be? Nobody's interested in us, Dillon. They don't even know you haven't been to school in years. We've dropped off the radar.'

'Yes, but...' He bashed his cheeks with the heels of his palms. Soundless tears.

'Enough of your weeping, Dillon O'Brian,' Imogen said. 'You're the man of the house now, and you need to act like it.' She strutted towards the farmhouse, and he followed, head bent down.

Had they killed Tierney? Dumped him in the water? Laura trembled. Her torch fell through her fingers, clattering onto a pile of sticks. Imogen stopped and peered in her direction. *Can she see me?*

Laura froze; her heart pounding so hard she was amazed Imogen couldn't hear it. But after a long, painful moment, Imogen and Dillon continued into the house, and closed the door behind them.

Laura turned and ran. Should she call the Guards? If she didn't, was she an accessory after the fact? But Tierney was a cruel man, and the last thing she wanted was for Dillon to get into trouble. They'd be better off without Tierney, she knew that much. She picked up speed, tripping over branches, her hands catching on thorns – sharp and painful, blood running down her palms.

When she entered the house, Rachel was screaming, and Laura

raced up the stairs to see her standing in her cot, face red and smeared with tears, stomping her feet.

'I'm so sorry, sweetheart,' Laura cried. Flustered, she grabbed a blanket, and held it against her hand, blood spreading across the lemon wool. 'I'm an awful mother. You deserve someone better.' She lifted her out and attempted, for what must have been the millionth time, to comfort her. But the child wiggled and thrashed, until Laura put her down.

'Why do you hate me so much?' she said, a tear rolling down her cheek.

***

Dillon appeared at the back door around seven the following morning, drained of colour.

I saw you. I saw what you did.

'You look dreadful – rough night?' Laura said, wishing she could take back the words instantly. He didn't need her playing games with him.

'A bit.' He avoided her gaze. 'Rachel asleep?'

She nodded. 'Do you want some tea?'

'Na, had some.' He shoved his hands in his pockets, and looked everywhere but at her. 'Da's gone, Laura,' he said eventually.

I know.

She sat down at the kitchen table. 'Where's he gone, Dillon?'

'Just took off in the middle of the night. Took all his clothes and everything.' There was a wobble in his voice.

'Just like your mother?'

He bolted a look her way, but said nothing.

'Talk to me, Dillon,' Laura said.

'Imogen says we're better off without him.'

'Perhaps she's right.'

'I keep wishing me real ma was here. She'd know what to do.' He lowered his head into his hands. 'Imogen says I can come and see you now, if I want. She says she'll come too sometimes. You know, like she did before. That's if you want her to.'

Laura's mind whirred. Imogen had deserted her, bickered with her, and now she'd possibly murdered Tierney. Suddenly, the cold reality that Imogen was capable of murder – that Dillon had helped – shot through her like an injection of poison, and fear filled her senses. She had to find the courage to leave Ireland. Leave behind the memories of her cold, selfish parents, and Jude letting her down. It was time to shake them free. Stop allowing them to feed off her sanity, to somehow hold her here. This time she would find the strength to move on.

'You don't mind me coming over, do you?' Dillon said, seeming to pick up on her silence, and lowering himself on the chair opposite her.

She looked into his worried dark green eyes, bruised cushions of flesh beneath them from lack of sleep, and sighed. She leaned forward and touched his cheek gently. How could she leave him when he needed her most? 'Of course I don't mind, I love our chats. Always have.'

For a moment a smile touched his eyes, but it quickly departed, 'Thanks, Laura,' he said. 'Life's shite at the moment, and I desperately need a friend.'

Chapter 30

February 2018

Blobs of rain fell once more, and I turned and raced back to my hire car, the image of the poor cat prominent in my mind. *Had the cat drowned?*

I dived into my car, thrust the key into the ignition and turned it.

Nothing.

'Crap!' I muttered, turning it several more times, before leaning over to retrieve the car hire documents from the passenger seat. I tapped the company's phone number into my mobile and, following a time-consuming effort to get through and convey my problem, they promised to send someone out – in two hours.

I sat for some time aimlessly flicking through my contacts, eventually calling Zoe.

'Rach,' she said, in her usual singsong voice.

'Are you busy?' I asked.

'No, I'm on my break. How's Ireland?' And with a pretty good, if a little satirised, Irish accent, added, 'Slept with any leprechauns yet?'

'Only the one.' I was trying for upbeat, although I felt far from it.

She laughed hard, but my sense of humour had deserted me. 'So, seriously,' she said, as though my low mood had brought her down too. 'How's it going? Have you found the farm?'

'I have, yes.'

'And?'

'Truth is, it triggered some weird repressed memories.'

'Oh my God. What sort?'

'They were pretty awful. I think something happened there. I don't know what exactly. The place is really beautiful now though ...'

'Do you think you should be there on your own? I could always come over ...'

'No, I'm fine. Honestly. I'm making progress. I've found Marcus McCutcheon.'

'The bloke whose wife died in the accident?'

'Yes ... he collects gnomes, of all things – which is a bit freaky in itself. I was quite traumatised going round there. He's got so many, and I've always had a bit of a gnome phobia.'

She laughed. 'He's a bit of a weirdo then?'

'A little, perhaps, but I think it's more that he's still grieving, and dealing with it in the only way he knows how. Who am I to judge?'

'But it's been over thirty years, hasn't it?' she said, far too flippant.

'Some people never get over losing someone they love, Zoe.' I sounded like a mother telling a child. 'I guess we haven't had that kind of loss in our lives, so we can't understand.' I stopped, knowing I sounded preachy.

There was silence on the other end, as rain hammered on the roof of my car, penetrating my eardrums. I shuddered, already cold from sitting too long.

'You're right,' Zoe said eventually. 'I don't know what it's like to lose someone I love. To know I'll never see them again. It must be impossible to deal with.' She paused for a moment. 'I don't know what I'd do if I lost my parents.'

They lived in Cornwall and led a full life. She would sometimes go down to see them, and from photos she posted on Facebook of them hugging and laughing, it was clear they loved their daughter – and she loved them.

'I feel bad now,' she continued, her voice low, the brightness I'd come to depend on, gone.

'Don't be daft. When you haven't suffered loss, it's not always easy to empathise.'

'Well, it was hard enough breaking up with Hank.' A pause. 'He came round last night.'

'Oh God. Is he OK?'

'No, he's worse than ever.' Her voice was low, tearful, words catching in her throat. 'He's acting a bit weird. Doesn't seem to accept we're over. I need him to stay out of my life. File him under "crap" and lock him away.'

'Does he know you're seeing Connor?' I asked, glancing in my rear-view mirror. I could just make out, through the incessant rain, someone pulling up behind me, headlights on.

'No, I wouldn't deliberately hurt him.' A pause. 'Anyway, enough about me. How are things with Lawrence?'

I'd tried to put him out of my head. 'He's in Paris with Grace,' I said, distracted by the car behind.

'Oh yes, you said they were going.'

'Mmm, and I have this awful feeling Farrah could be with them, even though I insisted he didn't invite her.'

'Bastard.'

'Is the right answer,' I said. 'I can't be certain, but I think I saw her at the airport.'

'Un-fucking-believable. Listen, I'm sorry, Rach, I'd better go. Work calls.'

'OK. See you soon. Let's have a catch-up at the weekend, aye?'

'Sounds brilliant.'

The line went dead, and I leaned back and closed my eyes.

A sudden fist-thump on my window, and my eyes shot open again. 'Fuck!' The downpour blurred the figure standing beside my car, and my heart raced. How had I ended up so anxious? The figure bent down, and a face appeared close to the glass. It was Felix Clarke, bearing a wide smile.

I lowered my window.

'I thought it might be you,' he said. 'I saw you get into a blue Fiat when you left the teashop. Everything OK?'

'I've broken down,' I said. 'But it's totally fine. The hire company are sending someone out.'

I went to close my window, but he slammed his gloved hand on the glass, making me jump. 'Will they be long?'

'Another hour and a half – but it's fine,' I repeated. 'I've got my mobile to keep me occupied.' I wiggled my phone.

'You look freezing, Rachel. Why not come back to mine for a warm drink and wait in the comfort of my lounge? I'm parked just behind you. I can bring you back here later.'

'Honesty, I'll be just fine.' I'd used the word fine far too much. I had so many questions I needed to ask him, but I wasn't sure I could face going to the farmhouse again yet.

'You're going to freeze to death out here. I insist.'

The draw was too much. What was I doing in Ireland if I wasn't going to ask questions?

I got out of the car, pulled up the hood of my coat, and fumbling with my keys, locked the door.

I wasn't sure of the make of Felix's car, but when I climbed into the passenger seat, I had no doubt it would have cost a fortune, with its heated leather seats and more gadgets than *The Enterprise*. In fact, it looked as though it could drive itself.

'Nice car,' I said for something to say, as I fastened the seatbelt.

He started the engine, and pulled away, The Cranberries' 'Zombie' playing through the speakers. 'I bought it with my last royalties,' he said with a smile. 'I run out of things to spend my money on.'

'A great position to be in. I'm not jealous at all.' I laughed, and he smiled.

'Yes, I suppose it is.' There was something in his voice I couldn't quite read, and I realised I knew nothing about him. I was alone with a man I didn't know, going to his lonely farmhouse. What was I thinking?

'So, are you married?' I blurted, immediately wishing I'd chosen something less personal to say.

He shook his head. 'Not any more.' He looked across at me. 'What about you?'

I felt hot, realising even more how personal I'd been with him when the question bounced back to me. 'Long-term relationship. I have a daughter. She's four.' I left out that Lawrence was a complete bastard. That he'd walked out on me just when I needed him most.

'How lovely,' he said, sounding genuine, and I began to feel a bit more relaxed.

In less than a minute, he'd pulled up on the road next to the farmhouse, and pointed a remote at the automatic gates, which opened inwards. I swallowed hard. What if the memories came back again – the blood, the child? But while part of me was afraid of the traumatic memories returning, another part of me wanted them to surface so I could find out the truth.

'It's such a beautiful house,' I said, as he drove his car onto the cobbled drive, and the gates closed behind him.

'I like it,' he said, pulling on his handbrake.

My phone rang, and I stared at the word 'unknown' on the screen, knowing I would have to answer. *It could be the care home, or the car hire people.* I pressed answer, but remained silent.

'Hello, who is this?' It was a male voice. Was it the man who called me pretending to be Martin Walker? Or was I imagining it? Had all male voices morphed into every call?

'I could ask you the same thing,' I said, with more confidence than I felt, throwing Felix a little shrug and a roll of my eyes.

'This is Inspector Smyth from the Hertfordshire Constabulary.'

How would a policeman get my mobile number? Was he really a cop? I was on distrust autopilot, and felt sure it was the prankster who told me my mother died. The same prankster who'd called the TV studio. 'Please, just leave me alone.'

I cancelled the call with shaking hands, and Felix's eyes widened. 'Is everything OK, Rachel?'

'Yes,' I said. 'Yes, I'm a bit jittery, that's all.'

'I can see that.' He placed his hand on my arm. 'Let's get you inside, shall we? A nice cup of tea will help.'

Relief swam through me, as I entered the farmhouse and no memories invaded my head. In fact, the place was stunning in an old-fashioned, cosy kind of way. The lounge was square with quaint nooks where heavy, antique furniture stood, including a bookshelf full of hardbacks, mostly his own. There was a grandfather clock in the corner, ticking into the peace, and two large sofas positioned opposite each other, in front of an open fireplace where a fire blazed. There was an aroma of baking too, and my stomach rumbled.

'Take a seat,' Felix said. 'I'll put the kettle on.'

But I remained standing, looking at the paintings on the wall – mainly landscapes. One caught my eye, and I moved closer. It was one of my mother's, a picture of the lake I'd seen, and a tingle tickled my neck. I turned to glance at the photos on an antique dresser of Felix with various recognisable authors and celebrities.

'Ah, you've seen my hall of fame, then?' Felix said with a laugh, heading into the room with a tray rattling with mugs, a jug of milk, a pot of sugar, and two large slices of cake that looked absolutely yummy.

He sat down and I joined him on the sofa. 'Shall I be Mum?' he said. 'Sugar? Milk?'

'Just milk, thank you.' I looked about me again. 'Your house is amazing.'

'Why, thank you. I renovated and extended it a while back.' He handed me a mug. 'Cake?'

'Please,' I said. 'Red velvet – my favourite.'

'So what do you do, Rachel?' he said, leaning back in the soft-cushioned sofa.

'I'm a psychotherapist,' I said. 'I run a practice from my house.'

'And where's that?'

'Finsbury Park.'

'You're a long way from home.'

'Yes … as I said before, I'm researching my family history.' I sipped my tea and took a mouthful of cake. 'This is delicious,' I said.

'Did they live in this area?'

'Oh, yes, yes, my mother grew up around here.' He was asking so many questions. I was supposed to be doing the questioning.

'Fascinating,' he said. 'So what have you discovered so far?'

I looked into his eyes. There was no doubt they were warm and friendly – but something stopped me telling him any more about myself. I glanced back at the painting. 'What a lovely study,' I said.

He rose, and looked at it more closely. 'Painted by the artist Laura Hogan. She lived nearby, a long time ago.'

'So how long have you lived in the area?' I asked, as my phone rang again. Another withheld number.

I pressed answer, but again remained silent.

'Rachel Hogan?'

I didn't reply.

'Hello, is that you, Miss Hogan? This is Philip's Car Hire. Just to say I'm with your car now, but I can't see you.'

'Oh, OK. I'll be there in a few minutes,' I said, ending the call, and putting down my mug. I grabbed another bite of the cake,

176

before rising to my feet. 'The hire company are with my car,' I said through crumbs, oddly relieved I was leaving.

'That was quicker than you expected,' he said, rising too.

I glanced down at the cake, and up into his face.

'Take the cake if you like,' he said, seeming to read my mind, and I picked it up and took another bite.

We headed into the hall, and I was putting on my shoes and coat, when I heard a creak above my head. I looked up the stairs, but Felix didn't enlighten me.

Once we'd made the short journey to my car, and spotted the man from the hire company, I got out of the passenger seat, and closed the door, thankful the rain had stopped.

Felix buzzed down the window, and leaned over. 'Well, I hope to see you again, Rachel.'

'Yes. I'm sure we'll bump into each other,' I said, bending to look back into the car from the puddled pavement. 'I'm here for a few more days.'

'Miss Hogan!' the hire chap called, shoving his hand in the air.

I shot a look at Felix. 'I'd better go,' I said.

'Me too,' he said, sliding his car into first gear, and pulling away.

Chapter 31

February 2018

Once the bloke had fixed the car, I keyed the postcode of the bed and breakfast into the satnav, and, with a spin of tyres in wet mud, I set off.

The sky was dark, and heavy raindrops fell once more, splashing my windscreen. It was difficult to see, despite putting on my headlights and wipers, and I slowed to a steady twenty mph, crossing my fingers nothing would appear from the opposite direction. But I was uneasy: the roads were narrow, the bends sharp. I needed to pull over until the rain stopped.

But before I could, a beast of a car began tailgating – headlights on full beam, like a panther hunting a deer.

'Pass me, for God's sake,' I muttered, flashing looks in my wing mirror, but despite several opportunities, it didn't overtake.

With nowhere to pull over, I reluctantly put my foot down.

It speeded up too.

'Hey, just pass me, for Christ's sake,' I yelled, over the incessant rain, and the roar of its thunderous engine. 'I'm not going any faster, you idiot.'

A ram against my bumper jolted me forward, and my hands

flew off the steering wheel. 'Oh God, oh God, oh God,' I cried, thrusting my foot harder on the throttle. Was the driver going to drag me from my car? Kill me? My stomach lurched, and I thought I might throw up.

A screech of tyres, and it was parallel with me, getting closer to the side of my car. I snatched a look at the driver. Despite the teeming rain, I could just make out the figure behind the wheel. Whoever it was wearing a balaclava masking their face.

I swerved into the entrance to a field and slammed my foot on the brake, my heart thudding against my chest. The car continued onwards at speed, and despite trying to make out the number plate through the hammering rain on my windscreen, it was impossible. But before it was out of sight I noticed a round, yellow sticker in the back window.

My body shook, as I gripped the steering wheel and let out a sob. Had it been some random fool, or had I upset someone by snooping? I pulled out my phone. Should I call someone? The Guards? But what could I tell them?

My fingers shook as I brought up Zoe's number. I needed someone to talk to. But the call went straight to voicemail.

'Zoe,' I said, trying for calm. 'Can you call me? Please.'

I ended the call and threw my mobile onto the passenger seat. Once I'd stopped trembling, I glanced over my shoulder and reversed back onto the road. I was about to pull away when my phone rang. I grabbed it, and without looking at the screen, answered, expecting to hear Zoe's comforting voice.

'Rachel Hogan?' It was the man who'd called me earlier.

My heart sank. 'For God's sake! Just leave me alone.'

'Please don't hang up, Miss Hogan. I'm Inspector Smyth from the Hertfordshire Constabulary, and we're investigating the suspicious death …'

I didn't let him finish. Just ended the call, and threw my phone back onto the passenger seat. I drove away with a skid of tyres, windscreen wipers thumping to and fro, as my phone blasted again and again.

'Fuck off,' I screamed into the air, my foot fully down on the throttle. 'Leave me alone.'

Finally the phone stopped ringing and I slowed down, fat tears rolling down my face, dripping off my chin.

***

Back at the bed and breakfast, I splashed some of the rhubarb gin I'd picked up en route into a tumbler, and knocked it back in one swallow. The pale pink liquid warmed my throat and chest, calming me. Seconds later I'd poured another – then another.

It was moments like this that I missed my mum most. In my teens, she'd always made everything right with a mug of hot chocolate, a hug – her words turning something impossible, into the possible. I was desperate to call that version of her. But then, had that same mum kept something from me all these years? Something I should know? She'd rarely talked about her parents, or the night I was conceived, but I'd always assumed her secrets were personal, emotional ones, not tragic, dangerous ones.

I tried calling Zoe again, but she still didn't pick up, so called Angela instead. She was full of apologies when I got through to her, saying she was dashing out on a date. 'There's more chance of Theresa May turning lefty, than him being Mr Right,' she said with a laugh. 'But I keep trying. You can't say I'm not giving it my best shot.'

'Well, good luck,' I said, wondering why she felt such a strong need for a man in her life. They brought nothing but heartache, in my experience.

I flopped onto the bed, with the glass of gin resting on my chest, my head swimming. I closed my eyes – nothing made any sense any more.

Eventually I dozed, finding myself lost in a tangled nightmare, where I dashed through a wood, stumbling, scraping my arms on sharp brambles. Blood smeared my pale arms, and Marcus was chasing me, wielding a knife. I reached the water's edge, trapped, with no escape.

'Jump,' he said, but his voice wasn't his own. It was that of a child.

I woke, gasping, and shot to a sitting position, splashing gin over my top. I placed the tumbler on the bedside table, and cradled my knees. Maybe I should go home. Forget Sligo – forget the past. Truth was, I should have been getting on with my life without Lawrence, and thinking about my future with Grace, not running around as if I was Sherlock bloody Holmes.

But my trip wasn't over. Not yet.

I grabbed my notepad, and found the details of the first friend request I'd received. David Green. The cover photo had been a row of grey houses with red doors. Mandan Road. Tomorrow I would go there. The friend requests were linked to my past somehow – *and that means whatever happened in one of those houses is too.*

***

I woke at five, and began stacking the events of the previous day in my head, attempting to slot them into some sort of order. But each time I thought I was making sense of it, down the pieces fell, chaotic and disjointed, tumbling around my skull, making my head hurt.

I pummelled my forehead with my fingertips, and sat up in bed, huddled against the headboard. Maybe I should go and see Marcus again, or Felix, find out more about what they knew about the tragedy that happened before my mother moved away.

But first I would find the grey houses with red doors.

I left the bed and breakfast around nine. The sky was clear, and a milky sun was rising over Benbulbin – a stunning sight

– and I wished, for a moment, that Mum, Lawrence and Grace were with me, and things were as they had been, once upon time, before life took an axe and wrecked everything.

I breathed in the cool, fresh air as I headed for the hire car, checking the bumper wasn't damaged before getting in. As I slipped the key into the ignition, I looked about me, convincing myself that if the person behind the wheel of the black car had wanted to cause me harm, they could have. I felt sure it had been a warning to back off. But I couldn't. I was in too deep.

I took a deep breath, and keyed Mandan Road into my satnav, before pulling onto the quiet road.

Once I'd found the road I pulled into a lay-by and took in the houses. They were exactly like David Green's cover photo. Grey brick walls and although the doors were all red, they were different shades, and they weren't the same style, or even made of the same material. Some looked to be the original wooden doors, and others were PVC.

I looked both ways before racing across the road, plotting my reason for knocking on doors. Should I be honest – tell them about the friend request?

A dog barked behind the first door, but nobody answered. At the second a young woman holding a baby told me she'd only been there six months, and had never heard of David Green. I rang the bell of the third house and waited, sensing someone was inside. I was about to walk away, when an elderly woman opened the door.

'Can I help you?' she said, but before I could reply she raised her hand like a traffic cop. 'Wait! Guess how old I am?'

'Sorry?'

'Go on. Guess how old I am?' She had a pleasant face, a fair few lines, short grey hair. I suspected she was around eighty, but knocked a few years off, just in case.

'Seventy-six?'

'No! Guess again.'

'Seventy-eight?'

'Ninety-two,' she said, and clapped her hands. 'Nobody gets it right. The new postman, a dishy young man who looks a bit like Frank Sinatra, thought I was fifty-five and a half.'

'Well, you look amazing for your age,' I said, hiding a little smile at the 'and a half'.

'I know,' she said, gesturing for me to enter, and turning and heading down the hall.

'I just wanted to ask you a question,' I called after her, raising on my toes and leaning forward.

She glanced over her shoulder. 'Well, I'm not standing on the doorstep freezing my knickers off,' she said, disappearing.

I looked up and down the quiet road, before stepping in and closing the door behind me. The heat and the smell of cooking engulfed me – a casserole, I suspected.

'Cup of char?' she offered, when I entered the lounge, where ornaments and photos jostled for space on cluttered surfaces.

'No thank you, Mrs …?'

'Call me Alice, and please sit down, dear, you're making the place look untidy.' She settled herself into an armchair, and a cat jumped onto her lap and curled up.

I sat down, told her my name, and began the spiel of words I'd decided upon, as an alternative to the truth. I wasn't even sure Alice would know about Facebook friend requests anyway. 'I'm writing an article,' I said, not enjoying lying to a sweet old lady.

'How lovely.'

'And I wondered how long you've lived here.'

'All my life,' she said, tickling the cat's ear. 'This was my parents' house. I never married. Probably why I've lived so long.' She laughed, a tinkling mirth lighting her pale blue eyes.

Through the window, I could see her long, narrow back garden, mainly laid to lawn. The fences between each house were low, and I noted next door had a dilapidated summerhouse that looked as though it had been there for years. 'So,' I said, taking a breath, eyes back on the woman. 'I wondered if you remember David Green?'

'Yes, yes I do.' A pause. 'Is that what you're writing your article about? The fire?'

The fire? 'Yes, yes that's right.' I remembered the cartoon gif of the blazing fire on the friend request, the status update:

Here comes a candle to light you to bed
Here comes a chopper to chop off your head.

'Well, it was all a very long time ago, dear,' she said. 'Why would you want to write about that? I'm pretty sure nobody will be interested – no offence.'

'None taken,' I said, and couldn't help smiling.

'If you're looking to make money, why not write a nice piece about Prince William and young Kate; they're so popular these days. Or what about Harry and Meghan? Such a sweet couple – their wedding is coming up soon. I've booked seats in front of my TV.' She laughed before adding, 'Did you know they had chicken for tea the night he proposed?'

I needed to stop her.

'He got down on one knee, you know.'

Confess why I was really there.

'The thing is …' I cut in. 'I just …' I clammed up, looking down – fiddling with my fingers.

'Are you really writing an article?' she said. I looked up and met her eye. 'I've lived a long time,' she continued. 'I can tell a porky when I hear it.'

'I should probably go.' I rose.

She looked up at me. 'The fire was next door at number fourteen. A young family live there now. The place was renovated after the fire by one of these do-up and move-on before it falls down types.'

I perched back down on the edge of the sofa.

'Since then it's had more changes than a baby with a tummy upset,' she went on. 'The fire happened in the mid-Nineties, if my memory serves me. They said David and Janet Green left a candle burning near their bed.' She shook her head as though remembering. 'Such a terrible tragedy. The flame caught the duvet while they were sleeping, and they both died. Thankfully their child survived.'

'What were the couple like?' I said.

'I couldn't say. I tried to be friendly, but they weren't interested, so I gave up trying in the end. I used to see their little one going off to school some days, but even she kept herself to herself – the apple never falls far from the tree, as they say.'

'What happened to her?'

She shrugged. 'I've no idea. Are you sure you won't have a cup of tea?'

'I really shouldn't, but OK,' I said, feeling she liked having visitors.

'I'll get my photo albums,' she said, and I knew the subject of David and Janet Green was closed.

I sat for half an hour thumbing through photos of people I didn't know, learning all about Alice's family history, before making my exit.

A black saloon was parked in a lay-by some distance away, facing away from me, and I cautioned my paranoid self. Told *her* there were thousands of black cars on the road, that I hadn't even seen the make of the one that had bamboozled me off the road the day before. But then I saw it – the round yellow sticker in the back window. I couldn't see what it said, but there was no doubting it was the same car.

I raced across the road, fumbling with my keys, dropping them on the road as I faffed and flicked glances at the vehicle. Someone was sitting in the driver's seat, and part of me wanted to rush over – find out who'd caused me to career off the road. But my sensible side won. I got into my car, started my engine, and raced away.

'Crap!' I said, as I turned the corner. I hadn't noted the number plate.

***

Once I was back at the bed and breakfast, relieved that the black car hadn't followed me this time, Grace FaceTimed.

'Are you having a good time, my little cuppy cake?' I said, her little face helping me to get things into perspective. I missed her so much.

'It's brilliant, Mummy,' she said, eyes glowing. 'Amaze balls.'

I laughed. 'I've never heard you say that before.'

'Farrah says it,' she said, her smile dimpling her cheeks.

I felt a prick behind my eyes. *When? When did Farrah say it?*

'I hope Daddy's spoiling you,' I said.

She nodded, and giggled. 'Beauty from *Beauty and the Beast* hugged me. Can you believe it? And I've got some Mickey Mouse ears. It's just so brilliant.'

And then the words fell out of my mouth. 'It must be nice being with just Daddy.'

She didn't seem to get I was fishing to find out if Farrah was with them. She just shrugged. 'I'd like it bestest if you were here too, Mummy.' Her voice cracked, losing its sparkle, and there was a blur on the screen, and Lawrence's voice saying, 'It's OK, chipmunk,' before his grumpy face appeared in front of me.

'What was that about?' he said, his tone sharp.

'What?'

'You've upset her, Rachel.'

'Oh God, I didn't mean to. Put her back on, please.'

'No, we're heading for a swim. We'll call you tomorrow.'

And then he was gone – and so was Grace.

I refused to cry, and bit down hard on my bottom lip, tasting

186

blood, as I ploughed through my contacts, pressing Zoe's number.

'Can you talk?' I said, with a sniff, when she picked up.

'It's not easy; I'm in the middle of a manicure. You OK, lovely?' If she was sick of me bugging her, she certainly didn't let on. 'You sound a bit …'

'It's Lawrence …'

'Ah, say no more. We all know he's a dick, and not a very big one.'

I laughed. 'Thanks, Zoe – although I'm not sure how you know.'

She laughed. 'Listen, I really can't talk right now. We'll catch up at the weekend, Rach. You can tell me everything then. Keep strong, and please take no notice of Lawrence.'

'You're right. He's not worth it.'

'Exactly.'

Once she'd rung off, I jumped to my feet, and began throwing clothes into my holdall. But it was no good. I had unfinished business in Sligo, and I knew, despite my instincts telling me otherwise, I would venture out again.

Chapter 32

October 1990

A month had gone by since Laura had seen Dillon and Imogen in the boat. A month since she'd heard *that* splash in the lake.

Recurring nightmares had haunted her sleep: Tierney's corpse at the bottom of the water, seaweed spiralling his body like a death robe, lake crustaceans feeding on his flesh. Each time, Laura woke hot and sweating, telling herself she was right not to report it. That he'd been a cruel man. Imogen and the children were safe now. He'd deserved to die.

She hadn't put the house on the market, like she'd promised herself she would. Dillon needed her. She couldn't abandon him. But it was more than that. It was the fear of starting somewhere new.

Rachel spooned in her cereal, darting looks at Laura.

'Is that nice?' Laura asked, but there was no response. She wished the child would talk more – jabber like Caitlin. But some days she was saying less than before, and becoming increasingly lost in her own world. It wouldn't be long before she started nursery school. Would it bring her out of herself, or make her worse? What if she got branded the spiteful girl mothers told their little ones to avoid? Perhaps she could home-school the child.

Rachel pushed her bowl away, slipped down from the chair, and headed into the lounge, where Laura knew she would sit at the table and draw for hours. She'd inherited Laura's talent, and her pictures were amazing for a three-year-old. Perhaps art would be Rachel's saviour, as it had been hers.

Once her daughter had disappeared, Laura pressed play on her tape recorder, and as Kate Bush sang from the speakers, she lit joss sticks, breathing them in, in an attempt to capture her younger self. Times she'd spent with Jude. She swayed to and fro to the music as she collected up china bowls and cups, losing herself as she twirled across the kitchen, before dropping the china into frothy water.

As she washed up, she looked out at the road, lost in thought – her mind somewhere else entirely. Suddenly a face appeared at the window, startling her.

'Christ!' she cried, holding her chest, her bubble-covered hands soaking her kaftan. 'Marcus, you scared me,' she added, as a child's grinning face appeared too. 'Yolanda.' She hadn't seen them since that day in the village – the one and only time she'd taken Rachel to toddler group.

She dried her hands and opened the front door. 'What brings you here?' she said, hoping they wouldn't want to come in.

'We were just passing,' Yolanda said, 'and thought we'd say hello.' She was precocious, dressed in a pink dress with embroidered flowers, and pink tights, her hair scooped into a high ponytail, a chunky, cream cardigan over the whole ensemble.

Marcus shrugged, and after an awkward silence, Laura opened the door wider and gestured for them to enter.

'Would you like a drink?' she said, as they followed her into the kitchen, Marcus carrying a plastic carrier bag.

'Yes please. Have you anything fizzy?' Yolanda asked.

'Think of your teeth, Yolly,' Marcus cautioned, and gave Laura a sheepish look as he sat down.

'I haven't got any pop, I'm afraid,' Laura said. 'I'm trying a

189

no-sugar regime with Rachel.' She'd tried changing her daughter's diet so many times.

'Is Rachel your little girl?' Yolanda asked, plonking herself down at the table opposite her father.

Laura nodded. 'She's in the lounge, go and see her if you like.'

'OK.' The child jumped up and skipped through.

'Cup of tea?' Laura asked, meeting Marcus's eye.

'Love one.' He slipped off his checked jacket with leather elbows, and dropped it over the back of a chair. 'I hope you don't mind us popping in.'

Laura didn't reply. She did mind. Marcus and his daughter were the last people she wanted as friends. Her parents killed his wife, for God's sake.

She filled the kettle, flicked it on, and snuffed out Kate Bush mid-song. 'I'm afraid I'm going out shortly,' she said in her best assertive voice.

'That's fine. We won't stay long. We were just out walking. Went to the garden centre.' He pulled a gnome from the carrier bag he'd brought in. 'What do you think?' he continued, holding it up for inspection.

'It's cute, I suppose.'

'Yes,' he said, shoving it back into the bag. 'Yes it is. I think Jacqueline would have liked it.'

'So how are you and Yolanda?' Laura said, deciding to ignore his reference to his dead wife.

'It's hard, of course,' he said, now fiddling with the salt pot. 'Yolanda seems to be handling it better than I am.' He unscrewed the lid and poured a little heap of salt onto the table, not looking up. 'I get so lonely.'

Laura poured hot water over teabags in mugs, controlling an urge to snatch the salt pot. 'I'm sorry,' she said. 'I've never lost anyone I love, the way you loved your wife, but I can imagine how difficult it must be.'

'You lost your parents,' he said, as she walked towards him and handed over one of the mugs, taking the salt pot from him.

She sat down and took a slow sip of her drink. 'We were never close,' she said. 'I wish we had been. I'm left with a void inside that I'm not sure I'll ever fill.'

He placed his hand over hers. 'I'm so sorry, Laura,' he said.

She looked down at his hand. It felt warm and soothing, and she could tell by the look in his eyes he needed comforting too. But the last thing she needed was a relationship with a man she barely knew – one with the complication that they shared a painful past. No, there would only ever be one man for her.

But before she could pull her hand away, he leaned forward and pressed his lips against hers.

'Daddy?'

He leapt to his feet, as they both stared at Yolanda framed in the doorway. She was holding Laura's latest canvas – a study of Lough End Farm. 'What about Mummy?' she said, tears filling her eyes. 'Do you still love Mummy?'

'Of course, darling,' he said, entwining his fingers and pressing them down on his head, turning on the spot like a schoolboy caught breaking a window.

'But you kissed Laura. I just saw you.'

'It was nothing, Yolly, nothing at all,' he said. 'Laura got the wrong idea, that's all.'

Laura glared at him. 'I think you should leave,' she said, rising. 'Now!'

'Yes, yes,' he said. 'Of course, yes.'

Yolanda raced to her father and hugged his waist. She held out the painting towards Laura. There were thick blobs of black paint in the pale blue sky of Laura's latest artwork.

'Who did this?' Laura whispered, taking it from her, her eyes flicking over the ruined picture. She put it down on the table, her head spinning, and stared at the child.

'It was Rachel,' Yolanda said. 'She took a brush and blobbed black paint all over it.'

'We should go,' Marcus said, his normally pale cheeks flushed as they hurried towards the door.

'Don't come back, Marcus – ever,' she said, as they closed the door behind them.

Laura picked up the picture and headed into the lounge where Rachel sat at the table drawing. She perched down beside her daughter, and laid the painting on the table. 'Did you do this?' she said.

Rachel continued to draw.

'I asked you a question, Rachel. Did you do this?' She felt bubbles of anger rise. She'd spent so long on the picture. But it wasn't only that, it was Marcus – the way he'd humiliated her. 'Rachel!' she snapped, startling the child who looked up at her. 'Did you do this?'

'Yes,' she said nodding. 'You made it look too happy.'

'Too happy?'

Rachel bent her head down and continued drawing, and Laura stared, wondering if she would ever understand her daughter.

After a while, Rachel looked at the painting. She reached out her hand, and touched the black clouds, coating her small fingers with wet paint. 'Can I keep it?' she said.

Laura nodded. 'If you want,' she said, defeated. 'I'll paint a new one.'

***

Later, Laura and Dillon sat by the lake. Rachel was asleep in her buggy, and Bridie was showing Caitlin the fishes swimming under the water.

The ground was covered in leaves of every colour, and the sun was about to set on the far side of the water. There was no doubting its beauty, but it was tarnished for Laura by thoughts of Tierney lying at the bottom of the lake.

She hadn't seen Imogen since that awful night, despite Dillon saying she would come round. Laura was relieved, but often wondered if Imogen and her unborn child were OK.

'Do you like the fishes?' Bridie asked tucking her hair behind her ears.

'They're amazing,' Caitlin said, giggling and bouncing from foot to foot. 'All wiggly.'

Dillon cast a brotherly eye over the girls as they played. It was the first time they'd been out without Imogen – the first time Dillon was caring for them alone. It was reassuring to see them happy, and Laura consoled herself again that she'd been right not to report what she'd seen.

'How's Imogen?' she asked.

'Cries a lot.' Dillon dragged his fingers through his hair. 'Shuts herself away most of the time, and I get the girls their dinner, because she won't eat. She's so skinny, you'd never guess she's having a baby.'

'Do you think she'd let me visit?' Truth was, Laura didn't want to go near the woman, but she didn't like to think of her in such a state. 'She helped me when I was at my lowest,' she said. 'I owe her.'

He shrugged. 'I dunno, she acts odd all the time.' He paused. 'She's like she was when she first came to live with us.'

'When Bridie was a baby?'

He nodded. 'My real ma said I had to be nice to her because she'd been through so much, but I thought she was a bit weird. You can tell a lot from eyes – like yours are blue, with specks of yellow like sunshine, but hers were dead, nothing going on behind them. I tended to keep out of her way in the beginning.'

Laura rubbed his back gently, as he continued to stumble over his words.

'She was troubled, Ma said, and we had to be patient with her. But it was as though something bad was in Imogen's head – I can't explain it. Later, after Ma left, she seemed OK. Started to care more for Bridie and me. But now, since Da left ...' He shook his head, eyes shimmering with tears. 'Maybe it's just me. Perhaps I can't cope with what's happened to me da.'

Laura placed her hand on his and squeezed. 'What happened to him, Dillon?'

He stared out at the lake, as though deliberating what to say.

'Dillon!' Caitlin squealed, jumping onto him and grabbing him round his neck. 'Have you seen the fishes?'

'Fishes!' Rachel was awake, wiggling in her buggy. 'Fishes!'

Laura lifted her out, and placed her on the ground. And the little girl trotted towards the edge of the water where Bridie stood.

'Have you seen the fishes, Rachel?' Caitlin said, scrambling off Dillon's lap and heading towards the other girls.

'Caitlin,' Bridie said. 'Look at this big fish.'

Rachel went to walk towards her.

'Not you, Rachel,' Bridie said, putting up her hand like a miniature policeman. 'I want to show Caitlin first.'

Rachel clenched her fists, screwed up her face, and kicked Caitlin hard in the shin, and the little girl dropped to the ground crying, holding her leg.

'What the hell did you do that for?' Laura cried, as Rachel ran off into the wood.

'I'll get her,' Dillon said, leaping to his feet, as Laura picked up Caitlin, and held her until she stopped crying.

'She's not very nice, is she?' Bridie said.

'No, no she's not,' Laura said, as Dillon appeared once more, Rachel in his arms.

Half an hour later, the children had settled down, and were playing together as though nothing had happened, and Dillon had lain down on the dry earth and closed his eyes.

'Let's go to your house,' Laura said impulsively, rising. 'I'll talk to Imogen; try to find out what's troubling her. See if I can help.'

Dillon jumped to his feet, and grabbed his stick from where he'd propped it against a tree, and Laura noticed the end was stained red. Was it Tierney's blood?

'I'm not sure Imogen will like it if you just turn up,' he said, lifting Rachel into his arms.

'Well, we won't know if we don't try,' she said, beating down the sick feeling that his stick could have been used to bludgeon Tierney to death.

They walked the length of the wood: Rachel perched on Dillon's hip, Bridie and Caitlin walking along beside him, and Laura a few steps behind.

'I'm not sure this is such a good idea,' Dillon said, as they got closer. 'What if it makes her worse?'

'Well, why don't you go in and tell her I'm here?' Laura said, as they reached the edge of the wood. 'If she wants to see me, I'll come. If not, I'll leave her be.'

'OK,' he said, putting Rachel down, and dashing away with his sisters.

Laura waited with her daughter at the edge of the wood, watching as they disappeared inside – the door closing behind them.

Within moments the door shot open again, and Dillon raced towards her, his sisters appearing on the doorstep crying.

'Laura,' he yelled. 'Laura! Come quick. The blood. Oh my God, hurry. Please!'

Chapter 33

February 2018

The following day, I grabbed a pack of sandwiches from a local shop, and ate them in the car, looking out at the sea at Rosses Point.

I loved the beach in February, the peace radiating from it – just a man walking his dog, and the crash of waves breaking on the sand. A flock of seagulls flew over, squawking on their way to the beach, and as they settled, clustered together squabbling over a crab, the distant caws of others filled the cold air.

We'd always visited the beach in winter when I was a child, Mum and I. 'I don't like the summer crowds,' she would say, as we walked along the pier at Southwold, wrapped in our warmest winter coats, snuggled into our scarfs.

Now the wind had got up, and wild waves broke on the shoreline, and I felt some of the tension in my neck and shoulders lift.

Once I'd eaten my sandwiches, I closed my eyes against the watery sun, still tired from a restless night. I was in the place between awake and sleep, when a jolt ran through my body, as though I'd fallen, waking me.

My eyes sprang open, and I noticed a dark-haired man on the

grass near a huge statue of a woman holding out her arms towards the sea. He was staring my way.

I tried telling myself not to be paranoid, but my mind spun. Was he the driver of the black car that rammed me off the road? The anonymous caller? The man who'd arranged to meet me outside Emirates Stadium? I opened a bottle of water and took a sip. I was being ridiculous. Why would he be in Sligo?

But still the man stared, his dark eyes haunting.

I put down my drink, started the engine, and as I reversed, he turned, heading away from me, and out of sight.

I tried putting him out of my mind, as I drove along the beach road. If I didn't, I would end up back at the bed and breakfast behind a locked door, and I needed to see the farmhouse one more time.

The route took me, as it had before, along narrow, twisting country roads. As I slowed at a junction opposite a pretty church, I glimpsed Felix approaching the graveyard, dressed in a long coat, his hair blowing in the wind.

A toot from behind, and I turned the corner, but I promised myself I would go to the graveyard on my way back. Perhaps it held answers.

Just after three, I pulled up outside Evermore Farmhouse. With the knowledge Felix wasn't there, I could snoop about. Try to remember my childhood. Despite my fear, I needed to trigger those awful memories once more, learn what happened here.

After several deep breaths, I got out and locked the car.

The side gate was still ajar, so I headed through it and down the cobbled drive. Flashes of memory swooped – children crying, a woman screaming. I forced myself to go on, the farmhouse looming, my confidence sapping with every step, as the memory of a sharp blade on flesh came and went. I stopped and let out a scream.

I was wrong. *I can't do this.*

I spun round and ran back towards the gate, but someone was

standing there – the man who'd been staring at me earlier by the sea. He opened the gate, and strode towards me, hands deep in his jean pockets.

With memories fresh in mind of the car nudging me off the road, I turned and ran back down the drive towards the house, glancing over my shoulder, seeing him picking up speed. I darted right, and raced towards the woods, diving through a hole in the high fence that surrounded the farmhouse.

It was a mistake.

As I ran, I heard his heavy footfalls getting closer and closer, splintering twigs. 'I'll find you,' he called.

My attempts to pick up speed were scuppered, as I caught my foot on a branch and fell, scuffing my knees. *Fuck!* I dragged myself up, my breathing laboured, and looked over my shoulder, seeing him moving through the trees, like a hunter stalking his prey.

I darted in and out of the trees, but it was hopeless. I didn't know the woods. He was gaining on me.

Suddenly he was behind me, pushing me to the ground, and I fell with a thud face first, hurting my cheek, grazing my hands.

'Why are you snooping around?' he said. 'What do you want with us? Are you the press?'

'No.' Tears were close, as I pulled myself over and looked up at him. 'Please. I don't want anything. Honestly.'

He stared deep into my eyes for what felt like a minute, his own eyes dark, his pupils dilated. He furrowed his forehead as though trying to work me out.

'Who are you?' I cried, as he finally stumbled away, disappearing into the woods.

I didn't wait. I jumped to my feet and ran, not looking back, until I reached my car.

Whoever he was, he didn't follow.

***

It was almost nine o'clock, and I was dozing at the bed and breakfast, when my phone rang. I opened my eyes and grabbed my mobile from the bedside unit. It was Angela.

'Hey,' she said, when I answered. 'I've been trying to call you all day.'

'Sorry. The signal's a bit erratic here,' I croaked, rubbing sleep from my eyes. 'You OK?'

'Not really.' I picked up on a slur. 'But that's nothing new.'

'What's up? Can I help?'

'I doubt it. In fact, I'm sure you'd hate me if you knew me better.'

'What? Don't be silly. You're my friend.'

'So, would you stick by me whatever I'd done?'

'I've no idea what you're talking about, Angela.' I was barely awake, and struggling to understand. 'Have you been drinking?'

'A little,' she said. 'Drowning my sorrows, well, letting them have a paddle.'

'This isn't about a man is it? Because they're not worth it.'

'Ha – no – although in a way, I guess it is.' Her voice was huskier than ever. 'Rachel, the main reason I'm ringing is to let you know the police were round your house yesterday. I told them you were away.'

'Really?' My heart flipped, as I remembered the calls. 'Did they say why?'

'The one in charge said his name was Inspector Smith or Smyth, or something, and he needed to talk to you.' She paused, and I heard her take a gulp. 'Listen, I'm sorry I called. I should have waited until I was sober. It's not fair on you. You don't need this right now. Goodnight, Rachel.'

She ended the call before I could respond, leaving her words to thrash around in my head. What was it that I didn't know about her? And an inspector *had* been looking for me. Had the calls I'd received been genuine? Had I hung up on the police? I was so confused, and suddenly imagined the police tracking me down in Ireland, or catching up with me at the airport and arresting me for wasting their time. I needed to call them, to explain – to find out who *had* died in suspicious circumstances.

Chapter 34

October 1990

'I've got something for you.' Laura picked up her painting from where she'd propped it against the dressing table. Imogen had admired it at her house some time ago, and now she wanted her to have it.

Imogen raised a smile – the first since Laura found her in such a dreadful state.

'Thank you,' she said, eyes focused on Laura, her face pale against the pillow. Imogen was young, but tonight she looked tiny and helpless – like a lost little girl. The room was small with burgundy wallpaper burgundy, and lit only by a bedside lamp, the heavy curtains pulled against the window. A dark wood wardrobe stood in the corner next to a five-drawer chest, all polished to a shine. Books were piled on Tierney's bedside cabinet: three novels and a poetry book.

Laura leant the painting against the wall. 'Try to get some sleep, Imogen,' she said. 'I've heard it can be the best medicine.'

Imogen continued to gaze at Laura. 'I would swap places with you tomorrow,' she said. 'Not just now, but our memories.' She closed her eyes. 'It's the memories that hurt us most, don't you think?'

Laura stroked Imogen's hair from her face. 'You wouldn't want my life,' she whispered.

'Why not?' She opened her eyes. 'You have a lovely home, and you paint so beautifully. I know you lost your parents, and that must have been heart-breaking, but they were never cruel to you.'

Laura wanted to disagree. *There are different kinds of cruel.*

She mopped Imogen's forehead with a flannel.

'You would make a good nurse, Laura,' Imogen said. 'I wanted to be a nurse when I was young. I was booked on a training course before everything went wrong.'

'Don't upset yourself,' Laura said. 'Just get well.'

She'd helped her to shower, made her a hot water bottle, and dosed her up with painkillers, all the time unsure if she was doing the right thing. But Imogen had begged her not to call an ambulance or doctor. And Laura, as she always seemed to do, had been swayed away from her instincts – easily led.

Imogen turned her head away. 'Do you know what the worst thing is?' she said, her voice fading. 'It's not that I've miscarried, but it's the fact I didn't want the baby growing inside me. Tierney put him there without my permission. And now it's gone. What did the little thing do to deserve that?'

Tears filled Laura's eyes. 'I'm so sorry.'

Imogen turned back and rested her hand on Laura's. 'Don't be.' She closed her eyes. Laura stood up and padded towards the door. 'Don't go,' Imogen said.

'OK.' Laura returned to the chair by the bed, and took hold of Imogen's hand.

'Can I talk to you?' Imogen opened her eyes.

'Of course.'

'Can I tell you things I've never told anyone?'

'If it will help.'

'Yes, yes I think it will.' She took a breath.

'What is it you want to tell me?'

'I want to tell you how my parents threw me out when I couldn't hide her any longer,' she said. 'I was seventeen.'

'Bridie?'

Imogen nodded. 'Obsessively religious, they were. Set in their ways. They couldn't cope with a daughter who'd committed such a dreadful sin. Pregnant and unmarried – I didn't even have a boyfriend. They said they couldn't bear to look at me. They wanted me out of their sight, out of their minds.'

'And Bridie's father?'

Imogen's eyes filled with tears. 'I don't know.' There was a long silence, as her chin crinkled. She lifted her hand to cover her mouth, as though the words she was about to say hurt. 'I was attacked,' she said. 'He was wearing some sort of black mask. I couldn't see his face.'

'Oh, Imogen, I'm so sorry.'

'My own fault, Ma said, for staying out later than they allowed.'

'Oh, Imogen,' Laura repeated. 'Did you tell someone? The Guards?'

'No.' She closed her eyes, and a tear squeezed through her lashes and ran down her cheek. 'I was just grateful Tierney and his wife took me in. But now I wish I was dead, even plan how I would do it.'

Laura squeezed her hand, tears filling her eyes. 'I'm always here if you need to talk.' A pause. 'Promise me you will never do anything silly.'

'I can't promise that,' Imogen said, closing her eyes, and in moments she'd fallen asleep.

Laura left the room and descended the stairs, to where the children were watching TV – Dillon on the sofa, his arms around both his sisters, Rachel on the floor. Laura didn't want them to see her tears, so disappeared into the kitchen.

Dillon followed. 'Is Imogen going to be OK?' he said, his tone low and even, as he grabbed a packet of digestives from the work surface, and munched on one.

'She's had a miscarriage,' Laura said, picking up the kettle.

'Jesus.' He propped himself against the units, his jean-clad legs sprawled out in front of him. 'So there'll be no baby?'

She shook her head, tears stinging behind her eyes. 'Imogen seems OK physically, and doesn't want a doctor or anything, but I feel I should call someone to check her over.'

'She won't like it if you do. She hates people coming here.'

'Yes, but …' Laura streamed water into the kettle from the tap. She was already keeping secrets about the boat she'd seen. What if Imogen took a turn for the worse? Died? 'I'm just worried about her, that's all.'

'Well, let's wait a few hours,' he said, taking another biscuit from the packet and biting into it. 'See how she is then.'

'Yes, yes, OK. Do you want a hot drink?' she asked, opening a cupboard and reaching for a mug. Everywhere was spotlessly clean, and yet the place was so run-down – the children unkempt. Imogen was strange, but after what she'd just heard, it wasn't surprising.

Dillon shook his head, and sat down at the scrubbed pine table, his eyes wide. 'Laura …'

'What is it, Dillon?' she said, knowing by his face he needed to talk.

He blew out a sigh. 'OK … well … the thing is …' Another sigh, deep and long.

'Dillon?'

'The thing is,' he repeated, putting down the biscuits, his face draining of colour. 'You remember how Da used to burn Imogen's arms with cigarettes?'

'Yes, I remember.'

'Well, he's gone. And … well … I saw two fresh burns on Imogen's arms yesterday.' He demonstrated, pulling up his sleeves. 'I don't get it. This time it couldn't have been Da.' He paused. 'But I keep thinking, what if he never burnt her before?'

'You think she self-harms?'

'Maybe.' He shrugged. 'I asked her about them, but she said it was something and nothing. And then I got to thinking.' His voice was growing in volume, and he rose and began pacing the room. 'If me da didn't burn her, what if Imogen put the girls in the cupboard? I never saw him do it, see. I only had her word for it.'

'I'm sure she wouldn't, Dillon,' she said, grabbing his hand so he stopped and looked her way. 'You haven't found them in there since your da left, have you?'

He shook his head. 'No, no you're right.' He chewed on his lip. 'But, and it kills me to say it, I'm not sure what to believe any more.'

Before she could reply, screams came from the lounge, followed by tears. Dillon jumped up and raced through, Laura behind him.

Rachel and Caitlin sobbed, Rachel covering her forehead with her hand, blood trickling through her fingers, Caitlin holding her arm close to her body. Bridie, now five and big for her age, was standing over the two girls, her arms folded like a mini school-teacher.

Dillon whisked Caitlin into his arms and hugged her close, and Laura bent down near Rachel, and tugged the child's hand away from her forehead, to see a gash on her head.

'What happened?' she said, looking at Bridie, who shrugged.

'What happened, Bridie?' Dillon said, as he held a slightly calmer Caitlin on his hip. 'Tell us! Now!'

'Rachel hurt Caitlin,' Bridie said, shrugging again, unsmiling. She looped a straying hair behind her ear. 'She hit her hard.'

'And?' Dillon said.

'I hit her with that.' She pointed at a brass ornament, now on the floor. 'She mustn't hurt Caitlin. She mustn't. She mustn't.'

'No, you're right,' Laura said. 'But you shouldn't hurt Rachel either. You should have come to get me.'

'She hurts Caitlin all the time,' Bridie said. 'You don't see it, like I do.'

'I don't think she does,' said Laura, picking up Rachel. She took her into the kitchen, and sat her daughter on a work surface, where her chubby three-year-old legs dangled.

'Did you hurt Caitlin?' Laura said, dabbing away the blood on the child's forehead with a wet cotton-wool ball, and popping on a plaster. Hoping it would heal without stitches.

'Rachel?' Laura asked. 'Tell me what happened.'

But Rachel just smiled.

Chapter 35

February 2018

I called Inspector Smyth the following morning from the bed and breakfast.

'I'll let it go this time, Miss Hogan,' he said, when I apologised for yelling at him and hanging up the phone. 'But please remember in future, that non-cooperation and abusing the police could land you in trouble.'

'Yes, yes, I'm so sorry,' I said. 'So why did you want to get hold of me?'

'We don't any more. We're satisfied now that the man's death isn't suspicious.'

'Well, that's good news, I guess,' I said, rubbing my temples, as I perched on the edge of the bed. 'But that doesn't explain why you called in the first place.'

'Your number was the last he called before he died. We wanted to rule you out of our inquiries. But, as I say, there's no need now.'

'When was this? Who was he?' I said, trying to think who called me, if it was someone I knew. 'Oh God, it wasn't Lawrence …'

'No,' the inspector said. 'The dead man's name was Henry Derby. He called you last week. I hope he wasn't anyone close.'

'No,' I said, puzzled. 'I don't know anyone by that name.' *Unless* – I realised it must have been the man who'd called wanting to meet me at the entrance to the Emirates Stadium.

'Anyway,' the inspector concluded. 'As I say no suspicious circumstances. But thanks for getting in touch.'

'No, wait,' I said, wanting to tell him everything, spill it all, and hope they could sort it out.

'What is it, Miss Hogan?'

'Things have been happening to me,' I blurted.

'What kind of things?'

'I've been receiving strange friend requests on Facebook, and someone chased me in their car, and I've had some weird phone calls – that's why I didn't believe you when you said you were police. And it's odd, don't you think, that the man who called me is now dead?'

'Of natural causes.'

'Yes, but …'

'Can I suggest, Miss Hogan, that you get in touch with your local police as soon as possible, and give them a detailed account of what's been happening to you.'

'Yes, yes I will. Thank you.'

I ended the call, my mind whirring. The man who wanted to tell me what was happening was now dead. I desperately needed to find out who he was.

***

As I drove from Sligo, threatening black clouds following me, I knew I would return. I needed to ask more questions. Truth was, I'd made a right mess of things, and it felt as though I knew less now than I did before I visited.

Instead of getting the train, I planned to drop the car off at

Dublin Airport. I wanted to take a detour along the River Liffey. I'd Googled Glastons Insurance, and put the postcode into my satnav, leaving plenty of time to visit and ask questions about Ronan Murphy – the second friend request.

Glastons Insurance was set back from the river, reminding me of a workhouse, although tastefully renovated. I pulled into the car park, screwing up my eyes and scanning the office workers milling about reception. Had Ronan Murphy once worked here? Did he still work here?

I got out of the car, and was buzzed into reception, a spacious area with a curved desk, by a woman in her fifties with black bobbed hair and turquoise glasses. As I moved closer, her cloying perfume gave me an instant headache. She smiled. 'Can I help you?'

I hadn't thought things through, and delayed responding. She raised a finely plucked brow.

'The thing is,' I said. 'I'm doing a bit of research on a man I think may have worked here. Maybe still does.'

'OK.' She peered over her glasses. 'So are you a journalist or something?'

'No …'

'Police?'

'No … just researching my family history and trying to find a long-lost cousin.' I was amazed how the lie tripped off my tongue.

'I see.'

'His name's Ronan Murphy,' I said. 'I'm sure he must have worked here at some point.'

'Never heard of him.' Her phone rang. 'Excuse me.'

While she took the call, I glanced at the abstract paintings, the low, bright yellow chairs, a water machine gurgling. A man in jeans and a sweatshirt – dress-down Friday, I imagined – raced across reception and out through the door, talking on his mobile.

'Did I hear you right?'

I turned to see another man in his mid-sixties, his grey hair combed back from his face.

'Sorry?'

'You mentioned Ronan Murphy.'

'Yes ... do you know him?'

He shook his head. 'No, but I remember the name. When I first started here they talked about him a lot. He was murdered here back in the late Nineties.'

'Murdered?' *Oh my God!*

'Mmm, he always sticks out in my mind because he was so young, a lovely-looking lad if the pictures in the paper were anything to go by. Are you a relative?'

'No, I'm ...'

'I thought you said you were doing family research.' The receptionist had ended her call.

I ignored her. 'So who killed him?' My eyes were back on the man.

'God, now you've got me. It was almost twenty years ago.' He looked about him. 'As I said, it happened here, although it was a kids' home at the time – nasty death, it was, but that's all I can tell you.'

'Thanks,' I said, wondering if he could hear my heart thumping.

'You're welcome,' he said, heading on his way.

Back in the car, my mind whirred as I mulled over what the man said. If Ronan had been murdered, had the fire that killed David and Janet Green been deliberate too?

***

Later, I sat in departures browsing Facebook to try to soothe my tattered nerves. There was a photo on Lawrence's timeline of Grace in Disneyland, dressed as Snow White, her cheeks aglow, eyes sparkling. I clicked on the love symbol. They would be heading home too, and I couldn't wait to see her. I scrolled down his page, but apart from a few likes and comments by Farrah, there were no photos of them together. Perhaps I'd been wrong. Maybe she hadn't gone with him after all.

Curious, I clicked on Farrah's page. Her profile photo was of a cute labradoodle, and her cover photo was of boats bobbing on a river. There was nothing else to see. Her settings were private.

I moved on to Angela's timeline. She hadn't posted anything. But then she'd said she'd had difficulty setting up her profile, and was mainly using it to stalk her dates. I felt a pang of sadness, and a gnawing worry that Lawrence could have been right about her drinking.

Zoe's recent updates were beauty links, and there was a status that I'd missed about our spa day, so I quickly liked and commented that it had been an amazing evening.

I was about to come off Facebook, when another friend request appeared. I clicked on it.

Henry Derby: CONFIRM/DELETE REQUEST

I dropped my phone into my lap, and covered my face with trembling hands. It was the fourth request I'd received, and there was no doubting this man – Henry Derby – was dead, just like David Green and Ronan Murphy.

I had to tell the police. Someone was targeting me, and as fear bubbled inside me, threatening to take my breath away, I wondered if whoever it was wanted me dead too.

With trembling hands, I picked up my phone, and clicked on Henry Derby's Facebook page. The profile photo was of a man with his back to the camera, looking out at the ocean. The cover photo a modern terraced house.

As before there was one status update:

Half a pound of tuppenny rice,
Half a pound of treacle,
That's the way the money goes,
Pop! Goes the weasel.

Chapter 36

February 2018

The life drains from Henry Derby's body, and I ponder the fact I'm quite a good killer now. Feeling proud.

My earlier blundering attempts were quite different – especially Ronan. No wonder I got caught. Nobody can catch me now.

This is my fifth murder. Does that make me a serial killer? I straighten my back, and say the words out loud. Trying them on for size. Letting them hang in the air.

'Serial killer.'

But am I a serial killer? Do I fit the mould? I've read up on it, you see. Serial killers normally have no apparent motive. I have a motive – always. They follow a characteristic. That's not me – at least I don't think it is. And I'm definitely not following a predictable pattern – am I? They rarely know their victims.

No. I'm in a category of my own – special.

Truth is, if they'd taken the time to connect the dots, they would have caught me by now. Fools.

I feel a surge of excitement run through me – I still have two more deaths to look forward to.

Not long now, and it will all be over.

Chapter 37

I arrived home just after four, to see Angela crying on her doorstep – loud heart-wrenching sobs into her hands echoing down the street – as a man ran down her path and got into a car. He slammed the door, before screeching past me. I couldn't see his face, but I noticed a blue disability badge in his front window.

I jumped from my car, and headed up Angela's path. 'Oh God, whatever's wrong?' I said, taking her into my arms. She buried her face in my shoulder, a sour smell of wine on her breath. 'Was that the same man as before?'

She nodded. 'You wouldn't understand, Rachel.' She pulled away from me, wiping the backs of her hands across her cheeks and sniffing.

'Try me, please. I'm your friend. Whatever it is, I'd never judge you.'

She stared at me for a long moment, her eyes puffy and bloodshot, before opening her mouth as though to speak. But she closed it again, remaining silent, leaving a brick wall between me and whatever she was going through. She rummaged in the pocket of her cardigan, pulled out a threadbare tissue, and sniffed into it.

'I need to get on,' she said, touching my arm gently and tilting her head. 'We'll talk tomorrow, yes? You must tell me all about Ireland. I'll look forward to it.' She turned and went inside, and I glimpsed the rabbit slippers Grace had worn, before she closed the door behind her.

I lifted my arm to ring her bell, but retracted it, letting it fall to my side, defeated. I would go round in the morning, comfort her.

Once I'd lugged my holdall into my lounge and thrown it on the chair, I flopped onto the sofa and closed my eyes. I found flights tiring, even short ones.

My phone blasted, and my eyes shot open. It was a withheld number.

'Hello,' I said, apprehensive.

'Rachel?' It was a woman.

'Yes, who is this?'

'It's Margo, love, from Dream Meadows.' I recognised her voice. 'They've asked me to call you, as I had such a strong connection with your mother.'

'Had? What do you mean, had?'

'Love, your mum passed away this afternoon. It was her heart.'

I rose and paced the room, struggling to take in her words, to hold back tears. 'What? No! That can't be right. She was taking tablets for her heart.'

'For some reason she'd been stashing them away in her drawer. Not taking them.' My mind flashed to her saying she didn't want to take her medication – that it was poison. 'I know you've suffered a bogus call, Rachel, and I ...' Her voice broke off. She was crying. 'I'm so sorry ...'

'But she was only fifty-one.' I choked back tears.

I'd worried, after Mum's heart attack ten years ago, that I could lose her that way, but the reality was intolerable. 'This isn't right. This can't be true.'

'Come to the home, dear,' Margo said, her voice kind and warm.

'Yes, yes, I'll be there as soon as I can.'

'I'm so sorry, Rachel,' she repeated. 'I know it's nowhere near enough, and you would think I would have a thousand words, but it's such a shock.'

I ended the call, tears blurring my vision as I searched for my keys. I'd only had them a moment ago. I looked under the cushions, under the sofa, in the door. I was in shock, agitated, and the tears rolling down my face weren't helping.

I lifted my holdall from the chair and threw it on the floor. There they were – but my eyes had already drifted.

'Mr Snookum?' I whispered, picking up my toy rabbit, staring into his bead eyes. He'd been in the loft, hadn't he? How had he got down from there? In fact, with everything else, I'd never questioned how he'd got up there in the first place after I'd seen him with Mum. There was probably a perfectly reasonable explanation. But then the only person with a key was Lawrence who'd been in Disneyland – although I still wasn't sure if Angela had returned the spare set.

I put down the toy rabbit, and grabbed my keys. I would worry about Mr Snookum later.

I ran out into the cold afternoon, and jumped into my car, slapping my face to stop more tears flowing. I started the engine, pressing Lawrence's number on my phone.

'We've landed,' he said, before I could speak. 'We had a brilliant time.'

I sniffed back tears. 'Lawrence, can you take Grace to your place for tonight? I'll collect her in the morning.'

'For Christ's sake, Rach, she's desperate to see you. Why?'

'It's my mum,' I said in a whisper. If I said it out loud, it would be true.

'What's happened?'

'She died, Lawrence. She went and bloody well died.' I let out a cry, as I shoved the car into first gear, and released the hand-brake. 'I'm heading to Suffolk now.'

'Oh, Rach I'm gutted for you.' He sounded more sincere than he had for a long time. 'Are you OK? You sound distraught.'

'I'll be fine, just look after Grace, please,' I said. 'Tell her I'll see her soon.'

Chapter 38

February 2018

I turn up the music and close the door, watching Laura as she clutches her chest, and cries out. She looks at me pleadingly, as she stumbles towards the emergency cord. It's easy to guide her away from it, let her fall to the ground in pain. Encouraging her to stop taking her heart tablets had helped me no end.

When I know she's gone, her eyes like glass, I open the door and skip down the stairs, smiling at everyone I meet.

'Good morning.'

'Good morning.'

'Good morning.'

'She was alive when I left her, your honour,' I practise saying under my breath, and laugh and laugh to myself.

Chapter 39

November 1990

A month had gone by, and it seemed Imogen's miscarriage had brought the two women closer together. Or perhaps it was more that Laura wanted to keep an even closer watch over the children – over Imogen.

Today was a beautiful day, with clear blue skies, and a bright, watery sun. It wasn't warm enough to swim in the lake, which would be freezing this time of year, but with thick cardigans, Laura had been determined to have a picnic by the water to cheer everyone up.

Laura and Imogen followed the excitable, high-pitched voices of the girls through the wood, as they headed for a clearing, Laura carrying a picnic basket. Dillon had declined the outing. 'He's sixteen,' Imogen had said, when he glared at them and headed to his room. 'Let him wallow in his teenage angst.' She'd turned to Laura when he was out of sight. 'The apple doesn't fall far from the tree,' she'd said. 'He's so much like his father these days. In fact, I've suggested he join the army. It will make a man of him.'

Laura had noticed a change in Dillon since the day he'd confided his fears about Imogen. It was as though a deep sadness had crept in – along with a distrust of the woman he'd once spoken so highly of. 'Does he want to join up?' she'd asked, concerned. 'He's very young.'

'It's not what *he* wants, Laura. It's what's best for him. I've written him a permission letter. He's to move out by the end of the year.'

'Are you sure?'

'It's family business, Laura,' she'd concluded. And Laura took the subtext to mean 'mind your own'.

There was something surreal about today – almost storybook-like. As though they were characters in an Enid Blyton tale. Maybe it was the tinkling sound of children's laughter, the sun's rays breaking through the trees, casting yellow brick roads in every direction. It felt like an adventure.

But the truth was, inside Laura's book was the story of a useless mother, who still pined for Jude. A mother who'd wrecked her daughter's early years. And what would be in Imogen's novel? What kind of mother was she? Raped at seventeen, parents threw her onto the street, a woman who self-harmed? A killer? Truth was, beneath the covers of their books, maggots squirmed, burying themselves into the fleshy pages.

As they strolled, Laura asked, 'Do you think Tierney will ever come back?' She longed to tell her she'd seen them out in the boat that night, but if she had she would feel as though she was complicit. If she kept quiet she could pretend to herself that she hadn't seen anything.

Imogen shrugged. 'I can't say I miss him. I never wanted him near me, Laura,' she said. 'Not even at the start.'

'That's not surprising,' Laura said, 'not after what you went through. Maybe you could see a counsellor.'

'I don't want some counsellor knowing my business,' Imogen said, snatching a leaf from a twig. 'Can we talk about something else?' There was a painful pause, as she shredded the leaf, and discarded it. 'If you don't mind.'

'Sorry, I shouldn't …'

'Don't be sorry,' Imogen cut in. 'It's fine. I just want to forget him.'

'He was a cruel man.'

She nodded. 'All men are cruel, Laura.'

Laura's mind drifted to the men who'd featured in her own life: Jude and her father only thinking of themselves, Marcus with his inappropriate come-on. She looked at Imogen who was pushing ahead of her now through some brambles, and thought of the trail of destruction the woman had coped with. 'Perhaps you're right,' she called after her. 'You've had some dreadful experiences. But I still believe some men are different. That there are good ones out there somewhere.'

Imogen stopped and glanced over her shoulder. 'I thought Tierney was one of the good guys,' she said. 'He was kind at first. But he was like all men, Laura.' She kicked the undergrowth. 'Evil to the core.'

'Jump! Jump! Jump!' Rachel was yelling in the near distance, her words cutting through the still air, like a guillotine.

'What's happening?' Imogen cried, but Laura was pushing past her. Already running.

There was a splash, before Bridie yelled, 'She can't swim, you idiot. She'll drown.'

Laura appeared in the clearing to see Bridie run at Rachel. At five, she was bigger and stronger than the three-and-half-year old, and with one push Rachel was in the lake.

Laura raced to the water's edge to see Caitlin and Rachel thrashing their arms in the water, their eyes wide with fear. She kicked off her shoes.

'Caitlin can't swim,' Bridie cried from behind her, as Caitlin stopped fighting the water. 'She's going to die.' There was panic in Caitlin's eyes, as she attempted to lift her chin. She was defeated. One gulp, and she disappeared under the water.

Laura had to make a judgement call.

She jumped into the icy water, the cold numbing her. 'Rachel, keep paddling your legs and arms, like I taught you,' she cried. 'Try to get to the bank, darling. Can you do that for me?'

The child didn't reply, her little arms splashing the water, droplets landing on Laura's face. Laura took a deep breath and dived under to see Caitlin floating downwards. Without a second's hesitation, she swam down fast and strong to grab her.

Moments later she broke through the water with Caitlin, who spluttered and coughed, her dark hair clinging to her skull. The child was pale, exhausted, her eyes bloodshot. Laura hugged her close as she waded towards the edge, and scanning the area for Rachel, she lifted Caitlin into Imogen's waiting arms. 'Where's Rachel?' she said, her eyes flicking over the bank for her daughter.

'I couldn't go in, Laura, I can't swim,' Imogen said in a rush. 'And I couldn't reach her. I'm so sorry.'

Laura turned. There was no sign of her daughter. 'Rachel,' she screamed, panicking as she spun round in the water. 'Oh God, Rachel!'

She dived under once more, and opened her eyes, searching. She saw her child drifting downwards, arms splayed, her dress ballooned about her. For a split second the darkest thought oozed through her mind, like tar, thickening, swirling. Would life be easier if she let her float down to the bottom? She was clearly unconscious. She would feel no pain. She would be happy as an angel.

Coming to her senses, Laura kicked off a sunken tree trunk and dived down over ten metres after her daughter, deeper and deeper into the lake. Rachel could have hypothermia by now, Laura reasoned. She could lose her. *Perhaps this is how it's meant to be.*

She reached the bottom, where Rachel lay motionless, and picked up her small body. She swam up, up, up; until she broke through the surface, out of breath, her hair slicked to head.

On the grass verge, Caitlin – wrapped in Imogen's cardigan

– was huddled in Bridie's arms, her head on her sister's chest, teeth chattering. Bridie stared at Laura and Rachel, her anger at almost losing her sister tangible.

'Imogen,' Laura cried, and she turned.

'Oh God,' Imogen yelled, racing to the edge. 'Is she OK?'

'I don't know.' Laura pushed the child's soaking hair back from her face. As she reached the edge, she held her lifeless daughter up to Imogen. 'I don't know.'

Laura clambered onto the grass verge, trying to catch her breath, while Imogen laid Rachel down and attempted to revive her with anxious pushes on the child's chest and an awkward attempt at the kiss of life. Rachel spluttered, and water splurged from her mouth. The girl opened her eyes and stared at Imogen for some time, her hair clinging to her skull, her face so pale.

'Thank God you're OK,' Laura said, dropping to her knees and taking hold of her small hand.

But Rachel turned her head away, and closed her eyes.

Chapter 40

March 2018

Margo, wearing black trousers and a thoroughly buttoned cardigan, laid her hand on my arm as I stood with Grace outside the crematorium. 'A beautiful service, dear,' she said. 'You did your mum proud.'

'It's all too much,' I said through a lump in my throat, dashing a tissue across my nose, the aroma of the fresh flowers, woven into a beautiful display, irritating my nostrils. I gripped Grace's hand. She looked up at me bewildered, eyes wide and lost, and I wondered if I'd been right to bring her.

'I won't come back to the house, as I'm on duty at Dream Meadows later,' Margo continued. 'But I'm glad I came. I was fond of your mum.' She hurried away before I could answer, disappearing through a gap in a neat high hedge, and into the car park.

I'd noticed her earlier, when I got up to say a few words, sitting at the back, a handkerchief to her nose, next to a man in his fifties I hadn't recognised who'd gone now. It had been a small turnout, and it struck me as sad that Mum had so few friends, and barely any family. Her neighbour, Jessica, had turned up, but other than that, it was just Angela, Zoe, and Lawrence – people from my life.

I'd decided I would stay over at Mum's house, knowing I would want a drink after the ceremony, and Angela and Zoe had agreed to stay too. I was glad. I needed my friends more than ever.

Lawrence had declined coming back, saying he would take Grace home, and give me a chance 'to let it all out'. Looking relieved that I wouldn't be 'letting it all out' in front of him.

But I hadn't cried. Not since the rush of tears when Margo called with the awful news two weeks ago. In fact I felt numb, unable to function. Zoe reckoned I was in shock – *the tears will come, eventually.*

I tried telling myself it was better than seeing Mum decline. Better her weak heart gave out before the worst of dementia set in. But all I could see were the good times we'd had through the years. Times we would never share again.

I drove back to Mum's house, Jessica in the passenger seat, Zoe and Angela in the back. It was the first time my friends had met, and they were happily chatting about movies and London shows they'd both seen, and seemed to be getting on OK. Angela seemed to be her usual self, which I was thankful for.

'I need a drink,' I said like a desperate alcoholic, once I'd parked and Jessica had hurried across the road to her bungalow, Muffin greeting her. I grabbed a hessian carrier from the boot that clinked with wine bottles, and my overnight bag. 'Can you bring the sandwiches?' I asked Zoe, and she looped her hair behind her ears, and picked up four plastic boxes and her holdall.

'How many did you think were coming?' she said with a laugh, staggering towards the gate under the weight of them.

'Clearly more than did,' I said, following, and there was that sadness again. 'I thought people might come who loved her art.' I'd even put a piece about her death in the local paper. But I guess it had been a while since she sold anything. 'People have forgotten her.'

225

Zoe sighed. 'Don't think like that, hon. Her pictures are on so many walls, and the main thing is, you'll never forget her.'

'Zoe's right, Rachel,' Angela said, putting her arm round my shoulder as I opened the gate.

Once inside the house, we stepped over the boxes of Mum's stuff I'd collected from the care home, and had yet to sort through.

'Jesus, it's cold in here,' Angela said, wasting no time making a fire in the grate, and I turned on the central heating, which clanked and banged. I headed for the kitchen and poured three large glasses of white wine, while Zoe arranged sandwiches on a plate and poured crisps into a bowl. It was gone six, and none of us had eaten all day.

Back in the lounge we raised our glasses. 'To Mum,' I said, through a lump in my throat. But still no tears came.

'To your mum,' they said together.

'God, I needed that,' I said, almost draining my glass in one go, the alcohol warming my body. Angela refilled our glasses, and I grabbed a sandwich, needing something to soak it up.

'I'm not surprised you need a drink, sweetie,' Angela said. 'It's all so dreadfully sad. Your mother was too young to die. It doesn't seem possible.'

I stared at Angela. She'd lost weight, and heavy make-up couldn't hide the puffy shadows that cradled her eyes. I hadn't spoken to her about the day the man had taken off in his car, leaving her in tears. The death of my mother had dominated everything. I'd even cancelled my clients' appointments.

'Are your parents alive?' Angela's eyes were fixed on Zoe, who'd curled her legs under her and pulled her black dress over her knees. I smiled. The room, lit only by the flickering fire and a standard lamp, glowed orange, and I began to feel warm and cosy – secure with friends.

'Yes.' Zoe said. 'They live in Cornwall.'

'Do you visit them often?' She sounded like a cop questioning a suspect.

'Not as often as I would like. I own my own business in London, and never seem to find a window, somehow.'

'Have you got brothers or sisters?'

Zoe shook her head. 'I'm an only child.' She pulled her legs from under her, and placed her feet firmly on the floor, and threw me a 'save me' look.

'Do you live in London?' Angela went on, oblivious.

'Gosh, what is this, the third degree?' Zoe said.

'Sorry.' Angela shuffled uncomfortably. 'I didn't mean to pry.'

'It's fine,' Zoe said, now pushing her fingers through dark hair, and moving her gaze to Angela. And turning the tables she said, 'Do you work?'

'I retired just over a year ago from a London hospital.'

'I didn't realise,' I chipped in.

She took a gulp of wine. 'I worked in admin, updating patient records,' she said, fiddling with her earlobe, her eyes on the window. 'And now I'm as free as a bird, as they say, and loving every moment.' She glanced at me, her eyes wide, as though urging me not to dispute her happiness.

'It must be great not having to work,' Zoe said.

'It is, although it can be lonely at times.'

Zoe rose, as though placing a full stop at the end of the conversation. 'Where's the loo, Rach?' she said.

'Straight up the stairs, right in front of you.'

'Won't be a sec,' she said, dashing from the room.

'How are you now?' I said to Angela, as the door closed behind Zoe.

'Fine.' She looked confused. As though she had no idea why I was asking.

'You were so upset. When I saw you on your doorstep a couple of weeks ago.'

'Oh, that was nothing, Rach, honestly.'

I didn't push her. Not while Zoe was in the house. 'Well, you know I'm here for you,' I said.

227

We sipped our drinks in silence, and the air that had felt so warm a few moments ago, felt suddenly icy. I got up and looked out of the window. A movement in the shadows caught my eye. Someone was out there, I felt sure of it, and a memory flooded in of the footprints in the snow I'd seen when I visited with Grace – the fact that Jessica had seen someone hanging about.

'What's wrong?' Angela asked, as I moved closer to the glass, my heart thudding as I peered into the darkness.

'I thought I saw someone, that's all.'

Angela shuddered. 'Oh, please don't, Rachel, you'll give me the creeps.'

I snatched the curtains across the window. 'It was probably nothing,' I said, as Zoe reappeared.

'What was nothing?' she said.

'Rachel thought she saw someone in the front garden.'

'Ooh, a stalker – cue creepy music.' Zoe laughed, raced to the window, and pulled back the curtain. 'Where exactly?'

I joined her, and pointed towards the trees where I'd thought I'd seen a figure.

'Well, he's not there now.'

'It could have been a she,' I said, thankful Zoe had let the curtain fall closed again, blocking out the night.

'I'm pretty sure it's usually men who stalk, Rachel,' she said, walking across the room and flopping back into the chair she'd vacated earlier. She picked up her glass.

'And you're basing that on what, exactly?' I followed and sat down on the sofa next to Angela, and took a gulp of my wine. 'Anyway, it was my imagination.' But I was unsettled. It had been a long day, and I was drinking too fast. 'I think I'll head for my bed, if nobody minds.'

'What? It's not even seven,' Zoe said, as though ready for a fun night ahead. 'How old are you, five?'

'Rachel's had a difficult day, Zoe,' Angela said, giving her a warning look.

'Oh God, yes, sorry, I'm being insensitive,' Zoe responded, with a tilt of her head.

I picked up my glass and headed for the kitchen. As I put it down by the sink, I sensed someone behind me. A knife rack was close by, and I lunged forward, grabbed one, and spun round, brandishing the blade.

'Jesus Christ!' It was Zoe, her hands in the air. 'What the fuck?'

I lowered the knife. 'Sorry,' I said. 'I'm a bit jittery, that's all.' I laid the blade on the worktop.

'A bit? You scared the fucking life out of me.'

'Sorry,' I repeated. I hadn't realised my anxiety was quite so full on.

'It's OK,' she said, touching my arm. And in a whisper she said, 'What's with Angela?'

'What do you mean?'

'All the questions, and there's just something about her, don't you think? Sorry, I know she's your friend, and …'

'She's OK,' I said, defensive. 'Just a bit nosy, that's all.'

'Yeah, yeah, sorry, I didn't mean to be unkind about her. You know her better than I do.' I wasn't sure I did. 'Listen, I thought we could go to Southwold tomorrow, before we head home. I know you told me you went there with your mum. I just thought …'

'That's an amazing idea,' I said, giving her a hug, breathing in her perfume, before heading for the door. 'I'd like that.'

***

I fell asleep as soon as my head hit the pillow, but was woken in the early hours by a noise in my room.

'Mum?' It was a ridiculous assumption, but my dreams had been filled with her memory since her death. Dreams that wrapped me in a fantasy that she'd never left at all.

As my eyes adjusted to the darkness, I felt a presence close to me. Someone touched my hand with icy fingers.

'Christ!' I said, shooting to a sitting position, huddling myself against the headboard, my duvet pressed against my chin.

I could just make out the shape beside me, and reached out for the lamp, flicking it on.

'Angela, thank God,' I said, pressing my hand against my chest. She was still and silent, her eyes wide open, as though she was looking through me. 'What's wrong? What are you doing?'

She didn't reply.

'Angela? You're freaking me out here.'

Still nothing.

It didn't take me long to realise Angela was sleepwalking. Something she'd never mentioned, but then she'd told me so little about herself.

I climbed gingerly off the bed, and approached her. Turning her to face the door, I coaxed her out of my room and along the landing, flicking on the light as we went. 'This way,' I said, turning her so she walked back to her bed, and, once she was lying down, I covered her with the duvet. After a few moments she closed her eyes.

Was there an underlying reason for her sleepwalking? Stress or anxiety? Alcohol? Something that ran in her family? I found myself staring at her bedside cabinet. Next to a wine glass was a box of tablets:

56 Venlafaxine 150mg tabs.
Take ONE twice a day.
Take with or just after food or a meal.
Mrs Angela Frost

Mrs? I picked them up. They were strong antidepressants. How had I – a psychotherapist – missed that she suffered with depression? And why hadn't she told me she was married?

I put down the tablets, noticing her purse lying open. A photograph of a young lad with dark curly hair stared out at me through clear plastic, and there was an appointment card too. I slipped it out. It was for two weeks' time at Bell and Brooks – the clinic where I used to work.

I turned my gaze back to Angela and reached out my hand, about to stroke a straying hair from her face, but I pulled back, not wanting to wake her. I gave her one last look, before padding back to my bedroom, knowing I wouldn't sleep.

***

'This was such a great idea,' I said as I walked down the pier, my arms linked with Zoe and Angela's, trying to put the events of the early hours behind me.

Plaques pinned to the pier railings, where people remembered those they'd lost, caught my eye. I wondered if I could add one for my mum. It was one of her favourite places, after all. There were a few shops and cafés, and a quaint old-fashioned penny arcade. 'I love this place,' I said, looking down at the sea between the wooden slats we were walking on. Even in winter. In fact, especially in winter.'

Mum had always paddled in the sea at Southwold when I was a child. But I'd never got too close to the water, happy to sit on the craggy rocks, the multi-coloured beach huts behind me, watching as she ran along splashing her feet and laughing. Later we'd have chips, and she would paint, and I would watch her. Never bored – always happy.

Now we reached the end of the pier, and looked out at the choppy, brown sea, the sky almost white, like cream on weak coffee.

'Rachel?'

I turned to see the man who'd been at the funeral.

'Yes,' I said, as Angela and Zoe turned too.

231

'I wondered if we could talk.' He was well-spoken, pleasant.

'Sorry, who are you, exactly?'

He looked from Angela to Zoe, and back to me. 'Could we talk … alone?'

'I'd rather not,' I said. 'Whatever you've got to say, you can say in front of my friends.'

'OK.' There was a long pause, as he stared hard into my eyes. 'Well … the thing is, Rachel … my name is Jude Henshaw, and I'm your father.'

Chapter 41

I had so many questions. But now, as I sat opposite Jude Henshaw, a comforting drinking chocolate in front of me, I couldn't arrange the words in my head so they made sense.

Zoe and Angela sat at the other end of the café, watching over me like the secret police, and I wondered what they thought. Whether they believed this stranger could be my father.

'You don't look like your mother,' Jude said. He was handsome, with salt and pepper hair, casual in a chunky-knit jumper and jeans. It was clear he looked after himself, maybe going to the gym a couple of times a week. 'Although I'm guessing the red hair isn't natural,' he added.

I smiled. 'Why ever would you think that?'

He smiled back. Yes, he was likeable. But the truth was, he could be absolutely anyone. This strange man turning up with his paternal claims as soon as my mother died didn't ring true somehow, especially after the weird things that had happened to me lately. My body tensed. Was I being paranoid?

'How much do you know about me?' he asked.

I shook my head, my eyes veering towards the window. The

wind had got up, and frothy waves crashed on the deserted beach. 'Nothing at all.'

'She never told you anything about me?'

Another shake of my head, as my eyes met his once more. 'She told me my father was a one-night stand – said she didn't know his name.'

'That was never the case. Your mother and I dated at university,' he began. 'She told me she was pregnant, and the truth is I didn't stand by her. I was an idiot – far too young, and my parents expected so much from me.'

'And that's your excuse?'

'No, it's no excuse at all.' He reached into his pocket, brought out an envelope, and pulled a piece of thin, discoloured paper from it. 'And then I got this.' He handed it to me, and I unfolded it. It was in my mum's neat handwriting.

Dear Jude

I got your address from your mother, and I'm writing to let you know of the tragic death of your daughter, Rachel.

It breaks my heart to tell you this news – especially as you've never seen your child. But I wanted you to know, just in case one day in the distant future you get a prick of conscience – or merely become curious and come looking for her.

I hope you have a happy life.

Laura.

My eyes stung as I took in her strange words. 'I don't understand,' I said, looking up at him. 'Why would she tell you I was dead?' It was as though I didn't know my mother at all. 'When did you get this?'

'Many years ago, and if I'm honest, at the time I'd just got engaged – someone my parents approved of ...'

'They didn't approve of my mother?' I cut in, raising a brow.

He shrugged. 'They had nothing against her, as such. But they had grand plans for me, and I guess I had them too, at that time. I'd started at a law practice …'

'So basically you didn't give a shit that your daughter was dead,' I cut in, 'that I was dead?' The words sounded wrong on my tongue.

'That's a little harsh.'

'Is it? Not from where I'm sitting.'

'But you're alive, Rachel.'

'You didn't know that at the time.' I glanced at Zoe and Angela. *Maybe I should leave. This man, if he is my father, is an uncaring bastard.* I glared at him. 'So now you want to get to know me. Play happy families. Why? What's happened? Don't tell me, you're divorced, no kids.'

'It's not like that.' He rubbed his hand across his mouth. 'I'm widowed, no kids. But the point is, I'd thought you were dead all this time, but then I saw you on TV just before Christmas. Rachel Hogan talking about her mother, an artist. I needed to know if you were my daughter. If Laura had lied to me because she didn't think I deserved you. Which I know I didn't.'

'Too right.'

'I came to the TV studio.'

'You spoke to Emmy?'

He nodded. 'The TV presenter – yes.'

'And you phoned in?' My mind swooped to the strange call I'd received.

'No, no, I didn't call in,' he said, shaking his head. 'I just tried to find you, but had no luck. So I attempted to track down your mother instead. It was easy enough, online there are mentions of her living in Dunwich. After that locals pointed me in the right direction.' He paused for a moment. 'But there didn't seem to be anybody living at her house.'

'The footprints in the snow …'

'Yes, it was snowing one of the days I came to her house.'

235

'And you climbed over the gate?'

'Mmm, not my finest hour.'

'By then she was in the care home.'

'Yes, I gather.' He dragged his fingers through his hair. 'But I didn't know that, so I stayed in this area, hoping to find her. And then I saw her death notice in the paper.' He placed his hand on mine. 'I'm so sorry, Rachel. It doesn't seem possible she's gone. She was far too young.'

I stared deep into his eyes, a prod of tears behind my own. 'Did you love her?' I said, regretting my words as soon as they tumbled out.

He looked down. 'I regret not standing by her,' he said, like a politician avoiding a question. 'And I can't tell you how pleased I am to have found you.'

I snatched my hand away, picked up my drink, and looked at him over the mug as I took long sips. There was no connection. Surely there would be a spark if he was my father.

'I'm sorry,' I said, putting down the mug. 'Life's pretty crap at the moment. I'm not sure I've got room in my head, let alone life, for a long-lost dad. That's if you are who you say you are.' I got up.

'No wait, please,' he said rising too, gripping my hand. 'I am your father, Rachel. Can't you feel the bond between us?'

'If I'm honest, no,' I said. I noticed tears in his eyes and softened. 'Listen. What if we had some kind of test done?'

'A DNA test? Yes, yes, of course,' he said. 'Anything to make you believe me.'

I glanced over at Zoe and Angela, who were now deep in conversation – so much for being my bodyguards. I fished a card from my bag, one I'd had made for my psychotherapy sessions. 'Call me in a couple of days,' I said. 'I'll have had time to process things by then, and maybe we can organise something.' I went to walk away, then glanced back. 'Did you come to my mum's house yesterday evening?'

He was fumbling in his pocket – then handing me his card that told me he was lawyer. 'No, no I didn't. Why?'

'It doesn't matter,' I said.

'Although I came this morning – you were all getting into your car, just leaving. I'm ashamed to say I followed you here. God, that makes me sound like a stalker.'

'Yeah, it does,' I said, walking away.

***

'I've suggested a DNA test,' I said, as I drove along the M11 homewards. 'To prove he's not my father.'

'You don't think he is?' Angela said, from the back of the car. Zoe had jumped in the front when we set off, yelling, 'Shotgun'.

'I don't know. He could be, I guess. He seems certain I'm his daughter,' I said, looking in my rear-view mirror. A red car had been behind us since we left Suffolk, and I was beginning to get agitated. Maybe it was my constant state of angst. I tried hard not to focus on it.

'What if he's some weirdo trying to worm his way into your life?' Angela said, in her usual worry-filled tone. 'A serial killer, or worse.'

'Pretty sure he isn't a serial killer, Angela. He seems nice.' My tone was defensive. 'And surely there isn't anything worse than a serial killer.'

'Serial killers are top of my "wouldn't want to meet on a dark night" list,' Zoe said with a laugh.

'Ha, now I'd always fancied meeting one myself,' I said, but even though they were joking, I didn't like where the conversation was going.

'Careful what you wish for, Rachel,' Angela said. 'Although I admit he's far too cute to be one.'

'You fancy the man who could be my father?' I said. 'Yikes, you could end up being my wicked stepmother.'

237

We all laughed, as I pulled over into the slow lane, another glance in my rear-view telling me the red car had moved in too.

'What about Ted Bundy?' Zoe said. 'He was good-looking, wasn't he?'

'You do need to be careful, Rachel,' Angela chipped in. 'It seems a bit odd to me. Why wait until your mum's death to turn up? I mean what if he's the person sending you those weird friend requests? The bloke who called in to the TV studio?'

'He isn't,' I snapped. 'Listen, can we talk about something else?'

Silence fell, and my eyes drifted back on my rear-view mirror. The car behind was mimicking my every move, as though attached by an invisible rope. Each time I sped up and overtook, he did too. Each time I reduced my speed and moved into the slow lane, he did too.

'Are you OK?' Zoe asked after a while. 'You've gone a bit quiet.'

'I'm fine,' I said. 'Just fine.'

***

I was glad to drop Zoe at the station, to despatch her into central London to do a Zombie Escape Room with Connor, and drive the final half-mile home.

I'd lost the red car about five minutes ago, and was relieved once I'd parked outside my house, and Angela had hugged me goodbye and disappeared through her front door.

I carried the boxes of Mum's stuff inside, deciding I wanted the photographs and trinkets she'd had on display at the care home. Soon I would have to sort out her house. It had stood empty for long enough. I wasn't sure what I would do with the place. Perhaps I could rent it out – but it hadn't escaped me that I could move to Suffolk, maybe get a less stressful job. I'd loved growing up there, and Grace would too. After everything that had happened I needed some peace.

I called Lawrence, but it went straight to voicemail. 'I'm home,'

I said. 'I can come and get Grace whenever, just let me know when's a good time. I can't wait to see her.'

I sat down on the sofa, tapping my phone on my knee, as my thoughts drifted to Zoe's observations of Angela. I knew now that I couldn't let her look after Grace, not until I'd got to the root of what she was hiding. Why did she need strong antidepressants? Why was she attending the clinic in Kensington where I once worked? Why did she drink so much? Why did she think I would hate her?

I scrolled through my phone's address book, and landed on Aditi Chabra. She'd been another therapist at Bell and Brooks when I worked there, but I hadn't seen her since we worked together, although we often commented or liked each other's statuses on Facebook.

'Hey, Aditi,' I said in my brightest voice, as she picked up.

'Rachel!' She obviously still had my number in her phone, and I was unnaturally flattered. 'Oh my God. How are things with you?'

'Seriously, you don't want to know. What about you? I saw on Facebook that you're now a partner at Bell and Brooks. That's amazing.'

'Yep. It took seven years, but I'm finally living the dream.' She laughed. 'So is this just a catch-up call, or ...'

I took a deep breath. I knew deep down she wouldn't be able to tell me anything, but it was worth a try. 'I wanted to pick your brains.'

'Ah, well I'm not sure I've got any.'

I laughed. 'Listen, do you know a woman called Angela Frost?'

'The surgeon?'

I held in a gasp – had she got the right Angela Frost? 'Could be,' I said, as calmly as possible.

'She's a client, Rachel. You do know I can't discuss her case. You of all people should know that. What's this about?'

'It's nothing. Sorry, I probably shouldn't have called.'

239

'Well, I'm glad you did. We should catch up sometime, it's been too long.'

'I'd like that.'

'OK text me some dates, and we'll grab a pizza and a glass of wine, and you can catch me up on everything. Are you still madly in love with Lawrence?'

'How long have you got?'

'Ah, that doesn't sound good. Sorry, Rach, I thought you two were in it for the long haul.'

'Well, I'll tell you all about it when I see you,' I said, not wanting to go there.

Once we'd ended the call, I flopped back against the sofa.

If Angela had been a surgeon, why had she told us she worked in admin? But before I could let the strange news settle, my phone pinged. It was a message from Emmy:

So sorry to hear about your mum – I know what you must be going through. Call me if you need to talk. Emmy X

I closed my eyes, trying to unpack my thoughts. But they were so confused and unsettled, as though they'd been thrown in a case in a hurry, and I'd left the vital things behind. I opened my eyes, picked up my phone, and called Emmy.

'Rachel, it's so good to hear from you,' she said. 'Did you get my text? I heard about your mum. How are you?'

'Not great,' I said, honestly. 'You?'

'Still pregnant,' she said. 'I texted you some time ago, needed to talk, but I'm guessing you didn't get it.'

'No,' I lied, knowing I should have got back to her, but with everything that had happened it had gone out of my head. 'My phone's been playing up.'

'So, how did your mu – mu – mum die?'

What had brought on her stammer? Was she agitated, excited?

'I'm stammering, aren't I?' she said, as though she could read

240

my mind. 'I can feel my old anxieties rising. I keep worrying about the baby.'

'It's only natural, Emmy. Just try to remember the techniques we practised. Everything will be OK. Honestly.'

'Thanks, Rachel.' A pause. 'So, what happened to your mum? Unless you don't want to talk about it.'

'I don't mind,' I said. Although I wanted to put it in a box marked 'painful', and hide it away. 'She had a heart attack. I didn't want to lose her, Emmy. It was far too soon.'

'No, of course you didn't. But it's not like you're a child.'

Like you were?

'If I can handle my mother dying of cancer when I was eight,' she went on, 'you can handle this.' Her voice was soft and kind, but her words were sharp and careless. Could she not hear herself?

'You can't compare losses, Emmy. Every death is different. Everyone grieves differently.' I needed to get off the phone, before I undid all my good work as a therapist, and lost my cool. Truth was, I liked Emmy, even if she didn't know the meaning of the word tact, but she was so wrapped up in her own problems; she rarely considered that others might be suffering too. 'What did you need to talk to me about?' I asked. 'When you sent me the text a few weeks back?'

'Well, apart from feeling wobbly generally and desperately needing to talk with you, my producer asked if you'd be interested in coming on the show again. It would have to be soon, as I'm taking early maternity leave.'

'Sorry, Emmy, it's the last thing I want to do.'

'It's because of the Polly-put-the-kettle-on man, isn't it?'

The Polly-put-the-kettle-on man? Is that what we're calling him now?

'Partly, yes,' I said. 'But life is a bit messy all round at the moment.'

'Ah, OK,' she said. 'Well, the offer's there at the studio, and let's get together soon, please.'

'Yes, of course,' I said, knowing I didn't want to. Not at the moment, anyway. I needed to be alone – to have time to think. 'You take care of yourself and that baby of yours, won't you?'

'Will do. Bye for now,' she said, hanging up.

I rose and approached the boxes, packed with the last months of Mum's life. I dropped to my knees. The first box was full of the photographs that had stood on the dresser – a picture of me in school uniform grinning at the camera, my two front teeth missing; one of mum and me on my graduation; and a study of us on the beach at Southwold when I was eight or nine.

The tears came, quiet at first, followed by sobs, loud and abandoned, my shoulders shuddering.

Oh Mum, why did you leave me?

As I opened the second box, the shock hit me. 'Mr Snookum,' I whispered. I looked behind me at where I'd placed my toy rabbit on the shelf, after finding him the day Mum died. He was still there, and yet he was here in my hands. I fiddled with his waistcoat jacket, stunned and confused. There was a dark patch of red on his chest, and his fur was worn. One ear had almost fallen off. He looked different somehow.

I dropped the toy, and scrambled to my feet, my eyes snatching looks at both of them in turn as I tried to make sense of it. But I couldn't, and panic surged through me. I raced to the front door, and opened it, intending to go to Angela's.

'Jesus,' I yelled, looking down at my doorstep. A gnome with a cheesy grin, a red hat, and holding an axe had been put there.

I hurried by it, and as I dashed towards Angela's house, crying and breathless, I felt sure someone was staring at me from the end of the road. My stomach tipped and I darted up Angela's path and hammered on her door.

'Whatever's wrong, sweetie?' she said as she opened up, taking me into her arms, and hugging me close, the hum of alcohol now so familiar. 'Come in,' she continued. 'You look like you need a drink.'

Chapter 42

March 2018

'I don't want a drink,' I said.

Still, Angela splashed brandy into two crystal-glass tumblers. 'Well, you look as if you do,' she said, thrusting one towards me.

I took it and placed it on a silver coaster on her coffee table, my eyes skittering around the room – so cream, so clean. Impossible to believe anyone actually lived here.

'I'm guessing it's the loss of your mum that's getting to you,' she continued, as we sat down on the sofa. 'It's understandable.'

'No, and yes,' I said, rubbing my temples with outstretched fingers.

'It's such early days, Rachel. Give it time.'

'How can I when so many odd things are happening?' I picked up the glass, took a sip, and winced. Alcohol was the last thing I needed. 'I can't make sense of any of it. I think I'm going mad, if I'm honest.' I thumped the glass back down on the table.

'The friend requests?'

'Yes, and now there are two Mr Snookums and a fucking gnome.' It sounded funny – ridiculous – and I expected her to laugh. But she didn't.

'You'll need to explain that, I'm afraid,' she said, with a

243

concerned smile, pressing her hand down on my knee before taking a long gulp of her drink.

'Mr Snookum was my toy rabbit when I was a kid,' I began. 'There was one at Mum's care home when I visited a while back, and then I found one in the loft. But the one in the loft somehow ended up in my lounge. I have no idea how.' I was talking too fast, making little sense. 'And, God, I know this sounds ludicrous,' I went on, 'but now there's a bloody gnome on my doorstep. I can't help thinking this has something to do with Marcus McCutcheon.'

'The bloke in Ireland who collects gnomes?'

'Mmm.' Tears weren't far away. 'I'm so shaky, look.' I held out my hand. It wobbled, as though made of rubber. 'I'm a mess, quite frankly. And I wasn't going to mention it, but I think someone followed us home from Suffolk.'

'Oh my God.' She took another gulp of her drink.

'Someone's trying to send me crazy, Angela.'

'But why would anyone do that, sweetie?' She gripped my hand and squeezed.

'I don't know.' I shrugged helplessly, a pang of guilt rising that earlier I'd been snooping around, making phone calls about her. 'I should have gone to the police before, but then Mum died, and now things are getting worse.' I pulled my hand away from her, and buried my face in my palms. 'I don't know what to do,' I said through my fingers.

'Perhaps it's the way you're feeling at the moment. Perhaps the grief is making your mind spin out of control. It happens. Take my word for it.'

It was as though she was talking from experience, and I looked up and met her eye. She'd clearly had a shower since she arrived home, and was make-up free. Broken blood vessels speckled her pallid skin, and her eyes were puffy. And maybe it was a distraction from my own worries, but I needed to know what her problem was. Had she been a surgeon? What had gone wrong in her life that made her drink, take antidepressants – see a psycho-therapist?

She gulped down her brandy, finishing it.

'Is everything OK, Angela?' I ventured.

Her eyes widened. 'Of course, sweetie, why?'

'You know you can tell me anything. I'm always dumping my troubles on you.'

She stared at me for a long moment, and I leaned forward and placed my hand on her arm. 'I know there's something. You told me you were an administrator at the hospital, but you were a surgeon, weren't you? Why would you lie?'

Her eyes widened further. 'Who told you that?'

'It doesn't matter – the point is, it's obvious something is haunting you. Perhaps sharing it with a friend will help.'

Her eyes filled with tears, and she looked ahead of her, seeming lost in another place.

'You can tell me,' I said.

She turned to look at me. 'I'm fine. Maybe you should go, Rachel. I've got a bit of a headache.'

'OK, yes, sorry. I didn't mean to push you,' I said, rising. 'But if you need me, I'm right next door.' I padded across the room towards my shoes.

'It's the guilt,' she said, slamming her glass down on the table, and suddenly sobbing into her hands. 'It's all-consuming.'

'Oh, Angela.' I turned and raced to sit by her side. 'Whatever's wrong?' I said, rubbing her back.

'Nothing helps, Rachel.' She grabbed a handful of tissues from a box on the coffee table, and mopped her cheeks.

'Well, I'm here for you,' I said. 'Talk to me, please.'

She grabbed my hand. 'OK,' she said. 'OK. If you're sure.'

It was a few moments before she began again. 'I guess it all started unravelling when my husband left me for someone else. I can't blame him. I was never there. I even let him take our son, Adam.'

My mind drifted to the photograph of the boy I'd seen in her purse.

'He was six at the time, and I put my career first.' She moved her finger along her lower eyelid to catch a straying tear. I waited for her to go on. 'As time went by,' she continued, 'I knew I'd made a mistake letting my husband take him. I wanted Adam back. But I'd started drinking by then to cope with the pressure of my job, and Adam didn't want to spend time with me – always wanting to call his dad. Asking how long it would be before he picked him up.' She wiped a tear from her cheek with the back of her hand, and sniffed. 'In the end, he stopped coming,' she said slowly. 'I thought I was losing the plot at the time. It turns out I was.'

'I'm so sorry,' I said.

'And then, just over a year ago, I made an unforgiveable mistake.' She caught me in a gaze. 'They couldn't prove it was my fault, but they all knew I'd been drinking. Staff banded together, told management they could often smell drink on my breath. That they knew I operated when I'd had a drink.'

'But you didn't, did you?' I wasn't sure I wanted to know the answer and was beginning to wish I hadn't opened the box marked 'private.' Please say you didn't operate when you'd had a drink.'

'I can't, Rachel.' Her face contorted with grief. 'I wish to God I could.'

I let out a gasp. 'Oh God, how could you?'

She shook her head. 'Don't you think I ask myself that every day? I suppose I thought the occasional snort of gin or brandy wouldn't hurt. I know now I should have resigned.'

'And the mistake?' My heart thudded against my ribs. *Do I really want to know?*

'A little girl – Stacey – a straightforward procedure … but …'

'She died?' *Oh God, please say she didn't die.*

Angela shook her head, tears shimmering in her eyes. 'She's brain-damaged, Rachel. She was only four at the time.'

I covered my mouth with my hand.

'After that I tried to see the child, desperately needing the family's forgiveness, but they wouldn't let me near her – I was an absolute wreck.' She dabbed her face with the tissues. 'Then I moved in next to you, and tried hard to move on. I was drinking far less, and loved looking after Grace, having you as a friend; I even tried to meet someone who might love me despite my past. But, even though a nagging voice told me not to, I contacted the child's family again a couple of months ago. I just wanted to know how Stacey was.'

I glanced at the slippers Grace had worn – had they been for Stacey?

I looked back at Angela, who was still drinking. She must have looked after Grace while intoxicated, and I couldn't help a flood of despair that she would operate on a child with alcohol in her blood. And even now she was making no attempt to stop. It must have shown on my face.

'I knew you would hate me,' she said.

I rose. 'I don't hate you, Angela. I just ...'

'Can't believe I would do such a thing.'

'Something like that.' I paused for a moment. I didn't know the woman in front of me at all. 'Was the man at your door Stacey's father?'

She nodded. 'He doesn't want me near his daughter, and who can blame him?'

A tear rolled down her cheek, as she got up to fill her glass. 'I'm on tablets; I'm even going to the clinic where you used to work. But at the end of the day, what I did was unforgiveable.'

'And yet here you are still drinking.'

'It's not that simple. I've tried to give up. It's an addiction, fed by guilt.'

I so wanted to help her, say she wasn't at fault, comfort her – but I couldn't bring myself to. Instead, as she perched on the edge of the sofa, sobbing and dragging her fingers through her hair, I said, 'We'll talk tomorrow,' and closed the door behind me.

I raced from her house, my eyes coated with tears. At the end of my path I stopped suddenly, a feeling of being watched washing over me. I turned and scanned the road – the parked cars, the people, the houses – hating that I felt so vulnerable.

After I'd thrown the gnome in the bin, I spotted another friend request on Facebook. My stomach heaved, and my heart pounded. The picture was recent, taken in the grounds of the care home, and a familiar face smiled from the screen. *Mum.*

Laura Hogan: CONFIRM/DELETE REQUEST

There was, as there always seemed to be, just one status update:

There was an old woman who swallowed a fly,
I don't know why she swallowed a fly,
Perhaps she'll die.

Chapter 43

March 2018

The police officer behind the front desk – a tall chap with frizzy fair hair and a sharp nose – was approachable. He took down my details, and I explained how Inspector Smyth of the Hertfordshire Constabulary suggested I come.

'Take a seat,' he said. 'Someone will be with you shortly, Miss Hogan.'

I perched on the edge of the chair. Waiting. Practising what I wanted to say in my head, fiddling with my fingers. Taking my phone out of my bag. Turning it over and over in my hands. Putting it back.

I've received strange friend requests on Facebook, and two of those people are dead. In fact, Henry Derby called me before he died.

I took the journal from my bag, flicked through the pages, barely taking in the words.

And someone's been following me – watching me. They ran me off the road when I was in Ireland.

I shoved the journal back in my bag, catching sight of the plastic bag with the cigarette butt inside that I'd found at Mum's house. Why had I brought it with me? Why had I picked it up in the first place? Would they be able to find DNA on it to match a criminal?

There are two Mr Snookums. A gnome. A strange painting. Odd calls.

And something terrible happened at Evermore Farmhouse.

I know it did. I know it did.

It's all connected. It's all connected.

Anxiety consumed me, and a tremble spread through my body. The waiting area seemed to shrink, closing me in. The cop was busy talking on the phone. He smiled my way, his features blurring. *Jeez, I'm losing it big time.*

I looked at the door to the offices. Police officers had come through it since I'd been sitting there, but none looked my way.

They think I'm wasting their time.

They think I'm crazy.

I knew by the up-scaling of my heartbeat, and the way words jumped about my head making no sense at all, that I would come across delusional at best.

I rose, trying to control my erratic breathing, and pounded my way to the door, stealing a glance over my shoulder just once. The police officer now had his back to me.

Outside, I took a long deep breath. I needed clarity in the chaos and confusion. Something I could find an answer to.

I found a bench and sat with my head in my hands for ten minutes, before deciding to call Jude Henshaw. A DNA test would at least resolve that mystery. *And if he turns out to be my father, he may support me through this awful time.*

He sounded happy to hear from me, and I wondered, just for a moment, what it would be like if he was my father. I'd never had a paternal figure in my life, and often, especially around the age of eight or nine, I'd imagined him turning up, and my mum falling into his arms, and saying she loved him. And he would say he'd never stopped loving her. He would ruffle my hair, and hug me so close I would almost burst. And then he would bring an Ipswich Town Football Club signed football from behind his broad back, and suggest we go outside and have a kick about – somehow, in my fantasy, he'd known I was a tomboy.

'Love you, kiddo,' he would say.

'Love you more, Dad.'

And then he would vanish – never there at all, and, once more, it would be Mum and me against the world.

***

I met Jude at 11 a.m. at King's Cross Station. He'd booked an appointment, and insisted on paying.

'Dresden Clinic has fitted us in,' he explained as we forced our way through the London crowds. 'They've said we'll get the results quite quickly. I don't know about you,' he went on with a smile that reached his grey eyes. 'But I'm positive it will be a match.'

Why did he want me to be his daughter so much? Guilt? The fact he'd never had children? Loneliness? I smiled back, unsure what to say or how to feel.

From there our conversation was limited to films we'd both seen, music we liked, and I was relieved when he stopped at the foot of six white steps leading to a Georgian building, with a gold sign on the wall.

'Well, here we are,' he said, throwing me a warm smile.

Inside was elegant and minimalistic, and we sat in a small, brightly lit room. I took out my Kindle, reluctant to talk, but we were called within minutes. It didn't take long for a woman to take a swab from inside my mouth – a tiny sample that would tell me if Jude Henshaw was my father; a swab that could change our lives.

Outside again, we stood at the foot of the white steps, and Jude pulled out an e-cigarette and began puffing on it, the aroma of strawberries reaching my nostrils. 'Fancy a coffee?' he asked. 'Something to eat?'

I shook my head. I was beginning to like him, and the thought of getting to know him better, only to be told he wasn't my father, wasn't an option.

'Let's wait for the results first, shall we?' I said, turning to walk away.

'Yes, you're probably right.' His voice was low and sad, but I kept walking, heading towards the tube.

'I'll call you,' I said, but I didn't look back.

Could he be my father? I was annoyed that my pulse fluttered at the thought, as though I was the child I once was. But I knew it would be a mistake to let him in too soon.

The train thundered along the Northern Line, the carriage crowded with nameless people. My head felt heavy and woozy, but I didn't want to go home. I wanted to wander around London – a stranger in a city full of strangers. I needed to lose myself.

Lawrence had called the night before, saying he would keep Grace for another day, adding I sounded weepy and fragile. He was right, of course, but I had so wanted her back, to hold her in my arms and never let go. I missed her so much. But he'd convinced me it was better that way. 'Just until you get your act together, Rach,' he'd added.

As I left the underground at Angel, I pulled out my phone and called Zoe, hoping she might meet me for lunch, but it went straight to voicemail. I didn't leave a message. Instead I made my way along Upper Street, where she'd told me her salon was. I wanted to surprise her, and felt sure she wouldn't mind if I popped in unannounced. I trudged the length of the busy street, but when I reached the number she'd given me a while back, it was a café.

I spun on the spot, as though I expected the salon to be there once I'd turned full circle on the pavement. Maybe I'd jotted it down wrong. Feeling bewildered, I ventured into the café, and grabbed a coffee, before heading for a table in the corner. I tried Zoe's number once more. Again, it went to voicemail.

'Hey, it's me,' I said. 'I'm in Café Nero. I may be being a bit of a doughnut, but I can't find your salon. You did say 75 Upper Street, didn't you? Anyway, if you're free for lunch, I'm your gal. Call me!' I ended the call, and sipped my drink, lost in thought as sirens wailed and shoppers scurried by. Yes, London was the perfect place to get lost.

Later, as I made my way back along Upper Street towards the underground, I remembered Marcus McCutcheon telling me his daughter had a shop in Islington. I stopped and scanned the row of shops opposite, but I couldn't see anywhere called 'Yolanda's Heaven'. I carried on walking, keeping alert in case I saw it.

It was a few minutes later I spotted it on the other side of the road. 'Yes!' I muttered, as though I'd found lost treasure. I pressed the button on the first set of traffic lights I came to, curious to meet Yolanda McCutcheon.

Chapter 44

I peered through the shop window, and over the display of 1940s hats and bags, and a mannequin in a black and white Sixties-style dress, to see two women chatting at the counter. One was around twenty, the other, closer to forty, had honey-blonde hair held back from her face with a floral slide. They were wearing flared at the waist polka-dot dresses, under pale pink cardigans.

I opened the door and entered to find the air musty but perfumed – ageing furniture blended with potpourri making my nostrils twitch. I pushed my way through rails of vintage clothes and racks of shoes, and the women looked up and smiled as I reached the counter.

I opened my mouth to speak. Would Yolanda remember me? My mum? The children at Evermore Farmhouse?

'Is everything all right?' the younger woman said, and I realised I'd frozen up.

'Yes. Sorry. I'm looking for Yolanda.'

'Well, you've found her,' the older woman said, her underlying Irish accent drowned by upper-class English. 'How can I help?'

A customer approached, asking about an oval mirror on the wall, and the younger woman moved away to help.

'My name is Rachel Hogan,' I said.

Her eyes narrowed. There was no doubting she recognised the name. 'I remember you,' she said, and her mouth twitched with … what was that? Amusement?

'You do?'

'Not well, but you were a strange little thing when you were a kid.'

I'm not going to lie, she completely threw me. I felt my cheeks glow. Was I slightly offended? 'In what way?'

'Well, I remember you completely wrecking one of your mum's paintings. Blobbed black paint all over her hard work.'

I recalled my mother saying the same thing when I'd visited, but I'd dashed her words away, blaming her confusion.

'Well, I'm quite normal now,' I said, straightening my back, as though standing upright would convince her.

She smiled. 'I'm glad to hear it.'

I began fiddling with some marbles on the counter in a net bag, trying to gather my thoughts. 'I'm so sorry,' I said, an urge to apologise on my grandparents' behalf taking over, 'about your mother.'

She lowered her head. 'Thank you, but you were hardly responsible. I shouldn't think you were even born when it happened.' A tendril of hair escaped her clip, and she tucked it behind her ear.

'No, no, I wasn't. But it was my grandparents' fault.'

'Agreed. But I came to terms with my mother's death a long time ago. Yes, I still have moments when I wonder what life would have been like with her by my side, and what she would think of me now.'

'I can imagine,' I said, somehow tearing a hole in the net bag. The marbles tumbled out, rolling in different directions, some clattering to the floor. I fell to my knees and scrambled to catch them. She didn't help.

'I taught myself when I was a teenager how to accept death,' she said, looking down at me. 'My mother wouldn't have wanted me to lose my life too, pining over her loss. I know that because everyone tells me she was an unselfish woman.'

I rose, fists clutching the marbles.

'My one regret is I can't remember her.'

She seemed so rational, positive, and I hoped I would come to terms with my mother's death as she had.

'I met your father a few weeks ago,' I said, putting the marbles down on the counter.

'Ah, now he's a different story, I'm afraid.' She shook her head, another strand of hair falling loose. 'He's never got over her death. Always struggled with the fact there was nobody alive to atone for her death.' She paused for a moment. 'I worry about him, but with him in Ireland, and me here, I rarely get to see him. How did he seem?'

I thought of the invasion of gnomes. 'OK, I think,' I said. 'He was heading out to lunch with a friend.' There was a child's giggle from out the back of the shop, and Yolanda glanced over her shoulder. 'He's watching *Dennis and Gnasher Unleashed*. Always makes him laugh.'

'Your son?'

She nodded. 'His grandfather is missing out on his young years. I just wish he would see that life goes on – not the one you'd necessarily planned, but life all the same.' She looked towards an approaching customer cradling a pair of pastel-blue shoes with dainty heels.

'I'll let you get on,' I said, moving away, knowing our conversation was over.

I left the shop, and stood for a while looking at the window display – there were so many things my mother would have loved, and I gulped back a surge of sadness.

I was about to walk away, when the mannequin I'd seen earlier caught my eye. It was in a dress similar to the one in the photo

256

of Yolanda's mother I'd seen at Marcus McCutcheon's house. Even the wig was short and dark. I shook my head. I was being ridiculous. It was a vintage shop and the dress was old-fashioned. And even if Yolanda had kept her mother's dress, then it wasn't so strange, was it?

'Are you still here?' It was Yolanda, coming through the door, a pack of cigarettes, and a lighter in her hand.

I looked at my watch. 'Yes, but I should be getting home,' I said. 'Can I just ask you a quick question before I go?'

'Fire away,' she said, lighting a cigarette.

'Do you have any memory of the farmhouse near where my mother lived in Ireland?'

She nodded. 'Aha. Never went there myself, but I heard about the place when I was a child. It was the talk of our school for a while.'

'What was?'

'The death of a little girl, and the suicide.'

'There were two deaths?'

She nodded. 'I think so, but you know how these stories get twisted the more they are told.'

'Do you know the name of the child who died?'

She shrugged. 'Sorry, I honestly can't remember – although I believe she's buried in the graveyard near the farmhouse.' She threw down her cigarette and stubbed it out with her shoe.

I regretted that I hadn't visited the graveyard in Ireland like I'd hoped to. 'Well, thanks anyway,' I said, lifting my hand in a wave and heading away.

Later, as I was about to travel down the escalator towards the underground, Zoe called.

'Hey, Rach,' she said, her voice upbeat. 'How's things?'

'OK. I called earlier hoping to meet up for lunch. I was going to drop in on you, but couldn't find your salon.'

'Well, I'm here – 15 Upper Street.'

'Damn, I went to 75 – must have muddled the seven and the one up somehow. Probably my crap writing.'

'Aw, what a shame, but let's be ladies who lunch soon, yeah?'

'Sounds good to me.'

'So what were you doing in Islington?'

'I've had a DNA test, would you believe?'

'Wow! Does this mean you'll soon know if Jude's your long-lost father?'

'Yep.'

'Amazing. Hey, listen, do you fancy going to the spa tonight? It will do you good to relax, and you can tell me all about it.'

'I can't,' I said, moving out of the way of a rush of commuters. 'I'm collecting Grace from Lawrence at six, and I'm desperate to spend time with her. It seems ages since I saw her last.'

'OK, well if you change your mind …'

'Thanks, Zoe,' I said, ending the call, and stepping onto the escalator.

***

Back in Finsbury Park, I headed straight from the underground to Lawrence's apartment. Once I'd climbed the stairs, he flung open his front door. He'd clearly jumped in the shower after work, something he always did when we were together, and since thrown on a white T-shirt – wet in places where he hadn't towel-dried properly – and black jeans, his wet hair combed back from his face. I hated that he was good-looking and knew it. I'd definitely punched above my weight five years ago. Shame I'd got knocked out in the third round.

'Grace isn't here.' He sounded complacent.

'What? You said to pick her up at six.' I pushed past him and into his flat, which smelt of aftershave and cigarettes, feeling sure my daughter must be there. 'Where is she?' I said, spinning round, as he followed me into the room.

'Farrah's taken her out for a "girlie day".' He made quotes in the air with his fingers. *He never does air quotes.*

'Christ, Lawrence, you let our daughter out alone with a woman I don't even know.'

'But I know her, Rachel. Farrah loves Grace more than anything. It's like she's her own daughter. They'll be having an amazing time.'

'For God's sake! Just because she can't have kids, doesn't mean she can take mine. Call her! Get her back. Now!'

'You're over-reacting, Rachel.' His tone was patronising. 'You always do.'

'I do not!'

'You're not in a good place right now, after losing your mum.'

'No! This has nothing to do with my mum. This is about you taking advantage. You can't just let your girlfriend swan off with our daughter.' I snatched up Grace's toy rabbit from the floor, and held it to me.

'Listen to yourself, Rachel.'

'What? What?'

'You're a complete mess.'

I growled inside. 'No. I'm. Not. I'm fine – perfectly fine.' But I was shouting, struggling to keep control. 'So when will the home-wrecker bring my daughter back?'

'Our daughter.' He shook his head, and flopped onto the sofa, not rising to my anger. 'I'll bring Grace back tomorrow morning. It'll give you time to calm down.'

I sat on the edge of sofa, and pointed to his giant phone. He always had to have the latest gadgets. 'Call her!' I snapped.

'I can't. They'll be in the cinema. They won't be back for ages.'

'Jesus. How could you, Lawrence? I haven't seen Grace for ages. You knew I was picking her up at six.' I continued to clasp the toy rabbit to my chest, and took a deep breath. In my best calm voice I said, 'You're a complete shit, do you know that?'

He picked up his cigarettes, and shuffled one from the pack. Once he'd lit it, he took several long deliberate drags, blowing smoke towards me. 'I worry about you, Rachel, that's all,' he said eventually. 'You've had a rough time.'

'You have no idea.'

I sat in silence, watching as he puffed his way through his cigarette and finally stubbed it out in an ashtray.

He leaned forward. 'Listen, they won't be back until around eight.'

'What? For God's sake, Lawrence – why is she keeping her out so late?' I squeezed my hands into fists. 'She's only four.'

'I know how old she is, Rachel. She's my daughter too. Just go home. Please. There's nothing you can do.'

'If this happens again, Lawrence, I swear I'll …'

'I'll bring Grace round in the morning. I promise.'

I rubbed my eyes. They stung from the smoke, and tears that were close to the surface. 'You're a fucking bastard,' I said as a parting shot, rising and heading for the door. 'You'll see. One of these days I'll take Grace to live as far away from you as I possibly can.'

Chapter 45

March 2018

'I'm so glad you changed your mind about the spa,' Zoe said, as we sped along the winding country road. 'I haven't called to book any treatments, but I'm sure this late they'll be able to fit us in.'

'I don't mind if they can't,' I said. 'I just needed to get out of the house. I would have wound myself up into a complete frenzy if I'd stayed at home. Or drained a bottle of wine. Or both.'

Her eyes flicked towards her rear-view mirror. 'I wish this idiot would just overtake. I've given them enough chances. They've been up my arse for ages.' She paused for a moment. 'Sorry,' she said, eyes back on the road. 'You were saying.'

'It's nothing. Just glad to be out, that's all.'

'Cool. Well we'll have a great time.'

She indicated to turn in to the spa, as my phone rang. I pulled it from my bag, and looked at the screen. 'It's Emmy,' I muttered.

'The woman from TV?' Zoe asked, driving into the car park and pulling on the handbrake.

'Mmm, I can't face her right now,' I said, cancelling the call, and slipping my phone back into my bag. 'I'll get back to her tomorrow.'

'Where is everybody?' I said, as we climbed out of the car, scanning the empty car park.

She smiled. 'Looks as though we've got the place to ourselves.'

I glanced towards the spa. 'It's in darkness,' I said. 'It looks as though it's closed.'

Zoe looked at her watch. 'But it's only nine. I thought it was open late on a Saturday.'

We approached and peered though the glass doors. 'That's a shame. Shall we go for a drink instead?'

'I guess,' Zoe said, and we both turned and headed towards the car.

'Hey, wait,' Zoe said. 'I've got Connor's keys. He gave me his spare set.' She dragged them from her bag. 'We could go in, relax on the loungers. I could have a swim.'

I looked back at the building, not thinking much of the idea.

'I'm desperate for a dip in the pool. We don't have to stay long.'

I hesitated, as she dashed towards the door. 'I don't know, Zoe. Are we allowed?' I called after her. 'Won't Connor be mad?'

'He can't really say anything. We've been here after hours before. Oh come on, Rach, it'll be fun.'

'I suppose,' I said, setting out after her just as the skies opened and it started to rain.

Once we were at the door, Zoe unlocked it, and we sneaked in like burglars about to ransack the place. It was so quiet, and an eerie hum touched my nape with invisible fingers, making it tingle – as though a thousand troubled eyes were watching me.

'Are you going to lock the door?' I called, but she was ahead of me, turning off the alarm, and excitedly flicking on fluorescent lights that buzzed and crackled into life. She grabbed two white rolled-up towels from the counter.

I pushed down the fear of police finding us here, and locking us in a cell overnight. 'Surely Connor could get fired, couldn't he?' I said as I reached her side, and she handed me a robe.

'I guess so.' A shrug. 'But he's not that bothered. He's thinking of chucking the job in anyway to go travelling.'

'Will you go with him?' I dreaded the thought of losing her from my life.

'He's asked me to,' she said, as we headed down a corridor. 'But there's the salon to think of.' She paused. 'It feels weird being here, along with the ghosts and ghouls from the asylum.' She made a daft spooky noise.

'Stop it!' I was jittery. The place was too quiet. 'You're freaking me out.'

'Sorry,' she said, linking arms with me. 'I'm only messing with ya.'

'No, it's me. I'm a bit wobbly at the moment.'

'Well, it will do you good to unwind a bit.'

We headed down some stairs towards the changing rooms, Zoe flicking on more lights as we went.

I disappeared into a cubicle, and changed into my faded denim shorts, and a cropped top I'd slung into my bag before I left home. I looked dreadful, my pale legs dangling from the hem of my shorts. But it didn't matter. It was just the two of us. When I reappeared, Zoe was in the communal area pulling up the straps of her yellow one-piece. It suited her. She had the complexion for it. But then she could wear almost anything and look good.

We shuffled into our robes, and I pushed my feet into a pair of flip-flops, before we took more stairs down to the pool area.

Zoe flicked on the lights, and we headed through a brick archway towards the loungers, where she spread out her towel. The ceiling was low, and being deep underground there were no windows.

The pool glinted blue under spotlights, some distance away, and the whole area was dimly lit, which was relaxing and yet a little unnerving. Despite my reluctance to believe in the paranormal, I imagined phantoms hiding in the shadows.

'Sit, Rach,' Zoe said. 'Relax. You've had such an awful time lately, you deserve a bit of me-time.'

I perched on the edge of a lounger, picturing what it may have been like when it was a morgue. The thought of so many dead bodies sent a shiver down my spine. I spread out my towel, moved my body fully onto the lounger, and leaned my head back. 'I've received another friend request,' I said.

'Oh, Rachel, you must go to the police.'

'I already have.'

Zoe's eyes widened. 'You did? What did they say?'

'I didn't stick around long enough to find out. I got it in my head they'd think I was crazy.'

'Oh, Rachel,' she said again. 'Who was the friend request from this time?'

I took a deep breath. 'My mum.' As I said the words, tears came. I'd blocked it out – tried to ignore it – but now the thought that someone could play such an awful trick was too much.

'Your mum? Oh my God, Rachel.' She leaned over, and put her arm around my shoulder. 'Why would someone do something so cruel? This is getting out of hand, hon. Let's go to the police station together tomorrow.'

'OK, yes,' I said, drying my eyes on the sleeve of my robe, and sniffing. 'Thank you – but what about work?'

'This is much more important,' she said, removing her arm.

We stretched out on the loungers, remaining silent for a while, before I said, 'You know what? I actually hope Jude Henshaw is my father. I guess with losing my mum, I think he may help fill this painful void inside me.'

She smiled. 'I hope he is too,' she said, rising. 'Well, I'm going for a swim,' she went on, and before I could say another word, she raced towards the water and jumped in with a splash, droplets of water sprinkling my skin.

I pulled my Kindle from my bag, and began reading. Apart from the slightly creepy vibe, I suddenly felt more settled than I had in a while. The sheer peace, the gurgle of the nearby spa bath, and the sound of Zoe's arms thrashing through the water, relaxed me. My eyes grew heavy, and eventually I switched off my Kindle, and dropped off to sleep.

I was woken sometime later by the sensation of cold water on my face.

'Wake up, sleepy head.' Zoe laughed, and rubbed water from her body with a towel, her hair slicked against her skull. She pushed her finger into her ear and wiggled it. 'It's lovely in the pool,' she said, looking over her shoulder at the glistening water. 'I wish you liked it.' Her eyes were back on me. 'What happened, Rach?'

'What do you mean?'

'Why are you so frightened of water?'

I shrugged. 'I don't know. I just panic if I get too close. It's a phobia, I suppose.'

'Like your gnome phobia,' she said with a laugh.

'Much worse than that.' I gave a shrug.

'It's just a bit odd that you can't recall why. Didn't your mother ever tell you?'

I shook my head. 'To be honest, I don't even know if there is a reason. I mean you don't have to have had a bad experience with a spider to be afraid of them. But the fear is real enough.'

Zoe threw down her towel. 'I'll grab us a hot drink, shall I? There's a machine in the foyer.'

I went to get up.

'No, no, you stay here and unwind. I won't be long. What do you fancy?'

'A drinking chocolate, please. Thanks, Zoe.'

'OK.' She pulled on her robe, grabbed her bag, and headed away.

Once she was out of sight, I got up and made my way towards the pool, challenging myself. Why was I so afraid? I stepped closer, and my heartbeat picked up speed, and my body shook. I turned

265

and raced back across the wet flagstones towards the lounger, and sat back down.

Once my heart had calmed to an even beat, I lay down once more, and was about to close my eyes again when my phone pinged in my bag. I fished it out, and my stomach tipped as I took in another friend request:

Rachel Hogan: CONFIRM/DELETE REQUEST

My body trembled when I saw the profile picture was a gravestone. It was real enough, but the inscription must have been Photoshopped to read Rachel Hogan.

The cover photo was of Evermore Farmhouse. There was one status update:

Hush a bye baby on a treetop,
When the wind blows the cradle will rock,
When the bow breaks the cradle will fall,
And down will come Rachel, cradle, and all.

I jumped to my feet. 'Zoe,' I cried, blundering towards the door, my phone pinging, informing me I had another Facebook notification.

I froze yards from the door. A figure stood on the other side of the frosted glass. I narrowed my eyes. Whoever it was looked bigger than Zoe, but it was impossible to work out their features through the glass.

'Zoe?' I called, my stomach flipping. But the person behind the glass stood statue-still – silent.

Chapter 46

December 1990

'There you go, Rachel.' Laura zipped up her daughter's dress and spun her round to face her. 'You look so pretty in pink.'

Rachel gave a little shrug, and Laura touched her face gently. Her daughter almost drowning a month ago had switched a button inside her, and she'd been trying so hard with Rachel since. But there was still a long way to go.

'Are you sure you want to go?' she asked her daughter. It was Caitlin's fourth birthday, and Imogen was putting on a tea party for the three girls, which was out of character. But then Imogen hadn't been the same since she miscarried, or had it been before that – since Tierney disappeared? She'd almost been manic at times. Too high one moment, too low the next. Even suggested they might all go away together, far away from Ireland, which Laura had declined – if she was going away, it wouldn't be with Imogen. 'You don't have to go.'

Rachel shrugged again. Laura didn't want to stop her going – it would be good if her daughter could mix with other children – but the girls didn't always get on and Rachel had often been unkind to Caitlin.

'You're not taking all of that, are you?' Laura said, seeing Rachel filling a canvas bag with her things. 'You might lose Mr Snookum.'

But Rachel gripped the bulging bag to her chest.

'OK, well, don't blame me if things go missing.'

Once at Lough End Farm, Bridie and Caitlin ran out to greet them, Bridie in a purple velvet dress and cream shoes, her dark hair loose and curly to her shoulders, and Caitlin in a pale blue dress with identical cream shoes, her dark hair tied into a ponytail with a blue ribbon. They smiled widely, excitement in their eyes.

'Ma's done a special tea,' Caitlin said to Rachel, but Rachel didn't respond.

Dillon appeared, ragged in jeans and a sweatshirt.

'Can I take a photo of you all?' Laura asked, lifting the camera that hung round her neck.

Dillon shook his head, on his way to the barn. 'Count me out, I'm about to chop wood.'

'Please, Dillon,' Laura called after him.

'For feck's sake, what do you want a picture of us for?' He turned and padded towards her, hands deep in his pockets.

'I want to paint a picture, Dillon,' she said.

Once the children were lined up, Laura snapped a photo. 'I'll send the film off to be developed tomorrow,' she said, as Bridie and Caitlin ran inside, and Dillon disappeared into the barn, clearly disinterested.

'Let's go in, shall we?' Laura said to Rachel, taking her hand.

'I don't want to go any more,' Rachel said, pulling back.

'But Imogen has made tea, and it's Caitlin's birthday – and you've bought her a gift.' She kneeled in front of her daughter, tucking her hair behind her ears and smiling. 'You'll have a lovely time, and I won't be long.' She paused, staring into her eyes, finally seeing how beautiful they were. 'I love you, darling,' she found herself saying. Realising, for the first time, that she meant it.

'I love you more,' the little girl said, and Laura's heart gave a flutter, and her eyes filled with tears. Had she finally reached her daughter? 'I want to go home, Mummy.'

Imogen appeared at the door, and raced towards them. She whisked Rachel into her arms. 'Now come along,' she said. 'Don't spoil Caitlin's birthday.'

Rachel looked at her mother, and then at Imogen, the canvas bag of toys dangling from her hand.

'I'm not sure she's quite ready to be without me,' Laura said feebly, reaching out to touch her daughter's hand.

'Well, she never will be if you fuss all over her,' Imogen said, waltzing towards the door. 'Come and collect her in two hours,' she called, disappearing inside the house, the door closing behind them.

Laura sat on a log for some time, listening out for Rachel's tears. But they never came. Perhaps Imogen was right. Laura had certainly isolated the child too much, kept her inside like a dog you never take for walks, because it barks at other dogs.

Maybe this was exactly what Rachel needed.

***

The hammering on the door grew louder. 'Laura! Answer the fecking door. It's me. Dillon.'

'Whatever's the matter?' she said, opening up, and knowing from the tears on his cheeks, and the blots of blood on his T-shirt, something terrible had happened.

'Imogen's dead.'

'What?'

'I came in through the back door, and there she was in the kitchen.' He began to sob. 'She's cut open her wrists. There's blood everywhere.'

'And the girls?' Laura cried, shoving her feet into her trainers, and almost tripping through the door. 'Is Rachel OK?'

'I didn't go into the house, Laura. I just grabbed my bag and ran.'

'You didn't check on them? Oh God, Dillon. What the hell were you thinking? They'll be so scared,' she said, slamming the door behind her.

'I'm so sorry. I just panicked and ran.' He swallowed hard, eyes wide, and Laura noticed he was clutching a piece of screwed-up paper. 'There was so much blood,' he cried. 'I just had to get out of there.' He darted a look around the wood, as though someone was about to rush from behind a tree and grab him, and he rubbed his wide, vulnerable eyes with the heels of his hands. 'I've got to get away from here, Laura.' He dragged up a rucksack from the ground, and slung it over his shoulder, grabbing the stick he always carried. 'Have a good life, Laura,' he said, turning and taking off, racing through the trees like a convict on the run.

'Dillon!' she cried after him, as he slung the stick into the lake with a splash.

'I'm never coming back, Laura,' he yelled. 'I can't take any more. Tell Bridie and Caitlin I'm sorry.' His voice faded, and he was soon out of sight.

Laura took off towards the farmhouse, her mind spinning with scenarios as she raced through the hedgerow. Had Tierney returned? Had Imogen hurt the children? Had Dillon done something awful? *Oh God, please let Rachel be OK.*

When she reached the edge of the wood, she stopped, catching her breath. Hens pecked the ground. Kids' clothes swung, pegged on the makeshift washing-line that squeaked and moaned in the wind. The door stood ajar. It was far too quiet.

She shuddered, suddenly sure someone was watching her. She scanned the area, trying to pick out shapes, before walking hesitantly towards the door.

'Imogen,' she called into the house. 'Are you there? Rachel? Girls?'

She stepped in, and Bridie came into view, sitting on the floor with Caitlin huddled in her arms. Laura ran towards the girls, and crouched down in front of them. 'What's happened?' Her voice trembled. 'Are you OK? Where's Rachel?'

Neither girl spoke, their eyes dark and heavy in their intensely pale faces, and she noticed Caitlin had a gash on her forehead. She leaned over and touched her face. 'What happened, darling?' she said, but the child remained silent.

Laura went into the kitchen. The sight that greeted her made her stomach turn.

'Oh my God, Imogen,' she yelled, rushing towards her, and grabbing a tea towel from the cooker handle. She bent to where Imogen was lying on the floor, and wrapped it around one of her bloody wrists, noticing how deep the gashes were, as fresh blood dripped and pooled on the floor. 'Stay with me, please stay with me.'

But Imogen's wide staring eyes were lifeless. Laura knew she was too late.

In tears, she rose, and left the kitchen – searching for her daughter.

'Rachel?' she called, venturing into the small hallway, where coats of all sizes fought for space on a rack, and kids' shoes lined the wall. And there she was, her tiny body crumpled at the foot of the stairs. Laura let out a painful wail.

She fell to her knees. 'Oh God, oh God, oh God, Rachel, no, no, no, please be OK,' she cried, bending over the child, tears flooding her eyes. She'd never felt such agony. Despite everything, she'd grown to love her daughter. 'Rachel, please wake up,' she continued, her cheeks sodden, her nose running, tears dripping from her chin. 'Wake up, wake up, wake up.'

***

When the Guards and paramedics arrived, Laura was still by Rachel's side, her daughter's head on her lap. An unbearable numbness had stunned her into a trancelike silence, as though she wasn't there at all. As though she'd entered another realm she would never escape from.

Through the door, she saw Bridie had withdrawn into the corner of the room, her head buried into her knees. She was singing, her voice haunted, her words bouncing around the room. 'Polly put the kettle on, Polly put the kettle on, Polly put the kettle on, we'll all have tea. Suki take it off again, Suki take it off again, Suki take it off again, they've all gone away.'

Caitlin had found her way to Laura's side, and was now sitting next to her. She laid her head against Laura, blood drying on her forehead.

When the pathologist pronounced Rachel dead, Laura let out a piercing scream. Sheer pain thrust through the numbness, crippling her, and Caitlin burst into tears.

Rachel had gone. The little girl she was just beginning to reach had left her, and another painful sob racked her body.

Later, when her sobs subsided, she became aware of an officer talking to Bridie. The woman was crouched down in front of the child, holding both her hands.

'What's your name, sweetheart?' she said, but Bridie was silent.

Laura looked down at Caitlin by her side, the child's eyes puffy and red from crying, her dark hair damp from tears. She looked so helpless. So bewildered. Laura lifted her into her arms, stood, and swayed, as the child snuffled and hiccoughed, her breathing erratic. Within moments Caitlin had drifted off to sleep on Laura's shoulder.

'Do you know what the arrangement is here?' the officer asked Laura as she entered the room. 'The woman who took her own life, do you know who she was?'

Laura nodded, continuing to sway, the child's warm body comforting in her arms. 'She is … was Imogen O'Brian,' she told the officer. But then she couldn't have been. If Dillon had never discovered where his mother went to, Imogen couldn't have married Tierney without him getting a divorce. 'Actually, I don't know what her surname is, but her partner was Tierney O'Brian. He hasn't been around for months. And Bridie ...' she nodded at the little girl huddled into herself in the corner '... is Imogen's daughter. Tierney has a sixteen-year-old son, Dillon, but I don't know where he is.'

'And the child who died?'

My little girl. My Rachel.

Laura swallowed hard – the officer's words were so final. She looked down at Caitlin in her arms, and kissed the child's head. The thought of these girls losing both parents didn't bear thinking about. They would be better off with her than in care, surely. The words were out before she could think them through. 'The dead girl is Caitlin O'Brian,' she said. 'Tierney and Imogen's daughter.'

Bridie's head shot up, and she glared at Laura. 'Caitlin isn't dead,' she cried.

'Oh, sweetheart,' the officer said, pulling her into her arms. 'I know how hard this is for you.'

'But she isn't dead,' Bridie cried, pulling away from the officer. She rose to her feet, and ran at Laura, punching her legs hard, and crying.

'Come with me, Bridie,' said another officer, taking hold of the child's hand. 'Let's get you somewhere safe.'

Bridie was sobbing so hard now her words were incoherent. She grabbed Rachel's bag of toys, before being picked up by an officer, and taken outside. Laura wanted to stop her – explain – but she'd already lied, she couldn't go back on it.

'Oh God, what will happen to her?' Laura cried, as the door closed behind Bridie's screams.

'A foster home, I expect,' the original officer said.

Laura's heart pounded, and tears came again. 'I could take her. Let me take her. Please.'

'It's not that simple,' the officer said. 'I'm sure you could put in a request, but she's a dear little thing – they shouldn't have any difficulty finding her a good home.' She paused. 'One more thing, would you be happy to come down to the station and officially identify the bodies?'

Laura nodded. 'Yes,' she said.

Once they'd gone, Laura looked around the farmhouse. *What happened here?* How had Rachel ended up at the foot of the stairs? Why had Imogen taken her own life when the little ones were in the house? And why had Dillon taken off?

She headed through the open door, wondering if she would ever know the truth.

'We're going to call you Rachel from now on,' she whispered to the child asleep on her shoulder, as the trees swallowed them, and guilt consumed her as she thought of Bridie out there alone in the world.

Tears came quickly, the sobs waking the child. 'Don't cry,' she said, touching Laura's face softly.

'I'm not crying, sweetheart. I've got something in my eye.'

She took a deep breath, trying to battle down thoughts of her daughter lying dead at the bottom of the stairs, of Bridie now lost in the system. If only she could go back – take her too. But if she did it would come out eventually that she'd taken the wrong child. She would have to move as far away as possible, and quickly – before Dillon returned, if he ever did. She would book flights to England and put the house on the market. She couldn't stay around, not even for Bridie.

Chapter 47

March 2018

I raced to the far end of the pool area, hoping to find another exit, panic swelling. *What the hell's the matter with me?*

With no second exit, I pushed myself into the far corner and slipped down the wall into the shadows. I gripped my knees, making myself as small as I could, close to tears and feeling helpless.

I took several deep breaths – my shaking body rooted to the floor – and tried to reach my rational side. Lawrence's voice was in my head: *'You're over-reacting, Rachel.'*

After several moments, I leaned over to look through the door. Whoever had been there, had gone.

Oh God, had I imagined it? Or had it been Zoe, and through the frosted glass she'd looked bigger than she was? Or a caretaker perhaps? Or was this place really haunted?

My heart, which had picked up speed, began to slow, but my hands wouldn't stop shaking. I needed to get my act together. I levered myself to my feet with the aid of the wall, and, with a deep breath, padded towards the door.

'Zoe?' I called, as I cautiously peered into the quiet corridor.

'Zoe,' I repeated, as I crept towards the first set of stairs. As I reached the top, I noticed a cup lying on its side, a swirl of hot chocolate spreading over the varnished pine floor, dripping onto the second step. 'Zoe,' I called again. 'Is everything OK?'

I was about to take the second set of stairs, when a sound like something falling over down towards the gym area, caught my attention. 'Is that you, Zo?'

As I made my way along the corridor, I scanned the fitness machines, their shapes menacing in the half-light, and turned into the café area, where a chair was on its side. I cast my eyes around the deserted room, and caught a glimpse of someone disappearing through a door at the far end.

My courage made a run for it, and I turned and raced back the way I came, and took the stairs two at a time to the foyer.

Rain hammering on the roof of the reception area, after the silence I'd left behind, felt somehow reassuring. 'Zoe,' I said, looking about me. 'Zoe, where are you?' But she wasn't by the coffee machine, and a desperate need to get out of the building took over. I flung open the door, and breathed in the cold, wet air for several moments, trying to clear my head. Had I imagined someone else in the building? But as my eyes fell on a car parked next to Zoe's, I knew I hadn't.

I looked back over my shoulder, knowing I couldn't leave Zoe. I pulled my phone from my robe pocket, but there was no signal.

Without thinking it through, I raced back inside and down the two flights of stairs, hoping she'd somehow made her way back to the poolroom, calling her name as I went.

'Thank God, Zoe,' I yelled as I lunged through the door, to see her lying on a lounger, looking at her phone.

'Hey, Rachel,' she said, lifting herself onto her elbows. 'Sorry I was so long – I dropped your hot chocolate.' A pause. 'Are you OK, hon?'

'No, no, I'm far from it,' I said, heading towards her, my voice raspy.

276

'Christ, what's wrong?' she said. 'You look as if you've seen a ghost. You haven't, have you?' She looked about her wide-eyed, as though a grey lady might appear through the wall.

'Someone else is here,' I spluttered, gripping my phone like it was a hand grenade. 'A man, I think. But I can't be sure.'

She pretended to shudder. 'God, don't say that, Rach. You'll give me the heebie-jeebies.'

'I'm not joking. I saw him through the glass door. We need to leave. Now!' I was talking way too fast. 'You didn't lock the door when we arrived, and I think whoever it is followed us in.'

'But I'm sure I locked it.' Her brow lifted. 'And I didn't see anyone when I went to the coffee machine.'

Frustration was turning to anger. 'I've just been up there, for God's sake. The door's unlocked.'

She took my hand, and, as if I was a child making up stories, said, 'Calm down. It's pretty creepy, I'll give you that, but it's just you and me here.'

I wanted to argue, but she beckoned me to sit down next to her. 'You're meant to be relaxing, Rachel,' she said, with a wide smile.

I stared at the door. Had I imagined it? Lawrence said I over-reacted all the time. Maybe he was right.

But I hadn't imagined the friend request.

'And there's something else,' I said, remaining standing as I faffed with my mobile, attempting to get the friend request up. And then I saw it – *another friend request*. I almost dropped my phone as I opened it, despite a nagging voice telling me not to.

Caitlin O'Brian: CONFIRM/DELETE REQUEST

The profile photo was a recent photo of me. The cover photo was the spa. I read the update:

Caitlin O'Brian went to the spa, in a shower of rain
She stepped in a puddle, right up to her middle, and never
was seen again.

'For Christ's sake,' I cried, tears in my eyes as I showed Zoe the screen. 'I can't take any more.'

'Caitlin O'Brian?' she said, taking my phone, and furrowing her forehead as she looked at the screen. 'Do you know anyone called Caitlin O'Brian?' She raised eyes to meet my mine. 'Does she ring any bells?'

Memories I couldn't quite reach drifted in, and disappeared once more. 'Caitlin,' I muttered, lowering myself down next to Zoe, who placed my phone on the table. 'In the picture I found at my mum's house I was with three children I can't recall.' I dashed a tear from the corner of my eye. 'Perhaps one of those is Caitlin.'

I darted a look towards the door, and my body stiffened. 'Oh God,' I whispered, seeing the ominous dark shape behind the glass.

'Fuck!' Zoe cried on seeing it, jumping to her feet, but I couldn't move.

'I told you,' I said. 'I told you I saw someone. Hello!' I called out.

'Shhh,' she said, putting her finger to her lips.

'I just thought he might answer, if he's harmless,' I said, my voice low and jittery.

'Pass me that,' Zoe whispered, pointing to a broom propped against the wall.

Struggling to rise, I stepped towards it. 'What for?'

She glared. 'Just get it.'

I took a deep breath and reached for the broom, passing it over to her. She yanked off the brush head, and tiptoed towards the door.

'Be careful.' My heart thudded in my chest, but I somehow

found the strength to trail behind her, as she made her way across the room and out through the door. The man, who was now making his way down the corridor, didn't have time to react. The sound of the thuds of the broom hitting his head twice, his cries of pain, made my stomach heave. As he slumped to the floor face down, I let out a scream. 'Oh God, Zoe,' I cried. 'What the hell have you done?'

I went to kneel down, hoping to take his pulse, but Zoe grabbed my shaking hand, and pulled me back along the corridor and into the poolroom, still gripping the broom handle, now covered in blood. This was too much. We needed to leave. Now!

'Zoe,' I said, my voice trembling. 'Who do you think he was – is?'

She shrugged, a sudden coldness about her. As though knocking the man out had left her numb. 'No idea.'

'What if he wasn't after us? What if he was just an employee or something?' A lump lodged in my throat, as I dashed away tears. Everything was spiralling out of control. 'We should get out of here. Call the police. An ambulance.'

'No,' she said. 'I'd like one more swim before we go.' She slipped off her robe, and threw it on a chair.

'What? Don't be daft, Zo. What if that bloke wakes up? We need to get out of here. Call someone. I mean what if he's dead?'

'Dead?' She turned, her eyes stabbing into me.

And that's when I saw her necklace. I hadn't noticed it before. 'Where did you get that?' I said. It was just like my mum's locket, the locket that held a photo of me when I was a baby – the locket Mum had said was stolen.

'What, this ol' thing?' she said, looking down at it – flicking it open then closed. 'I can't recall exactly.'

I was going off on a tangent. We needed to leave. I grabbed my bag.

'I did so much for you,' she said, as I slung my bag over my shoulder, her eyes meeting mine once more. She sounded different, serious, *Irish*, but not in the satirical way she had when she'd called me in Ireland. She turned sharply and rummaged in her rucksack.

'Yes, you've always been there for me, Zoe,' I said, feeling even more uneasy, 'and I'm grateful for that.'

'But you left me.'

'What? Don't be silly, I never left you – I'm here, aren't I?' My words were coming out fast again, and I felt breathless.

'You went off with Laura, and didn't care what happened to me, neither of you did.'

'My mother?'

She laughed ironically. 'If you like.'

'We should go home, Zoe. Now.'

She stepped forward, so close to my face that there was barely any air between us. 'I want you to stay,' she said.

'But we must go,' I said, heading away, but she was quicker, stronger, taller than me, and I felt the cold steel of a blade against my neck, before I'd reached the door.

Chapter 48

Zoe dragged me towards the water, and lowered me to the floor. A tear I hadn't known was there, rolled down my cheek, and dripped off my chin.

'Please let me go,' I whimpered, my body drained of strength. 'I thought we were friends.'

'We're not friends, Caitlin.'

Caitlin?

'I'm Bridie O'Brian, and you're my little sister.'

I tried to take in her words, as she ran the flat side of the knife across my neck.

'Rachel died, you see,' she went on. 'And Laura took you from me, pretended you were her daughter.'

'No, that can't be right. You're mistaken. Please.' My body trembled. My heart thumped. 'I'm Laura's daughter. I'm Rachel.'

'No!' she yelled, gripping my hair and dragging my head backwards. 'You're Caitlin O'Brian, and it's your fault I've always been so alone – fostered, and later dumped in a children's home, then a psychiatric hospital. It's your fault for going with Laura – for leaving me.'

She let go of my hair and moved, and I let out a yelp like a

281

wounded pup, as she pushed the sharp blade into my neck – a surge of pain telling me she'd drawn blood.

'They freed me eighteen months ago, and I went to Ireland – to Lough End Farm. Of course it's called Evermore Farmhouse now.

'There it was all so vivid. Memories of how Laura lied to the Guards. The way you snuggled into her, abandoning me. I thought I might finally come to terms with it. My stepfather seemed pleased to see me. The daughter he'd never searched for. He never searched for you either, Caitlin, but then why would he? He thought you were dead, and I wasn't about to tell him different. I certainly didn't want to share him with you.'

'You know who my father is?'

'Mmm, Tierney O'Brian – although you know him by his pen name, Felix Clarke.'

'Felix Clarke is my father?' Fear and confusion swirled inside me, turning my body to liquid.

She laughed. 'When I told Tierney about my past, in an attempt to free myself of it, he wanted rid of me. I was bad news. A famous writer with a killer daughter.' She grabbed my hair and pulled my head backwards.

'Stop! Please,' I cried out.

She released my hair. 'He told me I was just like my ma. That she'd tried to kill him. *The apple doesn't fall far from the tree,* that's what he said.' She fidgeted, restless.

I'm going to die.

'He needed to be punished.' There was a long pause. The only sound her rasping breath in my ear, and the spa bubbling like a kettle that would never boil. 'So I pushed a pillow over his face when he was sleeping,' she went on. 'I wanted to snatch every ounce of life from him, because he let me down like everyone else. But he woke, fought me off, grabbed my throat, and I thought he was going to squeeze the life out of me. In some ways I hoped he would. But Dillon appeared. Told him to think of his writing career – the life he has now. I like Dillon.

'Tierney gave me money to *feck off out of his life*. He would top it up regularly, if I never returned, or shared my story with the press. So I came to London, searching for you and Laura.'

Suddenly the door crashed open. Zoe turned, bringing me with her, the knife still at my neck, and I saw the man from the corridor staggering into the poolroom, holding his head, blood on his fingers.

'Christ! Dillon!' Zoe cried. 'I didn't know it was you.'

'You could have cracked open my skull, Bridie,' he said, continuing to stumble towards us. 'You're fecking crazy at times.'

Through a haze of panic and confusion I watched him continue towards us, his dark green eyes on me. It was the same man who'd chased me through the wood in Ireland, and fear slammed into me. Had they been in it together all this time? Hating me for leaving? Tormenting me with friend requests and hoax calls? I thought it wasn't possible to be more frightened than I already was, but I was wrong.

Zoe's face closed in on me, her breath hot on my ear. 'This is our brother, Caitlin. Our lovely brother.'

Dillon began to sway, toppling and dropping onto a nearby plastic chair. 'You could have killed me,' he said, his Irish accent strong. 'What the hell were you thinking?'

'I told you, I had no idea it was you. It's your own fault, turning up without telling me, creeping around like some bloody phantom, scaring the bejesus out of me.' She laughed. 'But it's so good to see you, Dillon.'

'So, what will you be doing with that knife?' His speech was slurred, and he continued to hold his head with bloodied hands.

'I'm going to kill Caitlin,' she said, like she was talking about the weather. 'That's what I'm doing with this knife, silly.'

Another feeling of helplessness filled my senses. Nobody was going to save me. Nobody was going to appear and stop Zoe from killing me. 'She left us, Dillon. She didn't care about us. She has to die.'

I darted Dillon a look. His eyelids were growing heavy. 'I ran away too, Bridie,' he said, his words barely audible.

'You were scared, like me,' Zoe said, as his eyelids dropped closed.

Zoe kicked me hard. 'It's time for a swim, Caitlin. Get up.'

I rose, knowing my only hope was to keep her talking. 'So you left Ireland searching for me …'

'Yes.' A pause, and I could almost hear her mind ticking over. I felt sure she wouldn't be able to resist telling me everything. 'But then I met Hank. We bought a nice little modern terraced house in Hatfield, and I thought things were going to be OK. That my life had finally made a U-turn.' She moved the blade away from my neck, and my body for a second relaxed. 'We were so in love. And then he tried to help you – arranged to meet you.'

And then it hit me, *Henry Derby*. Hank was short for Henry. 'Did you kill him?'

'I killed them all, Caitlin.' The knife's point was back, pressing against my larynx. I almost choked, and cried out as I felt another nick in my flesh. 'And now I'm going to kill you.'

'But if I'm your sister …' I cried, desperate. But I knew before she answered, it made no difference.

'Not a very good one though, are you? I protected you from Rachel, and our crap ma, but you let me down. Everyone let me down.' She sighed. 'It was a shame about Hank. He was useless by the end. Pathetic. I hadn't realised he was an addict when I met him. I suppose if things had stayed OK, I may never have come looking for you. But he had his uses. If I fed his addiction with Tierney's money, he did jobs for me in return.'

'He rang the TV studio?'

'Ten out of ten, Caitlin – go to the top of the class. He rang to tell you your mother had died too – the first time.' She laughed. 'But then he let me down, you see. Arranged to meet you at the

Emirates Stadium. He couldn't live with himself. Wanted to let you know what was going on. I hadn't planned to kill him, but I had no choice. An overdose finished him off, poor love. Pop went the weasel. He was the only death I got no pleasure from.'

I racked my mind for something else to say, something that would keep her talking. Something to give me time – *I don't want to die.* 'So how did you find me?'

'Questions, questions, questions,' she said, but she still couldn't resist telling me. 'I found Laura from articles online about nine months ago. They pointed me towards Dunwich, and an old woman told me she was in care. I went to see her a few times. Stole her locket.

'She was proud of you, Caitlin. Quite happy to rattle on about you, which could be a bit tedious, truth be told. She even told me where you lived. I watched you for a while. Joined your yoga group. Befriended you. Simple.' A smile. 'I even told her you and Lawrence had split up. She was sad about that.'

I swallowed hard, keeping very still.

'Laura was so confused, even thought I was her daughter a couple of times. But then we all know her daughter died many years ago.'

I could feel her heart pounding, as she pressed her body against my back.

'And then you told me in December that you were going on morning TV – that's when my little game began. The friend requests were so much fun. You do know you were responsible for all those deaths. If you hadn't left me I wouldn't have been so alone. So messed up by the care system.'

Panic seared through my blood. 'Please don't kill me,' I spluttered. 'I was far too young to know any different, please stop.' It was a pathetic attempt. She wasn't going to stop. She was enjoying herself too much.

'Did you kill my mother?' It came out so quiet, the words drowned by fear.

'I would have, but she conveniently had a heart attack when I told her who I was – that I was going to kill her and you. The shock, I suppose. Well that, and the fact I'd convinced her not to take her heart tablets. It didn't take much – it was easy to plant fear in her that they were doing her harm.'

'You're pure evil,' I said.

'I am. Yes,' she said. 'In fact only fifteen per cent of serial killers are women, so that makes me special, don't you think?'

A tear rolled down my cheek. How could something I'd done when I was four years old have made her so tormented? My heart thudded with fear, but not only that, I was also angry with my mother for not telling me. How could she have kept this from me?

'Walk!' she yelled, a wicked sharpness in her voice, as she moved the blade away from my throat, and I felt its point nudging into the small of my back. 'Hurry up!'

I was shaking from head to foot as she guided me to the water's edge, the cold water on the floor against my bare feet making me shudder, and the room started spinning.

'Jump,' she whispered into my ear, as she pushed the blade deeper into the towelling robe, the fabric splitting. I wanted to scream, but I was paralysed by fear.

'I can't swim,' I croaked, sudden memories of almost drowning as a child flooding my mind – *Jump, jump, jump.*

'I know,' she said, and I turned to see a long thin smile stretch across her beautiful face. 'That's what makes it so much fun.'

With a shove, she launched me into the deepest part of the pool, the water striking my face like a blade, the thick towelling robe pulling me down.

I flailed my arms in an attempt to stay afloat, gasping for breath, memories of almost drowning as a child continuing to flood my mind. 'Help me, please.'

'Nobody's going to help you, Caitlin,' Zoe said, crouching on the edge, her eyes piercing me, her painted-on smile doll-like.

'How long can you stay alive underwater?' she continued. 'My guess is not long. Two minutes perhaps?'

Within moments, her words became muffled and inaudible as I dipped under the water, and then somehow scrambled to the surface once more.

'Don't waste your time,' she said. 'You might as well give in to it. You're not coming out of there alive.'

But the strength that left me earlier surged through me, as I thought of Grace – my precious daughter. If I left her now, at just four years old, I would become less than a memory – a photograph in an album, someone she was told about. The thought of my darling girl crying at my funeral, unable to understand where I'd gone, shot adrenaline through my body. I carried on splashing, heaving my body up above the water, choking and spluttering. I couldn't give up on life. I wouldn't give up out without a fight.

Suddenly a shape emerged behind her. 'What the hell are you doing, Bridie?' It was Dillon.

Through blurred vision, I saw her rise to her full height, and attempt to embrace him. But he tugged away. 'For Christ sake, get her out of there. She's going to drown.'

He went to pass her, but she lunged at him with the knife, slicing his face. He pushed her aside with a lash of his arm, and jumped into the pool, the blood from his cheek swirling in the water, as he dragged me, choking, to the side, where we both held on to the edge.

'Thank you, thank you,' I said, breathlessly.

I looked up. There was no sign of Zoe.

Once he'd caught his breath, Dillon levered himself out of the pool, his dark hair dripping, his clothes heavy with water. I continued to grip on to the side, exhausted, shaking, my breath rasping in my chest.

'Take my hand,' he said, leaning down, his arm outstretched. And I was about to grab it, when Zoe appeared from nowhere, and, yelling manically, she hurtled towards him. I let out a scream, catching the glint of the blade as he turned and she plunged it into his stomach. He cried out in pain, eyes wide with shock as he crashed backwards onto the floor, blood oozing from his body as he held his side.

'You let me down, Dillon,' she yelled, tugging at her damp hair, making it stand on end. 'Why does everyone let me down?'

I continued to grip the side of the pool, my breaths loud and uneven, tears streaming down my face. 'You can't let him die,' I said, wanting to climb out of the pool, but conscious she was still holding the knife. 'He loves you. He's your brother.' I had no idea if what I was saying would make her see sense, or provoke her further. But I didn't know what else to do.

She glared down at me. 'He doesn't love me,' she snapped.

'Yes, he does. I could tell you had a strong and special bond.'

I looked at Dillon, moaning in agony. He was conscious, for now, but I wasn't sure how long he would survive. If she'd hit an organ with the knife, he would need help fast.

'Then why did he save you?' she said, narrowing her eyes as she glared my way.

'To save you from killing again, Zoe.'

'Bridie,' she yelled. 'My name's Bridie.'

'If we call for help, he may live,' I said, trying to ignore her anger.

'I hadn't meant for him to die,' she said, her face softening as she looked at him groaning in pain. 'He wasn't on my to-kill list.'

'Then save him – he's never hurt you, has he?'

She shook her head. 'Dillon,' she said, almost childlike. 'Are you OK?'

'He will be, if you help him. He needs you, Bridie.'

She dropped to her knees by his side. 'Dillon, I'm sorry,' she cried, taking hold of his hand. 'I didn't want to hurt you. You just got in my way.'

I dragged myself out of the pool, and stumbled towards my

mobile, discarding the heavy robe as I went. 'Ambulance and police,' I cried into the phone, darting looks at Zoe. But she'd laid her head on his chest, unaware of me now. 'Sorry,' she was saying, over and over.

Chapter 49

Once the police had taken Zoe away, and the paramedics had made Dillon stable enough for transportation, I called a taxi.

I left the poolroom, and headed up the stairs to get dressed, looking at my phone. *Who can I call? Who can I trust? Who will listen now?* It felt as though I had no one.

The rain was tipping down when I raced from the building, head down as I avoided puddles on my way to the waiting taxi.

'Jesus!' I'd slammed into Connor dashing the other way. 'Rachel, isn't it?'

Is it?

'The cops called me to lock up,' he went on, 'but I can't find my keys. I've made a call to the owner, and I'll meet her here.' He glanced up at a waiting policeman in the foyer. 'They said there's been an incident.' He was a little breathless. 'Has there been a break-in?'

'Something like that,' I said, as a raindrop slipped down my collar, making me shudder. Zoe must have lifted his keys. 'It was Zoe, Connor,' I added, feeling he should be prepared.

'Is she OK? She came round earlier.' He paused. 'I know I sound like a jerk, but I've been trying to end things – she's … well she's nice enough, but a bit clingy and intense.'

'You've had a lucky escape,' I said, stepping out towards the taxi. 'She isn't who we thought she was.'

And neither am I.

***

'So, it seems we share the same father,' Dillon said, as I walked towards his hospital bed. He was in the corner of the ward, sitting up, his broad shoulders resting against the pillows. In my panic at the pool, I'd barely registered his dark, wavy hair, and rugged complexion, but I could see now he was a kindly-looking man, with deep green eyes. He looked well considering what he'd been through. Thankfully, the knife hadn't hit any major organs, although another inch and it would have struck his liver. He was lucky. At least that's what he said.

I sat down in the chair next to his bed. 'It seems we do,' I said. I hadn't yet fully come to terms with what my mother had done. I felt as though my identity had been ripped from me, and I was no longer Rachel the psychotherapist, I was Caitlin the changeling.

It was as though I was coping with losing her for a second time. But I was working through the trauma. Trying to understand why Laura – my mum – did what she did. Had she tried to save Caitlin, or replace Rachel? I knew she must have been psycho-logically scarred as she held the truth inside her all those years, lost in her paintings – rarely leaving the house. Perhaps she didn't tell me for fear I would leave her. It had always been the two of us against the world.

'I'm looking forward to seeing Felix again,' I said to Dillon. 'Or should I call him Tierney?'

'My guess is he'll want you to call him da.'

I smiled. 'I'm so relieved you're going to be OK.' And I was. I'd visited the hospital a couple of times when he was unconscious, and I was beginning to feel a connection.

'Why did you come to the spa?' I asked him. There was so much I didn't know.

'Well, I came to England to talk to you. I felt sure you were Caitlin the moment I looked into your eyes that day in the woods. I'm good with eyes. Never forget them. But I couldn't be sure.' He paused. 'I'm sorry about the day I saw you at the farmhouse.'

'You scared the shit out of me,' I said, but added a small smile.

'Da thought you were press, was worried you would uncover Bridie's past.'

'But I told him I was a psychotherapist …'

'And he didn't believe you. So I chased you, hoping to scare you off. When I became convinced you were Caitlin, I asked Da what you'd told him. When I found out your name was Rachel, alarm bells rang. I felt sure something strange happened the day Imogen died.' He shifted his body up the bed, and winced.

'Are you OK?' I said. 'Do you need painkillers?'

'I'm fine,' he said.

'Did you tell Tierney you thought I might be Caitlin?'

He shook his head. 'It would have sounded bizarre, basing a whole theory on your eyes and your name, plus I didn't want him to get his hopes up. But I was desperate to find you, find out more about you. Da said you'd told him you live in Finsbury Park, so I took a flight over, and tracked you down. I wanted to talk to you, that's all, but couldn't find the right words. I even followed you to Suffolk and back.'

'In a red car?'

He nodded. 'A hire car – I felt like a stalker.'

'Well, you were, by definition.' I smiled.

'Then I saw Bridie with you a few times, and knew then you must be Caitlin. I didn't trust Bridie, after what I knew about her, and how she tried to kill Da. And when I saw her put something on your doorstep and run away, my fear grew. She was dangerous, and I found myself watching you all the time – guarding you, I suppose. And then, last week, I saw her pick you up, and I followed you. It seemed odd to me that the two of you went into the spa alone. The rest is history, as they say.'

'I have you to thank for my life.'

He shrugged. 'I ran away when you were a child – left you when you needed me most. I wasn't about to leave you again.' He paused. 'It's hard to take in what your mother ... I mean Laura, did,' he said, as a correction. But the truth was Laura would always be my mother. 'But she was good to me when I was a teenager, so I'll find a way to understand. We were good friends,' he finished. And I hoped I'd come to understand too.

I spent another half an hour with him, and before I left, I found myself taking hold of his hand and squeezing. 'I'd like to get to know you even better, Dillon,' I said. 'Shall we exchange numbers?'

'I'd like that,' he said.

It was later that day that my mobile rang. An unknown number. But I no longer felt a sense of dread as I picked up.

'Miss Hogan?'

'Yes.'

'Dresden Clinic here.'

'Oh, hi there.' I didn't say I knew what she was about to tell me.

'I'm ringing to let you know that there is no DNA match between yourself and Mr Jude Henshaw.'

Chapter 50

From the first moment I saw Caitlin, I loved her. A precious gift. A beautiful baby sister. I would cherish her always.

People say it's rare to recall things that happened before the age of three or four. But I remember. I remember my mother showing her to me, telling me to be careful, she might break.

On my fifth birthday I asked Ma who my father was. 'He raped me,' was her cold reply. I didn't understand what she meant at the time. I do now.

I couldn't always protect Caitlin from Ma's strange moods. But I could protect her from Rachel. She was bigger than Caitlin, despite being six months younger. But she wasn't bigger than me.

She was a spiteful child. I didn't like her at all. I don't care that she's dead.

I remember the day I threw her cat in the lake, to get her into trouble. It worked. Rachel lost her cat. Serves her right. She was horrid to it anyway.

But the truth was, I didn't mean for her to die.

In fact, it had been a nice day. It was Caitlin's birthday, and Ma had made nice things to eat. She even sung nursery rhymes to us from Rachel's book. But then Caitlin, Rachel, and I went upstairs, and a squabble broke out. Rachel hit Caitlin, leaving a nasty gash on her forehead, and Caitlin cried and cried. I chased Rachel out of our bedroom and across the landing to the top of the stairs. She missed her footing. She fell.

Ma came rushing through when she heard the clatter. She just stared at Rachel's twisted body at the foot of the stairs, and back up at me.

'I'll put the kettle on,' she said, disappearing into the kitchen.

Eventually, Caitlin went downstairs, but I just sat on the top step, looking down at Rachel. It was a long while before Caitlin let out a scream – and I dashed downstairs to see Ma's bloody arms. I grabbed Caitlin's hand and we hid in the cupboard under the stairs.

Later we heard Dillon cry out, and the back door slam – his footfalls heading away. That's when we ventured out once more.

Later Laura came and stole Caitlin away.

I had thought she would come for me too, but I realised, when David and Janet Green took me to their grey house with the bright red door, she never would.

I liked David and Janet, and lived happily with them for five years before they told me they couldn't care for me any more, that they were only my foster parents. I hadn't realised it meant they would never be my forever parents. 'We're moving to Australia,' David said.

If only they'd said, 'And we're taking you too, Bridie.'

But they couldn't see how much I loved them – needed them – how I'd thought they loved me too.

Often, David would let me sleep in the summerhouse at the foot of their long garden. It was always a great adventure. I had a bed in there, and would snuggle up with Mr Snookum.

Mr Snookum had been Rachel's favourite toy. In fact, there were lots of her things in the canvas bag I took that awful day: her book of nursery rhymes, a sad-looking doll I threw away – even a painting of Lough End Farm with black splodges for clouds.

That night. The night David and Janet told me I would be going to another set of foster parents – who, they said, would love me as much as they did – I asked to sleep in the summerhouse, and they said, 'Yes, darling, of course.'

I waited until they were in bed, and headed inside – they always left the back door open, in case I needed the loo – and I crept up the stairs. I lit a candle and laid it at the foot of their bed, before leaving them, and closing the door behind me.

I wedged a chair under the door handle, and ran like the wind to the summerhouse. I saw him die – not her though. She must have suffocated with the thick black fumes. They deserved to die. They let me down.

I went back inside once he'd fallen to the floor, and I raced upstairs. Thick smoke seeped under the door, and I choked as I removed the chair.

They couldn't find another set of foster parents to love me as David and Janet had – it gets trickier as you get older to find people to care for you. That's what the lady with the big hair and cabbage in her teeth told me, when I was taken to the children's home, next to the River Liffey in Dublin.

I didn't mind it there. I made friends easily. I was fifteen when I started going out with Ronan.

He told me he loved me, so I gave him my virginity. But, like everyone else, he let me down. 'It's over,' he said – right there in front of everyone. 'You're like a leech, Bridie, the way you cling to me all the time.' They all laughed, and I hated him after that. The knife was easy to get from the kitchens; they don't guard them 24/7 – they really should. He deserved to die. I hate him even now.

They knew it was me – I knew they would.

Given my age, and the fact psychologists at the children's home had already been seeing me for what they called abnormal behaviour, they admitted me to a psychiatric hospital. The only good thing there was the field of daffodils I could see from my window in spring. Well, until, some years later, Flora Phillips started as a psychiatric nurse. I hadn't had myself down as bisexual, but there'd been something about Flora that turned my head.

We would meet in places nobody frequented much – and at first the passion between us was amazing. I loved her, and she told me she loved me too; that once I was out – which wouldn't be long now – we'd be together, always.

She'd trained as a hairdresser before changing vocations, and she taught me to cut hair – said it would give me a career when I was released.

Then she met someone else. A bloke. She'd made a mistake – she was straight.

Well, of course she had to die.

But this time they didn't know it was me and eventually they let me out.

Free, I was determined to find any family I had left, and went to Sligo. I remembered Lough End Farm, and everything that had happened there. I was shocked to find Tierney alive, but recognised him straight away. Dillon too. But once Tierney found out about my past, he didn't want me there, and deported me to England with the promise of money.

After my attempt at a normal life with Hank, I set out to find my sister and her fake mother.

It was easy to set up a few Facebook accounts, and I took care to use different IP addresses, just in case. I even set up my own profile, with a few Photoshopped photos of my fake family in Cornwall

It was easy to steal Rachel's spare keys, and bring the second Mr Snookum down from the attic to spook her. It had all been rather fun.

In fact, everything went so well – my only sadness now is I didn't kill Caitlin.

Chapter 51

May 2018

I fastened Grace's seatbelt, as we waited for the plane to take off.

'So I have a brand new grandpa and uncle,' she said, and I knew she was struggling to take it all in. 'I've never had a grandpa before,' she said, holding her fluffy rabbit tight against her chest.

I was about to correct her. Tell her she does have a grandpa in Australia who she'd never met, but I felt sure it would confuse her further. She'd already been through enough with my breakup with Lawrence.

'Are they nice?' she asked, looking up at me.

'Dillon is lovely.' *He saved my life.* 'And Grandpa writes books.'

'Like *Winnie the Pooh*?'

'Something like that.'

'Cool,' she said, closing her eyes.

I wondered if I'd arranged for her to meet Tierney and Dillon too soon. But it was too late now. The plane was moving down the runway.

I looked out of the window, the rumble of the plane's engine causing a surge of apprehension. But I felt sure I was getting there – beginning to feel better. Everything had started to settle down, as though someone had stopped shaking the snow-globe with my life inside.

Angela and I were OK. She'd come round to see me about a month ago to tell me she was going to put her house on the market. 'I need a fresh start,' she'd said, and told me how she was moving in with her elderly mother, who needed her care. 'My son often visits his gran,' she'd gone on. 'It could be a chance to make things right between us.' I hoped it would be.

She'd handed me the slippers the man had refused. 'Will you take them for Grace?' she'd said. 'Please.'

I'd taken them from her, and she'd thanked me as though I'd given her the gift.

Lawrence had introduced me to Farrah – *for Grace's sake*. I didn't like her, although if she'd been the kindest person alive I probably wouldn't have. She suited Lawrence better than I ever could, in her figure-hugging dresses and heels. She'd added me on Facebook, and, against my better judgement, I'd trawled through her photos and found pictures of her with Lawrence and Grace in Disneyland, but my heart had taken such a bashing over the last few months, I barely reacted.

Zoe, no, *Bridie O'Brian* awaited trial. I'd learnt how she'd been in a psychiatric hospital for murdering Ronan Murphy. They'd been in a children's home together – the building I'd seen in Dublin.

Now she was up on four counts of murder – Flora Phillips, Henry Derby, and the Greens – as well as the attempted murder of Dillon and me. Tierney hadn't pressed charges.

I knew my mother had been her victim too, but the lawyer said it would be difficult to prove.

I'd contacted Jude Henshaw to explain what the letter from my mother had meant all those years ago – that when she'd told him that his daughter, Rachel, had died, she was telling the truth. He'd wept down the phone, and I'd cried too, but I couldn't help thinking if he'd been the person he was now, back then, none of this would have happened.

I often wondered if we are three different people in our lifetime. The child. The adult. And the person we become when we realise the mistakes we've made.

***

I'd agreed to meet Dillon and Tierney at the cemetery near Evermore Farmhouse. It would be the first time I'd seen Tierney since Bridie attacked mem and now it felt surreal kneeling in front of the grave of 'Caitlin O'Brian 1986–1990' when I knew the child lying in the ground was Rachel Hogan – that Caitlin O'Brian was me.

A chill raced down my spine, and I felt suddenly weak and nauseous. Everything I thought I knew about myself was wrong. I wasn't even sure if I could go on using the name Rachel, although a search of the Internet had told me I could use any name, as long as it wasn't for illegal purposes.

But this had been illegal, hadn't it? I would need to talk to a solicitor, when I could face it.

I ran my fingers over the inscription. How had my mother lived with such a dreadful secret? But the truth was she hadn't. I'd discovered her trips every November, when I'd spent time with Jessica as a child, were to see the grave of her *real* daughter.

'There're talk of exhuming her body,' Tierney said, and I looked up to see him standing with Duke. I smiled hello. He was my father, and I wondered if I would ever get used to that, or the fact he was Grace's grandfather.

'I heard,' I said, rising and fussing over the dog. 'What good would that do? My mother's dead.'

He shrugged. 'I hope they leave the child in peace.'

Dillon appeared and smiled first at Grace, who was picking daisies under a nearby tree, and then my way.

'It's so good to see you both,' I said, greeting them with a hug. Now things had fallen into place, I realised, even more, how lucky I'd been that day at the pool. Bridie had intended to watch me drown.

Later at the farmhouse, once Grace was asleep, and Duke was lying by the fire, Dillon told me how he'd thought for a long time that his father – *my father* – was dead. He leaned forward and handed me a folded piece of paper. It was creased and stained dark red in places.

'Read it, please,' he said. 'I hope it will help you understand why I left the day I found Imogen.'

I unfolded it and scanned the words on the page:

I must confess, before I leave this world, in the hope my God will forgive me.

I know my parents would say taking my own life is a mortal sin, but I have nowhere else to turn, and I hope my God will understand that.

Where to begin?

When Tierney and his wife took Bridie and me in, I thought everything would be OK. He was a kind man, although he had a pair of lungs on him – his bark always worse than his bite. His wife was kind too, always looking out for me.

When his wife left him, I became Tierney's partner. However hard I tried, I couldn't bear him near me, but he never forced himself on me.

I couldn't bear living with him. I blame my awful past. I had to be rid of him, and if I could turn Dillon against him – convince the boy he was ill-treating the girls and me – he would help. The burns on my arms were my own doing – Tierney never hurt me.

One night I grabbed Dillon's stick and crashed it over Tierney's head. I wasn't sure he was dead, but Dillon helped

me take him out in the rowing boat, and push him into the
lake.

   But now the guilt consumes me. I can't go on. I'm sorry.
   Imogen

Dillon shuffled and twitched on the chair opposite me, nibbling on his thumbnail.

'I walked in the back door and found her,' he said. 'I knew instantly she was dead. That she'd killed herself.' There was a sob in his voice, but he took a deep breath and carried on. 'The note was by her side, and when I read it, I panicked. If the Guards found out I helped her, they would have thrown me in jail. So I filled my rucksack with money from the pot in the kitchen, as much food as I could carry, and took off.' He lowered his head. 'I'm ashamed to say I didn't think about you girls – that you were still in the house. I had no idea Rachel was dead. I just ran. And I beat myself up about that daily.'

'You were just a boy,' I said, leaning forward and touching his arm.

'I joined the army, ended up in Sierra Leone. But even there, with all the bloodshed, it felt safer than home.'

Tierney poured tea into mugs from a spotted pot. 'It turned out she'd convinced Dillon I was abusing her, told him I'd locked the kids in the cupboard – but it was never me, it had always been her. She had so many issues, poor soul. It wasn't surprising, the awful life she'd led before I met her. Parents can make or break a kid.'

We sipped our tea in silence for some time, before I looked once more at Dillon. 'So you helped Imogen throw your father in the lake?' The words felt wrong on my tongue.

He nodded, and put down his mug. 'She told me she'd struck Da with the stick I used to carry about, in an attempt to stop him hurting her. She said he was dead, and I must help her get rid of the body. She was in a dreadful state, said if I didn't help,

302

the girls would end up in care.' He turned to look at Tierney, and with words I knew he must have said a thousand times, he said, 'I'm so sorry, Da.'

'It was a long time ago, son,' Tierney said. 'We're different people now.'

I turned my tear-filled eyes on Tierney. 'So how did you survive?'

'Picked up by a fisherman,' Tierney said, leaning back in his chair. 'The water's deep in the middle of that lake, some say it's fifty metres, but I was lucky. I was washed up, still alive. But I was in a coma for months. Nobody knew who I was. When I finally came round, and got back here, everyone had disappeared. Took me years to track down Dillon, and later Bridie appeared, God help her. Of course, we thought you were in the graveyard.'

Another chill ran through me, and I covered my mouth with my hands. I wasn't sure I'd ever come to terms with everything.

'Eventually I did the place up,' Tierney went on. 'Gave it a new name – a new start.'

'So what will you be doing now, Rachel?' Dillon asked, his eyes meeting mine.

I shrugged. Thoughts of Suffolk had played around my head recently – it would be peaceful there, and, for now at least, I was planning to give up psychotherapy. And yet Ireland with its beautiful scenery and a new father and stepbrother to get to know was enticing too.

'Who knows?' I said, studying them both, and feeling relaxed for the first time in a long time. 'I guess I'll take one day at a time.'

The following day, once I'd hugged Dillon goodbye, Tierney walked with Grace and me up the drive towards my hire car. He was talking about his latest book, and I was glancing about me. Taking everything in so I could revisit it in my thoughts once I got back to Finsbury Park. My eyes skittered over the farmhouse, with jasmine growing around the door, the apple tree by the lake now bubbling over with blossom – it was such a beautiful place, and I couldn't wait to return.

One of the doors of the double garage stood open. Inside was Tierney's car, and next to it a black saloon, facing forward. I averted my gaze. I'd never got to the bottom of who'd rammed me off the road that day, or worked out who'd been watching me when I visited the grey houses with the red doors. I shook the fear from my thoughts. There were thousands of black saloons on the road, I told myself, refusing to let paranoia spoil things.

'I can't wait to read it,' I said, realising Tierney had come to a stop, and was staring my way. 'Will all this coming out about Bridie's past reflect on your novels?'

He shook his head. 'I worried for nothing, as it turns out. They seem to have gone up in the charts, rather than down.'

'That must be a relief,' I said.

He nodded. 'I'll send you a signed copy as soon as it's published. And you'll have to come to the book launch. I'd like to show off my new-found daughter.'

'That would be brilliant.'

'Well bye, Rachel.' He leaned forward and kissed my cheek, then ruffled Grace's hair, making her giggle. 'I hope you'll come again.'

'Of course, you can bank on it,' I said, with a smile.

Chapter 52

It felt strange to see the sold sign on Angela's house propped against the wall, and an excited young couple carrying boxes up the path.

Angela had moved in with her mother as she'd planned, and I felt a sudden rush of sadness. I'd spoken to her just before she left. Told her I would never understand what she'd done, but I would be there for her if she needed me.

It had turned out that neither of my friends had been who I thought they were. Maybe I chose friends unwisely, or perhaps I'd simply been gullible.

I slipped my key into my front door, and opened up to my familiar lounge. Grace skipped in, bouncing onto her bottom to open her toy box. It was time for a change. I would move into Mum's house before Grace started school. Lawrence would have to accept that.

Once Grace was in bed, and I'd poured myself a glass of wine, my mind whirred for the millionth time over everything that had happened.

I looked at Mr Snookum still perched on the shelf. Bridie had admitted to stealing my spare key, and moving the rabbit from the loft, to scare me. She'd even given my mother the original rabbit that had belonged to the real Rachel – another ploy to unnerve me. I was still struggling with her duplicity. The fact I'd cried on her shoulder when my mother died, the way she'd showered me with comfort, helping me through. She'd been there for me when I needed her most. Had it all been a lie? I was being ridiculous. Of course it had.

I lowered my gaze to the books by Felix T Clarke on my bookshelf, and a flutter in my stomach reminded me that he was my father. *I've finally found my father.* I was proud to be the daughter of a famous author. All those years of wondering, and now I knew exactly who he was – who I was. Happiness simmered on a low light, but didn't boil over. Despite wanting to feel ecstatic – crack open a bottle of champagne; after all, this was something I'd dreamed of since childhood – I was still haunted by my real identity, which felt like a new pair of gloves that didn't quite fit, and in a style I'd never worn before. And however much I didn't want to feel anger towards at my mother – Laura – I wished she'd told me, confided in me.

And there was the niggling concern that someone had chased me in my car that day in Ireland, which I couldn't shake. Who had it been? It hadn't been Bridie. She would have gloried in mentioning it, wouldn't she?

I rose, and pulled out the book he'd signed for me the day I'd seen him in the bookshop, and smiled at his photograph on the back. *My father.*

I opened the book, and let out a gasp. It slipped through my fingers as though in slow motion, crashing to the ground with a thud.

Dear Rachel,
 I hope you enjoy the book.
 Very best wishes,
 Felix T Clarke

I stumbled towards the sofa, my eyes on the open book on the floor, its pages splayed like a dead bird's wings, Tierney's words swirling and curling on the page – the same handwriting that was on Imogen's suicide note.

I fell onto the sofa, my head spinning. What did it mean? Had Tierney written the letter?

Memories prodded my mind, vivid and frightening:

I'm heading down a narrow staircase. Looking at my cream shoes, splattered with blood, a pain in my forehead.

'Rachel,' I whisper, as I pass the child at the foot of the stairs. 'Rachel, are you OK?'

I hear raised voices in the kitchen. 'Da?'

I pad across the lounge, passing the table laden with half-eaten food, and peer through the crack in the kitchen door.

'You left me for dead.' It's Tierney – younger – spitting as he yells, a knife in his hand. 'You're a fecking madwoman.'

'Please don't hurt me,' the woman cries, stepping backwards, covering her face with her arm, as though he might hit her. I know her. It's my real mother.

'You have no idea what I'm capable of, Imogen,' Tierney continues, his free hand balled into a fist.

'I've a fair idea.' She steps back once more, and presses her body against the worktop. 'I know it was you.'

'What was?'

'You raped me, Tierney. I was just seventeen. You followed me from the pub, and you raped me.'

Tierney claps slowly. 'What took you so long?'

'I see you in Bridie. She has your eyes. You raped me, then you pretended to rescue me.'

'My wife rescued you, Imogen,' he spits. 'Do you think I wanted you here?'

'She knew what you did, didn't she?'

He grabs her hair, and she lets out a small cry. 'And now I'm going to kill you,' he says.

'What, like you killed your wife?' she cries. 'I saw you, Tierney. I saw you kill her and drag her outside – plant an apple tree where you buried her body. I saw it all.'

He lunges towards her. I turn. I run.

I covered my eyes with my hands, as the reality that Tierney was evil – that he killed Imogen and his wife – crumpled me into a heap. I heard my mum's words. *The cuts. They were exactly the same. They should have been different.* Had she noticed that the cuts on Imogen's wrists were both the same depth? That if she'd taken her own life, her second cut wouldn't have been as deep as the first?

And Tierney couldn't have been in a coma for months. He must have been rescued, and then he'd returned – watching them.

Had it been Tierney who rammed my car off the road in Sligo – worried I would uncover the truth about Lough End Farm?

But there was one thing I was certain of. My father – Tierney O'Brian – was a killer, just like his daughter Bridie. *The apple doesn't fall far from the tree.*

I shot up, and stumbled towards the downstairs loo, feeling sick. I'd liked him. Thought he was caring and kind. *Stupid, gullible Rachel.*

Had it been in Bridie's genes to kill like her father?

But where did that leave me? I was his daughter too.

Nurture is more important than nature, I told myself over and over as I threw up in the loo, my head pounding, my limbs shaking – even more determined to leave Finsbury Park, and start again somewhere new.

Chapter 53

May 2018

In the early hours, memories of what Tierney had done morphed with ghostly shadows of Bridie's cruelty. I'd woken with a start around two, my body clammy – my mind thick with tension. These people were my family. My sister. My father.

I'd finally got back to sleep around five, and now I could hear my daughter's voice calling me through the darkness of my dreams, and my eyes sprung open.

'Mummy?' Grace was tugging at the quilt, her curls chaotic, her cheeks flushed from sleep. She placed her hands on her hips, and with a tilt of her head, she said, as though we'd reversed roles, 'Get up. I've got to go to nursery.'

I grabbed my mobile, knocking an empty glass to the floor, and stared at the screen, the white numbers blurred before my eyes. It was gone 8.30. *Damn!*

'Of course, yes,' I said, diving out of bed. And taking her hand, I led her down the stairs.

I filled a bowl with Rice Krispies, and splashed on milk, before making myself a strong coffee. 'Eat up, sweetheart,' I said, my mind distracted as I looked through the kitchen window at a milky sun rising in the sky.

I needed to see the letter again that Dillon had showed me in Ireland, to compare the handwriting. Maybe I was mistaken – I desperately wanted to be. But truth was, I knew it was Tierney's. The writing was sharp and spiky, the letters large. It was so distinctive.

Should I call Dillon?

'Finished,' Grace said, dropping the spoon into the bowl with a clatter, and getting down from the table. I glanced at the time on the clock on the cooker. We should have left by now.

'OK, let's see how fast you can get dressed today,' I said with fake brightness.

She raced towards the stairs. 'Do I get a prize if I'm quick?' she said, beaming.

'You get a big hug,' I said, following her and tickling her waist, before she raced up the stairs. 'And don't forget to clean your teeth.'

I followed her up, and got dressed, the sheer burden of what I was carrying weighing heavy.

'Are you OK, Mummy?' Grace said, appearing in the doorway and catching me perched on the edge of the bed, head down.

'Of course, sweetheart,' I said, wishing I was.

***

Once I'd dropped Grace off at nursery, I headed back home. I'd cancelled my clients the night before, knowing I wouldn't be up to seeing them.

Another large coffee in front of me on the breakfast bar, I brought up Dillon's number on my phone. After hovering my finger over the screen for some time, trying to work out what I would say to him, I finally found the courage to call.

'Hello, Rachel.'

'Dillon?' I said.

'No, it's Tierney.' A pause. 'Your dad.'

My heart leaped. Why did he have to say that? I felt an odd mixture of guilt for thinking he'd killed Dillon's mother and Imogen, and fear that he had.

'Hi,' I said, attempting to sound upbeat. 'I was hoping to catch Dillon. Is he about?'

'He's out. Left his phone charging. Shall I get him to call you, Rachel? Is it important?'

'No, no it's fine. Don't worry. I'll call him later.'

'Right. Well, it was good hearing your voice. Hopefully we'll get to see you again soon.'

I needed to end the call. It was painful to talk to him. 'Yes, yes. That would be lovely. Well I'd better go, Grace is calling me.'

I hung up before he could speak again, my body turning to liquid, tears stinging my eyes. I desperately wanted to be wrong about him.

It was much later that Dillon called me back.

'All right, sis?' he said, and gave a small laugh. I hated what I was about to say.

'Dillon, is Tierney about?' My voice was a whisper, as though he might hear.

'Da? No, he's headed down the boozer. Why? Is something wrong?'

I caressed my neck, a fizz of tension tangible under my fingers. 'Can you do something for me?'

'Yep, of course, is everything OK? You sound a bit anxious, if you don't mind me saying.'

'Can you look at Imogen's suicide note and compare it with Tierney's handwriting?'

'Why?'

'For me, please …' I wondered why he hadn't noticed the similarity before. Surely he could see the writing was like his father's. Known it was the same but refused to believe. Or perhaps I was mistaken, after all.

'I don't know what you're talking about.'

'The thing is, I'm sure it's Tierney's writing,' I said in a rush.

'Jesus, Rachel. Of course it isn't.'

'And there's something else.' I paused, trying to find the courage. 'I think he killed your mother.'

'What? For fuck's sake, Rachel, what the hell are you trying to do here? Don't you think we've all been through enough shite?' His voice was cracking as it rose in volume. 'I don't want to hear this crap. Listen, I've got to go …'

'Wait, please, Dillon. Just ask the police to look under the apple tree.'

'Goodbye, Rachel.'

'Dillon …' I said, tears filling my eyes. But he'd gone.

***

Over the next month I gave up my psychotherapy, packed my things, and moved into my mum's house in Suffolk. Lawrence had complained at first, but he agreed, eventually, that Suffolk wasn't the other side of the world.

I couldn't quite comprehend how my life had shrunk like pure wool in a tumble-dryer. No mum, no Angela, no Lawrence, no Zoe. I hadn't heard from Emmy, although Facebook had informed me she'd given birth to a beautiful baby boy. I'd sent her a card and a gift, but hadn't heard back.

And just when I thought I'd found Tierney and Dillon, they'd vanished like wasps in winter. I hadn't heard from Dillon since he'd hung up on me. Perhaps it was better that way. I wouldn't go within a hundred miles of Tierney knowing what I knew, and he and Dillon came as a package – Dillon had made that clear.

I'd been tempted to go to the police, but, for now at least, my sanity couldn't cope with it. Anyway, I had no real evidence that Tierney murdered Imogen. No real proof that Dillon's real mother was buried under the apple tree, other than my unreliable childhood memories.

Chapter 54

July 2018

Grace, her sunhat pulled low over her curls, paddled in the sea, splashing her shorts and her Peter Rabbit T-shirt.

'Stay where it's shallow, sweetheart,' I called.

Letting her go into the water raised my anxiety levels, but I had never inflicted my fear on her. She was a strong swimmer – I'd made certain of that.

I sat nearby, the sun beaming down from a clear blue sky on the quiet stretch of beach. Pastel-coloured houses in Aldeburgh looked like a picture postcard in the distance, and in the other direction the 'House in the Clouds' at Thorpeness towered above the trees, as though hovering above the ground. My mind drifted.

What will I tell Grace about her family, when she's old enough to understand? Do I tell her that Laura was never her real grand-mother? That her real grandfather murdered her real grandmother, that her aunt is a killer? Do I tell her what my mum – Laura – did? If I shelter Grace from that, am I no different than Laura was? The truth always comes out, eventually – but for now, at least, I have time on my side.

A seagull flew low, squawking, bringing me out of my reverie. I still hadn't come to terms with all I'd lost, and it was fair to say I was lonely. The doctor had prescribed anti-depressants – *just temporary, a low dosage to help get you through*, she'd said. And I was determined I would get through, and come out the other side.

We'd been living in Mum's old house for two months, and we would stay for now at least, living off my inheritance until I felt I could move on with my life. My mother had spent little money over the years, and made a lot from her paintings. Even after the care homes costs, there was enough for Grace and I to live on for a while.

But the truth was, I now understood how lonely my mother must have been, tucked away in the Suffolk countryside with her terrible secret, and I made a promise to myself that I wouldn't end up the same way – for Grace's sake.

I fiddled with Mum's locket hanging around my neck. The police had returned it to me, and I wanted to honour my mum's and Rachel's memory by wearing it – always. It had never been a photograph of me. It had always been of the real Rachel – the little girl who, due to a dreadful accident, lost her young life. But she had always lived on in my mum's memory, and I would carry that baton onwards. Something of that child had been lodged inside me since that awful day at Lough End Farm, and she would never be forgotten.

As I watched Grace playing in the sea, I thought about how many years I'd spent wondering who my father was. How many moments dreaming I'd one day meet him – that, when I did, he would be amazing. The old saying, 'Be careful what you wish for' couldn't be more apt.

My phone rang. It was Dillon.

'Rachel,' he said, when I answered – and it hit me for the first time, that I would always be Rachel. Discovering the truth hadn't changed who I was, how much my mother had loved me.

'Yes.' I was cautious. We'd ended things so badly when we spoke in May.

'I looked at the handwriting.'

I rose, wondering what he was going to tell me. 'You did ...? And ...?'

'I should have been honest with myself years ago, Rachel. I'd always known it was similar – just couldn't face comparing it. I buried the fear. Told myself I was wrong to doubt my father. But when you called ...' I heard him catch his breath. 'It's the same, Rachel. You were right.'

I let out a breath I felt I'd been holding for months. 'I'm so sorry, Dillon.'

'Me too.'

'What will you do now?'

'It's done.' A long pause. 'He's in custody. I told the Guards about the apple tree and ...'

'Dillon?'

'They found my ma,' he said, his voice breaking into a sob. 'That bastard killed my ma, Rachel.'

I closed my eyes for a moment, and a tear slid down my cheek. I'd hoped I was wrong. 'I'm so sorry, Dillon,' I said again, dragging my fingers through my hair, trying to hold back more tears. But I knew sorry was nowhere near enough.

'How did you know?' he said through a sob.

'I remembered. It all came back to me – memories of Imogen and Tierney fighting in the kitchen on that awful day. Everything.' I paused for a moment, before quietly adding, 'Listen, why don't you come to England? Stay with me for a while. I've got lots of room.'

'I'd like that very much,' he said. 'Can I bring Duke?'

'Of course, Grace would love that. Shall I text you some dates?'

'That'll be grand.'

'Mummy,' Grace called, and I looked up to see her running up and down, splashing her feet in the water.

316

'Bye, Rachel,' Dillon said, and was gone before I could reply. But this time I knew I would see him again, and it may have been the hot sun on my neck, the beauty around me, but a feeling of peace washed over me.

Waves crashed against the stony beach, but instead of my usual anxiety, I found the sound oddly soothing, and I knew to move forward I had to face my demons.

'It's a bit cold,' Grace said, grinning into the sun, as I approached her. 'But it's really, really fun.'

'It looks it,' I said, smiling. 'But you may need to hold my hand.'

Grace held out her hand, and taking a deep breath, I kicked off my flip-flops, ventured over the pebbles to the water's edge, and dipped in my toe.

Acknowledgements

First thanks must go to my outstanding editors, Nia Beynon, Genevieve Pegg, Helena Newton and Dushi Horti, who inspired me with their brilliant suggestions, and provided me with excellent edits. Thanks too, to Anna Sikorska for her amazing cover design. I'm in awe of her talent. And huge thanks to everyone at HQ for all their fantastic support.

My acknowledgements wouldn't be complete without a massive thank you to Hannah Smith for signing me with HQ, and for giving me such a huge opportunity.

To Karen Clarke, Joanne Duncan and Diane Jeffrey for being absolutely marvellous. I can't thank them enough for all their help and support with *Tell the Truth*. And to Desiree for her brilliant suggestion of the spa setting – I loved writing those scenes.

Big thanks to everyone who has read and enjoyed my novels – you make it all worthwhile. And thanks to the brilliant bloggers, amazing writers and to everyone I know on social media who have given me such support over the last year. And thanks to my fantastic friends and extended family. You know who you are – I love you all.

Finally, my biggest thanks go to my close family. My sons: Daniel for his encouragement and brilliant support on social media, and Liam and Luke for fun brainstorming sessions, and suggestions that kept me on track.

And thanks to my daughter-in-law, Lucynda for reading an early draft of *Tell the Truth*, and for giving me great feedback.

To my mum, who tells everyone she meets that her daughter writes novels, whether they want to know or not, and to my dad and sister, no longer with us, but I like to think are still out there somewhere cheering me on.

And last but by no means least, to Kev. I couldn't do it without you.

I love you all so much.

The next book from Amanda Brittany
is coming in 2019

Dear Reader,

Thank you so much for reading *Tell the Truth*, I hope you enjoyed it. And thanks to those of you who have also read my debut *Her Last Lie*. At the time of writing this letter, almost £7,000 has been raised for Cancer Research UK in my sister's memory, from my eBook royalties of that book, which is amazing.

I had great fun writing *Tell the Truth*. The inspiration for the Irish scenes was from a trip to Cliffony in County Sligo, to visit my grandfather's birthplace. I loved the area so much, and based Laura's fictional home in County Sligo. Finsbury Park, where Rachel lives, was inspired by travelling to King's Cross by train regularly – and looking out of the window at the Emirates Stadium, Finsbury Park opening up behind it.

I love to hear from readers and can be contacted through Twitter @amandajbrittany or on my Facebook author page www.facebook.com/amandabrittany2 or through my website www.amandabrittany.co.uk

Finally, if you enjoyed reading *Tell the Truth*, it would be amazing if you could leave a review. It doesn't have to be very long – but positive reviews can make such a difference to a book's success. Thank you so much.

At the moment I'm writing my third psychological thriller, which will be published in 2019.

Love, Amanda X

Thank your for reading!

Thank you so much for taking the time to read this book – we hope you enjoyed it! If you did, we'd be so appreciative if you left a review.

Here at HQ Digital we are dedicated to publishing fiction that will keep you turning the pages into the early hours. We publish a variety of genres, from heartwarming romance, to thrilling crime and sweeping historical fiction.

To find out more about our books, enter competitions and discover exclusive content, please join our community of readers by following us at:

🐦 *@HQDigitalUK*

f *facebook.com/HQDigitalUK*

Are you a budding writer? We're also looking for authors to join the HQ Digital family!
Please submit your manuscript to:

HQDigital@harpercollins.co.uk.

Hope to hear from you soon!

ONE PLACE. MANY STORIES

Turn the page for an extract from Amanda Brittany's thrilling
Her Last Lie …

Prologue

Saturday, 23 July

NSW Newsroom Online

Serial killer Carl Jeffery convicted of triple hostel killings, granted appeal.

Six years ago, the so-called Hostel Killer, Carl Jeffery, now thirty-one, was found guilty of the murders of Sophie Stuart, nineteen, Bronwyn Bray, eighteen, and Clare Simpson, twenty-six. He got three life sentences.

Now his younger sister, Darleen Jeffery, hopes to get him acquitted.

Mr Jeffery was accused of targeting women travelling alone in Australia. He would gain their trust, and when the women ended their relationship with Jeffery, he would tap on their window in the dead of night, wearing a green beanie hat and scarf to disguise his appearance, striking fear. He later killed them.

The main prosecuting evidence came from his intended fourth victim, Isla Johnson from the UK, who survived his attack and identified him as her assailant. She suffered physical and psychological injuries. Following Mr Jeffery's trial, she returned to England where she now lives with boyfriend Jack Green.

During his trial, Jeffery broke down when questioned about his mother, who left the family home when he was eleven, leaving him and Darleen to live with their abusive father, who died three months before the first murder.

Darleen, who penned the bestseller *My Brother is Innocent*, has campaigned for her sibling's release for almost six years. She claims her brother's DNA was found on Bronwyn Bray's body because they had been in a relationship, and that this wasn't taken into account fully at the trial. She also insists the court should re-examine Isla's statements of what happened the night of her brother's arrest, suggesting there is no proof that he started the 'bloodbath' that unfolded that night.

Canberra's High Court granted permission today for an appeal, agreeing there are sufficient grounds for further consideration of the case. The hearing will take place on 30 September.

Leaving court today, Darleen, wearing a two-piece royal-blue skirt suit, told reporters, 'I'm over the moon. I believe we have a sound case, and I can't wait for my brother to be released.'

We contacted Isla Johnson in her hometown of Letchworth Garden City, England. She told us she wouldn't be attending the hearing. 'They have my original statements, and I've no more to offer,' she said.

PART 1

Chapter 1

It was hot.

Not the kind of heat you bask in on a Majorcan beach. No tickle of a warm breeze caressing your cheek. This was clammy, and had crept out of nowhere mid-afternoon, long after Isla had travelled into London in long sleeves and leggings, her camera over her shoulder, her notepad in hand.

Now Isla was crushed against a bosomy woman reading a freebie newspaper, on a packed, motionless train waiting to leave King's Cross. The air was heavy with stale body odour and – what was that? – fish? She looked towards the door. Should she wait for the next train?

She took two long, deep breaths in an attempt to relieve the fuzzy feeling in her chest. She rarely let her angst out of its box any more – proud of how far she'd come. But there were times when the buried-alive anxiety banged on the lid of that box, desperate to be freed. It had been worse since she'd received the letter about the appeal. Carl Jeffery had crawled back under her skin.

She'd hid the letter, knowing if she told Jack and her family they would worry about her. She didn't want that. She'd spent too much time as a victim. The one everyone worried about. She was stronger now. The woman she'd once been was in touching distance. She couldn't let the appeal ruin that.

She ran a finger over the rubber band on her wrist, and pinged it three times. Snap. Snap. Snap. It helped her focus – a weapon against unease.

'Hey, sit,' said a lad in his teens, leaping to his feet and smiling. Had he picked up on her breathing technique – those restless, twitching feelings?

I'm twenty-nine, not ninety, she almost said. But the truth was she was relieved. She had been on her feet all day taking pictures around Tower Bridge for an article she was working on, and that horrid heat was basting the backs of her knees, the curves of her elbows, making them sweat.

'Thanks,' she said, and thumped down in the vacated seat, realising instantly why the bloke had moved. A fish sandwich muncher was sitting right next to her.

Her phone rang in her canvas bag, and she pulled it out to see Jack's face beaming from the screen.

'Hey, you,' she said, pinning the phone to her ear.

'You OK?'

'Yeah, just delayed. Train's rammed.' It jolted forward, and headed on its way. 'Ooh, we're moving, thank the Lord. Should be home in about an hour.'

'Great. I'm cooking teriyaki chicken. Mary Berry style.'

She laughed, scooping her hair behind her ears. 'Lovely. I'll pick up wine.'

The line went dead as the train rumbled through a tunnel, and Isla slipped her phone in her bag, and took out her camera. She flicked through her photos. She would add one or two to Facebook later, and mention her long day in London.

Your life is so perfect, Millie had written on Isla's status a few months back, when she'd updated that she and Jack were back from France and she was closer to finishing her book. It had been an odd thing for Millie to say. Her sister knew Isla's history better than anyone. How could she think Isla's life was perfect, when she'd seen her at her most desperate? Felt the cruel slap of Isla's anger.

Eyes closed, Isla drifted into thoughts of Canada. She was going for a month. Alone. Canada. The place she would have gone to after Australia if life hadn't forced a sharp change of direction. Going abroad without Jack wouldn't be easy. But then he couldn't keep carrying her. She had to face it alone. And it would be the perfect escape from the pending appeal.

With a squeal of brakes, the train pulled in to Finsbury Park, and fish-sandwich man grunted, far too close to Isla's ear, that it was his stop. She moved so he could pass, and shuffled into the window seat.

Through the glass, overheated people poured onto the platform, and her eyes drifted from a woman with a crying, red-faced toddler, to a teenage boy slathering sun cream onto his bare shoulders.

'Isla?' Someone had sat down next to her, his aftershave too strong.

She turned, her chest tightening, squeezing as though it might crush her heart. 'Trevor,' she stuttered, suddenly desperate to get up and rush through the door before it hissed shut. But it did just that – sucking closed in front of her eyes, suffocating her, preventing any escape from her past.

'I thought it was you,' he said, as the train pulled away. He was still handsome and athletic. Gone were his blond curls, replaced by cropped hair that suited him. He was wearing an expensive-looking suit, a tie loose in the neck, his tanned face glowing in the heat.

Her heartbeat quickened. It always did when anything out of the ordinary happened, and seeing Trevor for the first time in years made her feel off-kilter. The man she'd hurt at university was sitting right next to her, his face creased into a pleasant smile, as though he'd forgotten how things had ended between them.

'You haven't changed,' he said. 'Still as beautiful as ever.' He threw her a playful wink, before his blue eyes latched on to hers. 'I can't believe it's been eight years. How are you?' She'd forgotten how soft his voice was, the slight hint of Scotland in his accent. He'd always been good to talk to. Always had time for everyone at university. But the chemistry had never been there – for her anyway – and they'd wanted different things from their lives.

'I'm good – you?' she said, as her heart slowed to an even beat.

He nodded, and a difficult silence fell between them. This was more like it. This was how things had been left – awkward and embarrassing. An urge to apologise took over. But it was far too late to say sorry for how she'd treated him. Wasn't it?

'I've often thought about you,' he said, and she tugged her eyes away from his. 'You know, wondering what you're up to. I heard what happened in Australia.'

'I prefer not to talk about it.' It came out sharp and defensive.

'Well, no, I can see why you wouldn't want to. Must have been awful for you. I'm so sorry.'

Quickly, Isla changed the subject, and they found themselves bouncing back and forth memories of university days, avoiding how it had ended.

'You're truly remarkable,' Trevor said eventually. 'You know, coming back from what you went through.'

After another silence, where she stared at her hands, she said, 'It was hard for a time … a really long time, in fact.' She hadn't spoken about it for so long, and could hear her voice cracking.

'But you're OK now?' He sounded so genuine, his eyes searching her face.

She shrugged. 'His sister …'

Would it be OK to talk to Trevor about the appeal? Tell him about Darleen Jeffery? Ask him what kind of woman fights their brother's innocence, when it's so obvious he's a monster? There was a huge part of Isla that desperately needed to talk. Say the words she couldn't say to Jack or her family for fear they would think she was taking a step back. Vocalise the fears that hovered under the surface. The desire to tell someone about the Facebook message she'd received from Darleen Jeffery several months ago was overwhelming. '*I need to discuss the truth, Isla,*' it had said.

'His sister fought for an appeal and won,' she went on, wishing immediately that she'd said nothing.

'Jesus.' He looked so concerned, his eyes wide and fully on her. 'When is it?'

'The end of September.' The words caught in her throat.

'Are you going?'

She shook her head. She'd contacted the Director of Public Prosecutions. Told them she wouldn't be attending, that she didn't want to know the outcome. Being in a courtroom with *him* again would be like resting her head on a block, Carl Jeffery controlling the blade.

'I can't face it,' she said, her voice a whisper.

'I don't blame you.' He shook his head. 'It's sickening that he killed three women. Unbelievable.'

She thought of lovely Jack, knowing how hurt he would be if he knew she was keeping the appeal – and the way it was affecting her – from him. He would be hurt if he knew that within a few minutes of meeting her ex, she was confiding in him – letting it all out. But there was something oddly comforting in the detached feeling of talking to an almost-stranger on a train – because that's what he was now. Someone she probably wouldn't see again for another eight years.

'I'll be in Canada when it takes place. I can forget it's even happening. And I've told them I don't want to know the outcome.' She pinged the band on her wrist, before turning and fixing her eyes hard on the window, a surge of tears waiting to fall. She needed to change the subject. 'So what are you up to now?'

'I'm a chemist,' he said, his tone upbeat.

'Not a forensic scientist, then?' That had been his dream.

'Never happened, sadly,' he said. 'I'm working on a trial drug at the moment.'

'Sounds interesting.' Her eyes were back on him.

He shrugged. 'Not really. Not as interesting as travel writing.'

She stared, narrowing her eyes. 'You know I'm a travel writer?'

He smiled. 'I guessed.' He nodded at her camera. 'You wanted to be the next Martha Gellhorn.'

'You remember that?'

He nodded, entwining his fingers on his lap, eyes darting over her face. 'You haven't changed,' he said again.

She knew she had. Her blonde hair came out of a bottle these days, and there was no doubting she was different on the inside. She looked away again, through the window where fields were blurs of green.

As seconds became minutes he said, 'Maybe we could catch up some time. Now we've found each other again.'

Words bounced around her head, as a prickle of sweat settled on her forehead. She didn't want to be unkind, but she was with Jack, and even if she wasn't, there was nothing there – not even a spark.

She turned to see his cheeks glowing red, and an urge to say sorry for hurting him all those years ago rose once more. 'I'm with someone,' she said instead.

'That's cool. Me too,' he said, with what seemed like a genuine smile. 'I meant as friends, that's all.' He pulled out his phone, the yellow Nokia he'd had at university. 'We could exchange numbers.' His shoulders rose in a shrug, making him look helpless. 'It would be good to meet up some time.'

***

Triple-glazed windows sealed against the noise of heavy traffic rattling along the road outside, and a whirring fan that was having little effect, meant the apartment felt even hotter than outside. Isla hated that she couldn't fling open the windows to let the fresh air in. Sometimes she would grab her camera, jump into her car, and head to the nearby fields to snap photographs of the countryside: birds and butterflies, wild flowers, sheep, horses, whatever she could find – pictures she would often put on Facebook or Instagram.

'Can you open that, please?' She plonked the chilled bottle of wine she'd picked up from the off-licence in front of Jack on the worktop. 'I desperately need a shower.'

He looked up from chopping vegetables. 'Well hello there, Jack, how was your day?'

'Sorry,' she said, tickling their cat, Luna, under the chin before stroking her sleek, grey body. 'I'm so, so hot. Sorry, sorry, sorry.' She disappeared into the bedroom, stripping off her clothes, and dropping them as she went.

Fifteen minutes later she was back, in shorts and a T-shirt, damp hair scooped into a messy bun. She picked up the glass of wine that Jack had poured. 'God, that's better,' she said, taking a swig. She smiled, and touched Jack's clean-shaven cheek. 'Well, hello there, Jack, how was your day?'

He laughed, and plonked a kiss on her nose. 'Well Tuesday's done. I'll be glad when I'm over hump Wednesday.'

'Wednesday's the new Thursday, and Thursday's the new Friday.'

'Must be the weekend then.' He raised his glass. 'Cheers.'

She pulled herself onto a stool. 'I saw an old boyfriend on the train home. Trevor Cooper.' The guilt of talking about the appeal made her want to tell Jack.

'The bloke you went out with at uni?'

'Aha.'

'Should I be jealous?' he teased.

'God no.' She took another gulp of wine, before adding, 'He was suggesting I meet with him some time.'

Jack's eyebrows rose, and a playful smile dimpled his cheeks. 'Do you fancy him?'

She shook her head. 'Of course not.'

He laughed as he put chicken onto plates. 'Well, go ahead then; you have my blessing.'

'I'd go without it, if I wanted to,' she said, with a laugh. They'd been together two years. He should be able to trust her. 'To be honest,' she continued, 'I'm not sure I want to meet up with him. I'll think of an excuse if he texts. Maybe come down with something contagious.'

Jack smiled and shoved a plate of delicious-looking food in front of her. She picked up a fork and began tucking in, making appreciative noises. 'I probably shouldn't have given him my number.'

'And you did, because?'

She shrugged, remembering. 'I suppose I didn't want to hurt his feelings *again*.'

There was a clatter, and Luna, green eyes flashing, jumped off the worktop with a huge piece of French bread in her mouth.

'Luna, you little sod,' Jack yelled, diving from his stool. 'Has that "how to train a cat" book arrived yet?'

Isla didn't respond, deep in thought.

'If you don't want to meet him, Isla,' he said, long legs leaping after Luna, 'just ignore him if he texts.' He grabbed the cat, wrestled free the bread, and chucked it in the bin. 'Simple.'

'Maybe,' she said.

Later, Isla sat on her mobile phone watching cute cats on YouTube, as Jack watched a documentary about Jack the Ripper.

Her phone buzzed. Trevor had sent her a friend request on Facebook, and a message saying how great it had been to see her again. She stared at the screen for some moments, and then looked at Jack sprawled full length on the sofa. Trevor was just being friendly, and anyway, her conscience wouldn't allow her to ignore him. She had loads of friends she barely knew any more on Facebook. What harm could another person do?

She added him as a friend.

Chapter 2

Three months later

Tuesday, 25 October

Isla dashed towards Heathrow Airport's luggage claim conveyors, and eased her tired body between a heavy man in his fifties with a mobile pinned to his ear, and a family with two teenage daughters staring at phone screens. She sighed. Just a solitary red case was going round and round and round. The cases hadn't been released yet.

Heavy-man turned and flashed her a smile. He'd sat next to her on the plane, taking up part of her seat as well as his own, his sickly aftershave making her head throb.

'Hold this,' one of the girls said, handing her sister an energy drink and stomping away, eyes still on her phone. 'I need the loo.'

Isla closed her eyes. Her head ached worse than it had on the plane. Drinking several small bottles of wine hadn't been a good idea. Her mouth was dry, as though someone had installed a dehumidifier on her tongue.

Thirty-six hours ago she'd been snapping incredible photographs from a train window. The ice-capped peaks and remarkable alpine lakes of the Canadian Rockies had been just two of the many things that had made the leap of faith to jump on a plane alone worth it.

'I landed about an hour ago, Sean, mate.' Heavy-man's tone jarred. 'Should be at yours by ten if the traffic isn't shit.'

A trolley bumped her ankle.

'Fuck,' she muttered under her breath, turning to give the culprit her best cross look. But the man was elderly with white hair and wire glasses, reminding her of her granddad. She would let him off, but still needed to free herself from the people-coffin she'd found herself in. The eight-hour flight from Canada had been bad enough, but *this*, when she was tired and hungry, was too much. She rubbed her cheeks and neck. She wanted to be at home in her shower, letting water flow over her, and then to fall into bed next to Jack and enjoy a long uninterrupted sleep.

At first she'd missed having Jack by her side, like a child deprived of her security blanket. Taking off on the trip alone hadn't been anywhere near as easy as it had been eight years before, when she'd raced into the unknown after university for what was meant to be a gap year, but had drifted into two. Back then, she'd travelled alone, clueless about where her next bed would be, or what job she might pick up along the way, all without fear. She longed to be that person again: the girl with her life ahead of her, before Carl Jeffery took a metaphorical sledge-hammer and wrecked the mechanics of her mind.

She pinged the rubber band on her wrist and, taking a long, deep breath, tucked her hair behind her ears, and moved away from the crowd, clinging to how perfect Canada had been.

She pulled her phone from her carry-on bag and turned it on. She'd avoided the Internet and social media while away, worried she might find out something about the appeal. But now a month had passed. Whatever the outcome, it would be old news. And being off the Internet meant she'd immersed herself in her Canadian adventure, and also worked on her book.

Her phone adjusted to the London time zone, and picked up her network, bleeping, pinging, buzzing, as she was sucked once more into the frenzy of social media. Within moments she was blocking newsfeeds on Facebook and Twitter, muting notifications – hiding friends who continually shared news articles – she didn't expect there to be any news about the appeal; it had been a month, after all – but she was taking no chances.

On WhatsApp, Millie had added her to a chat about a six-part murder mystery on Netflix. Isla hadn't seen it, but her sister had given away so many spoilers, adding emoticons, that it probably wasn't worth watching it now. Julian had added a comment: *You're totally useless, Millie.*

Isla sighed. Why did her sister stay with him?

On Instagram, Roxanne had put on a stream of photographs of struggling refugees – another cause for her best friend's over-crowded, want-to-help-everyone head.

Millie had put on twenty-or-so photographs of her new puppy, Larry, who looked good enough to eat. And Isla's mum, who didn't understand Instagram, and was pretty rubbish with anything to do with social media, had added a photograph of a chicken casserole for no apparent reason.

Twitter was dominated by Roxanne's pleas to save foxes and badgers, and there was a string of Tweets by a magazine Isla regularly wrote for, and several updates from UK Butterflies.

Facebook was crowded by engagements and late holidays to the Mediterranean all jostling for attention. There was a wedding of an online friend Isla had forgotten she had, and another friend's mother had passed away – *Expected, she was 91, but still gutted – feeling sad.*

There was a rare update by Trevor Cooper – *Really must get on here more, and stop being an Internet dinosaur.* Nobody had liked it, but then he didn't have many friends. When he'd failed to get in contact again three months ago, after their chance meeting on the train, Isla hadn't thought any more about him, pushing him far from her thoughts. Maybe she could unfriend him now.

As she scrolled, she realised she could whittle her eight hundred-or-so friends, mainly picked up from university and her travels, down to a hundred, and still not recognise some of them in the street. She wasn't sure she even liked Facebook. In fact, sometimes she'd go on there and feel exposed.

'Isla, nobody's looking at you, lovely lady,' Roxanne had said, when Isla had tried to explain her feelings. 'And I mean that in the nicest way. They're just having fun sharing what they've been up to.'

There was a thump behind her, and she turned to see a black case rumble down the conveyor. Heavy-man barged forward, grabbed it, and once it was on the floor in front of him he yanked out the handle as though gutting a fish. He pushed past the teenage girls and the elderly man, veins in his forehead pulsing as he marched towards Isla.

'Facebook,' he said, nodding towards Isla's open screen as he walked by. 'Dangerous place the Internet. You heard it here first.'

She watched him rush through Nothing to Declare.

Not if you use it right, surely.

ONE PLACE. MANY STORIES

If you enjoyed *Tell the Truth*, then why not try another heart-racing read from HQ Digital?

It's bad when the girls go MISSING
It's worse when the girls are FOUND

PRETTY LITTLE THINGS

T.M.E. WALSH

It was the one place she should have been safe

THE CLASSROOM

A.L. BIRD

No matter where you hide...

HE WILL FIND YOU

DIANE JEFFREY

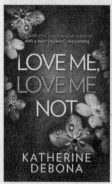

An addictive, psychological suspense with a twist you won't see coming

LOVE ME, LOVE ME NOT

KATHERINE DEBONA

DARREN O'SULLIVAN

CLOSE YOUR EYES

...and count to ten.

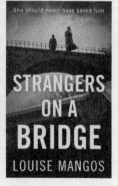

She should never have saved him

STRANGERS ON A BRIDGE

LOUISE MANGOS